A Done With novel

Found Pieces

WENDY LINDSTROM

NEW YORK TIMES BESTSELLING AUTHOR

All rights reserved.

No part of this publication may be sold, copied, distributed, reproduced or transmitted in any form or by any means, mechanical or digital, including photocopying and recording or by any information storage and retrieval system without the prior written permission of both the publisher, Oliver Heber Books and the author, Wendy Lindstrom, except in the case of brief quotations embodied in critical articles and reviews.

NO AI TRAINING: Without in any way limiting the author's [and publisher's] exclusive rights under copyright, any use of this publication to "train" generative artificial intelligence (AI) technologies and/or large language models to generate text, or any other medium, is expressly prohibited. The author reserves all rights to license uses of this work for the training and development of any generative AI and/or large language models.

PUBLISHER'S NOTE: This is a work of fiction. Names, characters, places, and incidents either are the product of the author's imagination or are used fictitiously. Any resemblance to actual persons, living or dead, business establishments, events, or locales is entirely coincidental.

Found Pieces Copyright 2026 © Wendy Lindstrom

Cover Design by Wicked Smart Designs

Published by Oliver-Heber Books

0 9 8 7 6 5 4 3 2 1

Chapter One

I should *not* have started my workday without coffee. There always seemed to be consequences when I wasn't properly caffeinated, but I simply couldn't abide the noxious swill at the hotel. Jonesing for a jolt of caffeine, I pulled into the Tamarack Gas-n-Go in Dunwith to fill my company car and grab a cup of strong brew. That's when I realized it was Thursday, not Friday. To make matters worse, my boss was lighting up my cellphone.

Before I could say good morning, he began pelting me with questions I'd already answered. Twice. Warning myself not to react, I swiped my company credit card. I needed my job, but his abusive treatment of me and the other female employees was straining my last nerve.

As the digital screen on the gas pump climbed with each belch of gasoline pumped into the tank of my company car, his voice grew louder. I released a sigh. It was just another day of dealing with the misogynistic ass and selling welding supplies that I'd rather be using.

A white van pulled up on the other side of the pumps and a woman about my age hopped out with an energetic spring I hadn't felt in months. She gave me a friendly nod, then noticed I was holding my phone away from my ear. A quizzical tilt of her eyebrows indicated she could hear my boss's loud tirade.

I glanced away, embarrassed that my boss sounded like an angry parent chastising a misbehaving child. I was a forty-three-year-old woman wondering how I'd ended up with a job I didn't love and a life that felt so empty and unfulfilling.

The hand nozzle jerked as the pump stopped, but the condescending drone of my boss spewing vitriol continued. I slipped the spout into the docking receptacle, wishing I could thrust nozzle-nose Norton into that narrow space and shut him off, too. I'd just spent two days on the road making sales calls and listening to noisy hotel guests laughing and planning fun adventures while I sat alone in rooms that made my skin itch. I was sleep-deprived, caffeine-deficient, and cranky. I tried to warn him to stop, that he was going too far, that I hadn't had coffee, but he cut me off again and again until the mounting pressure in my head became too intense to contain. Like a canister of acetylene gas exposed to extreme heat and relentless pressure, my temper exploded.

"I didn't lose the Quick-Fab account, you condescending jackass," I barked into the phone. "As I told you last week, Quick-Fab lost their biggest account, which cut their production by fifty percent. That means their demand for our welding supplies was cut fifty percent. So, for the third time, I didn't *lose* the account. And to set the record straight, I've brought in the highest sales, provided the most detailed reports, and have covered your ass at every turn from the day I took this job. Every accolade you've received has been earned on the backs of your sales team. But I'm done with your abuse and this whole shit-show. You can pick up the company car at the Tamarack Gas-n-Go in Dunwith, pump two."

"What are you doing in Dunwith?" he demanded, but I was done answering to him.

Jabbing my finger against the screen, I ended the call and cut him off mid-sentence. I tossed the company cellphone and car keys inside the vehicle and slammed the door shut on a part of my life I was desperate to escape.

From the other side of the gas pumps, I heard the woman laugh. She met my startled look with a sympathetic smile. "Bad day?"

Releasing a hard breath to unload some of the pressure ballooning in my chest, I nodded. "Yeah, it's an *I-need-a-freaking-cup-of-coffee* kind of bad day."

"Those are the worst," she said with a laugh. "Best coffee in town is at the Maple Leaf Café a few blocks from here, other side of the park." She glanced at my locked car. "I suspect you're looking for a place within walking distance?"

Realizing I'd not only left my briefcase in the car but also my purse, overnight bag, and personal items made me groan. "Damn it." I sagged against the car door. "I should have thought this through before locking the doors. The station owner will probably sue me for blocking the pumps."

"Nah, Jeff will cheer you on for standing up for yourself, although he might wish you'd left your car over there." She nodded toward an area in the lot with four open parking spaces.

I wrinkled my nose, embarrassed by my own shortsightedness. "I don't have a spare key with me."

"Well, I'm happy to help a sister in need," she said, screwing the cap on her gas tank. After taking her receipt, she retrieved her phone from the van and tapped in a number. "I'll tell Jeff you accidentally locked your keys in your car and that Jack will be over to open the door and move the vehicle."

"Who's Jack?" I asked.

The redhead, dressed in blue jeans, a white T-shirt, and a blue ball cap, leaned against her van, booted feet crossed at the ankles as if she hadn't a single care in the world, something I couldn't begin to imagine. "Jack is Jeff's twin brother," she said. "He's also a police officer who owes me a favor." Before I could comment, she spoke to someone at the other end, presumably Jack, who owed her a favor. Seconds later, she ended the call. "All set. You can get your coffee now."

"I need to wait for your police officer friend to retrieve my keys so I can move my car. And I need to get my other things out before my boss sends someone to retrieve it."

"No need to wait," she said. "I'll tell Jack to leave the keys with Jeff." She tapped out a text on her phone, then slipped it into a holster attached to the dash of her van. "I'm craving a cup of coffee now, too, so I'm heading to the café. You're welcome to ride over with me if you like."

My legs were beginning to tremble after the massive surge of adrenaline-fueled rage that had just ravaged my body. I was wearing uncomfortable heels and wanted to accept her offer, but I had no money. "Thank you, but I locked my purse and wallet in the car, so I need to wait for Jack."

Sympathy filled her eyes. "You know, it's days like this when a gal needs a pal. Let me buy you a cup of coffee and you can repay me by assuaging my curiosity about your jackass boss and if you really sell welding supplies."

Her comment made me laugh, and I could see that her offer was sincere. "Well, I'm in desperate need of a cup of coffee, so thank you," I said. "I'll reimburse you as soon as I can get my purse out of my car."

"Not necessary." She waved me over. "Come on, I've got you covered."

"Thank you." I climbed in on the passenger side. "I'm Andrea Arness, but I go by Andie, and I just quit a job I can't afford to quit."

Cranking the van to life, she replied, "I'm Maggie McKensie, and from what I heard, it sounded as if it was a job that cost you more than it paid."

Her comment struck me so profoundly, I sat mute for several seconds. "That's very insightful."

She shrugged. "If something makes me miserable, I stop doing it and try something else."

"That's a lovely way to live, but I need a steady income."

"It's possible to have a steady income *and* a job you enjoy." Maggie gave me an encouraging smile. "Regardless of why you changed lanes today, Andie, the fact is you did. Now you're free to go wherever you want to go."

As if a window in my life just opened and let in a gust of fresh air, I realized I didn't have to live another day in that crushing environment. I didn't have to answer the phone, chase orders, soothe irate customers, or tolerate my shithead boss. I was free. If only for today, I could enjoy a moment of independence.

Maggie drove the van down an alleyway that led to a parking lot behind the Maple Leaf Café. As we entered through the back door, the pungent aroma of coffee beans and spicy scent of chai lattes mingled with the sweet smell of baked goods. Colorful murals decorated the walls of the hip café. Patrons of all ages lounged on overstuffed furniture, talking, and laughing over their beverages. Wrought iron chairs with blue cushions sat prominently in the middle of the café, girded by low bookcases that created a cute reading nook. An antique hutch displaying tins of specialty teas, colorful tea kettles, and designer tea mugs with quotes on them stood beside a support pillar with a twining leaf design painted from floor to ceiling.

"Have you changed your mind about getting coffee?" Maggie asked, snapping me out of my awed inspection.

"God, no," I said, realizing I was still standing by the door. "If the coffee lives up to the décor, I can't wait to try it."

I followed her to a long glass bakery display case filled with delicious looking pastries. A pretty, blonde-haired woman wearing a crisp white blouse tucked into blue jeans stood behind the counter and greeted us with a warm smile. "Hey, Maggie. Where were you yesterday?"

"In Lake Placid trying to find the art pieces you want."

"Any luck?" the woman asked, her blue eyes lighting with excitement.

"Possibly. I'll let you know for sure tomorrow," Maggie said, then introduced me to her friend Sophie, owner of the café.

I complimented Sophie on her beautiful decor, and she insisted that first-time visitors to her café receive a free coffee.

"It's your lucky day," Maggie said with a laugh, and I readily agreed. Meeting Maggie and coming to a café filled with such beautiful energy was incredibly uplifting.

While Sophie waited on other customers, we studied the menu board posted high on the wall behind the counters. We both opted for dark roast coffee, a pastry for me, and blueberry scone for Maggie. Then, with steaming mugs of coffee in hand, we found a table near the front windows.

Savoring my first sip of robust, aromatic coffee, I said, "This day just got a thousand times better. If I'd had a cup of coffee this good before my boss called me, maybe I wouldn't have blown up my life."

With one knee draped over the other, Maggie relaxed back in her chair. "Maybe you didn't blow up your life, Andie. Maybe you just cleared a path so you can choose a more fulfilling direction."

"I hadn't been considering anything but getting a decent cup of coffee this morning, but maybe you're right."

"I usually am," she said with a smile.

I circled my hands around the blue porcelain mug and

released a long sigh. "God that call from my boss was a train wreck."

"I know. I was shamefully eavesdropping, but I couldn't look away."

Thinking about my unprofessional behavior made me wince. "I can't believe I just called my boss a condescending jackass."

"Your *ex*-boss," Maggie said, "and it was the best show I've seen since my friend Kate dumped her ex off a fishing dock because he was being an intolerable jerk."

I smiled. "That must have been wonderfully satisfying for Kate."

Maggie sat forward and braced her elbows on the table, her gaze intense. "Andie, no one should have to tolerate abusive behavior, whether you work for them or not."

"I agree. I've tolerated his verbal abuse because I needed the job, but each time he threw his freakishly small hand up like a roadblock to cut me off, I had to restrain myself from smacking it away from my face."

Maggie cracked up. "Freakishly small hands?"

"Yes. His hands are weirdly small for a man his size."

It took a moment for Maggie to contain her laughter. "Well, small hands or not, I can see how you'd want to smack him for sticking them in your face."

"I'm sure he'll do it again when I return my customer files to the office."

"Well, if you smack him, don't punch him in the mouth. You could get a fight-bite."

"What the heck is that?" I asked, having no intention of punching anyone.

"If you punch a person in the mouth their tooth can break off and lodge in your knuckle. A fight-bite is bad news for both parties. There are better ways to defend yourself."

It felt so good to laugh, I could have hugged her. "I'm suddenly a little scared and a lot in awe of you. Maybe I should hire you to go with me when I drop off my account files." Just the thought of facing my former boss and his obnoxious behavior made me feel powerless.

Maggie flapped a groomed hand at me. "Develop your own skills. That's something no one can take away from you. My friend Gayle owns a martial arts studio in town and gives a self-defense seminar on the last Tuesday evening of each month. If you're in town, you should go."

As Maggie's suggestion sank in, I realized somewhere along the line I'd lost my power. There wasn't a single event I could recall as the moment I gave in, or gave up, or just quit on myself. But I had. All I felt now was brittle and broken.

And lost.

"More coffee?" Sophie asked as she placed our orders in front of us. After topping off our cups, she asked if I'd be staying in town.

"I hadn't considered anything beyond getting coffee," I said, "but I think I just might take a couple days before heading home. I've been calling on the fab shop here but have never taken time to explore the town. Could you tell me where I can rent a room for the night?"

"The Eagle's Nest. My stepsister, Beth, runs the place," Sophie said. "It's just a couple blocks from here. Tell her I sent you over and she'll take good care of you."

"Thanks, I think I'll do that."

"What do you sell?" Sophie asked.

"I was selling welding supplies, but I guess nothing now because I quit my job this morning."

"Andie told her boss she was done with his shit show," Maggie said with a laugh. "I witnessed the whole thing at Jeff's station."

"Not my best moment," I said, "but in my defense, he was being an obnoxious bully."

Sophie scowled. "Sounds like my ex-brother-in-law. My sister finally got fed up with him and shoved him in the lake."

"I just told Andie about that," Maggie said, glancing at me, her eyes lit with humor. "I think you'd love Kate, and after witnessing your grand performance this morning, I suspect the feeling would be mutual."

My performance felt unprofessional rather than grand or courageous, but if Kate was anything like Maggie, I knew I'd like her.

"Let me know if you two need anything else," Sophie said, then headed to a neighboring table to top off their coffee.

"Andie, I'd love to know how you came to sell welding supplies," Maggie said, and began peppering me with questions.

While we ate our pastries, her interest in my welding and metal fabricating background was so genuine I found myself sharing details I hadn't talked about in years. I told her how my father started teaching me to weld and create metal sculptures when I was ten years old, and that I'd later earned a bachelor's degree in welding, then worked in a metal fabricating shop for several years before going into sales.

"How fascinating!" She steepled her fingers and leaned in wanting to know more. "Are you and your dad sculpting anything now?"

A familiar pang of grief cramped my chest, his absence a wound in my heart that wouldn't heal. "No, my dad passed away twenty years ago this October,"

"I'm so sorry." Her eyes dulled a little. "But what an extraordinary hobby you two shared."

It had never felt like a hobby because creating metal art was the only thing I ever wanted to do, but I'd pursued a welding degree that would provide more job options than an art degree.

Still, I could recall every lesson my father had given me, the first time I held a welding torch in my hand, his gentle guiding voice as he taught me hand control so the arc wouldn't shift away from the puddle. I could hear the buzzing sizzle of the torch, see the sparks behind my eyelids, and smell the metallic odor that lingered in my sinuses for hours after we finished working on our project. The memory of those moments with my father elicited such a deep, restless longing, the pain left me breathless.

"Are you okay?" Maggie asked, her expression concerned as she noticed me clenching my coffee mug.

"Um, yes, I'm just embarrassed for oversharing," I said.

"You're not at all. I'm truly intrigued with your interesting career." She leaned back in her chair and took a sip of her coffee. "With you being a woman working in a predominantly male industry, it makes me wonder if you had to deal with many jerks."

"Occasionally," I admitted, "but most of the people in the fab shop where I worked as a welding technician were respect-ful. And when I transitioned to my sales job four years ago, the customers I called on had no apparent issues discussing metal-working supplies and processes with me."

At Maggie's prodding, I summarized my years in sales selling welding materials, then explained how the time I spent in customer fab shops had deepened my knowledge of CAD programming and working with metal.

"That experience must help you create some amazing pieces of art."

"I haven't really had the time," I said, wanting to shift the conversation away from me, and because I was genuinely curious to learn more about this woman who'd befriended me at a gas station. "So, what is your gig?" I asked.

"I own an upscale consignment store and an antiques shop just down the street."

"Ah, that explains why you drive a van," I said, thinking a sporty car would be a more likely choice. But I was coming to understand there was nothing stereotypical about her. Despite her extraordinary beauty, Maggie's focus seemed to be directed outward with an avid interest in those around her.

"I also do a bit of interior design when I can," she added, then glanced at a clock mounted on the wall behind the counter. "Speaking of work, I need to get to my shop and relieve my assistant. If you don't mind, I'll take you back to your car now so you can get your things, then I'll drop you at the Eagle's Nest on my way in."

"Oh, gosh, I hadn't meant to hold you up," I said, realizing an hour had passed.

"You didn't at all." She placed her cup on the table. "I enjoyed this immensely and would love to hear more about your metal sculpting. I'm truly eager to see how you rewrite your story now that you're free to do so."

To imagine creating a new story for myself was something I'd never considered. But the possibility flashed so hot and bright, the idea welded itself to my brain.

* * *

I've been told I have a great poker face. Years of in-person sales meetings with customers, some lovely, some jerks, conditioned me to mask my thoughts behind a pleasant half-smile. Eighteen years with my husband, now my ex of ten months, who'd never been interested in my feelings or dreams, had taught me to conceal my pain behind an impassive façade.

But the sight of my company car parked at the station, a visual reminder of a high-paying job I'd just quit and really needed, shot a bolt of panic through my chest. I struggled to maintain a passive expression, but inside my head I was blurting, "*Oh my god, oh my god, oh my god!*"

Maggie pulled her van into the empty space beside my car. "Here you go!" Her chipper voice sounded wrong, as if she didn't realize we were at a funeral. I'd just killed my income, and I was already grieving the loss.

She waited while I went inside the station to get my keys from Jeff, a kind man with brown hair and farm-boy good looks. After thanking him, I hurried back outside, but as soon as I unlocked the door, my phone dinged. It was a text from my boss stating it was my responsibility to return the company car along with all account files, and he expected them to be delivered *tomorrow.*

But I wasn't ready to face the man who had driven me to upend my livelihood. I texted back that I wasn't feeling well, which was true because my stomach was in knots.

His reply to *STAY HOME!* came so quickly, I laughed.

Maggie raised an eyebrow as if inquiring what had hit my funny bone.

I told her Mr. Norton was such a fanatical germaphobe, he wouldn't allow me on the property until I could prove I wasn't ill. Then I showed her the texts I'd exchanged with him.

"Nicely played," she said with a laugh.

"Thanks, Maggie. Since I still have a car, for the moment at least, I can drive myself to the Eagle's Nest. But I'd like to meet you for coffee again before I leave town if you can manage it. Please don't feel pressured though. You've already been so kind and gone way beyond pointing a stranger in the direction of a coffee shop."

Maggie draped her elbow out the open window of her van. "Well, you were a very interesting stranger. I selfishly wanted to know more about the woman brave enough to tell her boss to bugger off. So, it was me who was being intrusive." She smiled and said, "I usually grab a coffee at the café around eight every morning. Hope to see you there." With a cheery wave, she drove out of the lot.

I stood beside my car feeling a bit stunned that Maggie, a confident woman with a vivacious personality and a job she loves, thought I was interesting. And brave.

I could barely remember a time when I'd felt either. Maybe during the year between graduating college and getting hired at the fab shop, when I'd gone backpacking in Australia with two of my college friends. At that time, I had adventures to talk about and stories to share. I'd planned to spend a year exploring the world, or at least a small part of it, but my father got sick.

Really sick.

I rushed home and began the hardest journey of my life—one that killed my joy as thoroughly as the cancer consumed my father. And I was so angry with my mother and sister for what they'd done, I hadn't spoken to them since.

The sudden blast of music coming from the open window of a silver SUV startled me. Two college-age girls bopped in their seats, singing along to a Taylor Swift song I recognized. I wasn't a hardcore fan, but I liked Swift's music and her messaging and admired her for setting a powerful example for young women. Apparently, the girls in the SUV did as well, because they were howling their hearts out as they pulled up to the gas pump, effectively diverting me from wandering into a swamp of quicksand memories.

I got in my car and headed in the direction of the Eagle's Nest. Until recently, I'd traveled to Dunwith every couple of months for my day job, but I'd never patronized any business other than the gas station because my tight schedule wouldn't allow it. I'd sold welding supplies to a small metal fabrication shop a few blocks from the gas station. When I met the owners, Rita Greenstone and her husband Walter, four years earlier, they were both in their seventies, wildly in love, and full of life. Rita was a talented, outspoken, whip-smart trailblazer I deeply admired, and Walter was a storyteller with a gentle sense of humor that reminded me of my father. When Rita died two months ago, Walter's heart wasn't the only one that broke. I adored them. Even though Walter had immediately closed their shop, and my company no longer had business in Dunwith, I still visited him because he'd become far more than a customer to me.

That's why my boss had demanded to know why I was here. I'd needed a quick visit to assure myself that Walter was holding up okay, to let him know I would keep coming back because I cared about him, and to selfishly enjoy a few minutes with a man who made me feel as if I mattered. I was eager to see him, but I needed to get a room first and take a few minutes to consider the consequences of my knee-jerk decision. Because without my job, I would have no car. No phone. No health insurance. No income.

What I did have were monthly bills and a son heading to college soon.

I had some savings and a decent retirement fund, so I could take a few days to regroup, but each week without an income would quickly drain those resources. I would need to get another job, but the thought of doing so was soul-crushing.

Chapter Two

The first thing I noticed about the Eagle's Nest Community Center was a large mural of a soaring eagle painted on a brick wall near the front entrance. The second was a petite dark-haired woman dressed in a dark pantsuit, wearing stylish, black-framed glasses, who seemed to be waiting for me. I suspected it was Beth but wasn't certain.

Feeling a bit awkward, I returned her smile and started up the wide concrete steps where she stood. The pipe railing wobbled beneath my hand, then unexpectedly broke loose at two of the joints. The unsecured section tipped inward and shoved me sideways a couple of steps.

The woman gasped and reached out to steady me. "Oh, my gosh! Are you all right?"

"Yes, I'm fine."

"I'm so sorry! I had no idea the railing was in such poor condition. Are you certain you're okay?" she asked, inspecting me with dark, concerned eyes.

"I'm fine. Truly," I said, reassuring her. "But your railing isn't." I set my travel bag on the steps, then knelt to inspect the damage. "Two of the weld joints have failed, and it appears at least two other joints need to be reinforced."

She glanced with dismay at the broken railing. "Shoot. The fab shop in town is closed, so I'll have to hunt down someone with a welder who is willing to do the work."

"I could do it for you." The words were out of my mouth before I realized I said them. I cringed and said, "I mean, if I had access to a welder."

Her eyes widened in surprise. "You can weld?"

"Yes, but I have no means to do so. Until you can get someone here to repair the railing, I'd suggest we secure it, so it doesn't fall in on anyone else," I said. "By the way, I'm Andie Arness, and I'm supposed to tell you that Sophie and Maggie sent me."

A warm smile tipped her mouth. "Sophie texted to let me know to expect you. I'm Beth Kingsley, and it's nice to meet you." Removing her glasses, she studied the railing. "Do you think duct tape would secure this thing?"

I laughed, appreciating her sense of humor, then peered over the railing to see freshly cut grass girding the concrete steps. "It might be a temporary fix if we can find a long, heavy stake or piece of pipe to support the railing. Cable ties would work better than tape if you have some. That might secure it until you can get someone to do a proper repair."

Popping her glasses back on her nose, she said, "All right, let's go inside and see what we can find."

I picked up my travel bag and followed Beth through two sets of heavy glass doors that opened into a lobby resembling a massive living room. Thick carpeting, soft lighting, and comfort-able-looking furniture created cozy sitting areas and reading nooks.

"This is beautiful. Did you do this?"

A sense of purpose filled her eyes. "Yes, with design help

from Maggie and Sophie, and many contributions from our community."

"Well, it's truly amazing." I took another moment to look around, feeling a sense of homecoming I rarely experienced in my own home.

"I can show you to your room before we repair the railing," she said. "I'm sure you're eager to settle in."

"I'm in no hurry," I said, knowing Walter would likely be home all day. "I just need a place to leave my bag."

She waved me into a cozy office adjacent to the lobby. After tucking my purse and bag inside a closet doubling as storage space for office supplies, she took me down a hallway leading to the back of the building where she unlocked a large metal door. She hit the lights and told me to help myself to whatever I might need.

The maintenance room was clean and well organized, and I immediately spotted two sections of rebar on a shelf and a hand maul on a steel pegboard. After Beth found the cable ties and three orange safety cones, we carried the items out to the front steps.

"If you can manage on your own for a minute, I'll make a sign to hang on the railing," she said.

"Go ahead. I'll need to sink the rebar in the ground outside the steps before we can secure the railing to it."

I'd just set the hand maul on the steps when she returned. While Beth held the railing against the rebar, I locked them together with nylon ties. We duct taped the sign to the railing, then placed safety cones along the broken section.

"That should do it," I said, dusting rebar rust off my hands.

She stepped back with a look of relief. "You have saved me a ton of worry and at least one sleepless night. How can I repay you?"

"How about a tour?" I asked, eager to see the rest of the

place. After washing my hands in the lobby bathroom, I followed Beth through the elementary school she'd converted into a dorm-style facility to temporarily house individuals or families in need. She also rented out available rooms to help sustain the facility. Everything had been painted in warm, uplifting colors, and decorated to give the place a homey feel. We passed other people in residence, and volunteer staff members working on premises, and people of various ages making use of the gym, pool, and game rooms.

We finished our tour back in her office where I collected my bag. Beth gave me a key to my third-floor room, promised to check on me later, then hurried off to a meeting. As I headed up to my room, I thought about Beth and her big vision. I could barely remember what it felt like to be that inspired. From the moment I learned I was pregnant with Tyler, my life had been so filled with doing and running and pleasing, it left no room for dreaming.

As I stepped into my rented room, sunlight streamed in through six tall windows, illuminating a suite straight out of an interior designer magazine. It was a large but cozy-feeling space with a kitchenette to the right of the door. On the far side of the room, white farmhouse-style bedroom furniture and a cedar wardrobe were arranged atop a thick gray and white carpet. Two blue and white pinstripe chairs created a cozy sitting area near the windows which gave me a view of the Dunwith River sparkling in the distance. Small shops and restaurants populated this side of the river, while a vast forest extended along the opposite side as far as I could see.

I'd expected a simple room with a bed and bathroom, but having this view and such a lovely place to rest my weary self for a couple of days was worth whatever Beth was charging.

Settling into one of the cushioned chairs, I kicked off my shoes and pressed my toes into a faux fur rug. With a long, satisfied sigh, I gazed at the river and let my eyelids droop as I dropped in and out of a lovely daydream. To relax and escape the world for a few minutes was a treat. Maybe it was the warmth of the luxurious suite and the dazzling view from my window that created an obsessive yearning in me, but whatever the cause, I ached for something more than the mundane life I'd been living.

* * *

I'd just freshened up and was ready to head out to visit Walter when my phone rang. Shocked and deeply concerned to see that my son was calling and not texting, I answered immediately.

"Hey, Mom." My son's voice had deepened long ago, but it could still catch me off guard to realize my baby would be embarking on his first year of college soon. In my mind's eye, Tyler would always be my sweet boy who'd wanted to cuddle and read books at bedtime. His voice was different now, not just deeper but distant. Because of me.

"Hey sweetie, are you okay?"

"Yes, Mom," he said, clearly exasperated with my need to be reassured. "I just called to ask when you'll be home so we can go car shopping."

I leaned against the bathroom vanity. "Since you're with your father this weekend, I figured we'd go Monday or Tuesday."

"Are you seriously working over a weekend?"

"No, Ty. I'm just taking a couple of days away to rest."

He was silent for a moment. "Are you spending the weekend with a guy?"

"What? *No*," I said, a little shocked. "I just need a minute to think about some things."

"Oh. Are you okay?" he asked, the first bit of concern I'd heard in his voice since I'd divorced his father. My leaving Clark had wounded Tyler, too, because I couldn't give either of them a clear reason for the divorce. All I could say was I couldn't breathe.

Which is exactly how I'd felt this morning when I quit my job.

"Mom? Are you there?"

"Yeah, sorry, Ty. I just had a rough morning at work and need a break is all."

"Ah," he said, intimately familiar with the stress I brought home with me. "You should tell your boss to back off."

"I did. In fact, I quit my job this morning."

"What?" Ty's voice cracked from bass to falsetto, making me snicker. "Are you serious?"

"Yeah. I really did it. I quit."

"Whoa," he said.

I knew I'd shocked him. My actions were so out of character and so unexpected, I knew he'd need a moment to process my news.

"Is this going to mess things up for me getting a car and going to college?"

It hurt a little that he was only considering how this would affect him, but he was eighteen, and I knew teenagers believed the world revolved around them.

"Of course not," I said. "I've earmarked savings for those expenses." I'd been working doggedly for years to create a fund for Ty's future needs. It had been easier during my marriage when Clark and I both contributed to our household needs, which allowed me to put more into savings. But in the ten months since our divorce, I'd barely banked any extra cash. Without an income, at least temporarily, I would need to be frugal with my expenses and protect the monies I'd set aside for Tyler.

"Okay, that's good," he said, "because I'll really need a car at college."

"I know, hon. We'll go on Tuesday."

"Or Dad could take me Monday," he haltingly suggested.

My heart cramped.

"I know you're helping me pay for the vehicle, Mom, but Dad knows a lot about cars."

He certainly did, and that single-minded passion of Clark's had destroyed us. We'd spent nearly every weekend of our marriage going to car-related events while Clark's unquenchable pursuit of buying and selling vintage cars and restoring them consumed our family. Tyler loved it, and early on I enjoyed it because it gave us something to do as a family. But years of Clark's obsession left no room in our lives for anything else.

Now, vehicle shopping was the last thing I wanted to do, but I'd anticipated spending the day with my son. I'd wanted to take him out for lunch and have the pleasure of helping him buy a newer car. He was still driving the starter car we'd gotten him at sixteen. But he was right. His father knew far more about vehicles than I did.

"Okay, Ty, it's probably a good idea to have your dad take you," I said, hoping my acquiescence wouldn't send the wrong message to his father. Despite our being divorced, Clark tended to interpret our joint parenting as the two of us still being together. He was underfoot now more than he'd been during our marriage. Several times a week he came by the house to dabble with his classic cars still stored in the garage that used to be my father's workshop. I did my best to avoid Clark, but somehow, he still managed to draw me into conversations and family-style evenings.

"How much can I spend?" Tyler asked.

"I've earmarked twenty thousand dollars for your car. Anything over that will be your responsibility."

"Got it. Thanks, Mom. Gotta call Dad now," Ty blurted, then ended the call.

I gaped at the phone for a second, then released a sad laugh. "Love you, too," I said to no one.

Barely five minutes had passed when Clark called. I groaned and let it go to voicemail because I knew exactly how the conversation would go. *What happened, Andie? Do you think you overreacted? Can you apologize to your boss and get your job back? Do you have a plan?*

No, I did not have a plan. But I needed one.

Chapter Three

I walked two blocks south, then crossed Fern Park, a gorgeous greenspace that stretched the length of town. The park sat between two main streets with bike trails running along each side. Sprawling maple trees dotted the park, and walking paths led to picnic pavilions, a covered farmers market, and designated game areas.

Lengthening my stride, I savored the feel of my lungs expanding and contracting. To enjoy a leisurely walk during a workday felt divine. Afternoon sunshine draped my shoulders like a lover's arm, something I hadn't felt in a long time. But I didn't feel lonely. I felt grateful to have a moment to myself.

As I approached the brown and tan structural steel building, I noticed Walter sitting on a wooden crate parked outside the open overhead door. He lifted his battered ball cap with one hand and scratched his head with the other, whipping his white hair into a milkweed tuft. He popped the hat back on, then leaned down to scratch the ears of his faithful companion Louie.

The memory of my first visit to their shop when I'd met them still made me smile. I'd just gotten out of my car that day when I heard a loud bang from inside the shop followed by a woman cursing. Knowing how dangerous metalwork could be, I sprinted inside to find an elderly woman, with a red bandana tied around her head, wrestling with a piece of partially fabricated aluminum sheet. One end of the material had kicked out of the machine, and she was struggling to wrangle it back in. I dropped my briefcase and stepped in to support the heavy end she was holding, but she refused to let me help with the *consarn piece of hell-metal* until I'd pulled on the pair of gloves lying on a nearby worktable.

After the two of us adjusted and finished bending the material, we carried it to a large worktable, then stepped back to rest our arms. Mopping her face with her kerchief, Rita introduced herself and thanked me for rescuing her. Then she scanned the shop and released a string of curses, saying her dagnab husband was a numpty fopdoodle for taking a stroll in the middle of a workday. Her cussing was so old-fashioned and colorful, I struggled to hide my smile.

I'd just introduced myself to her when an elderly man with white hair and a permanent squint etched around his eyes walked in followed by a scrawny brown and white dog. Rita called the man a bufflehead for walking the dog in the middle of their workday, but he just grinned and planted a loud smooch on her dirt-smudged cheek. Blushing, she introduced Walter and their dog Louie, then said she would literally expire if she didn't get a cup of coffee. I fell in love with the three of them on the spot.

To see Walter now, sitting on a crate and looking so forlorn without the woman he loved, wrenched my heart. As I approached, Louie's head came up, and he scrambled to his paws. Seeking the cause of the dog's excitement, Walter glanced in my direction and a slow smile creased his face.

I greeted Louie first, giving him a treat and a thorough scratching as I always did. Then I turned to Walter who had pushed to his feet and was waiting with open arms, as he always was, and we exchanged a warm hug. He'd been greeting me like this since my second visit to their shop. When he hugged me, I was so surprised by his sweet display, I apologized for not maintaining a modicum of professionalism. Walter just smiled and said friends and family greet each other with a hug, and from that day on that's how we said hello and goodbye.

When he released me, and sat back down on the wooden box, I asked, "What are you doing with the crate?"

"I'm contemplating how one might move a mountain with a hand trowel."

I laughed at his obvious exaggeration. "What's the problem?"

"I've completely destroyed Rita's shop."

Curious, I glanced inside. The interior lighting was dim after my sunny walk, but as my vision adjusted, the mess began to materialize. Tools lay scattered atop worktables. Bags and boxes buried the plasma table and nearly every other surface. What used to be organized standing metal racks of steel tubes, bars, and sheets were now a mixed jumble. Coffee cans and small boxes holding god-knows-what were stashed haphazardly atop the bar stock. Barrels and crates, spools of welding wire, tanks of acetylene gas, ladders, and other items I couldn't make out filled every corner of the shop. Utterly stunned to see Rita's clean, well-organized business in such disarray, I could only shake my head and gape at Walter.

"That's exactly how I feel each time I look at the mess," he said.

"What happened here?" I asked, truly bewildered.

"My wife died, and my life fell apart," he said with moist eyes.

"Oh, Walter, I'm so sorry." I gave his forearm a gentle squeeze.

With a sweeping glance at the building, he said, "It's just too empty here without her, so Louie and I are moving to The Grove where we have friends. I'm going to sell everything including the business, but I want to take Rita's pocket-pliers with me." At my confused look, he said, "It's a pair of needle nose pliers she carried with her everywhere. I can't imagine where they'd be. Every day I dig through more drawers and toolboxes looking for the dang things, but I just make more of a mess." He rubbed the back of his neck, his knobby fingers ruffling the worn collar of his work shirt. "Rita would string me up by my ears if she saw the place now. My realtor won't list the business until I get the mess cleaned up, but I'm just not up to the task." He gave a hopeless shrug.

"Of course you're not," I said, marveling that an eighty-two-year-old man had enough strength to move the heavy tools and materials that lay strewn around the shop. "How can I help?"

His mouth quirked in the lopsided smile I'd grown so fond of. "You could buy the place and save me the trouble of cleaning it up."

I laughed but also felt heartbroken for him. "Don't tempt me. I just quit my job and would love to have my own shop."

"Then let me make you an offer you can't refuse."

I glanced at the building where I'd discussed projects and life and old fashioned curse words with Rita and listened to Walter's stories that made me laugh myself to tears and where I fed Louie treats that earned me his slobbery affection. It had been a joyful place for me, and a happy home for them. I couldn't imagine the pain Walter must feel letting it all go. "If I lived in Dunwith, I'd buy the shop today, Walter, but I live two-and-a-half-hours away. That kind of commute would be impossible."

"You wouldn't have to commute if you lived in the loft apartment like Rita and I did."

A thump of excitement hit my chest, but it was simply a fantasy for me. "Buying a business can take months, so I'd still have to commute until the deal was done. Even if I got a quick sale on my house, our attorneys would have to push a mountain of paperwork through legal channels."

"None of that would have to hold you up, Andie. You could sign a purchase agreement and live right here in the apartment and run your business while you sell your house and the paperwork goes through." With a sly wink, Walter said, "Louie and I are already staying at The Grove, so I could give you the keys today."

The idea was wildly tempting. "I wish I could. More than you know. But I can't do anything with my life until Tyler heads off to college."

It seemed as if Walter wanted to say more but he let the conversation drop. "Did you say Tyler's going to Alfred State this year?"

"Yes, he's interested in design and animation."

"Not following in his mama's footsteps then?"

"Not even a little," I said. "He's all about cars and computers, but I want him to follow his bliss wherever it leads."

"Perhaps you should as well," Walter said, squinting up at me. "You have a solid set of skills and could easily run your own shop. Rita and I had a profitable business, and I'd be glad to show you the books, if you're interested."

Intense longing washed through me, followed by crushing disappointment because I didn't have the luxury of just picking up my life and relocating. "Thanks, but I'll just give you a hand cleaning up if you like. I'm staying in town this weekend and would be happy to help you move the rest of your things to your new place," I said, steering the subject back to his dilemma and away from my own wishful thinking.

"Thank you, dear, but this mess will take more than a

weekend to sort out. I'll hire someone to come in after I find what I'm looking for. Is there something special keeping you in town?" he asked.

"Not really. I just found myself with a bit of free time and decided to explore Dunwith before heading home." Because going back meant facing my ex-boss, starting a job search for work I didn't want to do, and dealing with unfinished business with my ex-husband. "While I'm here, though, I'd like to take care of a small repair for Beth over at the Eagle's Nest. May I rent your portable welder and a few tools?"

"You just take whatever you need, dear." With a wave of his hand, Walter beckoned me to follow him inside. "Watch your step," he said as we skirted boxes, metal debris, and hand tools, and sidled through narrow passages between stacked barrels and crates. Long metal bars sticking out of the racking system had Walter ducking and me playing limbo. It took nearly two hours to unearth the proper tools, appropriate gear, and a mobile welding screen. He offered to deliver everything to the Eagle's Nest on his old flatbed truck, but he looked tired.

"That would be wonderful," I said. "I could use your assistance if you're willing to help me, but would you mind if I do the job tomorrow?"

"Not at all. I'd like to help," he said, sounding pleased I asked. "Before you leave, Andie, would you give me a hand? I need to put that box in the back seat of my SUV." He pointed to a long wooden box sitting by the door to the office. "It's not heavy, just bulky and difficult for one person to manage."

"Of course. Whatever you need." After loading the box in the back seat, I retrieved a laundry basket of folded clothing and two small boxes from his office and loaded them inside. "Anything else need to go?" I asked.

"Just a few things I'll get tomorrow. Then the place is all

yours," he said, giving me a wink before opening the passenger door for the dog.

Louie climbed onto the seat, the tip of his tongue peeping from the front of his mouth as he watched Walter lock up the shop. The dog was so adorable, I couldn't resist kissing his knobby head and giving him a goodbye treat.

When Walter returned, he jangled the keys in the air. "Are you sure you don't want these tonight?"

I groaned and gave him a hug. "I do want them, so stop tormenting me."

"All right, I'll lay off for tonight."

He offered to give me a ride back to the Eagle's Nest, but I declined in favor of a walk along the river. Thirty minutes later, I found myself at a small pub on the river walk where I ordered a cheese pretzel and iced tea.

I sat at an outside table to get an unobstructed view of the stunning Dunwith River. The sparkling jewel moved with the slow, flowing grace of a ballerina, and I watched her dance for a long time. Blue and green reflections of sky and forest undulated on the glistening surface where my thoughts drifted like flotsam. A sense of peace permeated my body, and for the first time in a long time, I could breathe.

I ached for a place of my own, one that wasn't filled with memories. I missed the focused passion I felt when creating a sculpture. A deep, desperate longing for my lost art wrenched my gut, and I regretted not fighting harder to keep it. Somehow, I'd sacrificed the best parts of me. I hadn't intended to. My sacrifices were meant to be temporary, to briefly set aside my art until the needs of my infant son weren't so consuming. Bonding with my baby brought me intrinsic joy, and I didn't regret a single moment of those precious months of motherhood. I'd planned to get back to my studio when Tyler started walking, but my busy toddler, and Clark's car obsession, took over my workshop and every aspect of our lives.

I loved my family and believed my sacrifice was altruistic, that it was motivated by love, but now I wondered if I'd allowed the obliteration of my passion because it was easier to support someone else's dream than to pursue my own.

That disturbing question followed me to my room, haunted my dreams, and woke me at dawn with a rock in my gut.

Chapter Four

I pulled on my running shoes and ran a footpath along the Dunwith river, filling my lungs with fresh mountain air. The cadence of my sneakers lightly tapping the earth always lulled me into a state of meditation or gentle contemplation. Even as far back as high school, when I ran noisy track events, my thoughts would wrap around me like lotus petals closing at night. Encapsulated in my private space, I would focus on my breathing or follow gentle streams of thought wherever they led.

But this morning, an obsessive yearning flooded my brain, and it was all I could think about. I craved the freedom to spend my days pursuing my passion. I longed to build a life that suited *me*, however simple it might be. I wanted more spontaneity, joy, and laughter in my life. And I wanted mornings like this.

As the earthy scent of forest and river filled my lungs, I imagined owning Walter's shop, waking early in my loft apartment and pulling on my running shoes. After a brisk jog along the river, as I was doing now, I would stop at the café for coffee and a scone. I'd sit at a table by the front window and sketch out ideas in my journal the way my father taught me, then spend the day in my shop creating art from scrap metal.

Immersed in my dream, I soared along the river path as if I'd sprouted wings.

I was still flying high thirty minutes later when I entered the Maple Leaf Café and heard Maggie calling my name. I turned to find her sharing a table with two women of a similar age, one blonde, the other dark-haired, all three wearing T-shirts and ball caps with matching logos.

"Good morning," I said, giving them a small wave from where I stood at the counter.

With a head tilt that tossed her long ponytail like a chestnut-colored mane, Maggie said, "Come join us."

After dropping my change in the tip cup on the counter, I approached the table but hung back a couple feet.

She patted the chair beside her. "Have a seat. I want to introduce you to my friends Kate Weston"—she gestured toward the blonde—"and Chloe Saunders," she said, nodding toward the dark-haired woman.

"It's nice to meet you," I said, exchanging a warm smile with them.

They replied in kind and encouraged me to join them.

"I'm sweaty from my run and probably not the best table-mate right now."

Maggie dismissed my concern with a flip of her hand. "We've suffered far worse from Kate when she lived in her boathouse without electricity or running water."

Kate feigned insult. "Some friend you are."

Chloe wrinkled her nose. "Kate, I can attest to your appalling hygiene."

Their laughter was so warm and playful, I slid onto the chair beside Maggie and set my steaming mug on the table. "Don't say I didn't warn you ladies."

"Consider yourself warned in return," Maggie said. "We'll definitely be a bad influence."

I gestured to their matching ball caps and T-shirts. "Are you all on a ball team?"

Confusion crossed their faces, then Maggie laughed. "That would be spectacular! We could name our team Badass Broads. Just think of the after-parties we could have," she said, leaning in as if really trying to convince her friends.

"We already have after-parties," Chloe said. "They're called girl gabs." She turned to Kate. "You were right, though. We should have made our logo font larger."

That's when I noticed the words *Done With Landscaping* under the logo. "Okay, so you're not on a ball team. I like the layered meaning of your logo."

"It's intentional, and we're mostly part-timers," Kate said. "Maggie told us you're a welder and artist. You make metal sculptures, is that right?"

"Well, yes, but I'm not sculpting or working right now."

A knowing smile tipped Kate's lips. "Maggie told us you quit your job. Chloe and I couldn't wait to meet you."

"I'm sure," I said, happy to be part of their playful ribbing. "Maggie shared a bit about you, too, Kate. I'd love to see photos of your place and hear how you converted an old boathouse into a home."

"You're welcome to come by this evening and see it for yourself," Kate said.

I was so surprised by the invitation, I stuttered, "Um, yeah, sure, I'd love that."

"We'll be on a landscaping job all day, so let's plan on six o'clock."

"Okay." I glanced at Maggie. "I don't recall you mentioning that you do landscaping work."

They all laughed as if I'd said something funny.

"Maggie doesn't work with us," Chloe said. "We just make

her wear our gear because, well, she's gorgeous and everyone looks at her. She's our walking advertisement."

"I feel so used and unappreciated," Maggie said, as if sharing a confidence with me. "I only wear their gear because it's comfy, not because I like them."

But she did like them, and I marveled at their obvious love for each other and the deep connection they shared. I envied their friendship. I'd never had a relationship like that.

"We need to get to our job now," Kate said, pushing her chair back.

I gave her my number, and she texted me her address before she headed out with Chloe.

"Andie, I can pick you up. I'll be going to Kate's for our girl gab anyway," Maggie said. "I'll swing by at six to get you."

I wasn't entirely certain what all a girl gab involved, but the thought of hanging out with fun friends, or at least women my age, was something I hadn't experienced in a long, lonely time.

* * *

After I left the café, I met Walter at his shop and helped him load our gear on the truck. Louie sat between us as we headed to the Eagle's Nest.

We set out our tools and plugged in the welder, then put the welding screen in place to shield observers from the welding flash. Beth took Louie inside with her, and we got to work. To avoid having to dismantle the whole section of railing, we hammered the split pipe connectors back in place, then cleaned the areas to be welded.

"Okay, it's been a minute since I've run a bead," I said. "I might need a practice run."

Walter flapped a hand to dismiss my concern. "This old girl is a bit temperamental, so you can blame any mistakes on her."

"Thanks," I said with a laugh, but I felt a little nervous as I began welding the seams.

Wearing his own welding helmet, Walter looked over my shoulder, encouraging me while explaining how Rita would make small adjustments to the temperamental welder. Smiling behind my mask, I thanked him and followed his advice. His gentle instruction reminded me of my father and how he'd taught me to weld and encouraged my artistic passion.

I thought about the art we made from scrap metal, and the sculpture we'd never finished that Clark had pushed to a corner in my father's shop. I'd promised my dad I'd finish the piece we had been so excited about, but after he died, I couldn't look at it without breaking down. I wanted to blame Clark's car obsession for burying the sculpture, but the truth was it hurt too much to see the unfinished project that reminded me of my father's unfinished life.

"Better slow down a bit," Walter said, making me refocus and narrowly avoid undercutting my weld.

After I finished repairing and reinforcing the pipe fittings, we pulled off our helmets and inspected my work. With a decisive nod, Walter patted my shoulder. "You did a fine job, Andie."

His gentle praise, so like the words my father once said, had me blinking moisture from my eyes. "I really enjoyed this."

"I know you did. That's why you need your own shop, wherever that might be."

"Maybe someday," I said, wistfully.

"Someday isn't a real day, Andie. If now isn't the time, then when will you start living the life you want? In a month? In a year?" With a gentle pat on my shoulder, he said quietly, "You need to think about that."

Louie came bounding out the door, followed by Beth. "I can't thank you enough," she said, then asked what she owed us.

When we told her there was no charge, she insisted on buying Walter dinner and comping my stay in exchange, but we refused. Room rentals and volunteer services like this were vital to the continued health of the Eagle's Nest. I admired what Beth was doing and intended to fully support her however I could.

"Thank you," she said, pulling me into a hard hug.

I'd been hugged more in one weekend than in the whole previous year. Tyler claimed he was too old for hugs, and I had none left for Clark. With another round of thanks and a hug for Walter, Beth watched us gather our tools and equipment, then waved us off.

After Walter climbed in the truck, Louie bounded in and sat in the center of the bench seat. I sat beside him, and Walter cranked the engine to life. The radio was tuned to a country music station, and I smiled because Walter, a broken-hearted old man with a beater truck and a faithful dog, epitomized the song that was playing.

We were both quiet on the five-minute ride back to the shop. I couldn't guess what was on Walter's mind, but all I could think about was taking a hot shower, then finding out what a girl gab was all about.

After we took everything back in the shop, Walter said he wasn't feeling up to moving the last of his stuff from the apartment, so we planned to meet the next morning. But I suspected he had an ulterior motive like creating another opportunity to convince me to do the one thing I wanted to do with all my aching heart.

Chapter Five

I was used to going out for business lunches and dinners with customers I didn't know on a personal level, but Maggie wasn't my customer. Our conversations, however brief, had been fun, and I was looking forward to learning more about her and her friends.

She welcomed me with a warm smile as I got in her van. "Feeling up to a night out?"

I flopped back in my seat. "Absolutely. I need a distraction from the bedlam in my head."

"I can imagine." Pressing her sandal-covered foot on the accelerator, she pulled away from the curb. "Quitting your job is a big thing, Andie."

"Or a dumb thing," I said.

"Or a *courageous* thing," she countered, cruising slowly through town, weaving her way through two traffic circles. "Time will tell. Either way, you made a decision. That's important. Choosing to act is empowering."

I considered that as we headed out of town on Bear Hollow Road. I pushed my sunglasses up, using them as a headband to hold my hair back. "I suppose you're right. It was empowering, but I have no idea what I'm going to do now, and I can't stop obsessing about it."

"You don't need to have all the answers." She glanced over, her ponytail draped over one shoulder. "Why not give yourself permission to enjoy a few days off before thinking through all this stuff?"

Somehow the act of granting myself a longer reprieve from my real life felt strangely liberating. "That's a brilliant idea. I think I'll take a week off before starting my job search."

"Atta girl." With our forearms resting on the open windows, and the warm evening air tossing our hair, Maggie told me that Kate had left everything behind to escape her husband's cult-like religion, then started from broke and fought like hell to convert an old boathouse to a lakeside retreat. When we came to a crossroads a few minutes outside of town, she pointed out a white house with a connected garage and a large barn with a blue metal roof. "That's Chloe's place."

"That's a big house. Does she have kids?"

"She's widowed and has a college-aged son who lives with her during the summers." Before I could ask, Maggie added, "Kate has twin daughters about the same age as Chloe's son."

Maggie turned onto a gravel road that crunched beneath the tires and made the van vibrate.

"How about you? Any kids?" I asked, raising my voice a little to be heard over the road noise.

"No kids. Never married. Not happening."

"I admire your commitment, Maggie."

She shrugged. "I like my life. Why complicate things? So many people sabotage their happiness because they don't want to be alone."

A hot flush stole through my chest because I'd been one of

those people. I'd made one foolish decision after another. I had loved my ex-husband but shouldn't have married him. At the time, I needed someone who could navigate for me because I was floundering in an ocean of grief. But when I was finally strong enough to take back the oars, he refused to relinquish them.

"We're here," Maggie said, pulling into an unpaved driveway.

"Whoa! Wait a minute. Stop-stop-stop," I said, pointing to a wooden sign with a shoe nailed to it. "What is that?"

Maggie's face lit up. "That's Kate's handiwork."

As I read Kate's hand-painted sign stating she was done with religious nonsense, unfair tax laws, and misogyny and bigotry, I admired her declaration and her courage for openly displaying her position. "Would it be rude to ask if that's her ex's shoe nailed to the sign?"

Maggie laughed and pulled her phone from the holder on the dash "I'll show you exactly how the dumbass lost it." With a few swipes and taps, she opened a video, then handed the phone to me.

As I watched the drama between Kate and her ex unfolding on a wooden dock, I hoped I wasn't about to witness domestic violence. I winced when he grabbed her wrist, then gaped in surprise when her quick reaction caused him to fall in the lake. Whoever recorded the video panned from Kate's face to a close-up of her ex's enraged one as he surfaced. His arms slashed through the air flinging water as he released a verbal torrent of outrage. He sloshed ashore hobbling twice before limping angrily to his car. Grass flew from beneath the tires as he tore out, then swerved hard to miss an incoming vehicle, only to side-swipe a dump truck instead.

I hadn't realized I'd clapped my hand over my mouth and

was giggling like a teenage girl until I looked at Maggie. "I can't believe that really happened."

Maggie released a belt of laughter. "Wait until you see Kate's church walk. It was epic!" I expected her to cue up the video, but she popped the phone back in the cradle. "I'll let Kate decide if she wants to show you that one."

I hoped she would, but I understood these were moments captured from Kate's personal life and should be her decision whether to share.

Putting the van in gear, Maggie drove between two brick pylons with cameras mounted on them. She saw me noticing them. "Kate has justifiable reasons for having those cameras. Stick around long enough and I'm sure you'll hear all about her amusing incidents."

We drove out a narrow dirt road that Maggie called the lake trail. It meandered through a lush woodland and delivered us to a small lake nestled in a mountain basin. A driftwood-gray cottage with a blue gambrel roof sat several yards away from the sparkling lake. An awning spanning half the length of Kate's home was centered over white trimmed French Doors and a cozy arrangement of outdoor furniture. The peaceful beauty of the place took my breath away.

I glanced at Maggie. "This is straight out of a resort magazine."

"It wasn't like this when Kate first arrived. The lake trail we just drove in on was so overgrown it was difficult just walking out here. Waist-high weeds covered this whole lakefront area, and the boathouse was just a wooden shell."

"Did Kate do all of this herself?"

"Mostly. We helped when and where we could, but this is Kate's vision, and she had to fight like hell for it."

"I can see why she would."

Maggie's brows knotted. "But she shouldn't have had to. No

one should have to fight to have agency over their own life. And Kate is a certified badass for surviving all she went through."

The French doors opened, and Maggie's badass friend stepped outside. When Kate spotted the van, she waved.

Although we'd met at the coffee shop and exchanged a bit of fun conversation, I felt awkward entering her private life. But Kate surprised me with a hug and offered us a cold drink. We followed her inside, where I stopped and gawked at the beautiful interior.

Maggie puffed up like a proud mama and hooked her arm around Kate. "I love watching people see your house for the first time."

"Definitely different than the looks I got when I first moved in," Kate said.

I pressed a hand to my cheek and realized I was shaking my head in amazement. "My god, this is incredible." As I scanned the post-and-beam interior, I noted the cathedral ceiling with skylights over the main living area and a deep loft tucked over the kitchen. White shiplap walls, lots of windows, and white kitchen cabinets gave the cozy cottage a clean, open feel. "Was this really a boathouse?" I asked, struggling to imagine Kate's beautiful home as an empty wooden shell.

"Yes, and the first few nights I stayed here I slept in a canoe."

I laughed, thinking she was joking until Maggie assured me Kate was serious. "I know we just met and this might be intrusive, but I'm begging you to tell me that story."

"Happy to, but let me get our drinks first," Kate said. She carried a pitcher of cold tea and glasses to the living room and placed them on an old trunk sitting atop a smoky blue and charcoal gray rug. On each end of a gray sofa, antique wooden crates were stood on end and topped with matching lamps.

I sat in a chair opposite Maggie, marveling how the cozy

sitting area directed one's view to the sparkling lake outside the large picture window. "I would never be able to leave this place," I said, wishing with all my heart I didn't have to.

"I can't take credit for the interior decorating," Kate said, pouring our tea. "Without Maggie's artistic eye, my furniture would have been pushed against a wall with no thought to design."

"Exactly what I would have done," I admitted, thoroughly impressed with Maggie's vision. "How are you not booked twenty-four hours a day?"

Maggie shrugged. "I have no desire to fill my days working for other people."

"I can't fault you for that, but with your talent, you could make a fortune."

"But I don't need or want a fortune," she said. "I prefer to own the hours in my day, not sell them all."

"How does one manage to do that if you're not independently wealthy?" I asked, truly wanting to know her secret.

"Just figure out what you need to be happy." She shrugged as if the answer was obvious. "For me, I need to own my time, spend it with people I care about and do things I love to do. I don't want a big house or fancy car or to climb a corporate ladder. I'm not impressed by wealth or the trappings of that life. My days are filled with moments of wonder and joy, and I absorb them as they come. I don't go looking for more, and I don't feel as if I'm missing anything."

"That's the truth for me, too," Kate said, glancing up to the loft where a long-haired black-and-white cat sat on the half-wall watching us. "I live a richer life in my little paradise than I ever did in the multi-million dollar house I left behind." She told me how she'd come here alone in an RV, feeling lost and disconnected from her family and friends. When she refused to return home, her ex took the RV and left her destitute and without shelter in freezing temps.

Horrified, I glanced at Maggie, who assured me with a slight nod it was true.

"How did you manage to survive?" I asked, trying to imagine what she must have gone through in the wooded wilderness.

"I sheltered in the boathouse and slept in a canoe." Although she smiled, something in her eyes suggested the memory was painful. She glanced up at the loft again. "That little fur ball was living in my grandparents' dilapidated house," she said, "and he was as desperate as I was to find a safe, warm home. I figured things out one day at a time, and Sinatra has been with me every step of the way, haven't you, baby?" she said, speaking to the cat.

With a wide yawn, he stretched out on his perch, making us laugh. Maggie followed suit, relaxing back in her chair, long legs extended and crossed at the ankles.

While we drank our tea, I told Kate she was a lot braver than I would have been in similar circumstances.

"It was necessity more than bravery that kept me going," she said. "Starting with nothing forced me to figure out what I really needed. I realized how my old life crap had buried the most important parts of me." She eyed me for a moment, then said, "I hope I'm not getting too personal or sharing too much, but I know you quit your job, and I thought it might help you feel less worried to hear a bit about someone else's struggle. But if I'm intruding, just say so."

"If anyone is intruding, it's me. I'm basically a stranger Maggie rescued at a gas station. All I'd wanted was a cup of coffee. I didn't expect all this kindness." I glanced at Maggie who gave a one-shoulder shrug.

"Maggie's always bringing home strays," Kate said, then

glanced up at Sinatra who appeared to be sleeping. "But we love our strays and rescues, and you're more than welcome here, Andie."

To receive such unexpected warmth from strangers at one of the most chaotic moments of my life made my eyes mist. I cleared my throat twice before thanking them.

As if Maggie knew I needed a reprieve, she slapped her thighs and stood. "Why are we sitting inside on such a gorgeous evening? Come on, ladies." Pivoting on one strappy sandal, she was out the door in three strides.

We followed her down to the wooden dock where Kate's ex had plunged into the lake. She noticed me smiling, so I told her Maggie had shown me the video.

"Definitely a moment I won't forget," Kate said, then told me she'd grown up here with her younger sister, Sophie, and spent most summer days swimming and boating at the lake with Maggie and Chloe.

The sound of a car drew our attention to the lake trail, where Chloe was parking her SUV. We met her a few yards from the house where several lawn chairs sat around a sunken firepit. A thick bed of ashes suggested many campfires and likely many conversations had taken place here.

While Kate built a fire and Chloe pulled a variety of snack foods from a large shopping bag, I helped Maggie get two coolers from her van. "Whoa, what's in here?" I asked, giving the heavy cooler handle a jiggle as we headed back.

"Beer, wine, you know, the necessities."

I laughed, then I gasped. "Oh my god, I'm an idiot!" Heat blasted my face. "I should have thought to bring something."

"Not necessary, Andie. We invited you. You're our guest."

"That's even more reason I should have brought something. My brain has been in a spin since I quit my job, and I can't keep a straight thought in my head for a solid minute."

Clasping my shoulder, she pulled me to a gentle stop. "Hey, you can relax here. We've all been through shit. We get it. There are no expectations or requirements for our girl gabs. The only thing we ask of each other is honesty."

"That's one thing I always bring with me," I said.

Her expression softened. "Good, then let's go drink this beer."

Chapter Six

I had no idea how fun a girl gab would be. At times I felt a little outside the conversations and jokes because I didn't have the benefit of their shared history, but I never felt left out. Kate, Chloe, and Maggie showed genuine interest in my life and how I'd come to be at their Friday night campfire. Maggie delighted in retelling every beat of my conversation with my boss, and they cheered me with raised beer bottles. Not for one minute did they let me feel I was intruding in their circle.

It was as if they inherently understood the disconcerting angst of being untethered from your own life. When there was a slight lull in the conversation, I asked Kate if she was scared when she decided to leave her old life behind, and if she ever thought about going back.

Her hand paused mid-stroke on Sinatra's purring back. "Only once," she said, "but not because I was afraid of being on my own. I considered going back because my daughters begged me to come home. They didn't understand what was happening or why I'd left their father. They were confused, and one of my girls felt I'd abandoned her."

"That must have been a heart-wrenching decision," I said,

knowing my son might feel the same if I sold our home. I could empathize with Kate and the pain she must have experienced making that hard choice.

"It ripped my heart out," she said. "But going back would have taught my daughters the wrong lesson. They needed to learn that wanting independence and a life of one's own is not selfish, and that it's worth fighting for."

Chloe gave Kate's forearm a comforting squeeze. "Everything worked out, and your daughters are stronger, more independent women because of you."

"Yes, and they love this place and the new you," Maggie said, "and they adore their honorary aunts, of course."

"They sure do." The love in Kate's voice was palpable.

These three women were intrinsically linked like one beautiful day: Kate a luminous blonde with a radiant good-morning smile, Chloe a bronze-skinned beauty with sparkling eyes and midnight-black hair, and Maggie with her vibrant personality and dazzling looks sitting between them like a blazing orange sunset. But not one of them appeared to notice how spectacular they were.

Next to them, I felt like a brown mouse.

As the evening deepened and the fire burned down, my body sank lower in the chair. Frogs belched near the lake shore, and night critters fluttered and scurried in the forest. I looked up at the stars, so bright away from the glow of city lights, and released a long sigh.

"Are you all right, Andie?"

The concern in Kate's voice surprised me. "Sure. I'm just thinking about big decisions and what might be ahead."

"Life changes can be unnerving and upsetting as hell. Ask me how I know."

The way Kate said it made me want to delve deeper into her

life story, but I didn't ask. "I can't remember when I last felt this relaxed."

"Campfires will do that," Chloe said.

"Or beer," Maggie countered.

"Probably both," I said with a laugh. "Whatever the reason, it's great to be here. Thank you all for being so kind and—" My voice caught on a burr of emotion, and I had to clear my throat to continue. "I appreciate the warm welcome. And the beer," I added, toasting them with my bottle. "I'm ready for a second one if you don't mind."

Maggie looked at Chloe. "Well, well, well. The new girl likes beer and has a sense of humor. I think she'll fit in nicely with our girl gabs."

Chloe nodded. "Yeah, but she can bring the beer next time."

Next time?

"And the chips," Kate said. "Maggie always forgets the damn chips."

"I'd be happy to bring the beer *and* the chips," I said, "but I'm afraid I have to go home. I have a son and other responsibilities waiting for me."

"Didn't you say he would be heading off to college soon?" Maggie asked.

"Yes, which is why I need to figure out what I'm going to do for a job."

"There are plenty of jobs in Dunwith."

"Believe me, I'd love to work here, but I couldn't manage a two-and-a-half hour commute."

In the warm glow of firelight, I could see Maggie's brows dip in a slight frown. She looked at Kate and Chloe. "Maybe the new girl isn't very bright. She apparently doesn't understand that she could *move* here."

Chloe gave me the side-eye, then mock-whispered to Kate, "Would it be rude to uninvite her?"

Kate snickered. "We might have to."

Their exaggerated grimaces and playful heckling made me laugh. To be invited back by these women was deeply moving, and I was overcome with a fierce desire to stay in Dunwith, to become part of their community and easy friendship. The idea of upending my whole lonely life for one filled with campfires and girl gabs was incredibly tempting but felt so impossible it made my gut ache.

Releasing a hard breath, I asked, "Have any of you ever considered doing something totally crazy?"

"Every day," Maggie said, and Kate and Chloe assured me she was serious.

Then Kate added that walking away from her whole life to move here and start over with nothing could qualify as crazy.

"It sounds incredibly brave to me." I rubbed my temple. "I'd love to buy a fab shop in Dunwith, and I know it's impossible, but the idea is so relentless I can't stop thinking about it."

"Are you talking about Walter's business?" Chloe asked, setting aside her empty bottle.

"Yes, but he knows it's mostly a fantasy for me right now."

"Why?" Maggie asked. "Is he asking too much for the business?"

"No. His price is surprisingly reasonable, and I have enough in savings."

The three of them exchanged a look. "Then what's the problem?" Chloe asked.

"I'd have to sell my house, but it's the only home my son has known, and it's where he'll expect to spend his college breaks." It would also mean losing the workshop where my father had taught me how to create beautiful art from metal scraps, but I kept that heartache to myself.

"As someone with two kids in college," Kate said, "I can assure you they're rarely home during breaks."

"Ditto." Chloe pulled a bottle of iced tea out of a large cooler. "When Dylan comes home, he spends most of his time with his buddies. I'm lucky if I get one meal a week with him."

"Our point is you shouldn't be overly concerned with keeping your house just for your son's use during college breaks," Kate said. "He'll be moving out on his own at some point anyway. Until he does, why can't he spend his breaks here with you in Dunwith? If you haven't noticed, it's a pretty great place to hang out."

"Which is exactly why I'd love to live here," I said, slightly embarrassed by the whine in my voice. "But selling my house isn't the only issue. I'd have to pull everything out of my 401K, and I'd lose thousands of dollars in taxes and penalties, not to mention how it would affect my tax return."

"Don't do that!" Maggie blurted, rocking forward in her chair. "That's the worst thing you could do."

"I know, which is why this is just a fantasy for me."

"But it's not impossible," she said. "Just form a C-Corp, rollover your 401K, which you'll have to do anyway since you quit your job, to the C-Corp, then use that money to buy corporate stock. Then your C-Corp will have the money to finance your business purchase. Easy-peasy, and there will be no taxes or penalties."

I rubbed my temples, trying to make sense of what Maggie said, but she'd scrambled my brain. "I heard your words but don't understand any of them. And none of it sounded easy-peasy."

"It is if you use a good CPA, and it's the perfect option for you. If you're seriously considering this *crazy* venture," she said, using air quotes, "I'll introduce you to Eli. He's the CPA who set up my C-Corp. It's how I was able to buy the buildings for my consignment shop and antique business. I rolled over my personal IRAs to fund my corporation, but it would be the same principal for you to rollover a 401k."

In a general sense, I understood her, but to believe I could buy the fab shop and create a life here felt too big to take in.

"I can vouch for Eli," Chloe said. "He's my CPA. And Kate's, too."

Gripped by an intense state of indecision, I couldn't respond. To think I could really do this, that I could build a new life here, sent an electrifying rush through me that flipped my stomach one-hundred-eighty degrees.

Maggie eyed me with concern. "Just because you can do something doesn't mean you have to," she said gently. "But if buying the fab shop is what you truly want, you have every right to invest in yourself."

"Then why does it feel incredibly selfish to even think about doing this?"

Maggie scrunched her nose. "Following your passion is not selfish. It's *self-preservation*."

"She's right," Kate said, "and I wish it hadn't taken me so long to realize that."

"Intellectually, I understand what you're saying, but as a mom, I feel I'd be bailing on my kid if I moved here."

"Tyler's not a kid," Maggie reminded me. "And doing this would simply show him there are other ways to live. It's your life. You don't have to ask permission from anyone to choose how to live it."

"Unless you're living in cult-hell like I was," Kate said with a wry grin. "But you're not. You're an adult supporting yourself. Asking your partner or family for an opinion is one thing. That's being considerate. But your consideration should never equate to your asking permission."

They were right. I was divorced now. And I would look after my son no matter what path I took. I didn't have to ask anyone's permission. To realize I never had, was jolting. "I can't believe I'm about to say this, but can one of you text me Eli's number? It wouldn't hurt to talk to someone about my financial options."

Maggie's lips quirked. "I'll text it to you but let me contact Eli for you. It's the only way you'll get a meeting anytime soon. He's always booked out several weeks." She swiped her phone screen and tapped it a couple times. My phone dinged, but she continued to type. A minute later she lifted her head. "I sent Eli a text. He might not answer until tomorrow though."

I was surprised. "You have your CPA's private number?"

"Maggie has everyone's private number," Kate said, cracking them up.

I caught on seconds later. "Oh, I see the benefit now of having you make my appointment."

Maggie shrugged. "It's good for a girl to have friends." Her phone dinged and lit up. She typed a reply, then tucked the phone in her back pocket. "You're all set for Wednesday morning. Eli's office is right here in town."

I laughed in disbelief. "Wow, um, thanks, Maggie, but I don't know if I can make the appointment. I need to drop my car off at the office on Monday, and that means I'll be without a vehicle. Unless I rent one," I said, thinking out loud as I worked my way through the complications of losing not only my income but my transportation and phone. "I suppose I'll need to rent one anyway, but maybe I should think this over a bit more before I meet with Eli."

She gave me a mock scowl. "How can you give this any real thought without knowing your options?" she asked. "Meeting with Eli doesn't commit you to anything. Why not see what he has to say? At least then you'll know if your idea is worth the investment."

To imagine showing up each day for myself, pursuing my

passion, choosing my own direction felt surreal. *Wonderful* didn't begin to express what that freedom would mean to me.

"Sometimes the only way forward is to leap," Kate said.

There was a time I did that without hesitation, when I was a kid and my parents took my older sister, Pam, and me to our favorite swimming hole at the gorge. Pam would dip her toe and wade in, gasping and squeaking with each step. I'd scrabble up a ten-foot cliff and leap as far as my skinny legs would launch me. I relished the thrill, the anticipation, the shock of chilled water that would light up my whole body. I wasn't reckless. I was adventurous, brave, and wildly alive.

I wanted to live like that again, and so I said, "I'll find a way to keep the appointment with Eli."

Chapter Seven

It was after eleven o'clock when Maggie dropped me off at the Eagle's Nest. I sat outside on the concrete steps by the railing that Walter and I had repaired this morning. The series of highs and lows of an emotionally taxing couple of days had drained me, but I knew I wouldn't sleep. Anxious thoughts bounced and tumbled in my head like balls in a lottery cage, making me dizzy.

Bracing my elbows on my knees, I closed my eyes and leaned my forehead against my palms, rocking slightly side-to-side. According to my parents, this was how I comforted myself as a child. For me, though, it was simply a way to focus on breathing and calm my mind.

My life was upside down because of my boss and my knee-jerk reaction to his bullying. I wanted to be proud of myself for standing up to him, for putting a stop to his abuse, but I felt foolish rather than brave because I'd done it wrong. I didn't regret quitting, but I should have had another job lined up or a solid plan in place. Or at least had a freaking cup of coffee and kept my cool until I could do either of those things. But if I hadn't quit in the dramatic fashion that garnered

Maggie's attention at the gas station, she wouldn't have bought me a cup of coffee or introduced me to her friends. And I wouldn't be sitting here feeling torn about buying Walter's shop.

Dragging my palms down my face, I sat up and sucked in a breath of night air. A hint of smoke lingered in my sinuses and on my clothing. I thought about the simple pleasure of relaxing around a campfire with friends, of talking with brave women who spoke their truth, who openly razzed and supported each other, who talked about something other than fucking cars. I wanted that life, but I'd have to gamble everything I had to get it. And that scared me.

The faint sound of a band playing at a riverside pub mingled with voices that drifted in from various directions. Couples and small groups of people, most likely tourists, walked by, engaged in animated conversation as they enjoyed a Friday night in Dunwith. Clark and I almost never went out in the evening unless it was for a classic car cruise night or our son's school events. Our entertainment centered around swap meets, auctions, and vintage car shows that happened in mall parking lots during daylight hours.

After our divorce, I had no desire to go out on the town because I had no one to go with. The friends I'd made during my years with Clark were part of the classic car world to which I no longer belonged. Those weekend friendships faded away fast. The phone calls I received when I split with Clark, however sincere, were driven by shock and curiosity rather than deep bonds of friendship. I'd let them all go. They were good people, but they belonged in Clark's world, not mine. So, I filled all the empty hours with work and getting my son through his senior year.

The move I was now considering and the risk it involved scared me. But with Ty leaving in a few short weeks, no job in sight for me, and no girl gab buddies waiting for me at home, all those unscheduled lonely hours scared me far more.

* * *

After a shower and bracing cup of coffee in my room at the Eagle's Nest, I headed downstairs. Dressed in jeans, a T-shirt, and comfortable loafers, I headed to the fab shop to help Walter finish moving his remaining possessions to his new home.

The hatch was open on Walter's SUV, but he wasn't outside. I found him in the office closing a cardboard box. When he saw me, the determined expression on his face morphed into a welcoming smile. "You look lovely this morning," he said, opening his arms.

I stepped into the warmth of his hug, then asked where Louie was off to.

"Most likely hunting down all the treasures he's hidden away over the years. I suspect every nook and cranny in the place is home to one of his toys."

"Probably," I said, surprised to see the office was still somewhat organized. "What can I do to help? Do we need to box up the filing cabinets?"

"Oh, no," he said, dusting his hands together. "All the customer files will go with the business. I've already boxed up the few personal items I want. Everything else stays."

"All right, then. I can run the box out to your vehicle."

"Leave it for now. I'll get it when we finish up." With an inquisitive squint, he held my gaze. "Are you sure you want to bother with this today?"

The sorrow in his eyes expressed the depth of his struggle. "Of course. I really want to be here. What's in the box?" I asked, noticing how his hand rested protectively on it.

"Keepsakes." He gave the box a gentle pat. "Memories."

There wasn't a thing I could say that would offer comfort, but my slight nod let him know I understood.

A sad half-smile lifted one corner of his mouth. "Rita always wanted to be in the shop working with her hands. Didn't matter how dirty or difficult the job, she loved it. To sit at a desk to pay a bill was akin to torture for her. I gave her a hand in the shop when she needed one, but mainly I did the bookwork. I did our shopping and cooked our meals and kept our home. We were an oddity for our generation, but we were happy with our flip-flopped lifestyle." His smile faltered. "Don't know what to do with myself now that she's gone."

"What would she want you to do?" I asked, my heart aching for him.

His cheeks puffed on a forceful exhale. "She'd want me to quit caterwauling and get on with the business of living."

"Probably," I said, offering a sympathetic smile. "But it's not an easy thing to do. So, if you need to caterwaul, feel free."

A warm chuckle lifted his shoulders and brought a bit of light back to his eyes. "What I need is to get upstairs and finish carting out my boxes."

Just outside the office, we climbed a wide metal catwalk that spanned the building, had stairs at both ends, and provided access to the upstairs apartment. Walter and Rita's little home had been built above the office and storage rooms below, and I estimated the living space would be around six-hundred square feet. I followed him into his apartment. On the wall just inside the door were two occupied coat hooks and, on the floor below, a rubber boot tray holding Rita's beat up work boots.

Walter flicked a light switch, but the kitchen still felt dark. Perhaps it was the outdated décor, or maybe it was simply Walter's grief that cast the dingy shadow. He stood on the worn black-and-white linoleum as if paralyzed by the enormity of the task ahead. Chin in hand, his fingers worried the white stubble covering his jaw as he surveyed the room.

"Would you like me to box up the kitchen cupboards?" I asked.

For a moment, he didn't answer, then slowly shook his head. "There's nothing here I need."

"Okay," I said, unsure how to proceed. "Are there any boxes I can carry down to your SUV?"

"Just a couple in the living room."

"Maybe we should load your furniture first, then we can nest the boxes in the remaining space."

"I'm only taking the boxes." For the first time since we entered the apartment, he looked at me. "I'm leaving everything else for you."

I suspected he was jesting, but he wasn't smiling. "Is it obvious I'm considering your offer to buy the business? Because I am." The instant the words were out of my mouth, I knew this was the right path for me. However difficult it might be, I'd make the transition to my new life one step at a time.

His white eyebrows nearly touched the brim of his ball cap.

"I need to meet with a CPA to sort out the financial stuff first," I said, "so please don't sell to someone else until I can do that." For a moment, he didn't say anything, which shot a bolt of anxiety through me.

As if he didn't hear me, he said, "You know, Rita miscarried our daughter right here in this apartment. Only time I ever saw my wife cry, but she never talked about it. She just slept for two days, then went back to work as if it never happened." His eyes, black with pain, seemed to sink deeper into his skull. "I've never been able to let our baby go."

"My god, Walter. I'm so sorry."

"You remind me of her, the way I imagined our daughter anyway. She'd be older than you, though, in her fifties now."

The thought was both heartwarming and horrifying. "I can't even imagine your loss. If my being here is intrusive or causes you pain, I'll leave right now."

"What?" His eyebrows knit. "No, dear, I was trying to say you've been a comfort to me from the day we met. The first time I saw you, you were helping Rita wrangle a sheet of aluminum into the bending machine, and it was like seeing a vision of my own daughter. In my mind, I've watched her grow from a toddler to a gangly-legged girl playing with dolls to an angsty teen. But I struggled to see her as an adult until the day I saw you in our shop with Rita." Moisture beaded on his lower lids, and I felt my own eyes well-up. "It was like you were meant to be here with us."

"Well, that's how you've made me feel," I said, my voice wobbling.

"Rita loved this place, and I want to pass it on to someone who will love it like she did."

"I do, Walter."

"I know that." He backhanded one eye. "The place is yours if you want it." He dipped one hand into the pocket of his baggy work pants, pulled out a set of keys, and held them out to me.

"I can't take the keys until we have a legal agreement."

"All right," he said, dropping them on the kitchen table beside a wooden tray holding a pen and notepad. Leaning on one hand, he scribbled something on the pad. When he finished, he tore the page loose and handed it to me. "Consider this our purchase agreement. We can work out all the details after you talk with your financial guy."

Surprised, I glanced at the paper and read his shaky scrawl stating I agreed to purchase the business, all equipment, supplies, materials, and his 1990 flatbed truck for several thousand less than his asking price. He'd dated the paper and signed his name. All I needed to do was sign my own.

"Time is short, Andie. Do the things you want to do *now*."

"Okay, but I'm worried my accountant might point out issues I haven't thought of, or that things might not go according to plan."

"Whatever comes up, we'll work it out."

As if I were back standing on the edge of the gorge cliff, ready to leap, I worried there might be hidden debris in the water, that it might be too cold, but the brave, adventurous voice of my youth hadn't been completely silenced. *Just leap, damn it!* And so, I did. My hands shook as I signed and dated our handwritten agreement.

"I'll make a copy for you when we pick up the box in the office," he said, folding the paper and buttoning it in his shirt pocket.

Unable to do more than nod, I followed him into the living room, a cozy space cluttered by overstuffed furniture and enough plants to fill a nursery. Pots of every size and color overflowed three-tiered plant stands. Tall, leafy plants billowed outward from two corner planters. A large picture window was nearly obliterated by vines that climbed upward from several pots and twined around a sagging curtain rod.

"Rita must have loved plants," I said, taking in the domestic jungle.

A slight cringe deepened the creases in Walter's face. "They're all mine." With cloudy blue eyes, he surveyed his mini forest. "Just can't bring myself to let anything die. Same for bugs and critters. I can't kill a living thing."

I was of the same sentiment but not when it came to spiders. We could not coexist. "You're taking your plants with you, right?" I asked, but it was definitely a suggestion.

"I'd like to, but my new place is too small. I don't know what I'm going to do with them, but I can't let them die." I tried to ignore the hopeful look in his eyes by inspecting the ceiling fan. "Maybe you could keep them here?" he asked.

Dang it. I knew he was going to ask. "Why don't we wait until you're settled in your new place, then decide which ones you have room for? We can figure out what to do with the rest of them then."

"All right." He gestured to a stack of boxes. "I'm taking those and that small bookshelf."

"Okay. Show me everything that needs to go."

In a small room covered in floral wallpaper, there were three full laundry baskets sitting on a queen bed in what I assumed to be Walter and Rita's bedroom. I followed him to a fairly good size bathroom where he pointed out two boxes on the floor that he'd be taking. When I spotted the avocado green sink and toilet, I groaned.

Walter glanced over his shoulder. "I didn't catch that, dear. What did you say?"

"Um, I was just asking if this is everything."

"Yes," he said. "I'm leaving everything else for you."

He was? I released a quiet sigh, knowing it would take me a solid month to clean the place out if our deal went through. I wasn't dreading the work really, but what the hell was I going to do with the rainforest in the living room?

To avoid pressing him to take the plants, I picked up a box that had once contained printer paper. "Holy mackerel, this feels like a box of rocks."

"It's full of my books."

"Let me guess," I said, giving the box a slight bounce in my hands. "Mystery novels?"

"Nope. Plants, gardening, and nature books."

"Ah, all great choices."

"Let's load these on the elevator outside the door," he said. "That'll save us several trips up and down the stairs."

"You have an elevator?"

"Sort of. A few years ago, when climbing stairs started to become a chore for us, Rita designed a lift using a platform and electronic pulley system to make it easier for us to take out garbage or haul up laundry baskets and groceries and whatnot."

Curious, I followed him out of the apartment, where he pressed a button beside the door. I heard a motor kick on and the sound of gears and cables working. A few seconds later, Rita's elevator appeared in a caged section at the outside edge of the catwalk.

Walter unlatched and swung open a section of the catwalk safety rail, which allowed him to enter the elevator. "Come on in and set the box there," he said, pointing a gnarled finger to the back corner.

After I deposited the box, he pushed a button, and the lift descended in a safety cage, accessible from one side only, which prevented cross-traffic and potential injury to anyone below not paying attention. "This is really something, Walter. Your wife was brilliant!"

Pride lit his eyes. "Her talent was remarkable."

I agreed as the elevator settled quietly at the ground floor. The lift was large enough to accommodate a wheelchair. The thought that Rita might have been anticipating their future needs, believing they'd have more years together, wrung my heart.

"I'll run the box out to your SUV," I said, and we can stack the next load on the lift."

Despite all the unknowns I was facing, I felt an upwelling of happiness as I loaded the box in his vehicle. In my mind, I organized the messy shop and cleaned out the loft apartment to make a comfy home for myself. I imagined spending my days creating art and sculptures from scrap metal. Living here, I could walk to the café every morning for Sophie's delicious coffee and baked goods, and I could enjoy Friday night girl-gabs with the kind of friends I'd longed for all my life. No matter how impulsive or unnerving my leap into a new life might seem, I felt an admirable sense of courage for even pursuing the idea.

It took an hour to load the vehicle and round up Louie who was playing with a squeak toy Walter said he hadn't seen in months. In the office, Walter made a copy of our agreement, which I folded and tucked into the back pocket of my jeans. Then I carried his box of keepsakes and memories from his office out to his vehicle.

Together, the three of us headed to The Grove, a senior community set in a gorgeous park-like setting a few blocks east of the fab shop. Walter told me how an underhanded corporation with big plans for the area had built the sprawling two-story brick structure as a shopping center, but the Dunwith community wouldn't support it. They refused to allow their beautiful town to be overrun with big box stores, shopping malls, and chain hotels. That's when the Dunwith residents and board members went to work rezoning and restructuring their town. Their joint goal was to preserve the natural beauty of the area and support local businesses, and from what I'd seen so far, they'd succeeded admirably.

Every business had taken on a new name to represent the wildlife and natural beauty of the Adirondacks. Walter and Rita had morphed Greenstone Metal Fab into Evergreen Metal Fab, a name I hoped I could proudly keep.

According to Walter, the corporate monster that tried to gobble up their precious paradise was only too happy to sell their failing property back to Dunwith for half what they'd invested. "There hasn't been an entity since that has tried to move in," he said, puffing his chest a bit as if innately proud.

"Your tight-knit and protective community is highly unusual and truly commendable," I said.

"Wasn't always that way." He parked by a wide section of tall glass doors that appeared to be the main entrance. "Took a while to educate those folks who didn't understand how quickly corporate greed and urban sprawl can ruin a place. But after the town converted the mall to a mixed-use space with forty-eight micro-apartments, most everyone got onboard. A few stragglers had simply gone along or just didn't care. Either way, we've created a useful, functional space and saved Dunwith from being further encroached on and buried in concrete and blacktop."

"Is it ridiculous that I feel like cheering?" I asked, eliciting a chuckle from him.

"Not at all. It's something worth celebrating." He opened his door. "I need to get a cart so we can move everything in one go. I'll be back lickety-split," he said, then was out the door and rounding the back of the SUV with the vigor of a man half his age.

Louie's brown eyes tracked Walter all the way into the building, then he turned his questioning gaze on me.

"He'll be right back," I said, stroking Louie's adorable face. While the two of us watched the doors in anticipation, I gave Louie's head and ears a thorough massage that had his eyes drooping and his tongue slipping farther out of his mouth. He grinned up at me with his silly little face, and I wished I had a companion like Louie.

One set of the double glass doors swung open like welcoming arms, and a long, motorized cart came into view. Walter sat at the back end, steering it through the open doorway. Louie and I both bounded out of the SUV.

"That looks fun," I said, as Walter stopped the cart.

A child-like smile plumped his cheeks. "I only bring a couple of boxes over at a time just so I can drive the cart."

Laughing at his guilty admission, I was glad to see a bit of light in his eyes and his playful personality surfacing. "Just think how many trips you could make if you brought all your plants over," I said, hoping I wasn't being too obvious.

But I was, and he laughed, promising he'd try to find homes for his armchair-garden.

We loaded the cart, then Louie and I sat on the cart seat while Walter parked his SUV in the lot. His pace was slower when he returned, but he seemed lighter than he'd been that morning, which lifted my own heart a considerable amount.

We entered a space the size of a small department store with white walls and bright overhead lighting. Motorized carts, wheelchairs, and other walking aids were lined up on the front wall for easy access, and bicycles and golf carts were stored along the side wall.

We exited at the far end and drove into a vast park-like space with sunlight and blue sky visible through sections of clear dome roofs as far as I could see.

"Oh, my gosh," I said, trying to take it all in. "This place is enormous. Is all of this just for the residents?"

"Not at all. This place was created to provide added services for the aging at any level of independence, not to separate us from the community."

"It must have taken decades to convert this place."

"Just three years of around-the-clock working and sweating by a good many folks in our community," he said, pride thick in his voice.

As he navigated the cart through the vast space, leafy trees and robust bushes provided a green backdrop for raised garden boxes sporting brightly colored flowers and a community vegetable garden.

"I bet you were in charge of the planting and gardening."

For the first time since Rita's death, I saw a full smile on Walter's face, and it remained there as he negotiated the cart into a spacious elevator that took us to the second floor. His apartment couldn't have been more than four-hundred-square feet, but the open concept with the living space and kitchen area together made it feel larger. It was so different from his dark apartment, I worried he would never feel at home. But he seemed relieved when we carried the last box inside.

"Are you sure you'll be okay here?" I asked.

He glanced around the small space as if seeking the cause for my question. "As okay as I'd be anywhere. Why?"

"It's just so, well, it's quite different than your old apartment."

He gave a slow, thoughtful nod. "Sometimes different is what one needs to be able to go on."

I understood then. As beautiful as memories could be, constant reminders of what one lost could elicit paralyzing grief. Walter was bravely choosing a new space where he could cherish the memories without constant reminders of his loss. I wish I would have taken that brave path when my father died, but I'd stayed and wallowed in my heartbreak. By keeping our family home, I thought I was honoring his memory, but now I understood I'd simply been clinging to my fear of change and letting go.

"I'd better take the cart down now and give you a ride back," Walter said, snapping me out of my painful introspection.

"No need. I'm going to walk back to the Eagle's Nest and let you settle in. Would you like me to return the cart on my way out?"

"And rob Louie and me of the adventure?" He ruffled Louie's ears. "Not a chance."

Chapter Eight

Monday morning, after updating my new cellphone, I drove my company car into the office parking lot, desperate to be done with the unpalatable task of returning the car and account files. As I entered the office for the last time, I could hear the low murmur of voices from worker inmates occupying the cube-farm of half-walls topped with plexiglass partitions. Buzzing overhead lights cast pale shadows on avocado-colored walls and anemic-white window blinds. The stench of old coffee turned my stomach and made me pity my former co-workers.

I went directly to my boss's corner office and tapped my knuckles on the metal door frame to get his attention.

When he looked up, he shocked me with a greasy smile. "Good morning, Andie."

Instantly, my guard went up. He wanted something, but I had nothing to give him. "I'm dropping off the car and a box of customer files."

"If you'd rather apologize, Andie, you can keep the keys and get back to work."

I was so stunned by his offer I found myself locked in a

moment of indecision. To keep my high paying job was a huge temptation. In one hand, I held the keys to my company car and my income. In the other hand sunk deep in the pocket of my jeans, I held the keys to the fab shop. I experienced a dizzying swirl of second thoughts. Could I tolerate hell for a handful of money now, or would I dare to risk everything on a pocketful of dreams?

"I'm waiting," Mr. Norton said, condescension dripping from his voice as if he'd expected me to blurt out an apology and scamper back to work.

I'd rather scrub rest stop bathrooms on an Interstate than spend another moment in his presence. "The box of customer files is on the back seat of the car," I said, dropping the keys and my company cellphone on his desk.

The instant he realized I was declining his offer, he scowled. Mouth pursed, accentuating his beak-like nose, he said, "You're making a big mistake because you're going to lose your quarterly incentive pay. You haven't worked the full quarter."

I'd earned that money and was counting on it. "I'm only two weeks shy of finishing the quarter, so my incentive should be prorated—"

He threw his hand up to stop my argument. "We're done here. You need to leave the premises now."

The urge to bat his hand away from my face was strong, but I knew it was the last time I'd have to tolerate his rude behavior. "You can't deny me income I'm entitled to, but I'm not going to debate this with you. I'll take it up with HR," I said, then left without giving him the satisfaction of having the last word, something I knew infuriated the dumbass.

Outside, Tyler was waiting for me, impatiently tapping his thumbs on the steering wheel of his beater car. As I approached, he gave me a 'sup' chin tip that made me miss the days when his eyes would light up and a smile would fill his face when he saw me.

"You're late," he said, as I got in the passenger side.

"Hello to you, too."

"Sorry." He leaned over and gave me a quick hug. "I'm just in a rush to meet dad. We're going car shopping as soon as I get home."

"Okay, but don't trade in this car because I need it."

Tyler laughed. "It's all yours, Mom."

"Apparently, so is the mess," I said, noting several takeout containers, sneakers, and a snarl of workout clothing covering the floor and back seat. "I feel like I'm riding in your stinky gym locker."

He rolled his eyes. "I'll get my crap out later."

"What kind of car are you looking at?"

"There's a black SUV I've got my eye on. If it passes Dad's inspection, that's the one I want."

He began listing the merits of the vehicle, the great gas mileage, the excellent safety rating, and the spacious interior and hatchback that would make his move to college super simple. Tyler's excitement was something I hadn't seen much of since Clark left home, and I felt a little mesmerized by my son. He'd always been a cute kid. As a toddler with dark hair, brown eyes, and an infectious giggle, my curious boy had been deeply engaged in understanding the world around him. When he hit his teen years, he'd grown more serious and morphed into a handsome young man with a robust laugh I didn't hear often enough. To see him now, so animated and happy, made me wonder how I was going to tell him I was buying a business and selling our home.

While silently debating how or when to share my plan with him, my phone rang. When I saw it was Maggie calling, I answered with a smile.

"Hi, Andie, I'm just calling to see if we need to bail you out of jail."

I burst out laughing, and the sense of dread I'd felt all morning began to lift. "I'm doing great actually, especially after turning down my ex-boss's offer for me to stay."

"He said you could keep your job?" Maggie sounded as shocked as I'd felt.

"Yeah, but only if I apologized for my behavior."

"Ugh."

"Exactly. I dropped the car keys on his desk and walked out."

"Good for you, Andie. Sounds like you had a hell of a morning."

"I did, but I made sure to have coffee before dealing with that crap."

Maggie's laughter sang through the phone. "When you get back to town, stop by my shop and let me know how your meeting with Eli goes."

"I will," I said, ending the call, touched by her genuine interest.

"Who was that?" Tyler asked, noticing the smile I could still feel on my face.

"A friend of mine from Dunwith," I said, hoping I could introduce them one day.

* * *

With Tyler riding shotgun, I watched Clark back his vehicle out of my driveway and wondered why he couldn't just drive one of the classic cars that had been taking up space in my father's shop for well over a decade. I'd suggested it numerous times, but Clark insisted the cars were for showing, not for casual daily driving. He loved them, but I'd grown to despise Clark's obsession and the steel beasts that had taken over my shop.

My dad had erected the detached metal building forty years ago to do small fabrication jobs and create scrap metal art. The shop wasn't much bigger than a two-car garage, but in my childhood it felt enormous. Maybe it was the feeling of unlimited possibilities that filled my head as he introduced me to the world of creating art from junk. He would demonstrate how a simple metal spring could be used to create body parts, or fashion unique furniture pieces, or make trees and flowers and many other fascinating things. The ability to reimagine discarded scraps of metal as an integral part of something beautiful was one of the greatest gifts he'd given me.

I still had the first piece of art we made, and I wanted to find it. Braving the congested shop, I sidled alongside Clark's Chevy Bel Air but caught my toe on a replacement fender sitting on the floor. Releasing a growl of irritation, I stepped over scattered parts, tires, and tools as I made my way to the back of the building where he'd stacked boxes head-height across the wall. The box holding my first metal sculpture was surely buried now. There were still boxes from when Clark moved in with me nineteen years ago that he hadn't unpacked despite his repeated promises to clear out his mess.

Gritting my teeth, I slithered between the wall of boxes and the steel bumpers of Clark's Bel Air and Thunderbird to get to a back corner. The last sculpture my father and I worked on sat unfinished on a long wood pallet. After he died, I'd pulled a tarp over the sculpture like a mourner's veil and let Clark's passion nudge my own into a dark corner.

Dusty bins and boxes of car parts were stacked so high around the tarped sculpture I couldn't even get to it. Why had I allowed Clark to invade my space and bury me like he'd buried my sculpture. No wonder I hadn't been able to breathe. He'd left no room for *me*.

The only way to force Clark to get his crap out was to sell the house because as long as I was here, Clark would be, too.

Trying to find anything in the shop would be a waste of time, so I decided to clean out Tyler's car. Gathering a garbage bag, laundry basket, and cleaning supplies, I spent the next two hours hoeing out his filthy vehicle. Fast food containers and dirty floor mats went into the garbage bag. I piled his muddy shoes and stinky gym clothes in the laundry basket along with his gym bag and a sweat-stained ball cap holding three pairs of his sunglasses. I sanitized and scrubbed every surface, including the windows inside and out, and tossed the used towels in the garbage bag. By the time I finished vacuuming the vehicle, I was dripping sweat, covered in grime, and totally grossed out.

That's when Tyler pulled in with his new SUV, flashing me a wide smile through the windshield. It had been a long time since I'd seen him that happy, and I wanted to celebrate with him. But after spending two miserable hours cleaning his disgusting beater car, I felt he deserved a little playful torture. When he stepped out of his car, I pulled him into a big, sweaty hug.

"God, Mom, yuck!" he said, stepping back with a grimace. "That was gross."

I laughed. "So was your car."

"I told you I'd clean it out when I got home."

Ty was a procrastinator like his father, so I'd cleaned it because I wasn't about to drive to Dunwith in his gym bag on wheels. "Apparently, your dad approved of your SUV."

"Yeah, he was impressed it's so clean and it runs great." Ty hooked his palm over the open door, his gaze proudly roving the dark interior and freshly washed exterior. "Want to go for a ride?" he asked, then glanced at my disgusting self and added, "later."

To see Tyler so animated was such a treat, but I couldn't help teasing him a bit. "Let's go right now."

"Funny, Mom." Wearing a half-smile and shaking his head, he slid onto the driver's seat. "We can go after supper."

"Deal, but not too late because I have to leave early in the morning."

"Oh, did you get another job already?"

"No, I just have appointments and errands to run," I said, being intentionally vague. Until I was sure I could buy the fab shop, I was keeping my plans to myself. "I'll be back in the afternoon."

"All right," he said, popping on his sunglasses. "I'll see you later then."

I watched him leave, his proud smile so like the first time he'd driven our vehicle by himself. The two years since had transformed Tyler's boyish features into a young man's face, and my heart squeezed knowing my little boy would soon leave the nest. Everything was changing.

By the time I finished showering, I'd received a text from Tyler saying he'd made plans with his buddies. He wouldn't be home for supper but promised me a ride in his new vehicle tomorrow evening. I wasn't surprised, so I replied with a thumbs-up emoji. He spent most of his time with friends or crashing at Clark's apartment where they would watch sports and talk cars and do whatever guys do. I was glad they had such a close relationship, but being left out sucked. My empty, lonely life would be even worse when Tyler left for college.

Rolling my neck, I tried to release the tension that had clawed its way up my shoulders. It had been a long day, and I needed to look over my financial situation before my meeting with Eli tomorrow. After pulling on sweatpants and a T-shirt, I made a cup of coffee with a shot of espresso and headed to my office. For the first time in four years, I could see the top of my desk. Removing my work life seemed to expand my small office and let in more light from the window above the filing cabinets that now held only my personal files.

For two hours, I gathered tax returns and printed out statements from my retirement and bank accounts. The fees and costs involved in buying Walter's shop would cut my finances to the bone, and I felt my resolve wobble. Was I being selfish? Stupid perhaps? Or was the courageous side of me finally stepping up? I didn't know, but however difficult and scary the path ahead might be, it couldn't be as lonely and depressing as the one I'd been on.

* * *

After a ninety-minute meeting with Eli, a brilliant and sexy CPA who reaffirmed Maggie's advice and said I could afford to buy the fab shop, and agreed it would be a solid investment, I left his office with my entire body vibrating. I'd done it. I'd signed a dozen forms and asked him to proceed with everything I needed to purchase Walter's business.

Outside, I leaned against the brick building feeling light-headed and terrified and more excited than I'd been since my father and I started working on our last sculpture. I wished I could call him to share my news, or even just to hear his voice. He'd been my first call when I'd learned I was pregnant with Tyler, but my dad had been gone just over a year at that point, and a stranger answered the phone. Realizing my mistake, and my painful loss, I ended the call in tears but had never been able to delete my dad's number.

I closed my eyes, trying to settle the vortex of thoughts whirling in my head. I needed coffee, but first I wanted to tell

Walter our deal was underway so he could get a legal purchase agreement drawn up. Pushing away from the building, I left Tyler's beater car in the lot and headed to the fab shop on foot. It was only a few blocks away, so I figured I'd check there before heading to The Grove which was a few blocks farther on.

I found Walter sitting in a lawn chair parked on the concrete pad at the office entrance. Louie appeared to be sleeping on a chair beside him. The surprise and delight in Walter's eyes when he saw me warmed my heart even before he stood and wrapped me in his arms. "You're still in town!" he said, easing back as if to assure himself I was really there.

"Not still," I said. "I came back for my meeting with Eli." At his confused look, I said, "I met with my CPA today."

"Oh, yes!" He gave a quick nod, then concern clouded his eyes. "And how did it go?"

An upwelling of joy brought a smile to my face. "The paperwork is in process. I'm really buying your shop, Walter."

He clasped his hands to his chest and gasped, mumbling words I couldn't understand.

"Walter!" I clasped his forearm, worried he might be having a heart attack. "What's happening?"

He mumbled incoherently, backhanding his eyes.

My worry mushroomed. "I'm calling 9-1-1."

"No, dear...give me a minute."

Watching closely, I suggested he sit, which he did like a deflating balloon.

Pulling a red handkerchief from his pocket, he blew his nose, causing Louie to lift one droopy eyelid, then drop it closed a second later.

I'd expected Walter to greet my news with a happy smile, not a terrifying episode, which did not help my already shaky condition. "Are you all right?"

He nodded, sniffed once, and pushed his handkerchief into

his pants' pocket. "I'm sorry, dear. It just gave my old heart a squeeze to know how happy this would make Rita. Took me a minute to catch my breath is all, but I'm sorry I scared you."

"You really did," I said, releasing a harsh breath and sagging against Louie's chair. "Please don't do that again or I might be the one having heart failure."

With a soft chuckle, Walter clasped my forearm. "I'll do my best."

"Thank you," I said, then gestured to two cups of coffee sitting on a small table between the chairs. "Do you have company?"

"What's that?" His eyebrow lifted, so I gestured to the cups. Looking slightly embarrassed, he said, "The other cup is for Rita. Every night in bed, I would ask her to meet me for a coffee date in the morning. She would take my hand and say, 'I will always meet you for coffee.' Even if we'd had a bumpy day, we would fall asleep holding hands. The only time Rita didn't hold my hand was when she lost our daughter. That night, I held her in my arms, and in the morning, I brought her coffee in bed."

A claw gripped my throat and my eyes flooded.

For a moment, he was silent as if caught in a strong current of memory. A soft, faraway look came over his face, and he stroked Louie's head. The dog's ears twitched, but he didn't wake. "This is where we lived our life," he said with a slight hand gesture toward the building. "It's where we loved. Where we lost things. Where we made ordinary moments extraordinary." With a slight shrug, he looked up at me. "I just can't bring myself to end our coffee dates."

"Oh, Walter." I slipped my hand over his bony shoulder. "Rita was one lucky woman."

His lip quirked. "I used to tell her that all the time."

A sad laugh slipped from my throat. "I can imagine how she received that comment."

"With a bit of sass and bluster," he said, a melancholy smile barely touching his lips. "She was beautiful in her wild, passionate way. I have no idea what she saw in me, but I was unfairly blessed by her love and friendship."

"I can't even imagine," I said, then realized I'd spoken aloud.

With a trembling hand, he captured mine and gave it a gentle squeeze as if he could see I was missing pieces of myself. "Would you like a cup of coffee?"

"Always," I said, giving his hand a squeeze in return.

"It's probably cold now."

"I'll heat it in the office microwave."

"Do mine, too?" he asked, looking up at me.

"Of course." I picked up the cups and headed to the office where I could wipe my eyes and blow my nose. The man and his stories were ripping my heart out, but I couldn't have loved him more.

Chapter Nine

As soon as I got home, I texted Maggie that I was purchasing the fab shop and would let her know when I returned to Dunwith. I added that I understood why she had her sexy CPA's private number.

She relied with *Exactly, and congrats! We'll celebrate when you come back.*

Celebrating hadn't even occurred to me because I was worried how Tyler was going to take the news. Still, despite a healthy amount of fear, I was excited and felt lighter than I had since backpacking in Australia.

That feeling quickly dissipated, though, as I took a good look through my house filled with years of accumulated stuff that would need to be cleared out. Just peeking in the basement, attic, and storage areas made me hyperventilate. Especially since I couldn't recall what all had been packed in boxes or stashed in cupboards and on deep shelves.

In my bedroom closet, I found plastic storage bins and hanging clothes Clark had pushed to the back of the closet we once shared. I wondered why he hadn't taken his stuff. Had he really thought he might be back? A more disturbing question was, why hadn't I noticed that he'd never moved out?

Rolling my neck, I tried to release the tension gripping my shoulders. I was already overwhelmed just thinking about the task ahead and the conversation I needed to have with Tyler in a few minutes. After I freshened up in the master bath, I changed my shirt, then went outside and waited for him on the front porch.

When he arrived, he hopped out of the car and clomped up the steps. "Have to use the bathroom first," he said on the way inside, the screen door snapping shut behind him.

Leaning my head back, I exhaled a slow breath, hoping my new venture wouldn't hurt my son. I'd already put him through one major upset and life change by divorcing his father. To throw another one at him as he was preparing for a big move of his own was, well, it wasn't what I wanted to do.

"You okay, Mom?" he asked, the screen door banging closed behind him.

"Yeah, hon. I just have a lot on my mind." I patted the seat beside me. "I need to talk to you before we go for a ride."

The concern in his eyes turned wary.

"No one died, and you're not in trouble," I said, giving him a reassuring smile.

"All right, but the last talk we had was when you told me you were divorcing dad."

The arrow went straight through my heart. "Fair enough, but hopefully, this won't be as upsetting. Come on," I said, giving the seat another pat.

He sat in a chair facing me. "What's going on? Does this have anything to do with my car or college?"

"No, Tyler, it has to do with *me*," I said, a little irritated he assumed everything in my life revolved around him. I suppose it mostly had, but he wasn't a little boy anymore and it was time he started to understand that. "I've decided to buy a business and work for myself."

"Really?" he asked in surprise. "What kind of business?"

"Welding, metal fabricating, that sort of thing."

"Okay. Does dad know?"

"No," I said, feeling another flare of irritation that Tyler thought I needed to run everything past his father for approval. "I'm telling you because I'm going to sell our house and move to Dunwith."

"Whoa!" Tyler rocked back on the chair. "Are you serious?"

I nodded, wanting to explain all the reasons I needed to leave, to assure Tyler it had nothing to do with him, that I was sorry I had to sell the house, but his attention was already turned inward. I gave him time to absorb the idea and order his thoughts.

Finally, I said, "I'm sorry if this upsets you."

He blew out a breath, puffing his cheeks. "It does a little, but mostly I'm just wondering what it means. You'll be moving farther away. Our house will be sold, so I guess I won't have a home anymore."

"Of course you will, Ty. You'll always have a home with me or your father."

"That's not what I meant. Where will I keep my stuff? Where will I live when I'm not at school?"

I clasped his hand between my own. "At my place in Dunwith."

He wrinkled his nose and pulled away. "Mom, I'd be bored out of my mind there."

"It's not the quiet little town we drove through when you were six and we took you to Lake Placid. It's a gorgeous tourist town now with a lot going on all the time. And it's a great place to live, Ty. I really think you'll like it."

"Maybe, but my friends are here."

My hopes deflated. "You know you can live with your dad if you prefer. I just wanted to make it clear that you'll always have a home with me."

He winced a little, chagrined. "I know. Sorry. This is just a lot to take in."

"I know it is. That's why you need to understand that my moving doesn't mean I don't care how you feel about all of this. But you already spend most of your time with your dad or your friends, and with you leaving soon, the house is going to be really quiet. I guess I want something more in my life than an empty house and a job I hate."

He gave a slow nod as if really considering my words. "I understand. When do I need to move my stuff to Dad's?"

A painful clamp locked around my chest and made speaking impossible. My son had chosen his father. Tyler was his dad's "little man" and his "teammate", and I couldn't compete with that. Clearing my throat, I said, "Before you leave for college."

"Okay." He leaned forward and braced his forearms on his knees. For a moment, he seemed to be thinking, then he looked at me. "Dad's not going to like this. Where's he going to store his cars?"

It took everything I had not to shout that I didn't give a damn about his father's cars or what he wanted. That had been my only concern our entire marriage and I was done with catering to Clark. "Not my concern," I said. But it sort of was my concern because of the stupid agreement I'd made with Clark. I allowed him to store his cars in the shop so I wouldn't have to cash out part of my 401K to buy out his share in the house. He'd helped me buy it from my mother so I could be clear of her and the conspiracy world she and my sister lived in. If or when I sold the house, I would owe him a percentage of the net profit, if there was any. I needed to tell Clark sooner rather than later.

With a sigh, Ty pushed to his feet. The joy shining in his eyes earlier was long gone. "Would you mind if we went for a ride another night?"

It had been a hard conversation, and I knew he needed time to digest the changes that were, once again, going to affect his life. I stood and pulled him into a hug he barely returned. "No, hon. But I do want a ride in your car when you're ready, okay?"

He gave me a nod, then slipped from my arms. I watched my son descend the steps slowly, as if trying to lock in the memory of a place he would soon lose. I'd been doing the same thing in every room of our house. The urge to call him back and promise to keep his home, his childhood playground, his safe space, was strong, but I knew it was time for us both to start building our own independent lives.

There were many things I loved about the house where I'd grown up and raised my son. For me, it was the shop where I'd spent time with my dad. For Tyler, I assumed it was the back-yard where he'd played with neighbor kids and school friends, or our living room where he and Clark had flopped on the sofa and yelled at the television during hockey and football games. Or maybe it was the shop where he'd spent time with his own dad working on cars and discussing their shared passion.

I sat alone on the living room floor, thumbing through albums holding years of printed photos and those from our later years saved on thumb drives that I viewed in our digital photobook.

Pictures lay scattered around me like pieces to a puzzle. I found an image of Clark at a fifties-themed classic car event we attended early in our marriage. Wearing blue jeans, a white T-shirt with rolled sleeves, and his hair slicked back with hair oil, Clark stood with a cocked hip, thumbs hooked in his front pockets, beside the shiny red fender of his Thunderbird. Dressed like his dad, three-year-old Tyler stood beside Clark trying to imitate Clark's bad-boy pose.

I found another photo of Tyler at seven years old, imitating the donkey-ear gesture he found so funny in his favorite Christmas movie *It's a Wonderful Life*. He referred to it as the Hee-haw movie. Each year after Thanksgiving passed, Tyler would tuck in beside me on the couch each evening and we'd watch his Christmas shows. Clark was bored by them, so he spent his time in the garage, and I savored that rare precious alone-time with our son. All season long, Tyler would gallop through the house, flopping his pretend donkey ears and yelling *Hee-haw*. I would scoop him into a hug and threaten to bite his ears, making him squeal and squirm free in a fit of giggles.

I loved his silliness because he was a quiet, rather shy kid outside our home. That was the year his class put on a Christmas play, and Tyler was terrified of performing in front of people. We practiced his lines, but the night before the show, when he fumbled his words, he threw his notebook. Although I'd scolded him, the memory made me laugh because the little stinker stuck out his tongue and flapped his pretend donkey-ears at me.

The day of Tyler's school play was both heartwrenching and heartwarming for me. Clark and I sat in the auditorium chuckling as kids wandered around stage like a gaggle of confused geese. Some children waved at their parents, mumbling their lines incoherently, others forgot them completely until the teacher coached them word by word, but Tyler couldn't speak at all. His teacher encouraged him, but he just stared at me with big, frightened eyes. Seeing my little boy so terrified, wrung my heart, but I knew protecting him didn't mean sheltering him. It meant helping him push through his fear. So, I made a funny face and flopped pretend donkey-ears at him. Tyler hid a smile behind his fist, but I saw his shoulder's hunch and knew he was giggling. Then he surprised everyone by lifting his head and speaking his lines like a pro. I would never forget that moment or the triumph in his eyes and the joyful hug he gave me afterward. It was one of the sweetest moments I shared with my son, and I wondered if he remembered it, too.

Memory-surfing through photos of Tyler growing up was a bittersweet experience. I laughed and cried because I missed my adorable little boy and because those days of being a family were long gone. I couldn't remember the last time I'd looked at our albums. Maybe I hadn't wanted to see the early years of our marriage when my heart was filled with love for my family, when I believed my husband loved me, too. The changes in our marriage, and in me, were apparent now. The few images with me in the photos revealed my slowly fading smile and eyes that grew duller and more jaded by the year.

I exchanged the album for an older one with photos of my own childhood and the family I no longer had. I tried to skim past the images of my sister and mother, but even all these years later I couldn't seem to completely let go of my anger toward them. Or my love. I lingered over photos of my father, missing him and silently thanking him for everything he'd given me. There weren't many photos of us from those days, but the ones of me as a young girl with a smile beaming from my face and my eyes wide with curiosity made me wonder how I'd lost that part of myself.

Searching for clues, I spent hours thumbing through images,

visual documentation of the moments of joy and pain that made up my life and brought me to this crossroads. When I finished viewing the last album, I leaned back against the couch. The wildly curious girl who'd grown up here, the young mother who'd raised her son here, and the woman who had ended up alone and disillusioned here were part of my past. That life was over.

Now, it was time for me to build a new one.

* * *

After a night of memory-surfing and little sleep, I texted Clark in the morning and asked him to meet me at the house when he got out of work. I was waiting outside with the shop door open when Clark arrived.

"Hey, Andie," he said, tucking his T-shirt into the waist of his jeans as he strode toward me. Clark was a fit guy of average height and a muscular build. "What's up?" he asked, a look of uncertainty in his eyes. In other words, he gave me his usual greeting.

"I need you to clear out the shop and get the rest of your stuff out of the house."

He glanced at his cars and the clutter surrounding them. "We agreed I could keep them here."

"Yes, unless I decided to sell the house."

His eyebrows quirked, dark upward slashes like Tyler's that gave them both a perpetually inquisitive look. "I know that, so what's the problem?"

"I can't list the house with all your stuff in there," I said.

"Hold on." He gave his head a small shake as if he hadn't heard correctly. "Are you putting the house up for sale?"

"That's the plan. But I need to get the place cleaned out before I can even call a realtor."

"When did you decide this?" he asked, widening his stance and folding his arms across his chest.

His familiar pose warned me I was in for a debate I didn't want to have. "It doesn't matter. I'm telling you now so you can get your things moved out."

"What brought this on? Really, Andie, what's going on with you?"

I sighed because asking anything of him seemed to be an invitation for him to start questioning my thinking. "Clark, please just tell me when you can move your cars out so I can clean out my own boxes in the back of the shop."

"Where am I supposed to put my cars? My apartment has exactly two parking spaces and no storage. None, Andie. That's why my cars are here, and you haven't had to pay me for the house."

As soon as we married, Clark and I had gotten a loan to buy the house from my mother, and we'd contributed equally to our mortgage payments. "I'm familiar with our deal, and you'll get your money as soon as the house sells. I'm just asking you to rent a storage facility while the house is on the market."

"I can't afford to rent one," he said, "and it could take months or years to sell our house in this market. Have you thought this through? This is Tyler's home. It's where he learned to walk and ride his bike. Can you really sell those memories?"

"Don't be dense, Clark. I'm selling a house, not memories. Tyler can live with either of us. I've already talked to him about this, and he plans to stay with you during his breaks. With Tyler leaving soon, I don't need this big house."

"Is that really the reason? Because this seems like another one of the impulsive decisions you've been making lately."

"Impulsive? Like what exactly?"

"Like divorcing me, for one thing!"

His anger backed me up a step. It probably had seemed impulsive to him, but we'd been heading that direction for years. It had just taken a long time for me to see it, accept it, and speak up. "That has nothing to do with my decision to sell the house. I just want to move on with my life."

The drooping of his mouth and dulling of his eyes told me I'd hurt him. I hadn't meant to, but my need to speak my truth outweighed my need to protect his feelings.

"What does that mean?" he asked, the quiet strain in his voice tweaking my conscience. "Moving on? To someone else?"

"God, no. I bought a business in Dunwith. I can't live here and work there, so I'm moving."

His brows furrowed. "What kind of business?"

I told him about the fab shop, and that I planned to live in the apartment in the building.

For several seconds he looked at me as if I'd become a stranger to him. In some ways, I had. I was no longer willing to please and cater just to keep the peace or to blindly support whatever he wanted. He walked over to his Thunderbird, putting his back to me, another move I was too familiar with. But this time I refused to let his broad back end our discussion.

"I'd like you to rent a storage unit and move all your things out. Including your stuff in the house."

He didn't respond.

"Please don't make this more difficult than it already is."

He glanced at me over his shoulder. "Me? I'm making this difficult?"

"Ugh!" I groaned aloud. "Get. Your. Crap. Out. Of. My. Shop."

That turned him completely around, a deep scowl on his face.

"I mean it, Clark." Folding my arms across my chest, I tried to look as tough and unyielding as him. "No games. No stalling. Just do it."

"What if I want the house?" he asked.

"You? The guy who was constantly saying we should find a place with a bigger garage?"

"If it's just Tyler and me, well, it would work."

Eyeing him closely, I tried to see if he was messing with me. "You really want the house?"

"I hate living in an apartment. If I take this place, Tyler can keep his home."

"Is that your way of saying I'm a crappy mother?"

"Jesus, Andie, no. I was just making a point that I could make the place work."

"Okay, then what do you mean by *take this place*? Do you want to buy me out?"

"I don't have that kind of cash."

"You would if you sold those cars," I said, gesturing to the beasts that had taken over my shop.

"Not happening. No way." He scraped a stray lock of hair off his forehead, sweeping the dark strands back into the wavy mass twining around his ears.

"Well, what are you proposing then? Are you suggesting you could rent the house from me, or I suppose it would simply be you reducing your percentage of what I would owe you if or when I sell it?"

"Maybe. Yeah, I guess."

"Well, that's not very decisive." And it was something I wasn't going to consider because it would keep me linked to him. I wanted to be done with all of it. I needed a complete separation from him. "I'm not interested in that, but maybe there's another option."

"Such as?"

The idea had briefly skittered through my mind last night while I was caught in the emotional wringer looking at our photos. "If you're willing to provide health insurance for Tyler and pay his college tuition for as long as he remains in school and keep this house while he's a student and needs a place to live during school breaks, I'd consider signing a quit deed. You'll have to pay any legal fees to make this transaction happen, but you wouldn't have to pay me anything for the house."

"That's it?" Clark's eyebrows were working overtime today as they hovered near his hairline.

"What's the problem? That deal is more than fair."

"Exactly, Andie. Have you thought this through?"

"Swear to god, Clark, if you ask me that again I'll throw a rock through the window of your Thunderbird." His condescending questioning had strained my last nerve.

He raised his palms as if to fend me off. "Just double checking, but I got it."

"Good because I'm done with you questioning every decision I make or you telling me I'm being impulsive. I'm not an idiot, and I don't need you to understand me or my decisions. Do you want the deal on the house or not?"

"The deal works for me," he said quickly.

Signing the house over to him would save me the headache of cleaning it out and trying to sell it. I knew I was on the losing end financially, but I was willing to cut my losses to cut our ties. "Okay, I'll provide whatever information the attorney needs, but you have to get the paperwork drawn up. I'll pack the things I want from the house, but I need to get settled in Dunwith before I can take my stuff there. I'll leave most of the furnishings here for you and Tyler unless you don't want me to."

"That would be a big help," he said. "Thanks."

"All right, then please move your cars and tools out of the shop so I can get to my stuff in there. Please get it done while

I'm gone because when I come back I intend to move everything in one trip."

"I will, Andie, but are you sure—"

My loud growl cut him off. "I dare you to finish that sentence."

Chapter Ten

It took a week of hoeing out, throwing out, and packing up to get through decades of accumulated crap. I was ruthless in my attack as I sorted my personal items and the bits that had remained from when my parents had occupied the house. I kept clothes I could work in and a few nicer options for going out for dinner and drinks, something I hoped to do with my new friends. Everything else went to a donation center.

I filled a laundry basket with towels and bath items, another with bedding, and four large boxes and a suitcase with my shoes and clothing, then stored them in my office downstairs.

After giving Tyler a big motherly hug that made him groan, I headed to Dunwith to sort out the mess Walter had left behind.

Two-and-a-half hours later, I parked in front of the office and used my key for the first time. Despite signing Walter's handwritten purchase agreement, I felt I was trespassing. He had left so much of his personal life behind, especially in the apartment, it felt awkward to be here without him. I walked through my new home, flicking on every light as I went, and yet the apartment still felt dim and sad.

Walter's grief had saturated everything.

In every room, despair seemed to reach up from the floor and drag me down into the threadbare carpets. I fought the oppressive feeling until I couldn't breathe.

Rushing out the door, I shot down the metal stairs. Outside, I sank onto the lawn chair Louie had occupied during my last visit and dragged in deep breaths. As soon as I stopped hyperventilating, I called Maggie.

She'd barely said hello before I blurted, "I need your help! I think I made a mistake. I don't know, maybe not. But oh my god, Maggie, I don't know if I can live in Walter's old apartment."

"Whoa, girl, you might have had too much coffee today."

Her unexpected reply made me snort. "Yeah, maybe. But ugh, Maggie, this place is so depressing. I'm begging you to fix the apartment. Please let me hire you."

"What's wrong with the place?"

"It's filled with grief and darkness. Will you please just come over when you have some free time?"

"Of course," Maggie said with a light laugh. "But it sounds as if your apartment needs an energy cleanse rather than a facelift."

"Probably both."

"My assistant will be here in a few minutes. I'll head over then."

I waited for her outside, practicing my square breathing and trying to calm down. My reaction in the apartment had shaken me. During my drive up, I imagined the sense of freedom and excitement I'd feel to finally enter my new home, but all I felt was overwhelming panic. What was I doing? I'd just committed nearly all my resources to buying a business I wasn't sure I could manage successfully and an apartment I couldn't bear to live in. I'd just left everything behind to embark on a journey that had gone from exciting to terrifying. And I already missed my son.

He was leaving, too, I reminded myself. We were both figuring out our next steps, but I hated that our paths were leading us different directions. Maybe that was the issue. Perhaps I was experiencing empty-nest syndrome. Maybe it was my own grief, and not Walter's, that overwhelmed me in the apartment. Maybe the darkness was simply a lack of light in my own life. Rocking forward, I braced my elbows on my knees and buried my face in my palms. *Inhale for four, hold for four, exhale for four, hold for four...*

"Hello, miss. I'm looking for my badass friend."

Maggie's voice brought me upright and I saw her walking across the parking lot, arms swinging in sync with her long-legged stride.

"Have you seen her?" she asked, stopping in front of me.

I pushed to my feet. "No one here but a whiney baby."

Smiling, she surprised me with a quick hug. "Okay, baby-cakes, show me what's got your diaper in a twist."

A burble of laughter rolled up my throat, and I returned her hug. "Thank you for rushing over. Truly, Maggie, I appreciate you coming to my rescue *again*."

"Well, I appreciate you keeping my life interesting." She gestured to the door. "After you."

"All right, but prepare yourself," I said, then led her inside and up to the apartment where I swung the door open and nodded for her to enter first. "Welcome to my messy-closet-slash-armchair-garden."

I observed Maggie as she walked through the apartment, her green gaze taking in everything from floor to ceiling, room to room, making three slow passes through the place. Finally, she turned to me, hands on hips. "Paint, light fixtures, and low-cost flooring will completely change the look of this place."

A happy thrill rushed through me, followed quickly by concern. "I'd love to update the whole apartment, but my finances are tight right now. I can't afford to spend more than five thousand dollars. Any chance that amount could improve this space?"

Giving the apartment another assessing look, Maggie said, "Will you let me get creative?"

"Absolutely."

"Are you willing to trade services?" she asked.

"Of course, but what service can I possibly provide to you?"

"Provide our lunches and make a sign for me. The wood sign for my consignment shop is falling apart. I'd like a more durable metal sign if you can make one."

"Yeah, I definitely can, but it could take a while because I have to clean up the shop before it's safe for me to do any work there."

"I'm in no rush," she said. "When can I start in here?"

"As soon as you want to. Consider the place yours," I said, fanning my arms out like a game-show hostess, making her smile. "I can get cash for you today."

Maggie took another sweeping look around. "I'm going to paint the darkness and grief right out of this place, and when I'm done, this will be a bright, beautiful space where you can build your new life." She pinned me with a knowing look. "Just don't drag any ugly crap back in."

I wanted to promise I wouldn't, but grief had a way of shadowing a person and lurking in our blind spots.

"Hey," she said with a sympathetic tone. "That wasn't meant to be harsh. It was simply a reminder that you have a right to be happy and create a life you love. That's all."

"Well, it's a reminder I really needed to hear right now. Thanks for checking my little closet for monsters," I said, gesturing to the shadowy interior of the apartment. "I feel better knowing the only things lurking in here are my own doubts and too many plants."

Maggie's laugh filled me with hope. "The decor is a little scary, but it's time to pull on your big-girl pants and get to work." She surveyed Walter's armchair-garden. "Keep the bamboo palm in the corner, the braided money tree in that blue pot, and that beautiful anthurium in the white pot on the corner shelf," she said, pointing them out. "The rest need to go."

"Got it," I said, making a mental note, then followed her to the kitchen where she began opening cupboard doors and drawers.

"All these dishes, pans and utensils need to be boxed up and stored outside the apartment. Same for everything else that isn't too bulky or heavy to move out. As she made her way around the kitchen, she talked about painting everything including the cupboards and replacing the countertop with a budget-friendly option. She suggested laminate flooring through the whole apartment to give it a more expansive, cohesive feel, then headed back to the living room.

Out of my depth, I followed along watching her work, intrigued by how easily she envisioned the space as a canvas in her mind where she confidently brought her ideas to life.

I used to view scrap metal like that, welding odd pieces and shapes together in my mind, seeing a sculpture emerge into a complete piece. I'd get so excited that I'd want to grab my dad's welder and start melding metal together. But my father would ask me to show him my vision on paper first so he could see the amazing sculpture I intended to create. His interest flattered me, and I'd eagerly scribble lines and shapes in my notebook. He'd ask me about each piece, what type of metal I'd use, what size it would be, how I would shape it and attach it to reflect my vision. As we discussed my process, I'd see the issues I might come across, the inconsistencies in my mental calculations, and I would erase, adjust, and correct dimensions until my sculpture worked on paper.

Sketching slowed me down, but that was how my father taught me to draw and design sculptures, and to read blueprints. He would repeatedly remind me that the time spent planning would be time saved in the doing. And he was usually right.

"So, what do you think?" Maggie asked, snapping my attention back to her.

My face heated for allowing my mind to wander off. "I'm not sure," I said, hoping my reply was generic enough for my lapse to slide by unnoticed.

She screwed up her face. "Why are you not sure about getting boxes to pack this stuff in?"

"Oh, um, I just meant that, well, I'm not sure where to get them."

"I know a place. If you're hungry, we can grab a late lunch at the Bobcat Brewery and get boxes there."

"And maybe a glass of wine," I suggested.

She smiled. "You read my mind."

The Bobcat Brewery sat on a wide patch of gravel with the front entrance facing the park. As Maggie explained on our walk over, Bobbie Jo Kafferty, owner of the establishment, had converted a farm supply and feed store into what was now a trendy brewery.

Overhead duct pipes snaked across a high ceiling painted black, and a long bar at one end of the brewery. The interior walls were decorated with metal beer signage that made me eager to start creating my own art pieces. As I followed Maggie through the bar, nearly every booth, pub-style table, and barstool was occupied.

"Let's sit outside," she said, stepping out a back door onto a sprawling deck with a view of the Dunwith river. In a graveled area just off the deck several people relaxed in colorful Adirondack chairs circled around a brick fire pit.

"Weather permitting, Bobbie Jo lights the firepit in the evenings," Maggie said. "She also has live music here a few nights a week."

"Gosh, I can't remember the last time I heard a live band," I said as we crossed the deck strung with Edison style lights and sat at a table.

"It's mostly acoustic musicians here, but there are full bands in the park on Sundays, and you can almost always find live music somewhere in town."

"What a fascinating place," I said, wishing I'd taken time to explore Dunwith four years ago when I first visited the fab shop. Maybe I could have convinced Clark to spend a weekend here to reconnect with each other. We could have gone to dinner and listened to live music in the evening, maybe even danced together and made love in our room at night. Maybe it would have helped me breathe and saved our marriage. But probably not because he wouldn't have been interested in any of that.

The jangling sound of bracelets drew my attention to a striking woman who placed two menus on our table. She wore a blouse of forest-green that matched the color of her eyes and was tucked into tight blue jeans that emphasized her slender figure. Her silvery-blonde hair was loosely braided and fell to the middle of her back.

She glanced at Maggie. "Who is this beautiful lady with you?"

"Bobbie Jo, this badass is Andie Arness," Maggie said. "She just bought Walter's fab shop and is moving to Dunwith."

"That's fantastic." Bobbie Jo welcomed me with a wide smile. "I'm glad you'll be contributing to the female badassery in our town."

I laughed, knowing she must be one of Maggie's fun friends. "Nice to meet you, Bobbie Jo. Your brewery is gorgeous."

"Thank you. Let me grab drinks for you gals while you look at the menus."

Maggie and I both ordered white wine, and when Bobbie Jo returned with our drinks, we placed our orders.

"Join us if you have time," Maggie said.

Glancing around the deck, Bobbie Jo gave a nod. "The lunch crowd is thinning out now, so I should be able to visit for a few minutes when I deliver your lunch. I'll return shortly." She gathered our menus and headed inside.

While she was gone, Maggie shared her plan for updating my apartment. We'd stopped by the bank so I could get cash, but Maggie wouldn't take more than half until the job was done.

"I'll need to get measurements before I know how much flooring to buy," she said, "so let me know when you get everything cleared out and I can stop by."

"I'll get it all done tonight."

She smiled as if I were being naive. "There's a lot of packing to do in that little apartment. It might take you a few days."

"But it won't. Everything will be cleared out by tomorrow morning exactly as you instructed."

That made her laugh. "All right. I'll stop by around ten o'clock. Are there any colors you dislike?" she asked, and all I could think of were the avocado green walls in my old company office and the bathroom fixtures in my new apartment.

"I don't want to see avocado green *anywhere*, please."

"That goes without saying. Any other preferences?"

"Maggie, my only preference is to have an apartment I can live in. How or in what manner that's accomplished is entirely up to you. I not only trust your judgement, I'm in desperate need of it. With everything happening in my life right now, my brain aches. All I want is to mindlessly pack up the apartment then walk away until you finish working your magic there."

"Understood," she said. "I know exactly what to do."

"Thank god," I said, breathing a sigh of relief. For several minutes we sipped our wine and talked about the town.

I'd noticed a complex of sorts across the river, where a small plane took off and another one landed. "I didn't know Dunwith had an airport," I said, as Bobbie Jo delivered our meals.

Maggie pointed out an industrial size building with a flat roof. "That's a private airport with public access for small planes and light aircraft,"

I pointed to three large rectangular structures that resembled the longhouses Native American's once used. "What are those buildings?"

"They're plane hangars," Bobbie Jo said, sitting beside Maggie. "My friend rents one for his light sport and ultralight planes. Another guy I know keeps his hang glider in one."

As we ate our lunch and sipped our wine, our conversation shifted to the town. I learned that every Sunday the Dunwith community gathered in Fern Park, where people enjoyed a farmer's market, craft booths, music, games, contests, and picnics from morning to late evening. They called it their Sunday Fun-day. I called it wonderfully enlightened and couldn't wait to experience a Fun-day in my new town.

"Are you open for business yet?" Bobbie Jo asked me.

Chewing the last delicious bite of my salad, I shook my head. "Not yet. I need to get organized first and do a bit of packing." I didn't mention the mess in my shop I needed to clean up because I didn't want it to reflect on Walter. "Any chance you'd have some empty boxes you'd like to get rid of?"

"I have a storage room full of boxes," she said. "Take them all. Please."

* * *

I didn't take all the boxes in the brewery storage room, but I did pile several stacks on the back of Walter's old flatbed, then used Rita's elevator to cart them up to my apartment.

Opening the drapes to late afternoon sunlight helped brighten the apartment, but a feeling of sadness lingered in the place, and in me. Swiping on my phone, I opened a playlist I hadn't listened to in a long time, then turned up the volume, hoping music would fill the empty space in my chest.

I worked on the kitchen first, which took much longer than I'd anticipated because I was trying to group things as I packed. What to keep, what to donate, what to toss, and what items to ask Walter about before deciding what to do with them. Two hours in, I realized it would be more expedient to sort every-thing later before moving stuff back in.

I put aside a few things I would need now: a glass, a plate, a bowl, and a set of silverware and stored them in the downstairs office next to an old drip coffee maker and two stained porcelain cups.

Each time I descended Rita's lift with several heavy boxes, I admired her ingenuity and appreciated her creative forethought that was making an undesirable task tolerable. As the mounting stacks of boxes filled the downstairs storage room, the apartment upstairs seemed to expand. Box after box, room after room, I packed up Walter and Rita's life, gently making room for my own. Night shadows darkened my windows and my phone battery dwindled as I carried and stacked boxes I would eventually have to unpack, sort, and move again.

I muscled the mattress off the bed, then wrangled and pulled it through the apartment. When I finally got it out to the catwalk, I gave it a hard shove and sent it sliding and tumbling down the stairs, knowing I wouldn't be bringing it back up. The box spring was in great shape, but I planned to buy a new mattress and fresh bedding before Maggie finished updating the apartment.

After catching my breath, I pulled the bed frame apart and stacked the rails, headboard, and box spring against the back wall, glad the gaudy floral wallpaper would soon be gone. I wanted to move the dresser against the same wall, but it barely shifted when I pushed it. I tried again, using my shoulder, but only managed to rock it up on two legs. I thought removing the drawers might lighten the weight of the dresser, but to my surprise and slight horror, I found it full of Rita's clothing.

Oh, Walter... Did you forget about her things? Or was the task of clearing them out too heartbreaking for you to face?

I didn't know, and I couldn't ask. But the stuff needed to be moved. I dumped the drawer full of Rita's intimates into the garbage bag with cleaning rags and other items to be tossed out. The rest of her clothing went into boxes that Walter could sort through later or simply donate, whichever he preferred. The same for everything he'd left behind in the closet.

Hours later, after depositing the last box in the storage room downstairs, I slogged back up to the apartment. Walter's plants and stands still inhabited the living room along with a comfy-looking chair and a worn loveseat where I'd placed my overnight bag, a pillow, and a blanket. I was too wiped out to take the plants downstairs. When I plugged my phone into the charger, it was nearly four o'clock in the morning, but my aching, sweaty body demanded a shower.

Carrying my overnight bag, I slogged across worn carpeting and entered the bathroom. I pulled a bath towel, washcloth, and bodywash from my case, then shucked my filthy clothes. For a moment, I considered using the walk-in bathtub, imagining how good a hot soak and jetted massage would feel on my sore body, but I didn't want to wait for the tub to fill, and I wasn't certain how to use the unit. Opting for the stand-up shower adjacent to the tub, I turned on the faucet. Fat, beautiful streams of water burst from a large showerhead. I sighed in relief as hot water gently pummeled my tight shoulder muscles. Walter and Rita's outdated furnishings had indicated their frugality, but they had obviously splurged on these fixtures to offer their aging bodies a measure of relief and pleasure. While I mentally thanked them, I couldn't help wishing they'd updated the green toilet and sink to match the white tub and shower.

I would add the updates to my growing wish list.

Number one on the list was for my son to not only accept my new life but to become part of it. I missed him deeply. The truth was, I'd been missing my son for a long time. He'd been my baby and sweet chubby-cheeked toddler, and he'd needed me for sustenance and comfort. But I lost a piece of our boy when Clark claimed Tyler as his little buddy. Tyler loved Clark's strength, riding high on his daddy's shoulders and in his cool cars. I'd lost another piece of Tyler to his teenaged independence, and another to his disappointment and blame when I broke our family.

I hadn't meant to.

Tyler said I hadn't considered how my decision would affect him and his father, but they were all I'd considered during my entire marriage. When Clark and I married, I thought I'd found love, a home, and family. I poured my entire self into our family, utterly and completely, and my son and husband drank greedily from what seemed to be an unending stream of my love and devotion. I'd kept nothing for myself. I understand now how foolish that was, but I'd thought that's how a person showed their love for someone, so I'd given everything I had.

It was only when I couldn't dredge up another drop of energy, when I was so empty and depleted I couldn't function, that I understood a simple yet crucial fact. Without a source of water to refill a well, it goes dry, and all that's left are deep cracks and fissures.

Chapter Eleven

After four hours of fitful sleep on a couch that should have been retired years ago, I freshened up, dressed, and braided my hair, then headed downstairs to make coffee. I left it to brew while I moved the rest of the plants out of the apartment and put them downstairs near the office windows, hoping they'd survive until Walter found them a new home.

With a sense of accomplishment, I reached for the coffee pot and saw that the glass carafe was empty. The cord was plugged in and the buttons lit up when I pushed them, but nothing happened. *Noooo.* Gripped by a sense of desperation, I thumped the top of the coffeemaker, but nothing happened. I could not, would not, start another hardworking day without caffeine, and I knew just where to get a big-ass mug of great coffee. Grabbing my wallet, I headed outside to find Walter approaching with two travel mugs in his hands and Louie prancing happily at his heels.

When Walter saw me, his face lit up with a crooked smile. "Good morning!" he called, ambling toward me with a slight hitch in his gait. "How was your first night in town?"

"Busy," I said, kneeling to give Louie a snuggle. He gazed up at me with adoring eyes and a sloppy grin. I popped a kiss on his knobby head. "Your treats are in the office," I said, then spoke to Walter. "I'll be right back."

It took a minute to find the bag of treats in the clutter, but Louie was waiting patiently, and expectantly, when I returned.

"You're up early," I said to Walter while feeding Louie his treat.

"Always am," Walter said, stepping onto the concrete pad. "Brought you coffee. Didn't know if you used cream and sugar, so I tucked some in my shirt pocket."

"You are a lifesaver," I said, gratefully accepting the insulated travel cup he pressed into my eager hand. "I didn't realize the coffeemaker here didn't work."

His eyebrows beetled in surprise. "The old girl finally gave out, did she?" Releasing a small laugh, he said, "That thing has been creaking and sputtering for a year now, but I thought she might still have a bit of life left in her."

It struck me that Walter and Rita might have used that philosophy for deciding when to upgrade things. If there was still life left in it, they kept it. But the wafer thin couch cushions that disrupted my sleep and abused my body had, in my opinion, died long ago.

"How are you settling in at your place?" I asked as we both sat in the lawn chairs Walter had left here.

"Well enough." He stroked shaky fingers over Louie's head. The two seemed to draw comfort from one another, but Louie was avidly interested in the treat I was holding.

"Are you ready for this one?" I asked and was rewarded with a bark that lifted Louie's front paws off the concrete. "Here you go, sweetie." I gave him the treat, then used my pants leg to wipe the slobber off my fingers. "Walter, you might want to work on Louie's eating etiquette. It's a bit untidy."

Walter's warm chuckle filled the morning air. "That's what you get for spoiling him with those expensive treats," he said. "He sure does love 'em though."

"Well, I love this delicious coffee. Where did you get it?"

Walter leaned toward me as if sharing a secret. "I made it. I just add a little vanilla. Rita said drinking my coffee was so lovely it was like getting a warm hug."

The image was so sweet it hit me right in the heart, and I felt a little choked up thinking about Rita's clothing I'd had to box up.

"I suspect flattery was just Rita's way of getting me to make the coffee every morning," Walter said, releasing a soft chuckle.

"Probably. She was a smart lady."

"Too smart sometimes," he said. "I could be dead set against a thing, and she'd appear to agree with me, but then I'd find myself doing that very thing I didn't want to do." He shook his head. "Never could figure out how she'd turn me around so quickly."

Clark used to do the same thing to me, but I knew how he'd accomplished it. He'd simply taken advantage of my desire to please him and be a supportive wife. I know it had been my choice to do so, but he'd never once considered what giving myself away had cost me. Neither had I because I was so committed to my illusion that we were happy, I couldn't even acknowledge my own feelings. It was only years later, and one too many of his long-sighing-eyerolls, when everything came crashing down around us. Our marriage, like my illusion, lay in shattered pieces at my feet, all of it beyond repair.

Walter rested his mug on the arm of the lawn chair. "I wanted to let you know that our formal purchase agreement will be ready tomorrow," he said, redirecting my thoughts toward my future here. "Would you be able to meet me at my attorney's office at nine o'clock to sign the paperwork?"

"Of course," I said, both excited and a bit unnerved by the speed of our progress.

While we sipped our coffee, which really did feel like a warm hug, we shifted the conversation to other matters. "Do you have everything you need here?" he asked.

"Actually, I have more than I need. I'm having a few updates made in the apartment," I said, hoping it wouldn't offend him. "I've packed everything in boxes and stored them downstairs while the work is being done. But before I move anything back in, you should go through the boxes to see if there is anything you might have overlooked that you'd like to keep." I wouldn't tell him some of those boxes contained Rita's clothing, but I wanted him to consider looking through everything again and maybe spare him regrets later.

"Not necessary," he said, sinking back in his chair. "I have the necessities and my memories. That's all I need now."

"Are you sure, Walter? There are items in those boxes that might have sentimental value."

He held my gaze. "It's just stuff, Andie. You're free to use it or pass it along. At this age it just weighs me down. I have what I need. Everything here is yours."

The pain in his eyes suggested he might have intentionally left Rita's things behind. Hoping a little playful jesting would bring light back to his eyes and to our day, I asked, "Does every-thing include all the plants?"

A grin spread across his face. "I'd hoped you'd grown fond of them."

"I've fallen in love with three of them that I'd be happy to keep. But maybe your friends at The Grove would like to add a little love to their lives as well?"

"There's plenty of love happening in that place," he said with a teenage-like smirk, "but whatever the residents don't want, I'll plant in the community flower garden."

"I'd be happy to help with that," I said, and we agreed to move them in the morning before meeting with the attorney.

While we finished our coffee, I gave Louie a thorough scratching and probably too much snuggling because he seemed eager to trot off with Walter when he gathered our empty mugs and headed out.

I went to the shop, flipped on the lights, and hit the button to open the overhead door. As daylight flooded the shop, the enormity of the task ahead overwhelmed me, especially knowing I'd be doing it alone. Metal was heavy and dangerous to move. It could slice through clothing, skin, and bone. It could tip or fall and crush and break body parts or flat-out kill a person. One shifting bar in a rack could start a chain reaction and topple hundreds of pounds of bar stock onto an unsuspecting victim. I did not want to be that person, so my priority was to determine what equipment I had for safely handling and moving material.

But after another assessing look around, I knew I required a new plan because the forklift was blocked in by overturned barrels of scrap metal. How the hell had Walter managed to bury the one piece of equipment capable of moving stuff in here?

The challenge of sorting it all reminded me of the sliding puzzles Tyler had loved to play with. The puzzle tiles were locked into the board and could only be slid into an adjacent empty space. The goal was to eventually get all the tiles moved around to create a specific image. But sliding plastic tiles into their proper place on a boardgame was far different than moving metal and equipment around.

Not one thing was where it belonged. All I could think about was Rita. Her clean, organized shop had been her pride and joy. No matter how much she loved Walter and his *warm-hug coffee*, if she had seen this mess, she would have hung him by his ears. I loved the man, too, but I was beginning to understand why she'd called him a numpty fopdoodle.

With a loud sigh, I navigated my way to the least congested corner of the shop and pulled on my work gloves. For two hours, I gathered, carried, and dragged tools, equipment, and materials into designated spots. When I finished clearing a small area, I stood and stretched my sore back, relieved to finally have a section of floor space open enough to be able to slide in the next piece of my puzzle. But which piece?

I needed to think on it to avoid making mistakes and ultimately more work for myself, so I figured I might as well brush up on my welding skills. After plugging in Rita's temperamental portable welder, I pushed aside tools and a pile of cleaning rags to clear a space on the worktable.

After clamping two pieces of scrap metal to the table, I tugged on my leather gloves and slipped a welding helmet over my head. Rolling my tight shoulders, I leaned in and placed a few tack welds to reacquaint myself with the torch. Then I laid two stringer beads and a long weave bead. Not bad. Not great. My next weave bead was better, and the one after that far smoother and more consistent, and soon I was lost in the methodical movement and buzzing sound of the torch.

The smell of smoke snapped me out of my trance. Flipping the helmet up on my head, I saw flames dancing in the pile of cleaning cloths on the worktable.

"Oh, no! No-no-no!" I switched off the welder, then scooped the burning rags up with my leather gloves. I was going to drop them on the floor and stomp out the flames, but dark spots of oil or grease trailed across the concrete. Even a small fire in this mess could quickly engulf the whole place, and I refused to lose my business before it even opened. Panicked and cursing my stupidity, I ran for the open door.

"Shit-shit-shit!" With the flaming rags in my hands, I shot

out the door and crashed into a human brick wall, at least that's how it felt.

As I stumbled forward, a man with shocked blue eyes stumbled backward, my burning gloves jammed against his abdomen. "Holy hell," he said, sweeping the flaming mass of fabric out of my gloves. The clump landed on the ground between us, and he snuffed it out with his brown leather boat shoes.

For a moment, we stared at each other, mouths agape.

The tall, sandy-haired, clean-cut man recovered first, giving me a quick looking over then glancing behind me. "Should I call the fire department?"

"No," I said, my voice shaking.

"Are you sure? Is there a fire inside?"

"Not anymore."

"Are your hands burned?"

Glancing at my scorched, sooty gloves, I wasn't sure. Between my panicked sprint and unexpected crash into the man, I was stunned and off balance. "I think I'm okay. Are you?" I was so amped up and unnerved, my jaw was clenched and my body vibrated.

He looked down at his abdomen where my dirty flaming rags had left a large sooty stain on his crisp white shirt. "I'm okay, although I might have a few less chest hairs."

"I'm so sorry. I hope I didn't hurt you," I said, fighting a cough. Smoke residue coiled in my throat.

He smiled, and my shaky knees grew a lot weaker. "You didn't hurt me," he said, "but you did surprise me. I thought I was getting mugged."

My laugh came out of my tight smoke-clogged throat as a bizarre squawk. Clapping a hand over my mouth, I immediately realized my mistake when the smell of singed leather filled my nostrils, and I was seized by a fit of sneezing. Scrubbing my forearm across the tip of my nose, I sniffed and blinked, trying to stop an oncoming sneeze. I coughed, then sniffed a couple more times trying to get my shit together.

"Um, you have a smudge on your face," he said, his lips twitching, eyes lit with humor as he took in my appearance.

I stood there with a welding helmet wobbling on top of my head, filthy, sweat-stained, and smelling like I'd crawled out of a firepit. "Well, you have a smudge on your shirt," I said, my voice raspy. "I'll pay to have it cleaned or replaced. Just drop a bill in my mailbox by the office door."

"Not necessary. Do you need help with anything in there?" he asked, nodding toward the open shop door at my back.

"I need to blow my nose."

"Go ahead. I can wait."

"What? Why would you wait?" I couldn't think with those blue eyes assessing my soot-covered face and nostrils that probably looked like black holes.

"Because I'd like to hire you to do a job at the airport."

"I can't. I mean, I'm not open for business yet."

"The job is halfway done. Materials are already on site. You'd just need to bring a welder."

"But I'm not open yet," I said, feeling a sneeze coming on.

"Let me start over."

Please don't. It felt as if a hairy-legged spider was crawling up my nose. *Oh, god.*

"I'm Mason Scott and I'm the operations manager at the Dunwith Airport." He stuck out his hand and held it there, waiting for me to shake it, but I was utterly convulsed.

A loud, involuntary expulsion of air shot from my nose and mouth, wracking my body, and sending my helmet sailing. Through watering eyes, I saw it hit his extended hand with a hard clunk that made him yelp even as he fought to catch it. After a quick bobble, he clasped the helmet between his manly hands and held it out to me, his rolled shirt sleeves now smudged with grime.

"Will you consider it?" he asked as if he hadn't just been accosted by the grossest human on the planet.

Mortified beyond words, I grabbed my helmet and bolted back inside to the rat's nest where I belonged.

Chapter Twelve

Mason Scott didn't follow me inside, but he did leave a note in my mailbox with his name, number, and request to discuss the job. I put the note on my desk, utterly baffled that he would even consider hiring me after my stellar performance.

I was still so rattled after my shower, I dressed and headed to the closest furniture store where I bought a sofa sleeper and paid extra to have it delivered the next afternoon. On the way home, I bought a coffeemaker, a large cooler, a few groceries including beer, which I stashed in the cooler with two bags of ice. Then I stopped at Sophie's café for a Mediterranean panini with vegan cheese. Sophie wasn't there, nor were any of my girl gab friends, so I opted for takeout and walked down to the river.

In an open public area, a large group of people visited with frivolity, eating from a picnic table buffet, throwing frisbee, and playing horseshoes. I passed two empty benches and made my way down the grassy riverbank where I sat alone.

I took out my phone to call my son. I'd tried him four times since I'd been here, but each time he'd texted back that he would call me later. Later hadn't happened yet, and I wanted to know that he was okay. Clark was staying at the house with Tyler and would have called me had any issues come up. But I needed to connect with my son directly. To my surprise, Tyler answered on the second ring.

"Hi, sweetie, how's your new car running?" I asked, both curious and intentionally starting our conversation with a subject that would interest him.

"It's great. What's up?" he asked, sounding half distracted and rushed.

"I'm calling to see how you're doing. I miss you."

"I'm good. You?"

"All right, Ty, what am I interrupting?"

"I'm about to head over to the car wash to help Joey and his dad."

"Did you get a summer job?"

"Just for a couple of weeks to earn some money for my trip."

"What trip?" I asked, unable to recall him mentioning anything of the sort.

"The guys and I are going to Myrtle Beach for three weeks."

"Wait. Who are the guys? When did you plan this? And how are you going to afford to stay anywhere for three weeks?"

"Mom..." he said, dragging out the word I both loved and hated depending on his tone. "I'm going with Joey, Alex, and Eric."

"When? And where do you plan to stay?"

"We're leaving in two weeks and staying at Eric's aunt's house. We're house-sitting for her while she's on vacation in Europe."

I immediately thought the lady was insane for letting four teenage boys stay in her home but kept my opinion to myself. "Okay. That sounds fun," I said, biting back the urge to remind him to be respectful and careful and use good judgement.

"I'm kind of running late, Mom."

"I won't keep you. But, Tyler, I want to see you. I was thinking you could drive up for the day, and I'll show you around. We could get lunch and talk about your trip."

"Can't. I'll be working."

"Every day?"

"Well, no, but I've got other things to do."

"Then I'll drive down and see you at home. When will you be there?"

"I don't know, Mom. Jeez, can we talk about this later?"

"Sure, Ty. I'll call you tomorrow."

"K-Mom-love ya-bye," he said and ended the call.

Tossing my phone aside, I reminded myself that my son was a teenager, that he didn't mean to be rude or inconsiderate. But he was. And I was partly to blame for my disappointment and frustration because my son was simply struggling against my need to hang on too tightly.

He was about to leave home, and I needed to find a way to let him go.

I sighed and leaned back on my hands. It was a beautiful June evening, warm enough for short sleeves. A small plane droned high overhead, and off in the distance, horseshoes clanged against metal stakes. For the first time in days, I exhaled and focused on being present.

The gentle tones of the river began to soothe my rattled nerves, and I sat unmoving for a long time, just listening, just being. If not for my growling stomach, I might have drifted off to sleep. I longed for the moment when I could spend a night in my own bed in my own apartment.

Unwrapping my sandwich, I savored the smell of pesto and grilled sourdough bread for about two seconds before taking a ravenous bite. I hadn't realized how hungry I was. I should have bought chips to go with my sandwich and brought a beer with me. I could use one after the day I'd had. Recalling my disastrous mishap with Mason Scott made me mentally squirm in discomfort. Just my luck to be a walking disaster and run into the most gorgeous guy I'd laid eyes on in decades. I would never be able to face the man, but Dunwith was a close-knit town, and the likelihood of our paths crossing again made my brain ping-pong between *ooh-yeah* and *god-no*.

Releasing an audible groan, partly from embarrassment and because my abused muscles were protesting, I picked up my sandwich wrapper and headed back to my car.

When I arrived back at my shop, Maggie pulled in behind me but stayed in her van and lowered the window.

"I've got the flooring and paint for your apartment," she said. "We're starting tomorrow at ten o'clock, so I'd like to take everything up now, if that's all right."

"Oh my god, *yes*! That's fantastic."

Laughing at my stuttering excitement, Maggie stepped out of the van and opened the back doors. Inside were boxes of laminate flooring labeled Gray Oak. Several gallon cans of paint and one five gallon pail sat atop the boxes along with tarps, paint trays, brushes, and rollers. From the paint dots smeared on the lids, the colors appeared to be white and a taupe-gray color. I wouldn't have picked those colors, but I'd seen Maggie's work in Kate's place and trusted her judgement.

"We're going to get a workout on your stairs tonight," Maggie said, dragging out the heavy pail of paint and setting it on the ground. "Should we bet on how many trips we'll have to make?"

"What's the wager?"

"A drink?"

"I'm in. I bet we can do it in one trip."

She laughed. "You obviously don't understand betting, but I'm happy to let you buy me a drink." From the side door, she pulled out a large aluminum hand truck, then pulled out retractable back legs with wheels that tilted the trolley back at a forty-five degree angle.

"That's a sweet piece of equipment," I said. "I'm envious."

"This girl's a beast," she said. "We've moved a lot of things together. We should be able to manage several boxes per trip and save ourselves some steps."

"We can just take them up on my elevator."

Pausing with a case of flooring in her arms, Maggie gaped at me. "You have an elevator?"

"Yes," I said. "Rita built it."

"If we can haul this up in one trip, I'll gladly buy you a drink."

I picked up a box of flooring. "This stuff is heavier than I expected," I said, placing it on the hand truck. "It'll be safer to make two trips, and I already have beer here, so I'll buy."

We loaded the trolley, then rolled it inside and onto the lift. As it carried us to the loft, Maggie glanced down at the messy shop. "You could probably get Chloe to haul a lot of the junk steel in here to the scrapyard for you."

"What?" I followed her gaze, but instead of seeing a mess of junk, I saw gold. Every piece of scrap could be used to create a sculpture. "Thanks, I'll let her know if I need her," I said, but I knew I wouldn't be scrapping a single thing.

After depositing the first load in the apartment, we went back for the rest of the flooring and other supplies. When we finished, she loaded the trolley and closed her van while I got our drinks and a bag of chips. We sat in the lawn chairs on my small patio, and she told me that her brother, Ashe, would install the new light fixtures and help Kate lay the flooring.

"Why is Kate helping?" I asked in surprise.

"Because I asked her to. She knows how to do the work, and I can trust her."

"I can give you more money to pay her unless you already budgeted for it."

"She wouldn't take money if I tried to pay her."

"Maggie, I can't let her work for free," I said, embarrassed. "I can help with the flooring."

"Andie, we've got this. This is Kate's way of giving back so to speak. Chloe, Ashe, and I helped Kate for months because we *wanted* to. Because we love her and we all really enjoyed hanging out together while we helped her build her house. That's what friends do."

"Not any friends I've ever known."

"Then it's lucky for you that you're making new friends," she said with a playful wink.

I could barely swallow past the lump in my throat.

"Do you need a place to stay while I'm working on your apartment?" she asked.

"No. I have a bathroom downstairs, a coffeemaker, and a cooler to keep my beer cold. That's all I need. But, Maggie, I really can help with the work."

"Nope. It's my project, and I promise, you won't recognize the place when I'm done. Besides, from the looks of your shop, you'll have plenty of work there to keep you busy."

"Ugh. The place is a disaster. I don't know how Walter could have created such a mess just looking for a pair of Rita's pliers."

Sympathy filled Maggie's eyes, and her lips drooped a little. "I suspect Walter was in the shop raging rather than searching."

As her words sank in, I saw the mess in a new light. The overturned barrels, bar stock and materials ripped from the shelves, tools scattered across the floor, crates and boxes thrown haphazardly, their contents scattered in every direction as the entire shop was torn asunder by a man howling with grief. No wonder Walter couldn't bear to face the mess he'd made. I understood now why he'd needed to leave behind everything—right down to the nuts, bolts, and undergarments of Rita's life. It was probably the only way he could keep breathing and claw his way forward.

I told Maggie that Walter had been stopping by each morning with Louie and bringing me his special *warm-hug* coffee. When Maggie cracked up, I shared Walter's comment about Rita claiming his coffee was so smooth and lovely it felt like a warm hug, but I didn't share the story about their coffee dates. Those stories belonged to Walter.

"What a sweet couple they were," she said, then sadly shook her head. "Such a shame he lost her."

For a moment, we sat in silence both seemingly lost in thought. But Walter's grief, and my own, were not a place I wanted to hang out, so I asked, "Is your brother, Ashe, older or younger?"

"Older. Why?"

"Just curious is all. How many siblings do you have."

"Just one."

"Sometimes that's more than enough," I said, thinking of my own sister and her fucked-up beliefs.

"I take it you have a sibling?"

"A sister. Older. Not in touch with each other. Long story."

"Got it," Maggie said, glancing at the darkening sky. "I suppose I should get going, but first, do you have different furniture for the apartment? Or are you using what was there?"

"I just bought a sofa bed to replace the old loveseat upstairs, but I'll keep the chair."

"Perfect. When's the sofa being delivered?"

"Tomorrow afternoon."

She made a face. "Those suckers are heavy. Any chance we can keep it downstairs until the flooring is done so we don't have to move it around?"

"That's the plan since I'll be sleeping on it."

"All right then." She stood and stretched. "I'll see you in the morning."

After she left, I put the cooler and chips back in the office. Then I spent an hour clearing a space under the catwalk where I could park my new sofa when it was delivered. Once that was done, I locked up the building and headed upstairs.

There was no television to keep me company, so I grabbed my blanket and sat in the chair. To my surprise it rocked and swiveled and glided. After bopping around in it for a few minutes, I tucked my feet up, arranged my blanket, and opened my reading app. Then I eagerly read my way back into a story of a young man's harrowing journey alone through a snake-infested rainforest. His courageous struggle encouraged me to just keep moving forward in my own life.

* * *

I woke early, got dressed, then loaded and secured Walter's plants on his old flatbed truck. I texted to let him know I was on my way, and he was waiting outside with a cart and two cups of coffee when I arrived. After giving Louie his treat and greeting Walter with a morning hug, I helped him take the plants inside and deposit them in the garden area of the park. Then we headed to the attorney's office where Walter and I signed our formal purchase agreement. When we finished, Walter said he and Louie, who'd waited in my truck, were going to take a leisurely walk back to The Grove just a few blocks away.

So, on the way to my shop, I stopped by my CPA's office to drop off a copy of the agreement and ask his assistant to check on how my other paperwork was coming along. She promised to have Eli text me when he came out of his meeting, so I headed home.

I had just opened the overhead door of my shop when Maggie pulled in, followed by Kate, so I walked out to meet them. Maggie stepped out of her van wearing a ball cap, black T-shirt, and jeans covered with paint-spatter. Kate exited her Trailblazer in similar garb minus the paint marks, and a guy stepped from the passenger side of her vehicle. He was tall, dark-haired, athletic-looking and extremely handsome.

Maggie snickered a little and said, "Did I mention that my brother and Kate have a thing?"

She hadn't, but I could immediately see the *thing* they shared reflected in their eyes when they glanced at each other. Ashe McKensie approached me directly, hand extended, a warm smile on his handsome face. "I'm Maggie's brother Ashe."

"Andie Arness," I said, shaking his hand. "Thanks so much for whatever work you'll be doing in my apartment."

"Lights and flooring," he said.

"And the kitchen counter," Maggie added as if reminding him of a job she would not be doing.

"Hi, Andie," Kate said, giving me a quick hug.

"Oh, good morning," I replied. "There's a fresh pot of coffee in the office if anyone wants a cup. And I put cold drinks in the refrigerator upstairs, but I can move them to my cooler if you need to unplug the fridge."

"Not necessary. We can serve ourselves after we take every-thing upstairs," Maggie said, opening the side door of her van. She pulled out the hand truck we'd used last night. "Let's get this stuff loaded."

Kate opened the hatch on her Trailblazer, and Maggie swung open the back doors of her van. Together, the four of us moved a chop saw, jig saw, and other tools upstairs. When we finished, Maggie popped her hands on her hips. "Okay, Andie, if there's anything else you need in here, get it now because you're not allowed back until we finish."

Her desire to surprise me was heartwarming. "I have what I need," I said. "I promise not to enter my apartment again until you give me permission."

"Good, now get out," she said with a laugh, then gave me a gentle nudge toward the door.

I descended the catwalk stairs with a light heart, my day brightened by people I barely knew but already loved. To realize that a brief meeting or short-term relationship could yield such a warm connection surprised me. I'd only felt this immediate bond once, with my son, but not with Clark. I'd been physically attracted to my ex but felt little emotional connection until much later—after our son was born. I thought I'd just been too raw with grief at the time. My father had only recently died when I crossed paths with Clark at our company holiday party and ended up in his bed.

He wanted to see me again, but my grief left no room in my life for anyone else. Clark didn't give up. He made excuses to visit my area of the shop and playfully chat me up in the parking lot before or after work despite my effort to avoid him. Then I discovered I was pregnant, and our parking lot chat wasn't funny at all. Not for me anyway. It was the first time in months I'd felt any emotion other than grief. I wanted my baby but had no idea how I'd raise a child alone. Clark suggested we talk at his place, so we met there each evening, and a month later, he proposed. I accepted because I wanted my baby and a family of my own.

Our son brought us both great joy, and a lot of work, and I got caught up in our busy lives. Perpetually exhausted, I operated on automatic pilot and went along with whatever the day, or Clark, put in front of me.

Maybe that's why I'd felt a bit off balance since our divorce. Technically, I was free to make my own decisions and choose how to live my life, but Clark had remained so present, and

Tyler still expected my decisions to include his father, that I'd barely changed anything. But now, here in this new place, every decision was mine to make. I had no partner to consider, and no one to blame should I make any bad choices or decisions.

I was on my own here, guessing my way into a new life.

After pulling on my singed gloves. I began the slow process of gathering and organizing bar stock, depositing one piece at a time onto the waiting steel arms of the iron rack system secured to the back wall. The distant sound of an electric saw and thudding of hammers sounded overhead in the direction of my apartment. It was music to my ears as I sorted and organized materials scattered during Walter's *search for Rita's pliers.*

Flashlight in hand, I rescued tools from under the grinder, the hand shear, and the plasma table that I had to retrieve on hands and knees. Jeans were not adequate protection between boney knees and a concrete floor. Nor was my thin shirt a sufficient barrier when I had to lie on my belly to investigate the dark lump under a metal shelf.

Angling my head and adjusting the flashlight beam, I found myself nose to nose with a mouse. I reared back in surprise and banged my head on a metal tube sticking over a neighboring shelf. The noise startled the mouse, and it shot across the floor and out the open door. While I was glad for the serendipitous exit of the mouse from my building, I hoped it hadn't left behind a nest of babies.

It took several minutes to clean out the mess it had made beneath the shelf. I found no nest or any babies, but there was a good amount of Louie's dog food piled up under there and two of his squeak toys. I felt bad forcing the mouse to find a new home, especially since it had this one so well stocked, but I would be sleeping down here on my sofa bed and didn't want to share the space with a mouse no matter how cute it was. Still, its appearance made me wonder if there were any more critters hiding out here.

By the time I'd fished out a pipe wrench, a pair of vice grips, and three bench clamps, my elbows were scraped, and I was covered in spider webs. As I added the tools to the growing pile on the worktable, my phone alarm dinged, and I glanced at the screen in surprise. It was already time to order lunch, and I was dismayed at how little I'd achieved, especially when I'd been working diligently and steadily the whole time.

Barred from the apartment, I sent Maggie a text asking what they'd like for lunch and where to place the order. While I waited for her reply, I sat on an overturned five gallon pail and drank half the water in my thermos. After she replied, I called the café and placed our order, then washed my hands in the bathroom. Twenty minutes later, I picked up our food and returned to the shop.

We sat on the patio to eat lunch. Kate said the flooring was going down well. Maggie said she was kicking ass painting, as expected, then asked how I was managing in the shop. I said I was getting my ass kicked, which made them laugh. But I wasn't kidding. My ears were still ringing from banging my head and from dropping metal bars into racks to avoid pinching my fingers, which I'd done three times before changing my process, and my knees felt raw from retrieving tools and dog food from under equipment.

"Maggie tells me you're a welder," Ashe said, setting aside his empty bottle of iced tea. "And Kate said you're moving here from the Utica area."

"That's right. But they haven't told me a thing about you, Ashe." I was curious about the man who couldn't keep his eyes off Kate. "All Maggie said was you're an electrician and you and Kate have a thing."

He smiled and looked at Kate. "Is that what we're calling this? A *thing*?"

She gave a non-committal shrug, but humor sparkled in her eyes. "What thing?"

Her playful set-down made us laugh.

"Sounds as if I'm missing a party," a male voice said, drawing our attention to the sidewalk out front. When I saw Mason Scott walking across the paved parking area in front of my shop, I wanted to bolt into the building and hide.

"Hey, Mason!" Ashe said with genuine warmth. "We missed you at the tournament. Where the heck have you been?"

"At the airport mostly," he replied, shaking Ashe's outstretched hand, then greeting Maggie and Kate like close friends. When his blue-eyed gaze landed on me, his smile widened. "Hello again."

"Hi," I said, my monotone making it clear I didn't appreciate his presence.

I caught the odd look exchanged between Maggie, Ashe, and Kate, but wasn't about to explain my response or reveal my grand disaster with their friend.

Mason kept his gaze and his smile fixed on me. "I brought you something," he said, dangling a pair of olive-green gloves in the air. "They're flame retardant and cut resistant."

Every eye was on me, but my brain refused to produce any words.

"I also brought this for you." He pulled a folded letter from his shirt pocket and handed it to me along with the gloves.

I wasn't offended that he wanted to be reimbursed for his shirt. "Is it all right if I send a check to the airport address?"

His sandy-brown eyebrows furrowed. "Why would you send me a check?"

"This is a bill, isn't it?"

"No. It's my purchase order to Rita for work she was doing at the airport. I'm hoping you'll finish the job."

"I'm not open yet."

"I can wait."

"It might be a while," I said, wishing he would leave and that my new friends weren't watching with avid curiosity.

"You might want to look at the order," he suggested. "I haven't paid the bill yet."

When I unfolded the paper, the first thing I saw was the total for five-thousand dollars. "What the heck was Rita doing for you?" I asked.

"She was installing man doors in sliding hangar doors. She installed three before she..." He paused and his eyes darkened, the four of us silently acknowledging Rita's death. "There are seven doors that still need to be done."

"Why wouldn't you hire a door company for that work?"

"Because they want to replace the entire hangar door at ten times the cost. All we need is a simple egress so that the main door doesn't have to be opened to access the hangar. Rita's solution was exactly what we need."

I glanced at Maggie who gave a slight lift of her eyebrows as if suggesting I should take the work. I could use the income, especially since it would offset some of the updating cost on my apartment, but I hesitated.

"I know you're busy," he said, "but could we discuss this over coffee tomorrow morning?"

"I already have a coffee date," I said, thinking of Walter and Louie.

He slid a wary look at Ashe who was failing to hide a grin behind his fist. "I wasn't asking for a date."

"I know," I blurted, realizing my mistake. "I just meant I'm busy in the morning. I'll stop by the airport tomorrow afternoon if you'll be there."

"I will. Just text me when you get there and I'll walk you out to the hangars. I wrote my cell number on the purchase order."

"Okay. Goodbye, then."

Ashe snorted and Maggie outright laughed. "We need to get back to work," she said, rocking to her feet and pulling her brother up with her. Kate stood, too, and the three of them deserted me.

As soon as they went inside, Mason said, "I didn't want to point this out with your friends here, but you have a spider on your shoulder."

"What?" I glanced down.

"Other shoulder."

"Ack!" I flicked a black spider off my shoulder.

"It's dangling at your elbow now."

I bolted to my feet, swiping madly at my elbow.

"I think it's attached to that blob of web stuck to your shirt."

I rolled my shoulder forward and saw a silky white ball stuck high on the back of my right sleeve. Using a napkin, I plucked it off, then made a wide arc with my arm to carry the spider, still attached to the web, away from me. The arachnid landed on the concrete pad and scurried off into the grass. "How long was that thing on my shoulder?"

"I noticed it when I got here," he said.

For a moment, I was speechless. Then I laughed. "Okay, I suppose I deserved that after nearly setting you on fire."

Warm, robust laughter rolled from his throat, and I couldn't take my eyes off his gorgeous face. He winked at me. "See you tomorrow."

Chapter Thirteen

After a decent night of sleep, thanks to my new sofa bed delivered the previous afternoon and the sound of rain pummeling the metal roof all night, I woke early. I washed up in the downstairs bathroom and pulled on work clothes. While Maggie, Ashe, and Kate worked upstairs, I continued cleaning up the shop. At noon, I ran out in the rain to pick up lunch, then handed it off to Kate at the apartment door and told her I had to head to the airport to look at the job Rita had started.

With a sunny smile, Kate thanked me for lunch and told me to have fun.

My face heated a little over how awkward I'd been during Mason's unexpected visit yesterday. "Let me know if you guys need anything," I said, then hurried downstairs to clean myself up again.

I examined my appearance in the mirror on the back of the bathroom door. Face washed. *Check.* Teeth brushed, hair combed and braided. *Check.* Clean clothes free of shop grime and spider webs. *Check.*

The rain let up, and the sun poked out as I drove to the airport. I texted Mason to let him know I'd arrived, and he replied quickly saying he was on his way. While I waited, I saw a small plane in the distant sky. From where I sat, it appeared around the size of an eagle. I couldn't tell if it was approaching or leaving, but it seemed to float in the air, so graceful and unattached to the world below, I felt a sense of envy.

"Hey there," Mason said, startling me as he rounded the front of my truck. "Rita was working on a hangar at the other end of the lot." He gestured toward three long buildings lined up like barracks with a long, green carpet of grass stretching across the far end. "We can drive back or walk, whichever you prefer."

"We can walk." I stepped out of the truck into the humid afternoon and gestured toward a distant stretch of asphalt lined on either side with short yellow posts. "Are those lights on top of the posts?" I asked.

"Yes, that's edge lighting for our main runway and it's always on, but we're a non-towered airport so we also use pilot-controlled automated runway lights, reflectors, and other navigational lighting."

"Wait, are you saying that a pilot in a plane can turn the lights on down here?"

"Yes. They click their microphone, and it sends electrical pulses to activate the lights."

I squinted a little. "I have so many questions, but no time for them."

He smiled. "Go to dinner with me tonight and I'll explain runway lighting and how it all works."

I wasn't a shy person, but when our eyes met, I glanced away from his warm gaze. "Thanks, but I have my own lighting to worry about."

"Another time then," he said, and pointed to the long stretch of mowed grass beyond the hangars that sat at a ninety-degree angle from the main runway. "That's our turf runway for ultralights and pilots with tailwheel planes who preferred to land on grass. That's the one I use most often."

"It looks like a huge, green bowling lane and a big job to mow."

"It's not bad. Nora usually mows it," he said.

"Is she a pilot, too?"

"Yes, and a very good one albeit a bit nutty."

"She sounds fun," I said, privately wondering what their relationship was, then deciding I didn't want to know. "How many people work here?" I asked, following him into what appeared to be the main airport building.

"Nora and I work full time, and her husband, Jim, fills in when we need him.

Ah, question answered.

"This is the main facility," he continued, guiding me into a lounge with comfy furniture, an oversized couch for pilots who needed rest, and a television for anyone in need of news or who was grounded for hours due to storms. There was a full kitchen stocked with food, and restrooms with showers across the hall. I followed him through a clean and compact office, like mine would be someday, and out a back entrance that opened into a huge maintenance room with bright overhead lighting I envied.

Mason hooked his hand over the steel frame of a beastly machine. "This is the multi-deck reel mower we use to mow the green bowling lane."

His teasing made me smile, but I felt a little foolish for having made the comment.

He walked me past a vertical lift and snow removal equipment to where Rita had stored materials for the job I would be doing. "All the frames for the man doors are finished," he said. "They just need to be installed."

We headed outside, and he didn't speak again until we arrived at the hangar where Rita had created a smaller entrance within the huge sliding door. I followed Mason through the small door, and it was like stepping through a portal. I had to lift my foot over the bottom of the frame while ducking slightly to ensure my head wouldn't scrape the top of the doorway. "I'm glad I'm not any taller," I said, wondering how many times Mason had hit his head.

Inside, he turned on overhead lighting, I immediately understood why the door was on the short side. The fourteen-by-twenty-foot sliding hangar door was framed out with steel and had a support bar running horizontally across its center. The only way for Rita to add a man door without cutting through the solid support bar was to nest it beneath the center support and off to one corner.

"We can't afford to retrofit our hangars just yet," Mason said. "We needed an inexpensive way to give our renters an egress. Let me show you why we're doing this." As he slid open the massive hangar door, roller wheels rumbled along the overhead track and the metal door banged and thundered.

Squinting against the abusive noise, I said, "Okay, I get it. Do you know if Rita had the hinges and welding materials here?"

"Yes, she stored everything in the maintenance bay."

The job was mostly cutting and welding angle iron and sheet metal. I had the skills, but I wondered why he wouldn't do it himself, so I asked him.

"Not my lane," he said. "I played sports, then I flew planes for a living. Now, I run this airport and fly my own planes. So, will you finish the job?" he asked, sticking out his hand, reminding me he was a paying customer.

"Yes." I offered a firm handshake, but he gave my hand a light squeeze that sent tingling warmth up my forearm. I pulled away. "I need to get back to my shop."

"Okay, I'll walk you to your truck."

"No need," I said, already ducking out the door, but he was right behind me. "I'll start Monday morning."

"Great. I'll be here," he said, matching my lengthening stride. "Are you a runner by chance?"

"Sort of. Why?" I asked glancing over at him.

"You move fast."

"So do you, Mr. Scott."

Delighted laughter tipped his head back and bathed his face in sunshine, his teeth as straight and white as runway lights.

* * *

On the way home, I stopped at the Bobcat Brewery and talked to Bobbie Jo about delivering lunch to my shop for Maggie, Kate, and Ashe each day unless I texted otherwise. I wanted to get the airport hangar job done as quickly as possible which meant starting early and working late. Then I stopped at the Eagle's Nest to ask Beth if I could pay to use the locker room showers until my apartment was ready. She said the showers were free to anyone in need of them, then offered me a free room that I couldn't accept. She seemed sincerely happy to see me and to hear that I'd bought the fab shop.

I drove home with a smile on my face because I was making real friends here.

Then I remembered Tyler hadn't called me back, so I texted asking him to check in. His reply was fast. *I'm good. Talk soon.*

I'm good, too, not that you asked.

When I got back to the shop, Kate's trailblazer was gone, and Maggie was getting in her van.

"Hi, Andie. I was just going to send you a text," she said. "Just wanted you to know we were done for the weekend and that we'll meet you in the park tomorrow afternoon if you'll be around."

"What's going on in the park?"

"It's Sunday Fun-day tomorrow. You know, music, dancing, people having fun?"

"Oh, yes, that's right." I'd lost track of the days. "What time are you all meeting?"

"Craft booths and farmer's market open in the morning at nine. Music starts at noon. We usually meet near the bandstand around five o'clock."

"I'm going to try to see my son tomorrow, but if I'm back in town by then, I'll walk over. But before you leave, Maggie, do you need any money for the apartment work?"

"I'm good," she said. "I won't know the total until I finish, so don't worry about it until then."

"All right, thank you. Really. *Thank you.*"

She gave me a thumb's up. "Don't peek," she said, then backed out and drove down the street.

I couldn't face the mess in the shop, so I spent the evening puttering in the office. Several books and a stack basket overflowing with handwritten quotes Rita had worked up for fabricating jobs sat atop the filing cabinets. Some of them were two years old, but if the recent ones were still open jobs, the potential income was enticing. Still, the thought of having to do repair and fabricating work to survive sent a surge of anxiety through my belly.

I wanted to earn a living creating art, but maybe it was simply a naïve dream as Clark had insisted.

As I glanced at the debris on the floor and the mess out in the shop, I knew none of it mattered until I got things in order here. I would give myself one week to do the airport job and another to get my shop in order. Then I would have to decide if I had the talent, commitment, and more importantly the backbone to pursue my art.

Chapter Fourteen

After a long, uncomfortable drive in my son's beater car, I arrived at my house to find Clark's Thunderbird parked in the driveway. For an instant, I felt hopeful he was cleaning out the shop like I'd asked him to do. But then I saw him and Tyler poking their heads out from under the hood to see who was pulling in.

I should have known why Clark had moved the car out. It was Sunday. He would be driving his pride-and-joy to a car show today. He would spit-polish his *girl* until he could see his reflection in her custom-painted body, then show her off to fellow car buddies who would admire his workmanship. Clark reveled in their attention, but I grew bored with those one-subject circular conversations and the endless running that always led to the same place.

After parking Tyler's car on the front lawn, I walked over to see what they were working on. My son, a younger, slimmer version of his father, glanced up. "Hey, Mom. What are you doing here?" he asked.

"I came to see you," I said, a little annoyed by his question because I'd texted to let him know I was heading down. "When you didn't reply to my text last night, I figured I'd better check in to make sure you're still alive."

He rolled his eyes, a habit he'd picked up from his father, and one I loathed. "I've been busy working."

"So have I, but that's no excuse not to let each other know we're okay. If you can't do that, then I'll come back home until you leave for college."

He glanced at his dad who just gave a one-shoulder shrug as if he wasn't getting involved. "I'm fine, Mom. Sorry I haven't texted much."

I nodded to let him know I'd heard him but wasn't entirely letting him off the hook. "I'd like to take you to lunch and hear more about your vacation plans."

Tyler cast a help-me look at his father, but Clark remained silent. "Um, my buddies and I planned on going to the car show, then to a movie."

Disappointment compressed my chest. "Tyler, I've barely seen you in weeks. Could you skip the car show today and meet your buddies after lunch?"

"We're helping Dad at the show," he said, exchanging a look with Clark.

"It's okay, Ty," Clark said, wiping his hands on the soft cloth he'd been cleaning the engine with. "You should go to lunch with your mom."

Tyler's shoulders drooped. "I'm not hungry, and I promised the guys I'd pick them up in half an hour."

As much as I wanted to spend time with my son, I knew forcing him to give up his plans wouldn't make our visit enjoyable for either of us. "Okay, Tyler, you go ahead with your plans today. But I fully intend to spend some time with you before you go on vacation. Figure out your schedule and make some time for us, okay?"

"I will," he said.

"I mean it, Ty. I expect a text this week letting me know when you'll be available."

"Okay."

I gave him the look that said I meant business.

"I promise, Mom. Jeez!" He shoved his fingers into his hair and swiped it back, another habit of his father's.

"Okay, then how about greeting your mother with a hug instead of an attitude?"

I heard him sigh as he walked over and gave me a quick, hard hug.

"Hey..." I clasped his arms and gently kept him in front of me. "I'm not here to hassle you. I just miss you and want to spend a little time with you before you head off to college. All right?"

"Yeah," he said with a sheepish nod. "I'm sorry. I've just been kind of busy is all."

"I know. Life is like that, but we need to make time for each other."

He nodded, then gave me a real hug, one that said he loved his mother even when she was annoying the hell out of him.

"What are you and your buddies doing at the car show today?" I asked, guiding him into a calmer and hopefully more enjoyable conversation.

"We're cooking burgers and stuff for Dad's club."

"That will be a hot, sweaty job," I said, having years of first-hand experience manning food booths at the car shows we attended.

"Yeah, but we can eat for free and have as many burgers as we want," Tyler said.

The bright anticipation in his eyes made me laugh. "Sounds like the perfect job for teenage guys."

"It is," he said. "I've got to get going now." He surprised me with another hug, then headed to his SUV.

"Text me," I called to his back.

"I will," he said over his shoulder, then got in his car and left.

"If it's any consolation," Clark said, "I don't see him much either."

"It's not." I turned to face him. "And, yes, you do. In fact, it would help if you didn't gobble up his free time."

"What's that supposed to mean?" he asked looking a little bewildered.

"It means that maybe you could stop pulling him into your activities and give him space for other things. Like spending some time with me, for example."

Tilting his head slightly, Clark approached me with a placating smile. Cupping my shoulders in his large hands, he said softly, "You know I wouldn't do that to you."

I shrugged him off, hating the way he tried to disarm me with a smile while discounting my feelings, hating the way his hands made me feel trapped.

He sighed and raked his hair back. "Why don't you come to the car show with us?"

"God, no." That's the last place I wanted to go, and I did not want to spend the day with Clark.

He frowned at me. "Sorry I asked. I just thought it would give you time with Tyler and solve your problem."

"*You* are my problem, Clark." I took a step back to put some distance between us. "You need to give our son some space."

"How Tyler spends his time is up to him," Clark said, offense thick in his voice. "I'm not going to stop asking Tyler to do things with me."

I knew their shared interests bonded them, but it hurt that our son preferred to spend time with his father. "You know I'm not asking that. But he's *our* son, Clark, and I'm just asking you to remember that he needs both of us in his life."

"Exactly, which is why I'll never understand why you wanted a divorce," he said with a slight shake of his head. "We had a great home, a wonderful family, and a perfect life. What more could you have asked for?"

"Room to breathe," I said. "And we're not having this conversation *again*."

"Fine. Was there something else you wanted?" he asked.

"Yeah. When can I expect the quit deed paperwork from the attorney?"

Despite his agitation with me, his gaze skittered away. "I'll make an appointment this week."

"You haven't done that yet?"

"I've been busy."

"Oh my god, Clark, you're making excuses like our teenaged son. What the hell? Do you want the house or not?"

He pinned me with a hard look, his face red. "I told you I did."

"Then get that paperwork drawn up immediately."

"What's the rush, Andie?"

"I'm paying the freaking mortgage until the agreement is signed. So, unless you want to make the loan payments, quit playing with your cars and get the paperwork done."

He turned away and returned to polishing his car. "I'll call the attorney tomorrow, but I don't know how soon I'll be able to get an appointment."

"It had better happen before the next mortgage payment is due," I said to his back, "or you're going to pay it."

He spun around to face me. "I can't pay a mortgage and rent, too. I'm locked into a lease on my apartment for another three months because you wanted a divorce."

"Then feel free to live in your apartment, and I'll put the house on the market."

His jaw clenched and he slipped inside his precious Thunderbird. From the open window, he said, "This situation is a result of *your* impulsive actions, Andie, not my lack of planning. I'm staying here with Tyler as you asked, so maybe you shouldn't complain about paying the mortgage while I'm stuck paying for a place you forced me to rent in the first place."

"Good god, Clark, has it ever occurred to you that it was *your* actions that brought us to this place?" His eyeroll just reaffirmed my decision to leave. This conversation was a repeat of every discussion we'd ever had. Clark simply couldn't see that he was anything but the good guy, and he always chocked up my feelings as the result of my own rash behavior, or my job dissatisfaction, or worse, my hormones.

He cranked his Thunderbird to life, the four-barrel supercharged engine rumbling so loudly I felt it in my chest. "Got to go," he said, shifting into reverse.

As he backed down the driveway, I walked beside his car. "Clark, I'm not paying for you to live here."

He cut the wheel, backed into the street, then started to pull away.

"Get the paperwork done or get out," I said, but he just cruised off down the street in his souped-up car, my request, like every conversation we'd ever had, already in his rearview mirror.

Before I headed to the airport on Monday morning, I texted Mason to let him know I'd be there soon. My gloves were on my workbench, but they stank of smoke and were so grimy that I changed my mind and grabbed the new gloves Mason had given me. I hooked a tape rule on the pocket of my jeans, and tucked a pencil behind my ear, then headed outside to my truck.

As soon as I arrived at the airport, I saw Mason striding across the asphalt. His unbuttoned jean shirt flapped in the breeze, exposing a fitted white T-shirt molded to the athletic cut of his torso. His eyes were hidden behind dark aviator-style sunglasses, but I sensed he was looking straight at me.

To camouflage my unintentional ogling, I stepped out of the truck.

"Good morning," he called as he approached. "Coffee is on if you'd like a cup."

"I've got one with me," I said, hoping Walter wasn't too disappointed I had to cancel our morning coffee visits this week. I didn't want to tell him I was finishing a job Rita had started, so I'd simply texted that I wouldn't be available but promised we'd get back to our regular schedule next week.

Mason gave my truck a fond pat on the hood. "Can't believe this old girl is still running. I swear Rita was driving this truck back when I was in grade school."

His comment, and the idea of Mason as a sandy-haired boy, made me smile. "Probably. It's a rough ride now, but the wheels haven't fallen off yet."

He laughed. "What can I help with? I'm available all day."

"I think the job will go faster if we move the welded door frames and other materials from the maintenance room out to the hangars."

"I can do that."

"Great. It will help if you put one of the frames in each hangar that needs a man door installed."

"Sure."

"And leave a length of angle iron in each one, too."

"Got it."

"My welder and cutting torch are in the back." I nodded toward the flatbed. "Is it okay for me to drive out to the hangars so I don't have to carry my tools out there?"

"Of course." He skirted the front of the truck. "I'll ride out with you and help you unload your equipment." Before I could respond, he opened the door and slid in the passenger side.

When I got in, I noticed he was smooshed between the door and my gear bag. "Sorry," I said, dragging it closer to me. "I wasn't expecting to have a passenger."

"Not a problem. I'm used to sitting in tight spaces," he said. "This is about as much room as I have in my ultralight."

"I assume that's a plane?"

"Yeah, and it's the best kind of flying as far as I'm concerned."

"How so?" I asked, genuinely interested as I drove out to the hangars.

"Well, for several years, I flew commercial jets that averaged more than three hundred tons takeoff weight. It's a complex and challenging job, but the planes were mainly computer controlled, less susceptible to turbulence but slow to maneuver. When I started flying my one-seater ultralight, I learned fast that it takes a completely different skillset to fly a plane weighing less than two-hundred-fifty pounds."

"That can't be right," I said, mentally calculating the weight of various metals and arriving at numbers far above his claim. "Walter's scooter probably weighs more than that."

"Probably," he said. "I'm sure it's designed with more metal than my plane. My ultralight is basically aircraft fabric stretched over a chrome-moly tubing frame. A carbon fiber propeller, single cylinder forty-pound engine, and a five-gallon gas tank, keep the weight down."

"That's like flying a kite! Or parasailing."

He laughed, a warm sound I was growing to like. "It might feel like that for a non-powered craft," he said. "They weigh in around one-hundred-fifty pounds. But my ultralight is a fixed-wing tailwheel with an engine so it's easier to maneuver and will cruise the currents like a falcon at sixty-plus miles per hour." His passion for flying was evident in his voice. "I could take you up in my two-seater sometime if you like."

I thought about the plane I'd seen in the distance that looked like an eagle floating in the air. At the time, I'd imagined how peaceful it must feel up there. But *not* in a kite. All I could do was shake my head. "Thanks, but I'll pass," I said, opening my door.

His laughter followed me out. I grabbed my gear bag containing my welding helmet and other items, as he exited the passenger side. After he slid open the huge hangar door and turned on the lights, we unloaded the welder, compressor, and plasma torch, then carried everything inside.

"I'll go get the door frames," he said, then disappeared outside.

Parking my hands on my hips, I stretched my back and inhaled as I mentally reviewed my plan of attack. Then I got to work, measuring and marking out the man door. I'd just finished torch-cutting the opening when Mason returned.

"You work fast," he said, taking in the rectangular opening. "At this pace, you'll finish today."

"Doubtful. There's still plenty of cutting and welding to do."

"I've delivered the materials to each hangar as you asked," he said. "How else can I help?"

"You can figure out why the radio in my truck is stuck on a country music station."

He grinned. "Not a country music fan?"

"I'm a fan of options."

"How about the option of taking a ride in my light sport two-seater?"

"I have my own two-seater out there," I said, giving a head tilt toward my truck.

"Yeah, but that ride is nothing like the one you'd get in my plane."

My head was filled with so many salacious thoughts about taking a ride with the man, I couldn't even reply.

With a playful wink, he said, "Call me when you need a hand." Then he stepped outside and left me with a head full of thoughts about him I did not want to be having.

It took effort to shift my focus to my work, but I cut, welded, and prepared the door for installation in just under an hour. At this rate, and barring any issues, I could possibly finish the job tomorrow. I texted Mason to let him know I needed assistance hanging the door, and he arrived almost immediately.

On the way in, he caught the toe of his boot on the door frame and stumbled inside. Sweeping his arm out wide, then tucking it against his belly as he executed a sloppy bow, he said, "At your service, milady."

I burst out laughing.

Eyes twinkling, he looked at me. "You have a great laugh."

All I could do was shake my head because I had no idea how to respond to his comment or silly bow. "Have you been drinking on the job?"

"Not a drop, but we could get a drink after you finish here if you like." He wiggled his eyebrows, making me laugh again.

"Will you please just hold the door up while I screw the hinges into the frame?"

With a defeated sigh, he stood the fabricated man door upright. Together, we moved it into position, which brought our bodies so close I could smell a subtle hint of cedar and sage on him. Struggling to ignore the man, I secured the heavy-duty door hinges, then stepped back.

"Okay, this is the moment of truth," I said, swinging the door open, then closed, where it nested perfectly within the frame.

"Nice work," he said.

"Thanks. Only six more to go." I gestured to the tools and equipment. "I need to move this stuff to the next hangar. If you'll take the compressor first, I can start cutting the door while you come back to get the welder and tools. That's if you don't mind helping. The job will go faster that way."

"I don't mind at all," he said, but he didn't move.

"What's wrong?" I wiped my face and swiped my hair back, fearing I was smeared with grime or had singed my hair while welding.

"Not a thing. I'm just impressed with your work."

"Why? It's just cutting and welding."

A half-smile tipped his lips. "I'd say the job is a bit more involved than that."

"Well, making a door is a far cry from building a plane."

"I don't build planes. I fly them."

"Okay." Our eyes met for a moment. "Are you feeling as lost in this conversation as I am?"

His warm laughter filled the hangar. "I thought it was just getting interesting," he said, then went over and unplugged the compressor.

We moved on to the next hangar where I went through the same process. Mason popped in when I needed his help. I'd completed work on the third hangar when he suggested we break for a late lunch.

"I didn't plan to eat," I said, belatedly realizing I should have brought a granola bar.

"I ordered subs for us," he said. "Figured you wouldn't mind a short break and a hot cup of coffee."

Coffee and a break sounded wonderful, so we walked back to the main building. He took our lunch outside to a picnic table while I washed my hands and face in the bathroom. When I met him outside at the picnic table, he put a bag in front of me.

"Didn't know if you were vegetarian or not, so I figured a veggie sub would be a safe bet."

"It's perfect, thank you," I said, sitting opposite him. I hadn't felt hungry until the smell of the baked bread and Italian dressing reached my nose. Clasping the oily sub between my fingers, I took a bite.

"I have to admit, Andie, I'm duly impressed with your skills."

"Why?" I asked, trying and failing to talk clearly with a full mouth. "It's just cutting and welding metal."

Mason smiled as if he found my lack of feminine etiquette adorable. "Where did you learn to weld?"

I finished chewing and swallowed, then took a sip of surprisingly good coffee. "In my dad's shop, and four years of college for welding."

He seemed genuinely surprised. "There are actually college courses for welding?"

"Sure. Why wouldn't there be?"

He shrugged. "I don't know. I guess I assumed it was just a handy skill one picked up working in a repair shop."

I felt a little insulted. "There's a lot more to welding than just the physical aspect."

"Like what?" he asked. "Really, I'm curious. I know nothing about welding."

"Obviously."

He laughed. "Then please educate me."

I tapped my chin as if giving the subject deep consideration. "How to summarize four years of college and over thirty years of welding and fabricating work into a twenty-minute lunch break lesson?"

"You made your point," he said with a laugh. "But I really am curious."

I took pity on him, flattered by his interest. "The first thing my dad taught me, and I learned immediately in college, was safety. Welding can be dangerous and even deadly if you're not careful."

"Like catching yourself on fire?" he asked, barely suppressing his laughter.

"Exactly," I said, still embarrassed over our first meeting but appreciating his sense of humor. "You can also electrocute yourself."

He sobered a little. "I had no idea."

"The danger is real, so safety is imperative. You need good math skills for layout and fit up, joint design, preparation and fitting techniques. You have to know how to determine correct amperage, travel speed, and what filler metal to use. Understanding welding codes and specifications and how to read blueprints are a must, and so is a basic understanding of metallurgy so you know how to join various metals together without burning through the material. And you need to know what type of welding to use."

"There's more than one type?" he asked.

"Ah, yeah, there are several types like gas welding that uses filler wire, and shielded metal arc welding that uses stick filler, and there is plasma arc welding, electroslag welding, and friction welding to name just a few types."

By the time I finished, he was shaking his head. "I think I might be bleeding from my ears."

I laughed. "Then I'll have mercy and stop talking so I can eat this delicious sub and drink my coffee before it gets cold."

"Of course," he said. "I apologize for keeping you from it. I just find you and your profession fascinating. I'll help spread the word about your talent and business."

"Please don't." The words were out of my mouth before I realized I'd said them. "I mean, I'm not sure I'll be offering this kind of work. I bought the fab shop to have a place where I could make metal sculptures and signs."

His eyebrows shot up. "Sculptures? Are you an artist?"

"No. I mean, maybe. I don't know," I said, releasing a laugh of embarrassment. "I haven't done that sort of work in years so I'm not sure I have enough talent to call myself an artist."

"I'm more intrigued by the minute," he said, his gaze roving my face. "Have you seen the metal sculptures at the Wild Center in Tupper Lake?"

"Not yet," I said, "but I know about them, and I plan to go as soon as I get things settled at the shop."

"You need to. The sculptures are in the forest along a dirt path covered in pine needles. As you walk through, you can hear music and drumming sounds all around you. One minute the sound is coming from behind you, then it's off in the distance, and then it's right in front of you. The experience of viewing the sculptures and being immersed in the forest and music is one you won't forget."

"That sounds amazing."

"I think it would inspire you."

"I'm sure it would. One of the most powerful scrap metal sculptures I ever saw was *Ecstasy* sculpted by Karen Cusolito. It's a woman with her head slung back in ecstasy, and the flow of her pose is incredibly graceful and yet powerful. The artist used chains to sculpt the hair, and I think she used huge springs for the ribs. The thing is massive, like thirty feet tall, and profoundly beautiful. I spent an entire day looking at it. I can't even list all the pieces she used or how she brought them all together with such artistry because there was so much to take in, my brain sort of exploded," I said, laughing at my own fan-girl moment. "But someday I'd love to create a large sculpture like that. And one with movement, too."

"The way you talk about your art, I'm betting you'll do it," he said so sincerely I believed him.

Maybe it was his genuine interest in me, something I'd never felt from Clark, that had made me share one of the most moving moments in my artistic life.

"How many sculptures have you made?" he asked.

"Several small pieces, and one life-size half-finished piece."

Resting his forearms on the table, he looked at me, his eyes filled with sincere interest. "What was the first one?"

"A horse made from bolts, springs, and nuts," I said, awash with guilt for burying it in a box with the journal my father had given me.

"I'm sorry to say I've never viewed scrap metal as anything but junk," Mason said as if making a confession. "At least, not until I saw the sculptures at the Wild Center. Now, hearing you describe the beauty and power of metal sculptures makes me want to see more of them."

His interest encouraged me to tell him about Scrap Fest and how I've always wanted to go. "I missed it again this year," I said, but I hope to make it to the Metal Madness Festival in the fall. It's a similar event in the Albany area."

"The leaves will be turning then, and it would be a perfect time to fly there."

"I'm sure. But not in an ultralight," I said with a laugh. "You indicated you'd been flying for years. How did you get started?"

"My dad was a pilot. I got my sport pilot license when I was sixteen. In my twenties, I worked as a commercial pilot for several years, then I met an ag pilot during one of my flights and found his job far more interesting than my own. I transitioned to an agricultural pilot and did that for ten years."

"Are you referring to crop dusting?"

"Yes. It's highly skilled flying and a fun, lucrative career. I really enjoyed it, but after a decade of doing it, I was ready for a change. I retired early to take this job as operations manager. I'm also a certified flight instructor, so I can teach you to fly ultralights or light sport planes if you're interested."

I laughed. "Not at all, but I envy your ability to do the thing you love doing. Following your bliss is brave and admirable."

"Or maybe it's just a simple fact of not getting sucked into what others consider normal." He shrugged. "Whatever it was that got me here, I'm happy with the life I chose."

"You sound like Maggie," I said. "You two might make the perfect couple."

He released a belt of laughter. "Not a chance. Maggie is like a little sister to me."

The relief I felt surprised me and I realized I was enjoying our interaction too much and that our conversation had grown too personal. "I'd better get back to work," I said, picking up my oily sub wrapper.

"I'll take care of that," he said, slipping the rolled papers from my hands.

"All right. Well, thank you for lunch."

His eyes held mine. "Thank *you* for the most interesting conversation I've had in a long time."

I walked away thinking the same thing. The man intrigued me. And I was flattered by his sincere interest in my work, my background, my goals, and in me. Not for one minute did his interest seem feigned for the purpose of creating intimacy. That didn't mean we weren't noticing each other or that there wasn't an electricity humming between us. My hormones were wide awake and vibrating but I warned them to settle the hell down because I needed to get back to work.

Chapter Fifteen

Watching Walter drive up on a mobility scooter with Louie sitting on his lap gave my heart a happy squeeze. I hadn't seen them for three days. Although I'd been busy working at the airport and engaging in interesting conversations with Mason Scott, who piqued my curiosity on several levels, I was glad to be done with the job and back to my morning coffee dates with Walter and Louie.

As soon as Walter brought the scooter to a stop, Louie leapt down and greeted me with a sloppy wet-nosed-tongue-swish across the back of my hand. His slobbery dog-kiss was gross, but I loved his sweet affection.

"Hello, beautiful boy." I pulled two treats out of my pocket and gave him one while Walter slowly stepped off the scooter. "It's wonderful to see you guys," I said, wiping dog slobber on the leg of my jeans.

"We sure missed our coffee dates," Walter said, lifting two travel mugs from cupholders mounted in the dash of the scooter.

"That's a pretty luxurious ride," I said, moving in to get a closer look at the stylish maroon and black four-wheel scooter with a roof and windshield. "Does this thing have a stereo?"

"Oh, no. I didn't want one."

"I was joking about the stereo."

"Well, you can get a scooter with doors that lock, a heater, a stereo, foldout windows, and backup cameras."

By the time he finished, I was laughing. "I think you're pulling my leg, Walter."

"Not at all. Look them up if you don't believe me."

I did, and I was blown away. "Oh my god, these things are amazing. They're like little cars."

"Yeah, but they're not street legal." He shrugged. "If I wanted to ride in a closed box, I'd just drive my SUV. Louie and I prefer the fresh air, don't we boy?"

Louie gave him a wheezy grin as if he understood and agreed with every word.

I felt so much love for them, I couldn't resist giving Walter a big hug. "I missed you guys. Thanks for bringing your warm-hug coffee. I could use one today."

He pressed a mug into my hand. "Then let me do this right, sweetheart." With that, he wrapped me in his arms and said, "We missed you, too."

My eyes were a watery mess by the time he released me, so I tipped the mug to my lips and tried to hide my face. Once I marshalled my emotions, I asked, "Will you be attending the Independence Day fireworks tonight?"

"No, dear, we don't do them here."

I thought he might be toying with me to lighten the mood. "You're joking, of course."

"Not at all. Our community voted overwhelmingly to stop the nonsense several years ago. Fireworks are expensive, danger-ous, and noisy. They scare our furry friends, pollute the air, and litter the earth. We're dedicated to protecting the environment and wildlife here, so fireworks are out."

"That's admirable. And fiscally smart."

"The town saves almost twenty-thousand dollars each year by not participating in that nonsense. Instead, we celebrate our independence and community every Sunday in the park where everyone, including our furry friends, can enjoy the day."

"What an amazing, forward-thinking town," I said, hardly able to believe one like this existed and that I was actually living in it.

"We've made a lot of progress in the last ten years. But how about you? How are you making out here?" he asked, glancing toward the shop.

"I'm still cleaning up," I said as we ambled to the patio.

A guilty grimace deepened the wrinkles in Walter's face. "I'm so sorry. Please let me hire someone to get things cleaned up."

"Absolutely not," I said, sitting beside him.

"Andie, it wasn't right of me to dump that mess on you. I'm sorry I did."

I slipped my hand over his boney knuckles. "Cleaning up is allowing me to reorganize and take inventory. Those are jobs I'd have wanted to do anyway. So please don't give this another thought. And the only reason I haven't finished cleaning up is because I was out of the shop doing a job at the airport."

"Is that so?" he asked, interest lighting his eyes.

"Yes, and I need to tell you about it, but I'm worried it will upset you."

His forehead creased. "Why would I be upset by your work?"

"Because I was finishing a job Rita started." I waited a moment for my words to sink in, but he seemed confused rather than upset. "Walter, I finished the job because she wasn't... because she..." I couldn't finish the sentence, but as understanding dawned in Walter's eyes, I knew he got it. "This is for you," I said, pulling the check I'd written earlier out of my pocket and handing it to him. "It's for the work Rita did at the airport."

The tremor in his hand, or perhaps his aging eyes, made him squint to read the check. "I don't want this," he said, handing it back to me.

"Rita did half that job, Walter. She earned that money. Please take it."

"I don't want or need it. I have more than I'll ever need. And Rita would have loved the idea of you working with her on a job." He captured my hand and pressed the check against my palm. "Please don't ask me to take this."

"But I didn't earn it. Rita did."

For a moment, we sat in a stalemate, then he gave me a lopsided smile and closed my fingers around the check. "Consider this payment for cleaning up the mess I made in the shop." Despite his smile, the guilt in his eyes suggested he needed to make restitution.

"This doesn't feel right, Walter."

"But it is," he replied, giving my hand a final pat. "Now, tell me how the apartment update is coming along."

Though I didn't feel right keeping money Rita earned, I worried that pressing the issue would insult Walter, so I told him I'd put it aside until I could find a suitable solution for both of us. I could see the topic was painful for him, so I let him know that Maggie would finish updating the apartment by Friday.

"That's wonderful. Are you excited?"

"Very," I said, reaching down to rub Louie's knobby head and scratch around his ears. With a growly moan, he dropped against me like dead weight, making my legs shift sideways and my chair legs squeak on the concrete.

Walter's laughter mingled with my own. "You're spoiling him, Andie."

Slipping my fingers beneath Louie's chin, I lifted his nose and looked into his dazed eyes. "This is just some well-deserved loving for a sweet boy." I glanced over to see such a tender look in Walter's eyes, I wondered if he was thinking about his lost daughter, or maybe how he and Rita used to sit here together, or perhaps he was just enjoying our friendship.

"He sure does love you," Walter said.

Louie was flopped like a sandbag against my legs. "Maybe, or he just loves treats and rubs."

"It's more than that," Walter said. "Louie understands you're family and that I think the world of you."

"The feeling is mutual," I said, shifting my attention from Louie to Walter. "Before I forget, I found a glass gallon jug with money in it that you left in the office. It was pushed to a corner under the desk."

"That's Rita's rainbow jar!" he said, so animated he looked ten years younger.

"Sorry, but what the heck is that?"

A deep chuckle rocked his thin shoulders. "Rita made it the day she told me I was acting like an arse."

I wasn't following, so I waited for Walter to bring his gaze back from whatever past memory it was focused on. Louie sneezed, licked his nose, and noisily smacked his chops as he stretched out across my feet, garnering Walter's attention.

"My Rita could have happily spent every moment in her shop," Walter said. "But I never felt that way." He glanced at me and shrugged. "I preferred doing other things, like fishing, which is what I wanted to do one Sunday when she needed my help in the shop. I was clomping around wearing a deep scowl and grousing about everything, when Rita planted her work boots directly in my path. She told me I was like a black cloud raining all over the day." A mischievous smile slanted his mouth. "I made a cheeky comment about fishing in the rain, and she nearly thumped me upside the head."

I laughed. "I could see her doing just that," I said, knowing how strong and passionate she was.

"Rita didn't thump me, but she said my attitude and actions emitted colors and she'd much rather see a rainbow than a rain cloud. I knew she was agitated because she stood with her hands on her hips, so I stopped giving her guff. But she wasn't done with me. She said she intended to emit vibrant colors and bring more beauty to the world." He paused, his gaze distant again as if reflecting on that private moment between them. "She dug out our old glass milk jug, the one you found in the office, and told me it was for our rainbow money that we would use to help other people. I had no idea what she was talking about, but I put twenty dollars in the jug which seemed to make her happy. From that day on, she took ten percent of her fee from each job and put it in the jug."

"Sounds like tithing to a church."

"It was better," he said, "because *every* penny was donated to special causes or used to purchase materials to make things people needed and couldn't afford."

"What a beautiful vision," I said, admiring Rita's generosity.

"Yes, and Rita lived it. Every day she painted my life with color and joy and laughter, and a good kick in the arse when I needed it."

I laughed but my eyes misted because the story and their love for one another was so heartwarming and heartbreaking. "Your Rainbow Rita was certainly one in a million."

"She certainly was," he said, "and she would have loved that name." With eyes drenched in sorrow, he slowly shook his head. "I still can't believe she's gone."

"Neither can I," I said softly. It didn't seem real or at all fair.

"It'll be three months tomorrow. Feels like I've been sleepwalking ever since." He raised sorrowful eyes to mine. "Thank you for giving me a reason to get out of bed and make coffee each morning."

This man with his warm-hug coffee, heartfelt stories, and sweet words bowled me over. "I will *always* give you a reason, Walter," I said, deeply grateful to have this fatherly man and his silly slobbery dog in my life. I pulled the check I'd written to him out of my pocket. "Let's put this money in Rita's Rainbow Jar."

Slipping his hand over my wrist, he gave it a gentle squeeze. "That would be wonderful, but keep the jar and the money, Andie. Be someone's rainbow like you are for Louie and me."

* * *

Shortly after four o'clock on Friday, Kate left and Maggie hurried me upstairs to my apartment. "Welcome to your new home," she said, then let me inside.

The kitchen was so bright and beautiful, I felt as if I'd entered a luxury suite. "Oh my gosh, Maggie, there's no dingy darkness anywhere, and it looks twice the size."

"That was the goal."

"It's just so gorgeous, I can't believe it's the same place!"

"Come on, I'll show you what we did." She stepped around me and gestured toward the cupboards. "We painted the kitchen cabinets Dover white. You can see how the gray undertone ties in with the dark gray countertop. We used antique gray cabinet hardware that really pops against the white cabinets and pulls together the gray oak flooring, the dark gray countertop, and this light wall color which has a hint of taupe and gray undertones."

The way she'd brought subtle colors and elements together to contrast and complement each other was masterful. She'd even added a rectangular planter full of herbs on the window ledge above the sink and a white porcelain bowl filled with lemons on the table. "I couldn't have ever visualized this," I said. "I'm blown away, Maggie."

"It was fun giving this place a fresh new look," she said. "Come on, I'll show you the living room."

As I followed her, I noted that the flooring and wall color continued through the apartment. "Oh, wow, you brought my heavy sofa sleeper upstairs!" I said, seeing that she'd arranged the couch and chair at a ninety-degree angle to the large window. They faced the long shelving unit Walter had left behind. It had been too heavy for me to move downstairs, so I'd left it in the living room. The tall bamboo plant in the corner, and two smaller plants on the shelving unit she'd told me to keep, complemented the room rather than overwhelmed it.

"Yeah, we thought you might want to sleep in your apartment tonight but noticed you didn't have a mattress on your bed, so we brought your sofa upstairs."

"It's all so stylish and perfect," I said, unable to stop looking around the gorgeous room. "The wall color seems a tad deeper and richer in here, but with all the white trim it's bright and cozy at the same time."

She seemed pleased that I'd noticed. "This is just a place to start, Andie. You get the fun part of making it your own. Come on, I'll show you the bedrooms. I normally wouldn't have pulled the wall color through the entire house, but in this small space using the same color scheme opens it up."

"It really does. It feels twice the size, Maggie."

"Just add a few nice area rugs and understated curtains. That will pull everything together and make this a cozy, beautiful space," she said.

"I work with metal design, not interior design."

She patted my shoulder. "Relax. I'll help, just text me photos of things you like, and I'll let you know if I come across rugs or curtains for your place." Stepping into the hall, she said, "Time to see your bathroom."

The instant she opened the door, I squealed in surprise. "You added a vanity! And you got rid of the avocado-colored sink and toilet!"

"Yeah, those things needed to go."

"How did you manage all of this? You couldn't have possibly done it on my meager budget."

"I didn't," she said, and my gut contracted a little. I couldn't afford to give up much more cash, but the place was so gorgeous, it was worth whatever she spent. "Your grand total is four thousand seven hundred forty-six dollars and fifty-two cents," she said, pulling an envelope from her back pocket. "Receipts are all here."

"That can't be right."

"It is."

I did a mental scan of everything she'd just showed me. "How is that possible?"

"Well, you didn't have to pay for labor which saved you a bundle," she said. "I had gallons of leftover paint that was perfect for your space, and I was so glad to be able to use it up. I picked up the vanity and cabinet hardware months ago at an estate sale along with the living room light fixture I'd found at an antique shop. I sold those things to you for two hundred dollars, which was more than fair to me, so no need for you to worry I undercharged you. The rest of your money went to flooring, lighting, and bathroom fixtures."

When she finished, I threw my arms around her. "How can I ever thank you?"

Laughing, she returned my hug. "You can buy the drinks and food for our girl gab."

I released her and stepped back. "Happy to! When and where are we meeting?"

"Here. Tonight. At six o'clock," she said, "so take a shower and put on your party clothes because we're going to bring some new life to this place."

Chapter Sixteen

To host my first girl gab in my own home felt so liberating, I wished I had decided to buy my own place years ago. But had I done so, I wouldn't have met Maggie or been invited into her fun circle of friends who were now camped out in my living room. It's said that everything happens in its own time, or when it's the right time. But I believe it's the hard decisions and sacrifices a person is willing to make that carries them forward. For me, those wrenching moments had brought me to a place where I was beginning to feel like my real self again.

I must have gotten lost in thought for a moment, because Maggie said, "Hey, Andie, are you daydreaming about that sexy pilot?"

"Actually, I was thinking how liberating it is to be with other independent women, especially artists like you three. I mean, just look at this place!" I gestured to my gorgeous apartment. "You completely changed the look and feel of my home."

"Don't give me artistic credit just for helping lay the floor," Chloe said. She'd filled in for Ashe one afternoon when he'd had another job to do. "All I did was cut and place boards on a flat surface."

"Same here," Kate said. "This was all Maggie."

"I know it was Maggie's design, but you two helped implement it and did an amazing job. In my mind, this floor is a work of art just like everything else Maggie did in here."

"That actually poses an interesting question," Maggie said. "What is art, really?"

"Self-expression and something you create," Kate said, slipping off her shoes and tucking her feet up on the sofa.

Chloe seemed to think about it for a moment before she said, "I think art is the thing you love spending time doing. For me, it's landscaping. But art could be interior design or any number of passionate pursuits."

"Absolutely," I said. "In fact, simply creating a joyful life is an art. I think the same is true for creating the kind of friendships you three share and that I'm privileged to participate in."

"Ooh, friendship as an artform, that's an interesting thought," Maggie said.

"Well, in my experience, not many people, especially busy, overworked women have the sort of friendship you three share. I've never had that. I remember thinking when we were at your house, Kate, that you were sunshine and blue sky, and Maggie, you were a flaming sunset, and Chloe, you were midnight and starlight," I said, directing my comments to each of them in turn. "Your unique personalities and the friendship and the connection you share is an artform."

The three of them exchanged varying looks of surprise and pleasure.

"That's really beautiful," Kate said, and Chloe verbally agreed.

Draping one leg over the other, Maggie lounged in my glider chair, holding the stem of a wineglass between her fingers. "That would make you the dawn in our group. You know, you're that moment of expectation and anticipation that heralds something new and exciting is about to happen."

My laughter bubbled out. "I don't know how exciting I am, but I love the idea of being the start of a new day."

"But the metaphor fits you," she said. "You're unexpected and on the verge of creating a whole new life."

"I suppose I am," I said, "but I feel so far behind."

"How so? You obviously achieved a lot in your profession, and now you own your own business," Maggie said. "That feels more like you're leading."

"Not with my art." I settled deeper into my corner of the sofa. "It's been so long since I've created a sculpture, I can't judge if my skill or talent is good enough for me to make a living doing it. Clark said I was a dreamer, that earning a living with my *hobby* wasn't very likely. He might be right, but I'd like to try anyway."

"What a clueless ass," Maggie said. "Why do people discount the importance of a person's creative passion?"

"Jealousy," Chloe suggested.

"Or control issues," Kate said. "Dan said my writing took too much time away from our girls and that my fantasy story was blasphemous and embarrassing."

Intrigued, I said, "I love the fantasy genre. I didn't know you were a writer."

"I'm trying to be," she said. "I'm getting close to finishing my first draft."

"That's truly impressive, Kate. How small-minded of your ex not to see that."

She shrugged. "In Dan's mind, if my time wasn't spent doing for him, our girls, or his church, I was being selfish. He just couldn't tolerate me having a passion of my own."

"Sounds like Clark," I said. "I thought that showing him a couple of my early sculptures and some of my sketches would help him understand what I wanted to do, but he couldn't feign interest for ten minutes. I asked why he couldn't support my passion like I did his, but he said my art was for me and that going to his car shows was a *family* thing for all of us. Our son enjoyed the shows, so I didn't bother debating the issue."

"It's crazy the things we'll do for our family even when it's to our own detriment," Kate said. "If not for my daughters, I would never have spent years of my life being hamstrung by Dan's absurd beliefs."

"I get it," I said. "My mother forced my older sister and I to go to church with her, and I hated it. I would fidget through the whole service while my mother whacked my leg with her hymnal and told me to sit still. We sat behind the same family, and the youngest boy would pick his nose, then try to shake my hand when we stood to wish each other peace. One Sunday, he nabbed my sister, and I let out an obnoxious donkey-laugh. My mother threatened to take me outside and spank me, but we stayed all the way through that long, boring service. When the priest finally walked up the aisle, flicking holy water across his sleepy congregants, I was yawning with my mouth wide open. Two fat droplets splatted on my tongue, and I puked up my breakfast of eggs. The booger-picker in the next row vomited, and it splattered the pew in front of them."

"Oh, god!" Kate pressed a hand to her chest and laughed. "What a scene."

"Yeah, the smell of sour puke caused utter disruption. People covered their noses and tried to avoid those who were gagging and losing their battle not to vomit. My mother was so embarrassed, she dragged my sister and I outside. Then she whipped me around to face the church and told me to look at what I'd done. I'm sure she expected me to be ashamed, but when I saw the mass exodus of people pushing through the doors gasping for fresh air, I started giggling. Honestly, I couldn't stop. She was furious with me and said she'd never be able to show her face there again, and we never went back."

Our laughter filled my apartment and was a balm for the childhood wound I suffered over the connection I never had with my mother.

"Does your mom still live in Utica?" Kate asked.

"No, after my dad died, she moved south with my sister and her dumbass husband. He's a conspiracy nutjob who convinced my sister and mother to give my father animal medication that would 'supposedly' cure his cancer."

Sympathy filled Kate's eyes. "Andie, I'm truly sorry you experienced that heartache."

I acknowledged her kind words with a nod. "My mother and sister loved my father, and I know they were desperately trying to help him, but the only thing they did was end his life sooner. I didn't know they were giving him that shit until after he died and we were cleaning out his things. That's when I cut ties with them because I simply couldn't tolerate their absurd beliefs and biases."

"Beliefs can certainly bring people together in community and for good purposes," Kate said, "but I've seen rigid and irrational beliefs tear too many families apart."

I nodded because I understood that only too well. "If it's any consolation, Kate, I wouldn't have known you'd been in a cult."

"Thanks," she said with a laugh. "That's a compliment because it took a lot of unlearning for me to break free of the propagandized opinions and rules they'd embedded in my brain."

"Oh, what an interesting concept," I said. "And it really makes sense because we learn biases from our parents who learned from their own parents and so on. So, it's likely we all have generational biases and beliefs we should unlearn."

"That's exactly what we're trying to accomplish here in

Dunwith," Chloe said. "We're standing up and making it clear we're done with all the bigoted, unjust nonsense breaking down communities and countries around the world. We'll be celebrating our first *Done With Day* in October."

"I'm in awe that a small town is successfully executing such a big vision," I said, "and I love the *Done With* wordplay."

"Yeah, nearly everyone in town has seen or heard about Kate's handmade sign," Maggie said, "so her little phrase was one of the first suggestions and won hands-down in a vote."

"I assume you're referring to the sign out front of Kate's place with the spike through Dan's shoe?" I asked.

"That's the one."

Kate wrinkled her nose. "This girl gab is getting stale. Let's circle back to whatever we were talking about before Andie's pukefest sent us down this path."

"We were talking about Clueless Clark and Dumbass Dan," Chloe said, cracking us up.

"Actually, we were talking about kids and sacrifices," I said. "I love my son, but if I had it to do over again, I think I'd take Maggie's happily-single-childless-by-choice life."

"If you hadn't had Tyler, what would you be doing with your life?" Maggie asked. When I shrugged, she said, "Really, where would you be?"

"Gosh, I don't know. Maybe I'd be traveling the world looking at all the amazing sculptures, or maybe I'd be tucked away in my studio making one of my own. At this point, I feel so far behind my peers, I don't think I'll ever catch up to their talent."

"If you need practice, I'd be happy to commission a small sculpture from you," Kate said.

"I'll gladly do a sculpture for you, but there is no way I'd accept a single cent from you after all the work you've done here. Same for you two," I said to Maggie and Chloe.

"You're already making a sign for my business," Maggie said.

"Just as soon as I get my shop cleaned up, your sign is my first job, and I'm really looking forward to it." I felt a buzz of excitement just thinking about the concept I'd come up with, and I couldn't wait to work on it. Maggie's shop was on a main street in the center of town, so the sign would be highly visible, which was as unnerving as it was exciting.

"Speaking of art, we need music," Maggie said, pushing to her feet. "And I need more wine."

I gestured to the small speaker on the shelf behind her. "If you have a playlist, you can connect with Bluetooth."

Maggie made a funny face at me as she whipped out her phone. "Girl, I always have a playlist." Amid our laughter, she cued up her music, and seconds later, a dance song filled my living room. "Okay, ladies, it's time to bring this apartment back to life!" With that, Maggie got her groove on and danced her way to the wine bottle sitting on an end table beside Kate. Still rocking her hips and shoulders, Maggie filled her glass in dribbles and spurts. "Glad you don't have carpets in here yet," she said as droplets of wine hit her bare toes and dripped onto the floor.

"Me, too," I said, but couldn't help laughing because she was so funny and fun and a little bit crazy.

To my surprise, Chloe and Kate rocked to their feet and pulled me up with them. "Time for the girl gab grind," Kate declared, then bent slightly at the waist and started twerking.

When Maggie and Chloe joined in, laughter bent me double, and I knew I'd never forget this night or these amazing women who couldn't twerk to save their lives.

* * *

It took five days of dirty backbreaking work to finish organizing the shop. By Thursday morning, I was able to scrub the concrete floor and wash the windows. The shop was finally ready for me to start working on Maggie's sign, but I was too sore and tired to do any more today.

I took a long shower and dressed in the only clean clothes I had left, a pair of faded jeans and an old T-shirt with a stain on the chest. I really needed to get the rest of my clothes from the house. Maybe I'd head down over the weekend and try to see Tyler while I was there.

For today, though, I needed groceries. My prorated incentive pay had been deposited in my bank account yesterday, so I braided my wet hair, then ran to the store.

I mindlessly wove my cart through the produce section, barely registering the man in front of me until he said hello. I looked up to see Ashe McKensie holding a bag of apples in one hand and a six pack of beer in the other.

"Hi, Ashe," I said, embarrassed that I'd been so zoned out. "Didn't see you standing there."

He smiled. "Not a problem. I hear you are back in your apartment now. How do you like the updates?"

"It's gorgeous and I love it. Thank you again for helping, Ashe. Really, I owe you."

"No payment necessary." He glanced at my cart containing a family-size bag of potato chips and a sack of dark chocolate I considered my necessary food items. "Got a party today?"

Heat flooded my face. "Nope. You?" I asked, nodding toward the six-pack he was holding.

"Nah. Just going fishing with Mason," he said, looking behind me.

I glanced over my shoulder to see Mason strolling up with two takeout containers in his hands.

"Hi, Andie," he said with a smile on his face and such warmth in his eyes it sent another flood of heat through me.

Damn it. I was forever destined to run into the man while I looked like hell. "I hear you're going fishing today."

"Yep. Good day to be on the river."

"Or to sit by the river and read a book," I said, planning to do just that when I finished shopping.

"That, too."

"I thought you'd be flying today," I said, then mentally kicked myself for letting him know I'd been thinking about him.

"It's a little sporty today for my ultralight."

"Sporty?"

"You know, windy, breezy, choppy," he said, his eyes roving my face and making me think *he* was being a little too sporty.

"Well, you boys have fun," I said, then turned my back and feigned interest in a pile of turnips, the only vegetable I didn't like. Examining one of the root veggies, I surreptitiously glanced over my shoulder to see Ashe and Mason walking away. Setting the turnip back in the bin, I sagged against the produce table. It slid away with a loud screech across the epoxy floor. Ashe, Mason, and three other people turned surprised looks in my direction. A sweeping glance of the otherwise empty produce section assured me I couldn't blame the horrendous noise on another shopper.

A knowing smile tilted Mason's lips, and he winked.

I hated that his smile made him more gorgeous and that I was the world's biggest klutz in his presence. Lifting my nose, I turned away but couldn't ignore his chuckle.

I finished shopping and got out of the store without running into the guys again. Back home, I decided to do my laundry and unpack a few of the things Walter had left here. I stocked the kitchen cupboards with dishes and pots and pans, and the drawers with silverware and linens, some of which I would replace when I had extra money. I brought up two lamps Walter hadn't wanted. They were outdated but in good shape and functional, so I placed them on the tables at each end of the sofa, then popped online and ordered new shades for them. I considered purchasing a mattress for my bed, but my budget was too tight. I could sleep on the sofa bed for now. I still needed to purchase curtains and area rugs and get my personal items from my house, or rather from Clark's house if he got the paperwork ready soon, but my little apartment already felt more like home.

I considered driving down in the morning to get my things from the house, but I couldn't do it without a trailer to haul my forklift, which I'd need to move the heavy sculpture my dad and I had made. I called Chloe, and after a short discussion, we agreed to go on Sunday morning when she could borrow a small forklift from a friend so we wouldn't have to transport the beastly machine in my shop.

That would give me two whole days to work on Maggie's sign, which I would do after morning coffee with Walter and Louie, of course. When Walter arrived the next morning, we had our coffee, then I showed him the apartment.

"My goodness!" he exclaimed as he stepped into the kitchen.

All I could think while he looked around with wide eyes and slack mouth is that he found my need to update his home offensive. "I kept some of the furniture and dishes and other things you left for me," I said, hoping he would see that I valued them, and him.

Lifting his ballcap, he scratched his head. "I had no idea it could look like this."

"I hope the change doesn't upset you," I said, swamped with guilt.

"Not at all." His gaze bounced from the ceiling fan to the

cupboards to the countertop and then to me. "Rita would have loved this."

"What about you?" I asked.

He shrugged. "I never thought much about this sort of thing. But the change is very nice and far more suited to you, I suspect."

"I guess I just like a lighter palette. Would you like to see the rest of the place? Louie is already two rooms ahead of us."

Walter chuckled. "Of course."

He followed me through the rest of the apartment, nodding as if he were an inspector there to approve the work. "Rita would have loved this bathroom," he said, taking it all in. "She hated that green sink and toilet and always wanted a vanity." He released a hard sigh. "I should have given her those things."

There were no words of comfort for that kind of regret, so I simply took his hand and led him back to the living room where Louie was sniffing the wall. "I think he smells the fresh paint."

"Probably. I hope he doesn't get high."

Walter's unexpected comment made me laugh. "He's probably trying to figure out where I'm stashing his treats."

"No doubt." Walter ran his weathered hand over the long shelving unit he left for me. "I used to imagine moving my daughter into her first apartment, giving her some of our old furniture to help her get set up. When Rita was expecting, we used to talk about those things. But after she lost the baby, well..." He shrugged. "I'm glad you're keeping some of this stuff."

My throat was so thick with sorrow I couldn't speak.

Louie headed to the kitchen, sniffing so loudly I knew he was looking for treats. "I'd better get Louie his goodies."

Walter followed me to the kitchen where I gave Louie a treat and kept two in my pocket for later. "I wanted to let you know that I got the shop cleaned up. I changed a couple of things around to give me more room to work, but Rita's shop is clean and bright again."

"That's good, Andie. This is your place, and you need to make it your own."

"I have, but I want you to know that I'm honoring all the love you and Rita shared here, and that you and Louie are *always* welcome. I really mean that."

"I know, dear," he said, pulling me into a warm hug. "You have no idea how happy it makes me to see you here."

Chapter Seventeen

Until today, I hadn't had the opportunity to deepen my friendship with Chloe as I'd done with Maggie, and with Kate to a lesser degree, simply because I hadn't spent as much time with her. But our trip to Utica in the dummy, as she referred to her dump truck, revealed her to be an intelligent, complex, very interesting woman. I knew she'd been widowed, but her comments about her marriage to Josh gave me a glimpse into their beautiful life together and the ravine of grief cutting through her.

I almost felt guilty for divorcing Clark when both Chloe and Walter would have given anything to get their spouses back.

But there was lightness in Chloe, too, and a fabulous streak of humor. She shared funny stories about Kate, Maggie, and her as teenagers, and I could imagine them as half-wild young girls. But it was the incidents that had taken place when Kate returned last year that had me laughing myself to tears, especially the one about the trifecta showing up to herd Kate back to church.

"I so wish I'd have seen that," I said.

"It's one of those scenes that lodges itself in your brain and replays at the most inappropriate moments," she said. "Last week I burst out laughing in the grocery store because that scene popped into my head while I was buying beer. I was alone in the cooler aisle, and I actually snorted!"

My belly hurt from laughing. "Thank you, Chloe. I really needed this trip."

"Me, too."

A few minutes later, Chloe backed the dummy and trailer into my driveway. There were no cars there, so I knew Clark and Tyler weren't home. But the instant I opened the overhead shop door, I saw that Clark hadn't cleared out a single thing. "Damn it!" I said, feeling my blood pressure spike.

Chloe raised her eyebrows in question.

"I told Clark I was coming down today and asked him to clear his stuff out of the garage so I could get my things."

"Apparently, he didn't get the message."

"He never does," I said, fuming inside.

"Got the car keys?" Chloe asked, giving a head tilt toward the Thunderbird and Bel Air.

I realized Clark was living here now and probably hung his keys on the wall hook where he used to keep them. "Be right back," I said, then ran inside.

It took us five minutes to move the cars onto the front lawn. Then I began dragging out anything that blocked access to my stuff. When I came across a For Sale sign with Clark's phone number on it, I walked out front and put it on the windshield of his Thunderbird.

Chloe smiled. "I wonder how long it will take before his phone starts ringing."

"We'll know when he shows up in a panic."

"You and Kate have some alarming similarities," Chloe said, laughing as she followed me into the shop.

"Thank you. I consider any comparison to Kate flattering."

"Not exactly what I meant, but okay." Chloe picked up a wood crate filled with small car parts. "Not your things, I suspect?"

"Nope. Stack it against the wall beside Clark's toolbox."

It took nearly an hour to move my tools and the small equipment I'd inherited from my father to Chloe's dump truck.

"Is this going?" Chloe asked, gesturing to the tarped beast taking up one corner of the shop. At my nod, she released a slow whistle. "That is a small mountain. Any idea how much it weighs?"

Her comment worried me. "I'm not sure. Are you afraid the forklift can't handle it?"

"Only one way to know," she said, then headed outside and climbed on the forklift.

It took considerable maneuvering to lift and load my tarped sculpture onto the trailer and secure it with straps, but Chloe was as determined as she was skilled. When she'd finished with the forklift, she drove it onto the lowboy trailer. While she secured the machine, I got the boxes I'd packed from the house. At the last second, I decided to take the new mattress I'd bought for my bed after Clark moved out.

Finally, we loaded my father's Beverly shear on the truck. I was eleven when he taught me to use the shear. He told me to think of it as a pair of scissors mounted to the workbench. Despite my dad's explanation, it had taken many attempts for me to grasp the process of working the shear handle while manipulating a piece of metal with my other hand. When I finally mastered the technique, it became one of my favorite pieces of equipment.

We had just nested the shear in the back of Chloe's dump truck when Clark pulled in. His eyes were the size of quarters when he saw the *For Sale* sign on his Thunderbird. "What the hell, Andie?" he asked, whipping the sign off the windshield.

Chloe and I exchanged a look, both of us failing to hide our smiles.

"What do you think you're doing?" he demanded, his face mottled with agitation.

"Look at your text, Clark. I'm doing exactly what I told you I was going to do. I said I'd be here today. I asked you to move your cars and stuff out of the way. You didn't do it. So, I did."

"Do you know how many phone calls I've gotten because of this sign?" he asked, shaking it at me.

"No, but I'm honestly curious. How many?"

Chloe snorted and moved deeper into the dump box.

"Too many!" Clark snapped. "I was at work earning double-time but had to leave because of this nonsense."

He was wearing his khaki work shirt with the company logo embroidered on the chest. "Then maybe my point was made, and you'll stop dismissing me. Did you get the paperwork started yet?"

"I have an appointment tomorrow, but I have to reschedule it because I'm working."

After digging through Clark's crap and shuffling boxes around, I had no energy left to argue with him. "Okay, you owe me nine hundred and fifty dollars for the mortgage payment. If you don't have papers for me to sign in two weeks, I'm listing the house with a realtor. I'm not kidding, Clark. No more leeway here. I'm done with whatever game you're playing. Now, please move your car so we can pull out."

He glanced into the dump box where Chloe was securing the shear with straps. "You're taking that?" he asked, his gaze roving my possessions, then widening. "And the welder, too?"

Bewildered, I just looked at him. "They were my father's."

As if he suddenly recalled that fact, his gaze softened a bit. "That's right. Sorry." He glanced at the mess flowing out of the garage. "What are you doing with that?" he asked.

"Nothing. It's all your crap that I had to move to get to my things. It's your mess to clean up."

He opened his mouth as if to argue, then snapped it closed. As he stalked to his car, I asked if he knew where Tyler was or when he'd be home.

"Tyler and his friends left early for their vacation," he said, then slammed his car door and backed onto the lawn to clear the driveway for our exit.

I was agitated that neither of them had bothered to tell me, but any complaint would fall on deaf ears, so I climbed in the cab where Chloe was waiting. "Thank you for helping me with this, Chloe. Sorry for the drama."

"Are you kidding? This was surprisingly fun," she said, then burst out laughing as she pulled the dummy onto the street. "Maggie was right. You are a legit badass."

As soon as Walter and Louie left after our Monday morning coffee date, I went back to work on my sign project for Maggie. Once I settled on the finished design, I opened Rita's CAD software to create a 3D model of my sculpture.

When I worked at the fab shop, I disliked this labor intensive design stage. I preferred hand sketching my ideas, as I'd done for the sculptures I'd made with my father. He would have me sketch out my sculptures and calculate dimensions before building them. We created free-form sculptures, too, where we would simply visualize an idea, then create it. Both approaches had broadened my abilities as an artist.

It took the better part of an hour in the CAD program to create an initial blockout. I'd learned advanced programing but hated the process of inputting dimension details and adjustments because it felt endless. Other than a short visit with

Walter on Tuesday and Wednesday morning, my only breaks were to steal a few hours of sleep or grab a quick bite to eat.

Late Wednesday afternoon it was finally time to cut the pieces for my sculpture. With the vacuum lift, I moved a sheet of eleven-gauge mild steel to the plasma table. After setting the origin point for the tool path and double checking to see that I'd nested the pieces efficiently and allowed for kerf, I entered the computer command to start cutting. When I noticed the torch wasn't cutting all the way through the material, I lowered the speed until I got a clean cut.

While the plasma torch did its job, I created a new design for the lettering on Maggie's sign, a much easier and quicker job. By late evening, I had my sculpture pieces cut and labeled with a permanent marker and all the scrap tossed in the scrap bin. I also had a pounding headache that drove me upstairs for pain reliever and a long shower.

Early the next morning, I woke eager to get back to my first artistic project in years. After eating a bowl of quick oats with apple slices and pecans, I took a steaming cup of coffee to the shop and turned on the lights.

The pieces of the sculpture would need to be deburred with a grinder. *A clean edge makes a clean weld* was one of my dad's many sayings, and he was right. His dedication to me and to fostering my artistic passion made me extremely grateful for not only his love but for the solid foundation he'd given me. I knew I was fortunate to have had a father like him, but I still felt cheated by his early death. When people would tell me he was in a better place now, that he was no longer suffering, blah, blah, I wondered why they couldn't just say his death sucked. Because it had. And it still did. Or people could just say they were sorry for my loss because it was one that I felt in the deepest part of my being. Clark once accused me of being too sensitive about my father's passing, so I'd asked him what level of grief or sensitivity was considered acceptable for losing someone you loved with your whole heart.

Thinking of Clark agitated me, so I turned on an old radio I'd found when cleaning the shop. The only station that would come in without crackling white noise was a country station. I checked the time on the wall clock above the workbench. Walter and Louie usually arrived between eight and nine each morning, so I had about an hour to finish deburring nearly a hundred metal pieces that would eventually become my 3D sculpture of a fox. Before I began, I loaded a sheet of brushed aluminum on the plasma table and started the program to cut out the letters for the *Red Fox Boutique and Antiques*.

It felt good to be back in my lane pursuing my passion, designing a sign for Maggie I hoped would be worthy of the apartment update she'd done for me. I became so lost in my work, I was startled by Louie's happy bark and the sound of two men talking outside.

I recognized those voices. Tugging off my gloves and eye protection, I ran my palms over my hair, hoping it wasn't sticking out like tentacles around my face. I had no idea why Mason was here with Walter, but there was no sense delaying the inevitable.

When I stepped outside, I saw Louie standing on his hind legs with his front paws on Mason's Khaki-clad thigh, thoroughly engrossed in the head scratching he was receiving. The second Mason's eyes met mine, a slow, warm smile lit his face. "Good morning," he said, then laughed when Louie spotted me and bolted to my side.

"Hey, sweet boy," I said, kneeling to give Louie one of the two doggie biscuits I almost always kept in my pocket now. "Were you making a new friend?"

"Oh, no, Louie knows Mason," Walter said, his voice more animated than usual as he handed me a mug of coffee. "I've known this young man since he was a little tyke riding his tricycle right out there on the sidewalk."

To imagine Mason as a little boy on a tricycle was heartwarming, and it made me more curious about him. But I knew curiosity often led to trouble, so I mentally shut the door and gave Louie another biscuit. Wiping my wet fingers on my jeans, I glanced at Mason and found myself ensnared in his knowing smile.

"You forgot this in one of the hangars," he said, pulling a pair of vintage needle nose pliers out of his back pocket and holding them up for me to inspect.

"There they are!" Walter exclaimed, his shoulders sagging in relief. "Those are Rita's pocket pliers. She carried those things everywhere."

Mason handed them over, and Walter pressed the pliers to his chest, his face awash with joy and heartbreak. "That woman was a walking toolbox. Only time she didn't have tools on her was when we went out dancing."

I understood then that Rita must have left the pliers at the hangar because she'd planned to go back and finish the job. Knowing she'd been unable to do so was freaking heartbreaking, and it squeezed the breath from my lungs.

"On dance nights," Walter continued, "you wouldn't have known she was the same woman who'd worn a welding helmet all day. Dance night was the only time she'd quit early to get herself gussied up in a dress and heels. With her hair down and her lips pink and those blue eyes of hers sparkling, she'd turn every head in the place." Walter's gaze seemed to turn inward as he slowly shook his head. "I couldn't take my eyes off her. She was breathtaking."

For a moment, he was silent, and I exchanged an uncomfortable look with Mason.

Walter looked at the pliers in his hand, his voice wobbly as he spoke. "Truth is, the woman with messy hair, dressed in work boots and covered in welding dust, was the one who melted my heart. That woman, *my* Rita, was magnificent."

Mason nodded sympathetically. "I understand."

A slight quiver in Walter's jaw revealed his emotional struggle.

"I didn't realize Rita was the dancing type," I said, trying to help him push through his grief.

"Oh, she was a great dancer," Walter replied with conviction. "Name a dance and she could do it. She especially loved the Jitterbug and Swing dancing. If not for me demanding breaks through the night that woman would wear the soles off our shoes."

"Sounds like a great time," I said, imagining the two of them cutting up a dance floor.

"We loved dance night," he said. "You should try it."

"I'll pass. I'm sure I'd be an utter failure."

He flapped a hand. "If I can learn with two left feet, you can manage just fine. You two should come to our dance night at The Grove. It's a week from this Saturday."

"What?" I shot a look at Mason. "We're not, ah, dance partners." I heard Mason cover a laugh with a cough and I wished I'd taken the pliers so I could pinch him with them.

"Anyone can be partners," Walter said. "Invite your friends and make a night of it."

"Are you planning to be there?" I asked, wondering if Walter was fishing for my support without wanting to ask outright.

His eyebrows settled low over his eyes as he released a long sigh. "Don't know if I can do it without Rita," he said.

"Are you in need of a dance partner?" I asked, willing to do anything for Walter, even if that meant volunteering to help him dance again but hoping I wouldn't have to.

"No, dear, everyone just partners up with whoever's handy when the music starts. But if you think you'll be there, I might wander down to watch for a spell."

Fighting a groan, I gave him a small nod. "I could stop in for a bit if that would help."

His eyes brightened. "That would be wonderful, Andie." He looked at Mason. "Will I see you there, too, young man?"

I glanced at Mason and gave a slight shake of my head, but he just smiled. "I'd love to go."

"Really," I said, hoping my putting him on the spot would make him as uncomfortable as I felt. "You want to go swing dancing?"

Without flinching, he said, "Why not? Sounds like a good time."

"Then it's a date," Walter said, clapping his hand on Mason's shoulder. "Music starts at seven so make sure you and Andie are there by six-thirty."

"We'll be there," Mason said with confidence.

It's not a date, I mouthed silently to him.

Ignoring me, he asked Walter if it was a dress up affair.

"Oh, yes, everyone enjoys getting gussied up for dance night. Wear something pretty, Andie," Walter said, then called to Louie who'd curled up in a lawn chair. "Time to go, buddy."

"Walter, aren't you staying for coffee?" I glanced at my mug. "I still have a full cup."

"I need to get Louie to the vet this morning to get his claws trimmed. Enjoy your coffee, and I'll get the mug tomorrow." With Louie perched on his lap, Walter drove away.

As soon as the scooter hit the sidewalk, Mason began chuckling. "I would have never guessed that Walter would be the ultimate wingman. I just got a date without even trying."

"It's not a date," I said. "And you might as well know right now that I'm not interested in romance or a relationship."

"How about friendship?" he asked.

Our understanding of what friendship meant could be very different, so I didn't reply.

"Andie, I like my life. I'm not looking to move into someone else's life or pull them into my own. But if you have room for friends, I'd like to be one of them. No strings. No expectations. Just companionship in whatever form suits you in the moment. That's it and that's all."

"Just friends?" I asked, still a bit suspicious of his motives.

"Yep. That's it. I think you're incredibly interesting and fun, and just the kind of friend I'd like to have."

"Okay, but I'm only going to the dance to support Walter."

"Me, too, but I'm also going because I want to learn how to swing dance."

I laughed. "I'm sure."

"I'll pick you up Saturday. Wear your pretty dress and dancing shoes."

"I'll be in jeans and my work boots. And I'll meet you there."

"Nope. I promised Walter that I'd get you there, and I'm not missing my chance to escort a gorgeous lady to the dance even though she doesn't know how to button her shirt properly."

"What?" I glanced down and realized I'd misaligned my buttons and holes. *Dang it.* I lifted my chin trying to affect a cocky look. "Yeah, I've been trying to impress you. It's about time you noticed."

His laughter floated across the parking lot. The man had such a nice laugh, one that illuminated his face and eyes and made it impossible for me to look away. "Oh, I noticed, Andie. Believe me, I haven't missed at thing," he said, still laughing.

"Good. Mission accomplished," I said, then pivoted on my boot heel, and took my disheveled self inside.

Chapter Eighteen

For six days, I worked on the three-dimensional fox sculpture for Maggie's sign. Welding precut pieces of sheet metal together was a different type of sculpting for me. My father and I had created most of our sculptures using nuts and bolts, springs and coils, tubing and pipe fittings, parts from machines and appliances, silverware and other kitchen items, wagon wheels and bike chains, and even old horseshoes. Any scrap metal was material for creating our pieces.

But creating Maggie's sculpture was complex work that required bending and aligning various shapes of flat metal profiles so the edges would marry-up with neighboring pieces and fit together like a puzzle. I made soft bends with my hands or used my knee as a fulcrum. At times, I tucked larger sections between my boot heel and the concrete floor to bend them. For tighter, more intricate bends I used pliers and tongs. After shaping each piece, I tack welded, hammered, and manipulated it, along with neighboring sections to make the pieces flow together.

The process was difficult and labor intensive, but when I

found myself wishing it was over, I remembered my father telling me to slow down. We had been working on our third sculpture when I complained there were too many pieces, that it was too difficult, and he told me it was more complex by design to broaden my experience and my artistic eye. He explained that art wasn't about the finished piece but rather about the story of its creation, the process, the labor of love, the skill, the tiny nuances that gave the sculpture shape, form, beauty, and life.

So when I felt tired, I would pause for a moment, straighten my back and take a deep, reviving breath. I wanted to create a sculpture that reflected the playful sass and vibrant beauty of Maggie's personality. The only way to do that was to bring it to life with my own aching hands. So, I settled in and worked one moment and one piece at a time, my tongs and pliers grating against steel as I bent the pieces, then clanking as I dropped the tools back on the workbench. For hours, all I heard was the sound of my hammer tapping metal into shape and the buzzing sound of my welder mingled with the small expulsions of breath I released with my exertion. Once the symmetry of the piece looked good, I ground down the tack welds, then began the long, methodical process of finish welding.

Hours later, when I finally removed my welding helmet and tossed my gloves on the workbench, I pulled on a respirator and eye protection, then applied exterior black paint to the frame and sign.

It was after nine o'clock when I finally slogged upstairs. While the tub was filling, I made a tomato and cheese sandwich and ate it while slumped over my kitchen table. I checked my phone for messages, hoping Tyler had texted. He hadn't. But he'd texted earlier in the week to say he was safe and having a great time at the beach with his buddies.

Clark had texted once to say he'd met with the attorney and

would let me know when papers were ready to sign. Then he asked what I was working on, how I was doing, and how I liked it here. I'd responded with a thumbs-up emoji because his sudden interest in my life was unusual and a little too late.

I headed to the bathroom for the hot bath I'd promised my aching, abused body. While I soaked, I thought about Clark's sudden interest in my life. Early in our marriage I'd tried to share my passion for sculpting, how it made me feel alive, but Clark had no interest. He would abruptly change the subject or walk away in the middle of our conversation, or worse, he'd sigh and roll his eyes as if he couldn't bear to hear another word. His dismissive attitude shut me down and I quit talking about my art. For him to pretend interest in me or my new life now, felt offensive because it was too late, and his curiosity wasn't real. He just felt left behind or left out because he was no longer the center of my attention.

Thinking about my ex and how I'd tolerated my submissive role in our relationship just agitated me, so I pulled the plug and let the memories go down the drain with my bathwater.

* * *

I woke early, bleary-eyed and sore, but I was eager to get back to work. The black paint was dry on the sign, so I glued on the silver letters. It created a nice dimension and gave the name of Maggie's business a classy look.

I'd gotten so engrossed in finish grinding and polishing the sculpture, I didn't realize anyone was in the shop until Louie nudged my leg. I yelped and dropped the grinder on the work-bench. Pulling off my respirator, I ruffled Louie's ears. "You scared the bejabbers out of me," I said, using one of Walter's expressions.

Popping up on his hind legs, Louie pawed my leg.

"All right, I know you're waiting, little man. Let me take off my gloves first." I'd just opened the bag of doggie biscuits on my workbench when Walter ambled in.

"G'morning, dear," he said, scanning the shop, his gaze landing on the sign, where he assessed the sassy tilt of the fox's head and playful swish of its tail. "This is a fine piece of work, Andie."

"Thanks, and good morning to you," I said while slipping a biscuit to Louie. "The other section of the sign is over there on the tarp."

Walter ambled over with his scuff-step and took a closer look. "Ah, I see what you're doing now. The fox will sit on top of the sign, right?"

"Yes. I'll set it at this corner, and its tail will swoop across the front of the sign just beneath the name of her business. I'll weld the sculpture onto the sign-body once the clear coat dries. Then I'll touch up the welds, and it'll be ready to install."

A smile creased his face. "Maggie is going to love this. And Rita would truly admire your talent. I think you're going to be very busy here."

On one hand, I hoped he was right. I needed an income. But on the other hand, making signs and sculptures out of sheet metal was only a small part of how I wanted to spend my time. Making sculptures with scrap metal junk was my goal.

Louie's impatient nudge against my leg reminded me he was waiting for his second biscuit. "Sorry, sweetie, I was distracted. Here you go," I said. He lipped the biscuit so aggressively and noisily, I laughed. "You have atrocious manners, little man. But I get it because that's exactly how I feel about coffee."

"Then let's go outside and enjoy ours before it gets cold," Walter said, heading toward the door.

As Louie and I followed him outside into a gorgeous sunny morning, I asked, "Where did you find this sweet boy anyway?"

"Out by our dumpster," he said as we settled in our lawn chairs. "Poor pup was all bones and big eyes, and I knew there wasn't a question in Rita's mind that he was coming home with us. She fed him, bathed him, and I kid you not, she rocked that poor wretch to sleep in her arms. From that moment on Louie was her constant companion. He ate with us, spent his day in the shop with us, and slept with us. One day we couldn't find the knucklehead anywhere. Rita was in a full panic and near tears when she finally found him sleeping under the plasma table. She was so relieved, she crawled right under the table and scooped him into her arms." Walter's shoulders sagged on a hard exhale. "I think her absence is as hard on Louie as it is on me."

Walter's memories were beautiful and wrenching as hell. "I'm glad you two have each other," I said, slipping my palm over Louie's knobby head. He looked up at me with dreamy eyes and his pink tongue peeping from the front of his mouth. I leaned down, gathered him in my arms, and gave him a warm snuggle. He licked my face with a big wet swipe from my chin to my eyebrow. I rocked back and wiped my cheek on my sleeve. "Thank you, Louie, but *yuck*."

Walter was convulsed with laughter, a lovely sound from a man filled with so much pain.

* * *

"Wow, Andie!" Maggie stood in my shop, gaping at the sign I'd made for her. Slowly, she drew her fingertips over the sculpture, from the sassy tilt of its head down its shapely body, and finally along the playful swish of its tail. "This is stunning. How did you make this?"

"Cutting, bending, welding, and polishing sheet metal," I said as if it were a simple task rather than the painful process I'd just spent two weeks engaged in. "The weathering steel I used to make the fox sculpture will form a rusty orange patina that will protect the surface and eventually turn the fox a brownish-orange color."

"You have real talent, Andie. If this is what you're planning to do here, you'll have no trouble building a great business."

I was proud of how the sign and sculpture turned out, but I was more relieved that Maggie liked it. I hoped it might in some way compensate her for the kindness she'd shown me from the moment we met at the gas station.

"Chloe will be stopping by soon to help me install your sign. I thought we'd mount it on the wrought iron fence in front of your store. It will look as if the sign is part of the fence, if that's okay?"

"It sounds fantastic." She let out a little squeal and pulled out her phone. "Honest to god, Andie, I'm so blown away by this I can't wait to see it in front of my shop. I'm going to call Chloe and tell her to hurry the hell up so we can get it installed."

We heard a phone ringing as Chloe entered the shop. She glanced at her phone, then gave Maggie a confused look. "Did you need something?"

"Yes! I need to get this gorgeous sign installed right this minute."

"That's why I'm here," Chloe said, her eyes going wide when she saw the sculpture. "I had no idea you were this talented, Andie."

I laughed. "Thanks, I think."

"Come on, come on, let's move this thing," Maggie said, nudging Chloe's shoulder.

Chloe eyed the sign. "Okay, but it looks pretty damn heavy."

"It's probably three hundred pounds without the frame," I said.

"I'll get some help." Maggie tapped her phone screen. "I think Ashe is in town this morning." When he answered, she browbeat him into helping us.

When he arrived, we decided to lay the sign on a pallet for easier lifting. "Okay, Mags, be sure to pull your weight," he said razzing her like any big brother worthy of the title would do.

At his count, we lifted and did a shuffling side-step to my flatbed. Ashe and Chloe lifted their side high enough to clear the bed, then we slid the pallet onto the truck and strapped it down. I ran back to get my tools, and Ashe helped Maggie load the frame.

I'd had plenty of time to think through the installation, but I was surprised at how quickly we'd accomplished the job. Wiping our hands and sweaty brows, we stepped back to admire our handiwork. The playful fox perched atop the designer sign was so perfect for Maggie and her business, I felt a happy thrill zip through me.

"Andie, this is really something," Ashe said, gracing me with his gorgeous smile. "Too bad Kate's not here to see it."

"Where is she today?" I asked, suspecting he would know.

"She's visiting one of her daughters. But she'll be back tomorrow in time for the dance."

"What dance?" Maggie asked as if she'd been left off the guest list.

"Swing dancing at The Grove," he said. "The notice went up on the Board last week." He glanced at me. "Mason told me you two are going, and he asked me to bring Kate."

To avoid questions about Mason, I asked, "What's the Board?"

"It's an online bulletin board in calendar format that lists all the events in Dunwith and sends out an alert when a new post goes up," Ashe said. "Just sign up and click *Alerts*."

While Maggie checked her phone, I pulled mine out and signed up.

"How did I miss that?" Maggie asked, then looked at Chloe. "Want to be my dance partner?"

"Always," Chloe replied without hesitation. "But I'm not ready for swing dancing."

Maggie affected a pout. "Phooey."

"Walter might need a partner," Ashe offered.

Maggie flicked her manicured fingers at him. "Go away."

He laughed and headed toward his van. "See you tomorrow."

I couldn't tell which one of us he was talking to, but I called out my thanks. He lifted his hand without turning around, so I knew he'd heard me.

"You should be nicer to your brother," I said to Maggie.

"He loves our verbal sparring," she said. "He's one of my favorite people and he knows it."

A deep sense of appreciation and envy filled me. The relationship they shared was something I wanted with all my heart but the one thing I'd never share with my sister. It was impossible for me to connect with someone filled with prejudiced beliefs, and who thought everything was a conspiracy.

Maggie fiddled with her phone, and a few seconds later her assistant, Jill, came outside to see the new sign. While Jill gushed over my work, I noted her slight British accent and easy confidence even as she stood beside Maggie. She was petite and pretty with brown hair and green eyes and wasn't wearing a wedding band. It made me wonder why Mason was bothering with me when there were attractive ladies like Jill in town. I didn't realize I was caught up in my own thoughts until Maggie swept me into a big hug.

"Thank you for such an incredible, beautiful, amazing,

perfect gift," she said, stringing together so many adjectives it made me laugh.

"It was the least I could do for everything you've done for me." When she released me, I double-checked the sign to assure myself it was straight and mounted securely. "While I'm here, I'd love to peek in your shop."

"That's right, you haven't visited yet," she said. "Come on, I'll give you a tour."

I'd expected Maggie's shop to be cute but immediately realized I'd grossly underestimated her talent. A light scent of pine teased my nose as we entered. The rooms of the Victorian mansion were beautifully decorated with period furniture and pottery that several patrons were ogling as they meandered and browsed. In what was once a formal parlor, Maggie had created a lovely seating area around a stone fireplace, where a couple sat discussing the purchase of a vintage table currently holding stylish handbags and other accessories. Throughout the shop, women's clothing, shoes, bags, and jewelry were artfully displayed on metal racks and wooden tables. Bewigged mannequins wearing stylish hats, scarves, and sunglasses were positioned near a display case where Jill was cashing out two teenage girls excitedly talking about their purchases.

"Maggie, you are incredibly gifted," I said. "I think I'll browse a little while I'm here."

"Wonderful. I need to give Jill a hand for a minute anyway," she said, gesturing to the four people waiting at the checkout counter.

As I wandered, I became immersed in browsing, noting tiny artistic details and admiring the tasteful items Maggie had chosen to sell. Not one piece of clothing looked used, and I checked several that caught my eye.

"Looking for anything particular?" Maggie asked when she

returned a few minutes later and approached the rack I was browsing through.

"Maybe. Well, I don't know." I shrugged at my own indecisive answer. "I could use a dress for the dance but haven't a clue what that might look like."

"I do," she said, spinning on her heel and striding out of the room before I could ask for details. A few seconds later she returned with a short, sleeveless dress draped over her arm. "If the size is right, this burnt orange color will look fabulous on you and compliment your brown hair and brown eyes."

"It's beautiful, but do you think it's too bright and too young for me?" I asked, but it was more of a suggestion.

"You *are* young, Andie, and you can wear whatever makes you feel good." She held up the dress and gave it a shake, making the skirt flare out a bit. "This is perfect for dancing. Come try it on." I followed her to a fitting room at the far side of the room. She hung the dress on a hook, then nudged me inside, and closed the door behind me. "If it fits, I'd love to see the dress on you."

"Okay," I said, and once I'd pulled it on, I was glad Maggie was standing by to give me her opinion. "I'm going to open the door, but only if you promise to be honest with me."

"Girl, I'll always be honest with you, and I wouldn't let any friend walk out of my shop with something they shouldn't be wearing."

"All right then." I swung open the door. "It fits."

Her eyes brightened. "I knew this would look amazing on you."

"Not too short or too young, then?" I asked, aware of air circulating around my bare legs.

"It's barely above your knees, Andie. The style is timeless, and the color is sophisticated and alluring, not young and playful. You look gorgeous."

I rubbed the soft fabric of the skirt between my thumb and fingers. "It's been a long time since I've worn anything other than business suits or jeans."

"As your friend, I'm not letting you leave my shop without this dress," she said. "It's perfect and you deserve it."

I still felt uncertain, but said, "Okay, would brown strappy sandals work with this dress because that's the only option I have?"

"They'll look great. After you finish in here, I'll show you the antique section of my business."

"Is that the barn out back?" I asked, closing the door and changing quickly.

"Yep, and it's where I live," she said.

We left my dress at the counter and exited the back door onto a short, paved walkway, girded by boxwood bushes and colorful urns full of yellow daisies, that took us to a large gambrel-roofed barn. When I stepped inside, I marveled at the size of the building, the warm Edison-style lighting, and the decorative staircases at each end of the building. As she'd done with her consignment shop, Maggie's antique barn was a creative display of vintage art, old travel trunks and period furniture and fixtures among a vast selection of other items. And her loft apartment was dreamy with a rustic chic vibe that made me want to move in. "You absolutely must select the curtains and rugs for my place," I said, gazing with awe at all she'd created in a space not much larger than mine.

"If you insist," she said. "Now, I really must get back and help Jill before she quits on me."

"No one who works in a place like this would quit," I said. "But I need to go, too, because I'm heading over to see Eli and check on the progress of my paperwork."

After purchasing my dress at half price, at Maggie's insistence, I drove over to my CPA's office. Eli popped out of a meeting to let me know everything was moving along well but would likely take another two to three weeks for the paperwork, transfers, and payments to be finalized.

To know I'd soon own the shop where I'd made my first sculpture in years—but without my father at my side—was bittersweet.

Chapter Nineteen

When I stepped outside to meet Mason, who was picking me up for the dance, the look on his face made me question my decision to buy a new dress.

He released a slow whistle, eyeing me from my painted lips to my sandal-clad feet and polished toenails. "Is Andie here?" he asked, his voice sounding a bit strained.

I'd dressed and primped and gussied myself up as Walter would say because I wanted Mason to know there was another dimension to me. I wasn't just a grubby work-boot-wearing-mismatched-buttoned-up klutz. I had a softer side I hadn't shown anyone in years because that side was too vulnerable. And yet, here I was revealing that side of me to Mason.

But why? I didn't want romance. I didn't want a relationship. Had I done this to shock him? To make him feel as unsettled as I felt in his presence? Or had I done this to prove something to myself?

It was a question I couldn't seem to answer so I opted for humor. "I'm Andie's twin sister Andrea. Andie told me she didn't want to go to the dance with you, so she is sending me."

A smile spread across his handsome face, lifting his lips, lighting his eyes. "Well, it's a pleasure to meet you, *Andrea*."

"Of course it is," I quipped with a haughty lift of my nose that made him laugh. "Now, if you're done gawking, we should go."

"I'm not done," he said, tilting his head slightly as he looked me over.

Feeling exposed, I tried not to squirm under his warm regard. "If you're checking for mismatched buttons, you'll be disappointed because my dress zips in the back."

"Thanks for the tip."

"What? That wasn't a tip. There's absolutely no need for you to know that."

"But now I do," he said, his smile fading as his gaze drank me in. "You are beautiful, Andrea."

The admiration in his eyes was a balm to part of me that had been too wounded to surface until now. And maybe that was the answer to my question of why I'd taken such care dressing for this evening. Maybe I was beginning to resurrect the pieces of myself that had been buried beneath Clark's disinterest.

"Can we please go now?" I asked, feeling woefully out of my depth.

With a sweep of his hand toward an olive-green SUV, he said, "After you."

I was surprised by his vehicle, thinking this sexy single pilot would drive a sports car. "Are you sure you're not a family man?"

"Positive. I just need room for my gear bags and such."

"Well, this beats an old flatbed truck and the hand-me-down beater car I took from my son."

Our conversation remained light, and we found our way to the common area of The Grove where the dance would take place. To my delight, Walter was there, and he greeted Mason with a hearty handshake. "Andie, you're quite the cookie in that dress," he said, giving me a hug.

"Thank you, but speaking of cookies, is Louie with you?"

"Not tonight. I left him in the apartment watching dog tv. He thinks he's on a car ride right now."

We were laughing when Ashe and Kate joined us along with Maggie and Eli, our super sexy CPA. We all sat with Walter at a large circular table near a makeshift bar that served wine, beer, and soft drinks. For twenty minutes, we engaged in fun conversation, but I was frequently tapped on the shoulder by people I didn't know wanting to compliment me on Maggie's sign. Even the mayor, who introduced herself as Savanna, mentioned the possibility of signage work for Dunwith.

When the dance instructor's voice sounded over the sound system, Mason asked the mayor to stop by my shop during business hours because tonight I was his dance partner. Then he playfully pulled me to my feet and whisked me onto the dance floor. But five minutes into the instruction, most dancers seemed to have two left feet and no rhythm.

"Triple step, or one-and-two, and triple step, or three-and-four," the dance instructor said. The man was a resident of The Grove and an accomplished dancer but not the best instructor based on the confused faces of those around us. "Then you execute a rock-step. Just take a small step back with one foot," he continued.

I could see Mason trying to work out the steps in his head. I found it a little satisfying to see him struggling but took pity on him. "It's simple. Just think cha-cha-cha, cha-cha-cha, yee-haw! Turn."

"What?" Mason erupted with laughter.

"Like this," I said, garnering his attention. "Cha-cha-cha is your triple step." I demonstrated a one-and-two step while saying cha-cha-cha. "Yee-haw is your rock-step back." I demonstrated the bouncy backstep. "Then you just turn and do it again."

Maggie, who'd been standing near us with Eli, said, "That's brilliant!" She turned to Ashe who was fumbling the steps with Kate. "Hold up, you two. Andie found a shortcut. Just think cha-cha-cha, cha-cha-cha, yee-haw! Turn."

The befuddled look on Ashe's face sent Mason into another fit of laughter.

"Try it," Maggie said, turning him back to Kate who was taking it all in with humor sparkling in her eyes. Ashe stalled as if trying to recall Maggie's instruction, so she gave him a gentle nudge. "I'll say it for you. Take Kate's hand. Here we go. Cha-cha-cha, cha-cha-cha, yee-haw! Turn."

As Ashe and Kate followed her commands they fell into step with each other, the first few a bit stiff, then they melted into a synchronized flow as if they'd been dancing together for years. Maybe it was just their obvious desire for each other that made them seem so connected, but I envied them all the same.

I looked at Mason. "Brave enough to try again?"

"Absolutely." He clasped my hand and placed his other one on my waist. With a slight tug, he set us in motion, chanting the mantra.

I was laughing so hard I lost my timing. "Stop chanting out loud."

"If I don't say it, I'll miss the steps."

Maggie and Eli moved into the dance, so at ease with each other it was obvious it wasn't their first time together. With each struggling couple they passed, Maggie gave them the shortcut mantra, and before long, the crowd was chanting *Cha-cha-cha, cha-cha-cha, yee-haw! Turn,* much to the instructor's horror.

"It really helps," Mason said to the instructor as we swung past.

I winced. "I hope he never learns I'm the one that started this nonsense."

"Why not? The man could save himself an hour of instruction if he'd just start with your shortcut. How did you come up with it?"

"I cheated," I admitted, enjoying Mason's surprise. "I watched a how-to video, but I kept forgetting the timing and steps, so I came up with the shortcut."

Mason's warm chuckle melted over me, beckoning me closer as the desire to move into his arms consumed me. I missed the feeling of a man's body against mine. I missed sex.

"Andie, when you look at me like that it's very difficult to see you as a friend."

My gaze darted away like a startled bird, then circled back but couldn't find a safe place to land.

"I'm not complaining," he said, giving my waist a gentle squeeze that brought my gaze back to his. "I'm just letting you know I couldn't resist if you followed that path. Because I wouldn't want to."

Cautioning myself to get a grip on my hormones, I drew in a breath to clear my head. "I was just lost in thought is all. Sorry."

"Nothing to apologize for. I just don't want to misread a situation."

He wasn't misreading anything, but I intentionally shifted the topic. "I was thinking about Walter," I said, gesturing with my chin to where Walter sat talking with a couple of his buddies. "I worry about him. He's heartbroken."

"Yeah, it's got to be hell for him, but at least he's making an effort to soldier on," Mason said. "He seems to be enjoying the evening at some level."

I knew too well how laughter could cover a world of heartache. Still, Walter was a wise man who knew how to recognize and appreciate small moments of joy in whatever manner they presented themselves. Even an hour or two joking with friends was something to be treasured.

My faltering steps brought my attention back to our dance and the fact that Mason was doing a better job than I was. "I think I need a break."

"Sure. I could use another drink," he said as we wormed our way through the dancers and headed to the makeshift bar set up for the event. "What can I get you?"

"I'd like another glass of wine, thanks."

While he ordered, I slipped away to the restroom where Kate and Maggie were washing their hands and chatting.

"Andie, your shortcut saved my toes," Kate said, drying her hands on a soft towel. "Ashe was willing to tough it out, but my bruised toes couldn't have tolerated much more abuse." Laughing, she tossed the towel in a tall purple laundry basket. "Thank you."

I cringed a little. "I don't think our instructor appreciated it. And I suspect I'll never hear the end of this now."

"Probably not, but it's all in fun," Maggie said, dropping her towel in the basket. "Mason seemed to enjoy your little cha-cha." She wiggled her eyebrows suggestively. "Did I see some heat in the looks you two exchanged?"

"We're just friends. I'm here for Walter."

"Okay, but a friendship can mean so much more if you want it to." She looked at Kate. "Don't you agree?"

"Absolutely," Kate said. "Friends with benefits is a perfect fit for some of us."

"There are no other benefits between me and Mason"

"From the way he looks at you, there could be," Kate said, surprising me with her bold statement. "That sort of friendship can be wonderfully liberating."

I hadn't considered that aspect, but maybe that's what Mason had meant when he said we could be friends in whatever manner suited me in the moment. Was that his way of letting me know he was open to an arrangement like that? One where our friendship would be multi-layered but without ties or commitments? The idea was tantalizing, enticing, and wildly exciting. But would he be satisfied with a monogamous layer in our friendship? Because I couldn't do multiple sex partners, nor could I expose myself to someone who did. It wasn't a judgement thing for me. It was a health thing. And a trust thing. Because I needed to trust the person I invited into my bed.

The conversation with Kate and Maggie circled my brain all evening. Like a train passing through a tunnel, it would disappear for a few minutes then reappear at inappropriate moments. My body vibrated with longing each time Mason touched me. The warmth of his palm cupping my waist made me hyper-aware of every brush of our bodies. I smelled the hint of sage and cedar I associated with his clean scent. Golden highlights in his sandy hair made me wonder if it was as soft as it looked. It was so thrilling and painful to remain in his arms, I had to break away to save myself, but he scooped me back and pulled me close. "May I have the last dance?"

I looked for Walter, hoping I could talk him into just one dance with me, but he and his buddies were gone. He'd told me earlier in the night he wouldn't stay long, but I was disappointed he didn't say goodbye. "If you don't mind, I'd like to go home now."

"Is my dancing that bad?" Mason asked, giving my hand a gentle squeeze.

"Of course not. I'm just getting tired. Moving and working hasn't left much time for resting."

"I hadn't considered that. Sorry," he said, his hand slipping from my waist as he released me.

We waved to Maggie and Eli and gestured that we were

leaving. I looked for Kate and Ashe, but it appeared they'd ducked out earlier.

On the way to Mason's SUV, I scoured my mind for small talk and came up empty. After a night of music and loud conversation, he seemed to appreciate the quiet night, too, as we made the short drive to my place. I didn't want him to walk me to my door because I didn't trust myself, but he did anyway.

"Thank you for a fun evening," I said, then tried to end the night with my clothes on by turning away to unlock the door.

The gentle pressure of his hand under my elbow turned me back. "I really want to be friends, Andrea. But you can't dress like this and look at me with those beautiful brown eyes and expect me not to kiss you," he said quietly, then lowered his head and made my world tilt off its axis.

We sank into each other with a low moan as he deepened the kiss. All my reservations disappeared in a flood of longing and bone-deep need. I'd been alone so long, an island without a single visitor, and I ached to be occupied by this man who'd stumbled onto my beach.

Could I allow a bit of romance in my life providing it didn't consume me? Before I could decide, he drew back and set me away from him with shaking hands.

"My god," he whispered, his eyes dark with need, and maybe a touch of fear. "I think this friendship is going to kill me. Please show me some mercy and go inside now."

Chapter Twenty

I avoided Sunday Funday in the park, an event I was dying to attend, because I didn't want to risk running into Mason. Other than morning visits with Walter and Louie, I worked alone in my shop, but all I could think about was the kiss and the man who'd rocked my world. Was a "friends with benefits" relationship with Mason possible?

I wondered how Kate and Ashe managed their relationship without consuming each other. How did they avoid encroaching on the other's time or space? Or developing expectations beyond those of a platonic friendship? Were they really friends? Or were they lovers simply afraid of commitment? They seemed to enjoy each other's company and were obviously attracted to each other. Kate had said their arrangement was perfect for her. But what about Ashe? Did he want more? And what if he did? How would that work if one party in the friendship wanted more? Would the friendship implode?

Argh. My head hurt just thinking about the complexity of it all. I reminded my waking libido that I'd moved to Dunwith to pursue my art, not a sexual relationship with any man. So, I studiously steered my mind toward the evening ahead.

Maggie had convinced me to join Kate, Chloe, and her for a self-defense class they attended on the last Tuesday of the month. It sounded like a good way to recenter my attention on empowering myself, so I walked to the martial arts studio seven blocks from my shop. My friends were already there, and they introduced me to Gayle, the owner and instructor. She was dark-haired with a medium build but uber fit with defined muscular arms, so I was surprised to learn she was celebrating her fiftieth birthday. As we slipped off our shoes and moved onto the padded floor of Gayle's dojo, Maggie told me that Gayle did a stint in the Army and held a Black Belt in jujitsu.

"All right, everyone circle-up and take a seat," Gayle said, joining us on the floor. She sat beside a box filled with an odd collection of items. After the group of nearly twenty people of various genders and ages settled in, Gayle explained that there were enough first-time attendees that she wanted to do a quick review of the basics, which would serve as a good reminder for those who'd been attending on a regular basis. "First, we're going to talk about concepts and why they're imperative in self-defense, then we'll get you all on your feet and move into the physical skills that will help you survive a violent attack. After that, you'll get to test your skills against my assistants who will each be wearing a heavily padded red-man suit. All right then, let's get started. Someone give me a concept that relates to self-defense."

"Anything can be used as a weapon," Maggie said.

"Exactly." Gayle pulled a ring of keys from the box. "This can be used as a weapon, but don't weave the keys between your fingers. If you strike something that way, you'll cut your webspace, which is a bad injury." She clutched the keys with the barbed ends sticking out the bottom of her fist. "You can strike and cut like this." She pulled a stapler from the box and demonstrated how it could be used as a weapon, then continued with several more common items like a ruler, a coffee mug, and even a rolled-up magazine. "These are considered improvised weapons," she said. "Now, who can give me another concept related to self-defense?"

"Know your personal doctrine," Chloe said.

"Right! You must determine how far you're willing to go to protect yourself or someone else, and you need to lock that in your brain now because you cannot try to make this decision in the heat of battle. Give me another concept," she said.

"Don't let the attacker take you somewhere else," Kate said.

"Damn right." Gayle slapped the mat so firmly it startled me. "You end the fight right where you are. And you don't quit until you get out. Your only goal is to survive."

For twenty minutes, I sat enthralled and a little scared as she went on talking about several concepts and how they applied to various scenarios. She told us to be aware and prepared, and that doing stupid shit like walking with earbuds in and being focused on your phone makes you a target. At that point, she got us on our feet and paired us with a partner. Kate and Chloe teamed up, so Maggie and I worked together.

Gayle said, "If you can't avoid a life-threatening altercation, here are some simple, effective techniques that work."

In addition to striking the eyes and throat, she showed us wristlocks and finger locks but said attacking joints with a hard twist or crank could yield a similar result. Then she demonstrated a series of strikes and kicks that popped with power and rocked the freestanding punching bags.

From that point forward, Maggie and I exchanged strikes using our palms, elbows, and knees, along with various kicks against pads that sometimes sent me sprawling on the mat. After one tumble, Gayle made me stay on the mat where she demonstrated how a good ground defense worked by using kicks to stop an attacker from moving in or getting around you. Then she stood me up and widened my narrow stance which had caused me to fall. Once I got it, she moved on to assist other groups.

It seemed like only minutes had passed, but the wall clock said we'd been engaged in class for an hour-and-a-half when Gayle clapped her hands and shouted, "All right everyone, stack the pads in that corner and line up along the wall. It's time to test your skillset."

I glanced at Maggie. "What does that mean?"

She gave me a sneaky smile. "You'll see."

A shriek from the far end of the line drew our attention to a person wearing a red padded suit and face cage moving in on one of the female attendees.

"Don't just stand there!" Gayle shouted. "Counter and attack. Move and get out!"

Near tears, the woman started punching her attacker who looked like a beast covered head to toe in a padded red suit with a metal face cage.

"Don't punch with your fist!" Gayle shouted, having cautioned us earlier about getting a fight-bite or a boxer's fracture that could result from striking with a closed fist.

The padded assailant bulldozed the woman all the way to the mat where she lay shrieking and trembling.

Both Gayle and the padded man pulled her gently to her feet and apologized for scaring her but thanked her for allowing them to demonstrate just how terrifying an attack could be and why applying concepts is so important. They asked her to try again, this time under less pressure so she could implement what she'd learned. To my surprise, the woman agreed, and the attacker moved in. Instead of screaming and flailing, the woman moved and struck his face shield with her palm, driving his head back. She cut around him and picked up a padded stick lying on the mat. He moved in, and she hit him, but he yanked the stick from her hand.

"Break!" Gayle shouted. "This is why weapons retention is so important and why so many people are injured or killed with their own weapon. If you can't keep the weapon in your possession, don't present it."

Suddenly, another padded assailant stepped onto the mat and stalked directly toward me. Until this moment, I'd hadn't understood the expression of ice-water running through your veins. My body felt liquid and heavy at the same time.

"Move!" Maggie said, giving me a hard nudge.

As if she'd hit me with a bolt of electricity, I shot my palm into the attacker's mask as I tried to dart away, but I felt two big arms lock around me. Dropping my weight to break his grip, I stomped on his padded foot, then shot my arm out and brought it back with a spinning back elbow strike to his head and followed with a palm strike to his face mask. As he stumbled back, I drove a sloppy heel kick into his abdomen and heard a satisfying *whoof.* Then I ran to the other end of the dojo and hid behind two tall freestanding punching bags we'd used earlier to practice our kicks.

With fear flooding my body and my heartbeat hammering in my ears, the sound of clapping and laughter slowly seeped in. I peeked around the bag, praying the attacker was down, hoping the warm feeling in my legs didn't mean I'd peed my pants.

"Come on out, Andie," Gayle said, laughing. "You did a great job. Exactly what you were supposed to do. You used your weight to disrupt his center and followed up with a combination of strikes that caused enough separation for you to get out." She turned to the man in the padded suit who had accosted me. "Are you okay?"

He gave her a thumbs-up sign, so she had both of her padded-up assistants continue attacking randomly and in various ways, some empty hand and some with a weapon. I wanted to stay hidden behind the freestanding bags, but she put us all through several more rounds of attacks before she told us to take a seat. As a group, we sank onto the mat like weary soldiers. Then Gayle had our attackers remove their protective headgear.

My gasp drew everyone's attention, but mine was locked on Gayle's assistants—Ashe McKensie and Mason Burke. Both men were red-faced and sweaty, their hair askew from headgear that had been pummeled, pulled, and twisted by their intended victims. Gayle started our debriefing, and I glanced at Maggie. "Did you know they were doing this?" I whispered.

She smiled. "Who do you think asked them?"

"You could have told me."

"And ruin the surprise?" She winked and turned her attention to Gayle who was doing a quick review of our training.

As I listened and made mental notes, I tried to avoid Mason's gaze and the humor dancing in his eyes. By the time Gayle wrapped up the evening, I told Maggie I was ready for a cold drink.

"Great, because we always go to the Brewery after fight-night."

I laughed and said I was in. "How long before we meet there?" I asked, drying my sweaty face with the hand towel I'd brought and looking forward to a soothing shower.

"We're going now," she said.

"Oh, I thought everyone would want to clean up first."

"Nope. A cold beer tastes best when you're a hot, sweaty mess."

I couldn't argue with that, so I hooked my towel around my neck and followed her outside into a warm July night where Kate and Chloe were waiting—with Ashe and Mason.

Realizing that Mason was a permanent part of this circle of friends and avoiding him wasn't an option, I said hello and asked how he felt after being used as a punching bag.

"Thirsty," he said, garnering avid agreement from the others.

"Kate and I parked at the brewery and walked down," Chloe said. "So we're all walking."

As the six of us headed to the brewery, Ashe and Mason fell in behind us. I was surprised that Ashe didn't pair up with Kate, that he didn't take her hand or lay claim to her. But they both seemed perfectly content being part of this group of friends. Over the course of several blocks, the group positions shifted and morphed as conversations moved between them. I thought about the events I'd attended with Clark and how we, and other couples, needed to sit together as if it were law. That mindset seemed so odd and restrictive now. I was so caught up observing my new group of friends that Maggie's squeal startled me.

"I love my sign!" she said, pointing it out as we walked past her shop. The others echoed her sentiments and complimented my talent.

"It's really impressive," Kate said. "Makes me wish I'd have had you make my Done With sign."

"Oh my god," I said with a laugh. "No sign could ever top that one. It's one-of-a-kind."

Kate's misadventures with her dumbass ex had us laughing as we crossed the brewery parking lot. Circling around back, we found Bobbie Jo and a blonde-haired lady sitting at a large table outside on the deck. When Bobbie Jo spotted our group, she called out a cheery greeting and told us to join them. As we sat, she introduced me to her friend Leila, who was on the town council, then told her I'd just bought the fab shop.

"Oh, I've been meaning to stop by to meet you," Leila said. "You're the artist who made that fabulous sign in front of Maggie's shop, right?"

"She is indeed!" Maggie said, giving me a side-armed hug and a little shake. "We ran into Mayor Savanna the other night who said you might want signs for the town, but you better order fast before Andie gets too busy."

Leila turned back to me. "Actually, we are interested in your work. We're considering a feature for the park to commemorate our inaugural *Done With Day*. I'd like to discuss the project and some ideas with you. Would you be willing to stop by the office this week?"

A little thrill zipped through me. "Of course, just let me know what works with your schedule."

"I'll be there at seven tomorrow morning. Give me your card, and I'll text you my schedule for the day."

I hadn't ordered cards because I wasn't sure what I'd be advertising. Welding? Fabricating? Or just metal art? "I don't have business cards yet, but I can give you my number. Anyone have a pen handy?"

"Let me give you my card," Leila said, slipping a blue card from her phone wallet and handing it to me. "Text me in the morning."

By the time our waiter refilled our drinks, we were hungry and craving salty food. We ordered fries, onion petals, and cheese pretzels and shared them family-style.

Mason gripped his jaw and made a show of wiggling it side to side. "Andie, I think your spinning elbow might have dislocated my jaw."

"Doubtful," I said. "My elbow hit your mask, and I've got the bruise to prove it."

"I don't doubt it's bruised," Ashe said. "You clocked him a good one."

"Well, I didn't know who was behind the mask," I said in my defense. "He looked like a big red beast, and I was so terrified I really thought I peed my pants."

A chorus of laughter erupted from around the table.

"I get it," Kate said. "I bit the guy's neck pads because my mouth was the only part of me not frozen in fear. It felt as if I'd levitated out of my body."

"Same here," Maggie said. "I locked my arms and legs around the guy and screamed in his ear. I think Jeff is still hard of hearing on that side."

"No wonder he refused when I asked him to assist in tonight's class," Chloe said, setting us off again.

As we ordered more food and drinks, I vowed to do whatever it took to succeed here because I couldn't bear the thought of losing this life or these wonderful friends.

Chapter Twenty-One

I texted Leila at seven-thirty to say my schedule was open all day, and she asked me to stop by at ten o'clock. I showered, dressed, and enjoyed a brief coffee date with Walter and Louie, then headed to her office.

It was such a gorgeous morning, I decided to walk. Allowing myself plenty of time, I took the river walk past the brewery, then crossed the Dunwith River on the west walking bridge. The unique shops occupying several blocks from Dunwith center to the riverfront were treasure troves of beautiful hand-made items I'd hoped to explore with Tyler, but he would be heading to college in less than three weeks. He was due to return from his buddy trip this coming weekend, and I'd let him know in my last text message that I fully intended to see him. He replied with a thumbs-up emoji that I knew meant *yeah, sure but no guarantee*. Well, we'd see about that.

My walk took me past the airport, and I wondered if Mason was there or up in his kite-sized plane. Shielding my eyes with one hand, I scouted the cloudless sky but didn't see any planes, then wondered if I'd even be able to see Mason's small ultra-light. Thinking about the sexy pilot was counterproductive to my day, so I focused on what kind of project the town might be looking for.

After stretching my legs, I doubled back the way I'd come. The town offices were located on my side of the park about five blocks down from my building.

Leila was waiting in her office when I arrived. With a cheery hello, she beckoned me inside. After offering me a beverage, which I declined, she jumped right into the project details. "We want to commemorate the purposeful evolution of our town with something that will symbolize our intentional unity, equality, and protection of nature and wildlife, which is what our community stands for. We're calling it *Done With Day*."

"Yes, I've been told about it," I said, loving this bold, forward-thinking town. "Did you want a sign of some sort?"

"Well, we don't know exactly. We just want something at the center of the park that can be seen by people traveling through town in either direction."

"Would you consider a metal sculpture?"

Her eyes brightened. "Oh, that would be fabulous. We've raised ten thousand dollars for the project. I know that's not a large amount, but would that be enough for a sculpture?"

"Maybe, depending on the size and type of materials used. One sheet of stainless steel can cost a thousand dollars, so it really depends on what you want."

"Oh, my gosh," she said with wide eyes. "I had no idea." A look of defeat crossed her face. "I suspect we'll have to settle for a sign."

"Not necessarily. Mild steel costs much less. Your budget would probably cover material costs, and I'd be willing to donate my time and labor," I said, wanting to support Leila and my new community in their admirable and important mission.

"Oh, I don't know, Andie. I feel we'd be taking advantage of you and your talent."

"Not at all. I'll get exposure for my work, so it would be a win for both of us. When would you need the sculpture delivered?"

"We're planning a commemoration celebration for the first Sunday in October. So, if you were to do a sculpture, we'd want to do an unveiling that day as well."

A fast mental calculation told me I'd have just under ten weeks to complete the sculpture. A tight window, but if I didn't take any other jobs, I felt confident I could do it. Still, I'd be committing to a job without pay. Not the best business decision perhaps, but it was a rare opportunity to establish myself as a resident artist. It was a big gamble. If the sculpture didn't meet their approval, my credibility as an artist would be lost before it was fully established. Maggie's sign wouldn't carry much weight if the sculpture in the park center was subpar.

"That's a pretty tight window," I said, the pressure already making me queasy.

"Yes, we are a bit short on time," Leila said, "but we're so excited about this event. The whole community will be there, so I hope you can make this work because I suspect the council will wholeheartedly want you for this project."

A wild thrill and sharp anxiety swirled through my belly.

"I'll need to get their approval, of course, and even though you're willing to donate your time this will be a work-for-hire project, so you'll need to sign a contract. The town would own the sculpture and be responsible for its upkeep, but you would retain the copyright."

"I understand. What type of sculpture would you want?"

She tapped her pen on a blotter calendar filled with notations that looked like meeting times. "I really don't know. The fox sign you created for Maggie's store is cute and perfect for her business, indicating you understand the subject matter and the vision of your client, and more importantly that you can convey that in the finished product. Something oriented toward wildlife would be nice, but I suspect we'll be thrilled with whatever you come up with."

"I hope so because it will be painfully awkward if you're not," I said with a nervous laugh.

She gave me a sympathetic smile as if she sensed my concern. "Surprise us and I bet you'll surprise yourself, too."

Frankly, I'd already surprised myself for agreeing to take a job under an extremely tight deadline and put my work on such a public stage.

"All right, Andie, the meeting today is mostly a formality," Leila said. "I'll let you know when the work-for-hire contract will be ready to sign."

I left with hope in my heart and knots in my stomach. The idea of creating another sculpture thrilled me, but I'd need to give the piece deep thought and careful consideration before diving in. I needed some inspiration.

I remembered Mason mentioning the metal sculptures at the Wild Center, so I texted Tyler to ask if he'd like to go with me when he returned from his trip.

His reply was an immediate *No thanks. Maybe dinner?*

Here in Dunwith? I texted back.

Can't. Pizza and wings at the Grill?

After years of Clark and Tyler's preferred diet, pizza or wings were the last thing I'd order, but I texted *Sure. Sunday?*

We'll be driving back. Monday okay?

After agreeing to drive down on Monday, I decided to head over to the Wild Center on my own. I needed to walk and think and be visually stimulated, which is exactly what the gorgeous grounds offered. I followed trails that crossed suspension bridges over ponds adorned with water lilies, colorful fish, and other amphibians. I wandered a bit and came across primitive type huts an artist had created primarily with tree saplings.

Observing how the thin saplings were woven, creating the structure's shape and tying everything together, reminded me how my dad and I had used quarter inch round bar to shape the sculpture we'd never had the chance to finish.

My curiosity led me down trails where signs revealed information about the wildlife, flora, and fauna of the area. Various scrap metal sculptures made by an artist named Bellinger began to appear amid towering trees and were visible from the winding path I was walking. My footfalls were softened by a fragrant bed of pine needles as I meandered through the forest. String instruments began to sound from hidden speakers, sometimes far away, sometimes right beside me. The low, soft tones of a marimba and other percussive instruments created a gentle pulse, an immersive experience that enveloped me in the womb of the forest. The music was so beautiful, so moving, I stood for a long time just listening with my eyes closed.

My dad would have enjoyed this place. He was always inspired by nature. Some of my best memories of my family involved visits to local parks. My mother and sister would sunbathe while my dad and I checked out hiking trails. He'd point out various trees and note the shape of their trunks and how their branches would reach out like arms as if to embrace the world. He said they communicated through their vast interconnected root system and that their strong foundation allowed them to tower high above us. The correlation he'd made between trees and sculptures stuck with me, but when he died, I ripped up the roots connecting me with family.

And I'd done it again when I divorced Clark.

Now, my new network of friends was helping me set down new roots here, but my son was moving farther away. I hoped one day our roots would grow strong again and keep us connected no matter how many miles separated us.

The sound of people talking steered my wandering thoughts

back to the metal sculpture I'd been studying. As the small family passed, we exchanged a nod of greeting, but they left me to my observation. The metal sculptures were interesting and creative. While obviously very talented, the artist's style was rougher cut, for lack of a better definition, than the work I envisioned doing. I leaned toward the style of John Walsh. His sculptures were so unbelievably amazing, I envied his talent as deeply as I admired it.

Moving on, I followed a trail that took me to the Oxbow on the Raquette River. For a long time, I sat on the canoe dock watching the river. Birds and fish and people paddling canoes disrupted the sparkling surface but not the serene beauty of the place. This is what I wanted my sculpture to represent. Serenity, beauty, wild freedom, and yet it had to emanate the power of the human spirit. A tall order I wasn't sure I could produce—and a big gamble for my career as an artist.

I'd been back at my shop about an hour and was digging through boxes when I heard a car pull in. Wondering if I was about to get a customer, I stood and dusted off my hands and knees. When I saw Clark step inside, my heart clenched in fear.

"What's happened?" I squawked, so terrified something had happened to our son that my vision swam.

"What?" He frowned. "Nothing's happened. Why?"

"Oh my god." I gasped and sagged against the workbench.

"Are you okay?" he asked, eyeing me with wary concern.

"Jesus, Clark, I thought you were here because something happened to Tyler."

"He's fine."

I released a shaky breath. "Then why are you here?"

"I brought paperwork for you to sign. For the house," he

said, waving the folder in his hand. "You need to get your signature notarized, then send the papers to my attorney."

"All right. I'll do it tomorrow."

Acknowledging my promise with a short nod, he directed his attention to my shop. "This is quite a place," he said, then gave me a playful smile. "Are you hiring? I've got plenty of fabricating experience."

While I appreciated his attempt to ease the chronic tension between us, I wasn't at all charmed by him. I didn't appreciate his penchant for barking at me as he had during our last meeting, then acting like nothing had transpired.

"You could do a lot of work in here," he said.

"On cars, you mean?"

He shrugged. "Sure. That too."

"It's a one-woman shop, and there won't be any freaking cars in my place," I said, not meaning for my words to come out so abrasive. But by the offended look on his face, I knew they had.

"Excuse me. I thought you liked my cars."

"I can appreciate that they're classic beauties. Doesn't mean I want them in my shop."

"Is that what all of this is about?" he asked, sweeping his hand out to encompass my business. "You divorced me because my cars were taking up space in the garage?"

"What? No. Well, yes but that's just the tip of a large iceberg."

"I thought you enjoyed going to car shows as a family."

"I did for the first few years but not every year of our marriage." My comment seemed to wound him. "Clark, that's all we did, week after week, year after year. Nothing ever changed. Your playlist was locked on repeat. Car shows and sporting events. If we weren't doing one of those things, you were miserable and had no interest in anything else."

"Why didn't you tell me you weren't happy?" he asked, his voice quiet and so sincere I knew it was if he was hearing this for the first time.

"I did, but you never heard me, and I shouldn't have had to anyway. You should have known I was in distress when I started talking to a therapist."

"I thought you were stressed out because of your job."

"No, Clark, I was falling apart because my husband was emotionally absent."

Frowning, he rubbed the back of his neck, a tendency of his when he was skeptical of something. "I don't remember those discussions."

"I'm not surprised."

He dropped his hand to his side. "What's that mean?"

"It means that I mentioned my concerns several times. When I tried to tell you about the conversations I had with my therapist, you'd just grunt and nod your head, but your attention was always centered on a football game or on a car engine you were puttering with. I came right out and asked you once if you were ever worried about our marriage, and you said no and started talking about a completely unrelated subject as if my question merited no thought or consideration. You didn't even acknowledge my feelings. You were completely checked out, and I couldn't live with your indifference any longer."

"But I did care about you, Andie. I didn't want to lose you."

"You didn't lose me, Clark. You erased me!"

My revelation was met with his blank stare.

"You left no room for me."

"I don't understand."

"That's because you choose not to. You didn't want to know anything that might upset your own world. Every time you shrugged off my concerns or changed the subject or walked away in the middle of a conversation, you erased me. Every time you sighed and rolled your eyes, you shut me out and shut me down. You made me feel I had to apologize for my presence, so I quit talking. Your need to control the way we lived and how we spent our time left no room for my needs that didn't align with yours. You consumed everything in your path and in my life. I couldn't freaking breathe, Clark!"

Releasing my truth, that I'd repressed for so long, left me trembling and Clark speechless. But it was a cathartic moment for me because I'd just gained a clear, albeit painful, insight to the man I'd married. I'd thought he was safe, like a meadow filled with morning glory where I could take refuge, heal, and learn to bloom again. I didn't realize I was planting myself with bindweed that would sink its roots deep in the earth and consume me and everything around it. I'd had to uproot myself completely to survive. And now he was here, continuing to send out runners, trying to link with me and sink his roots back in the rich soil of my new life.

Silence vibrated between us for several seconds before he spoke. "Are you saying you divorced me because we didn't talk enough?"

He was sincerely asking, and I wanted to weep because I knew he'd never get it. "Clark, I divorced you because I had nothing left to give you. I was empty and exhausted. I wanted a minute to myself, to rest, to take care of me for one fucking day without having to apologize for being selfish or shortchanging my family."

"You never shortchanged us. You were an amazing wife and mother, Andie."

"I know I was, and you took advantage of my love and my desire to make a happy life for you and Tyler. I gave myself away, and you took all of me without a single thought to my own needs or happiness. But I share the blame for allowing your behavior and for not valuing myself enough to demand better." I waved my hand to dismiss the subject. "It's a moot point now and a conversation that continues in an exhausting loop. Our marriage is over, Clark. Why it ended no longer matters. Just let it be. I'll get the agreement for the house signed tomorrow."

For a moment, he stood unmoving, as if trying to absorb the finality of our divorce. Then, with a slow nod, he passed the folder to me. "I'm sorry." Without another word, he squared his shoulders and headed outside to his car.

As he drove away, I wondered if he'd been apologizing for being so oblivious. Then I realized it didn't matter because that broken piece of my life was one I couldn't fix, and one I no longer wanted.

Chapter Twenty-Two

On Friday morning, I showed Leila three variations of a sculpture and gave her an estimate on materials for each one. She called an hour later and said the project was approved and they'd leave the design to me. I placed an order for sheet metal and welding wire with one of my former customers and scheduled the delivery for Monday morning.

I was working on the sculpture design in my CAD program when I received a text from Maggie letting me know there wouldn't be a girl gab tonight because she was still out of town and Chloe wasn't feeling well. I'd been looking forward to escaping the shop and my own anxieties for a few hours of fun with my new gal pals, but I was a little relieved that an evening alone would allow me to get some much-needed design work done.

But the more I did over the weekend, the less inspired I became. The town council was expecting a sculpture like the fox on Maggie's sign. It would be a painstaking, physically demanding job with only a modicum of reward for me in an artistic sense. But for this project, I had to work with sheet metal and support the community's mission to the best of my ability.

The only breaks I took were brief naps on the sofa and short morning visits with Walter and Louie. After they left on Sunday morning, I tried to sink back into my work, but my brain refused to cooperate.

I cleaned up, then walked over to the park to experience my first Sunday Funday. The joyful atmosphere lifted my spirits, and I wandered with blissful abandon for a long time, just enjoying the sights and sense of community. I bought a hand-made cloth shopping bag and filled it with fresh organic produce from the farmer's market.

Booths displaying handmade arts and crafts lined both sides of the park and stretched several blocks long. As I wandered, I admired gorgeous painted pottery and custom jewelry pieces. I sampled delicious baked goods and bought two jars of home-made preserves. I slathered my work-roughened hands with samples of homemade body lotion and purchased a small bottle of neroli-scented bath oil. A booth of handmade children's toys captivated me for several minutes. Memories of Tyler as a sweet toddler made me miss my little boy, and I hoped he might give me grandchildren one day.

As people gently negotiated around one another, some chat-ting, some wandering as aimlessly as I was, I found myself carried along in the flow. A booth of paintings caught my eye, and I stopped to examine the oil on canvas landscapes. The artist had not only captured the beauty of the Adirondacks in colorful, gorgeous detail but also in photographs of wildlife that took my breath away. I purchased a photograph of a colorful Cecropia moth perched on a daisy. As the artist slipped the photograph into a cardboard sleeve, she said the moth never eats, which boggled my mind. Apparently, they exist only to mate and lay eggs. I found that incredibly sad and wondered how many women would feel a kinship to the poor creature.

The next booth was filled with home décor items that made

me wish Maggie was with me to select some pieces for my apartment. There was so much to choose from I found myself overwhelmed and a little anxious. Finally, I purchased a wood plaque painted with green leaves and the words *relax, breathe, unwind.*

"Do you think the reminder will help?" a male voice asked from behind me.

I glanced over my shoulder to find Mason wearing dark sunglasses and a warm smile that caused a flutter in my belly.

"If it doesn't, I'm going to return it."

He laughed. "I hear you're working on a sculpture for our *Done With Day*. That's got to be rather rewarding and exciting."

I nodded, but this time the flutter in my belly was from anxiety. "It is, but it's also a bit of a challenge."

"Anything I can help with?"

"No, I'm just whining a little. Beginning a project is like hiking a mountain. Starting out is exciting and a little overwhelming, but once I get my rhythm, my focus will shift to the work at hand, and I should be fine."

"All right, but if you need someone to carry your backpack for a while, you've got my number."

I smiled. "I sure do."

He raised his palms and took a step back. "I haven't trespassed since our cha-cha dance."

He hadn't but I sort of wished he would. "Where is everyone?" I asked, glancing around to see if Ashe or any of my gal pals were with him.

"I came alone. We usually meet at the bandstand around five o'clock."

Maggie had texted me last night to say she was back in town and hoped I'd meet her Sunday afternoon in the park. "What time is it?"

Mason checked his wristwatch, a complex device I'd noticed before and wondered about. "It's four-thirty."

"I had no idea it was so late. I've been wandering the park for hours."

"It's easy to do with all this going on."

I gestured to the rows of vendors. "There's so much here, but I didn't notice much in the way of metal art. Would that sort of thing not sell here?" I asked, truly curious and hoping that wasn't the case.

"I suspect it's simply that no one local is making that sort of thing." He glanced over. "Are you thinking of selling metal art?"

I shrugged. "Maybe, if it's okay to sell it here."

"Anything except drugs and porn is acceptable. Maggie sells antiques and some of her consignment items here once a month."

The idea of selling my art here was exciting, but I kept my thoughts to myself. "Well, I'd better get going. I promised to meet Maggie at the bandstand, but I'm going to run this stuff home first."

"Mind if I join you?" he asked. "I'll carry your books for you."

I smiled at his schoolboy reference. "No books today, but you can carry this," I said, passing him the heavy cloth sack of produce and preserves. As we passed a large chalkboard on a rolling stand, I noticed a colorful display of work needed and help wanted notations along with business cards tucked along the bottom of the board. There were also offers from volunteers willing to do yard work, cooking, cleaning, childcare, pet sitting, chauffeuring, and other jobs at no charge. "Is that for real?" I asked, surprised to see services offered for free.

Mason nodded. "Some people really need help but can't afford it, so the folks who can give a bit of their time do so."

"What a weird and wonderful town," I said.

Mason laughed. "That would be a great town motto."

"I'll be sure to mention that to Leila at our next meeting," I said, flexing my stiff fingers. I nodded toward the wide band he was wearing around his wrist. "What kind of watch is that?"

He glanced at his forearm, then back at me. "It's an aviator smartwatch."

"Okay, that tells me nothing."

"It's basically a touchscreen computer with tools for navigation. When I fly my planes, I use it to track flight time and fuel burn. I get aviation weather information and customizable alerts and can use it to set my flight plan among other things."

I squinted hard. "I think my brain is bleeding," I said, pressing two fingertips to my temple.

He laughed. "Now you know how foolish and boggled I felt when you tried to educate me on welding."

"I do now. But I figured your watch was just a glorified compass and flashlight, so we're both guilty of making assumptions."

His mouth quirked up on one side. "You know what they say about making assumptions."

"Yeah, it seems we're both a couple of asses."

His laughter rang out as we crossed the park. "Well, I guess we have nothing left to prove to each other then."

The man was so damn charming I found him impossible to resist. But I fully intended to do so. After my recent conversation with Clark and realizing how I'd let him consume me, I wasn't allowing anyone to plant themselves in my field.

* * *

Tyler texted that he was running late and would meet me at his favorite pizza place. I'd been waiting ten minutes when he bolted in the door.

"Sorry, Mom. Crazy day," he said, popping a kiss on my cheek.

"Hold on a sec," I said, standing and pulling him into my lonely mommy arms. "I need to hug you."

"Jeez, Mom, we're in a restaurant," he said, but he returned my hug, then sat across from me on the worn vinyl seat of our window booth.

"How was your trip?" I asked, both eager and a bit apprehensive to hear how four teenaged boys managed on their own in a beach house.

"It was great," he said, looking at the menu and tapping his thumb on the table.

"What does 'great' mean?"

"No broken bones. No trashed house. No police. Everyone survived."

I placed my hand over his knobby knuckles. "I'm not digging for private information or trying to be intrusive. I'm just genuinely interested in your vacation. You know, did you swim in the ocean? Did you find any good places to eat? Did you guys have fun? That sort of thing."

Looking a little chagrinned, he leaned back in his seat. "It was nice. We swam every day. The beach was great. Joey fell asleep and got scorched. The dumbass is still peeling," Tyler said with a laugh. "We mostly ate at a burger joint down the beach, but we went to a real restaurant one night and I tried grouper for the first time."

"You did?" I asked in surprise.

"Yeah, and it was really good. There are several places we didn't get a chance to check out, so the guys and I are going back on our first long break." The spark of excitement in his eyes was one I didn't see often, so I didn't tell him I'd been hoping he'd come to Dunwith during his break. "Joey's kind of hung up on a girl he met down there," Tyler continued, "so he's definitely eager to go back."

"I suspect you boys met a lot of girls on the beach."

His mouth quirked. "We met a few."

I raised my palms. "Okay, that's all your mama wants to know."

He laughed and seemed more at ease, more like his old self. After we placed our order with the waiter, Ty rested his forearms on the table. They were muscled now, but I remembered so clearly how he'd stand on the booth seat beside me and whack his tiny fists on the tabletop.

"So how are things in Dunwith?" he asked. "Is your shop open for business yet?"

"Sort of. Like I mentioned last time we talked, I made a sign for my friend's business. Now I'm working on a sculpture for the town. Oh, and my apartment update is done." I pulled out my phone and showed him photos. "This will be your room. It's small, but you'll have your own space when you stay," I said, hinting and hoping he would.

"Looks about the size of my dorm room."

"Just about. Are you getting excited about college?"

He shrugged. "I'm looking forward to campus life."

I moaned dramatically. "I hope you aren't going to school just for the parties."

"Ha-ha, Mom."

I hoped that meant he intended to apply himself, but his intentions would only become clear with time. "Is there anything you need for college?"

He wiggled his eyebrows. "Just cash."

"Okay, let your father know what you need. College expenses are his obligation now."

As if I'd flicked his chin, Tyler drew his head back and seemed a little offended. "Jeez, Mom, you asked."

"I know, sweetie, and I didn't mean to sound harsh." I told him about the agreement I'd made with his father, giving Clark the house in exchange for covering Tyler's college expenses. "We did it this way to keep your home, Tyler, but the agreement was very lopsided in your father's favor, which is why he's responsible for your college expenses."

"Oh, okay. Sorry. I didn't know the situation."

"You didn't need to know. But now that you do, I want to make it clear I'm still here for you. I want you to know that."

"I do."

"All right then, when are you planning to move into your dorm?"

"On the first move-in day. Joey and I want to set up our room then check out the campus and more of the town."

"Good plan. I'll follow you down and help you get settled in."

"What?" He looked horrified. "No way, Mom."

His outburst rocked me back a little. "That was a bit strong."

"Well, I'm not heading off to kindergarten. You've already been to the campus with me, and I'm assigned a dorm room, so you know I can manage to move in on my own."

"I'm sure you can, but maybe for just one second you could consider how I might feel about this? That maybe I need to do this thing for my son who is leaving the nest?"

"Why, Mom? You left first."

He couldn't have wounded me more if he'd stabbed my hand with his fork. For a few seconds, I focused on breathing and keeping my eyes from welling up. Finally, when I could find my voice, I said, "Do you hate me for leaving?"

"What? God, no." He released a sigh, and his eyes filled with apology. "I wasn't trying to be mean, and I don't hate you. I understand why you moved to Dunwith. All I'm saying is I'd rather not have my mommy take me to school. Joey and I plan to go down together. His car is trashed right now, so he's going to ride with me. That's all."

"Okay," I said, reminding myself that this move was about Tyler and his needs, not my own. "But I can't say it doesn't hurt a little that you don't need me anymore."

His lips quirked and he cocked his head as if I were being childish. "It's not about my needing you. It's about me not wanting to be coddled like a five-year-old."

"I know. I'm just being whiney about you growing up and becoming so independent." I gave his hand a squeeze. "I have a new bedding set for you in my car. The sheets, blanket, and bedspread are washed and ready to use, if you want them."

"Sure, if they don't have cartoon characters on them."

I laughed. "I considered it," I said, teasing him a little. "Will solid brown and beige work?"

"That works. Thanks, Mom."

He sat back while our waiter placed our pizza on the table along with two plates and a small salad for me. Ty dug in, shoveling pizza into his mouth like a typical teenage guy, as if he hadn't eaten in a week. While I ate my salad and Tyler inhaled his pizza, I told him about my trip to the Wild Center and more about Dunwith. He talked about his animation classes and how he hoped to work for a large studio when he graduated. The idea of someday working on movies had him so excited, his expressions so animated, I saw flashes of my vibrant little boy. I relished his enthusiasm and encouraged him to share more about his chosen area of study and a career path I knew little about.

After I paid our bill, we walked outside together to get the bedding I'd brought down for him. "Whoa, you're still driving my old car?" he asked, giving the beater a sweeping glance.

"It works for now," I said, hoping it would work for a long time because I couldn't afford a car payment.

"Well, it's a lot cleaner than when I had it," he said, reaching in the back seat to get his bedding that I'd zipped into a plastic case I'd kept from an old comforter. "Smells better, too."

I followed him to his car where he tossed the bedding onto the passenger seat. Backpacks, gym bags, and a slew of food containers were strewn throughout his car. "This is starting to look like the mess you had in the beater. I'd hoped you'd take better care of this one."

"I do, Mom. This is all our crap from vacation. I haven't dropped Joey's stuff off or gotten mine out yet. We just got back last night."

"Okay, my mistake. I'd just hoped to get a ride in your new car. Maybe next time?"

"Yeah, for sure."

"Okay then. Please make sure you text me when you're settled in at school."

"I will, but I'll talk to you before then."

I hoped so, but I knew that "talking" for his generation meant texting, so I'd need to be the one to call. The trick would be getting him to answer the phone.

Chapter Twenty-Three

On the way home from visiting Tyler, I stopped at a garage sale and picked up a second-hand electric cable hoist for my shop. On Thursday morning, Ashe came over to run a separate electrical line for it.

While Ashe was up on a ladder installing the wire, I stood below answering his questions about the placement of the hoist. Walter sat on a stool with his back against the frame of the open overhead door, sipping his coffee. Louie lounged at his feet, drifting in and out of sleep. Two standing fans in the shop oscillated slowly, wafting warm August air through the building and creating a soft drone.

I was so engaged with what Ashe was doing overhead that I didn't realize we had company until a man called my name. The voice sounded so familiar, I turned in disbelief to see my former boss entering the shop with another man carrying a portfolio in one hand.

"Good morning, Andie!" Mr. Norton chirped as if we were the best of friends.

"What are you doing here?" I asked, utterly bewildered.

"I heard you opened your shop and thought I'd stop by and introduce you to the new rep for your area."

The rep who had taken my old job extended his hand with a bit of trepidation, as if he sensed my hostility toward his boss. "Pleased to meet you," he said.

Dumbstruck, I shook the man's hand while repeating my question to my former boss. "Why are you here?"

Nozzle-nose puffed up with importance. "We just made a call at Jonah's shop, and he said you placed an order with him. We stopped in to remind you that we can supply your welding wire."

"No, you can't," I said, finally snapping out of my stupor.

"Sure we can!" he countered, his tone condescending as a big smile bloomed beneath his hawkish nose. "We're making deliveries to the area once a week now."

"I don't care if you're delivering every day. I'm not buying anything from you."

"Now hold on, Andie. Let me finish," he said, thrusting his hand up a mere inch from my face.

Fury exploded behind my eyes, and I grabbed his stubby fingers and cranked them backwards, dropping him to his knees with a yelp of pain. "Get the hell out of my shop, you condescending jackass."

"What the hell, Andie?" he snapped, so outraged his face flamed red. He struggled to his feet, clutching his fingers against his abdomen. "I ought to have you charged with assault."

Walter straightened on the stool, and Louie sat up with a growl.

"Get out," I said.

He glowered and straightened his shoulders as if trying to back me off.

"Hey, fella. You heard the lady!" Walter said, his graveled

voice as menacing as Louie's growl. He thumbed toward the door. "Scram."

The rep headed outside, an odd expression on his face as if losing his struggle not to laugh.

Casting a scathing look in my direction, Nozzle-nose stalked outside, then yanked on the door handle and yelped. "God-dammit!" he said, shaking his abused hand, then opened the door with his other one. He slammed it behind him, and by the time they pulled out of the parking lot in front of my shop, Walter was hooting with laughter.

"Wow!" Ashe said stepping off the ladder. "Remind me to never piss you off."

My breath sailed out, and I pressed a hand to my belly. "Did I really just do that?" I asked, wondering if I'd just experienced a lucid dream.

"You did," Ashe said, wearing a delighted grin. "I was about to make my presence known when you dropped the dumbass." He released a belt of laughter. "The girls are going to love this story."

I cupped my burning cheeks between my palms. "God, I probably traumatized that poor sales rep." Glancing outside, I was relieved to see the lot empty. "Do you think Mr. Norton will file charges against me?"

"No way that guy's going to tell anyone a woman just dropped his sorry ass to his knees," Ashe said, chuckling and wiping his hands on a rag. "He'll lick his wounds in private. But I got to tell you, Andie, your self-defense instructor would be proud."

* * *

I'd been working ten days straight on the sculpture for the town when Maggie came by and convinced me to take a break. She waited in my living room while I took a quick shower and pulled on shorts and a T-shirt over my bathing suit that she'd insisted I wear. It was Sunday, and we were going to spend a day on the river is all she would tell me, so I slipped sunscreen, a sarong-style cover up, and a thick towel in my bag along with my wallet, house key, and sunglasses.

"Girl where are your curtains and area rugs?" she asked as I walked into the living room braiding my wet hair.

"I haven't had time to shop for anything but groceries. And even if I had time, I really don't know what to get. I was serious when I asked you to decorate for me."

She shook her head as if thoroughly disappointed in me. "I thought all artists had a sense of style."

"Not this one. I'm a plain-Jane, I guess." After securing the end of my braid with an elastic band, I dropped it behind my back and readjusted the shoulder strap of my bag. "Please put me out of my misery and say you'll finish the job."

"I guess I'll have to if you're ever going to have curtains in this place." Giving the room a final scan, she turned toward the kitchen. "Come on, let's get out of here and forget about curtains and sculptures for the day."

"Sounds wonderful," I said, pulling on a hat as I followed her out to her van. We both slipped our sunglasses on, then she drove to a boat ramp at the far end of town a short distance from the White Tail Winery. To my surprise, Sophie was there with Kate and Chloe. "I wonder how Sophie managed to escape her busy café for the day?"

"It doesn't happen often," Maggie said, "but she's fun to have around."

"Looks like this is shaping up to be a great girls' day, but I wish I would have picked up some drinks and food on the way over."

"We have plenty of both," Maggie said, gesturing for me to follow the others onto the boat.

With towels slung over their shoulders and coolers clutched in their hands, Kate, Sophie, and Chloe stepped off the dock onto the tan nonslip carpeting of a large pontoon boat. Bench seating ran along both sides in the rear. A canopy covered the back and driver's area, but the two seats up front were uncovered.

That's when I noticed Mason sitting in the captain's seat wearing dark sunglasses and a gray bucket-style hat with breathable mesh openings on the sides. I whispered to Maggie. "Is he coming with us?"

"Yeah, he rented the boat, and Ashe is coming, too," she said, pointing out her brother who was leaning over the side to release the lines tethering the boat to the dock. "It's just a bunch of friends getting together for a fun, relaxing day on the river, so chill and enjoy it."

"Okay," I said, following Maggie onto the boat, but I wasn't sure how relaxed I'd feel spending the day with Mason. I didn't have time to consider it further because everyone seemed to be greeting us at once and asking what we wanted to drink. As the boat undulated beneath me, I wobbled my way to a seat beside Kate and opted to start with water.

"Good idea," Chloe said, pulling two bottles from her cooler. "No alcohol if you're piloting the boat." She gave one to me, then to Maggie. "And always hydrate before alcohol, right, Maggie?"

Maggie leaned back against the tan vinyl seat and crossed her legs. "That was the worst hangover I've ever experienced. I think I have PTSD from that trauma."

"Me, too," Chloe said, sitting beside Sophie in the seat opposite us. "I was stuck on the boat with you barfing off the siderail for two hours."

Ashe pushed us away from the dock. "You were gross, Maggie."

"You guys suck," she said, making a face. "Mason, turn on the music so I don't have to listen to these mean women."

A chorus of *no's* came from her mean friends, but Mason apparently took Maggie's side because music started playing softly from the speakers. The sound was laid back and easy, and I felt myself sinking back in my seat.

I glanced at Mason whose smile softened, and he gave me a slight nod as if to say *I see you.*

I saw him, too. Every gorgeous inch of him from his white smile to his muscled forearms to his tan legs. He wore khaki shorts, brown boat loafers, and a white short-sleeved shirt that ruffled in the breeze as he navigated the boat out onto the river.

Maggie glanced at me. "See something you like?"

It took me a second to catch her meaning. "Just taking in the sights," I said, being flippant because I knew she was messing with me.

"I think our captain is taking in the sights as well."

"What are you whispering about?" Sophie asked. Barefoot, she sat across from us with one foot on the seat tucked beneath her thigh and one arm resting on the back of the seat behind Chloe. She was naturally pretty like Kate.

"Andie is ogling our captain," Maggie said.

Sophie grinned. "I noticed."

I turned to Kate. "Make them stop."

"Sorry," she said. "There's nothing I can do with this group. I guess you're stuck with us for the day."

I was, and I couldn't have felt more fortunate. Their easy comradery and playful banter recentered my thoughts on the beautiful day. As the boat glided through the water, a sense of peace and real happiness settled around my heart. I drank in my surroundings as we meandered downstream through a series of twists and turns, dipping into marshy areas and passing small tributaries that fed the river.

Navigating the boat became a group endeavor they all seemed to enjoy. I'd never piloted a boat, so I abstained and listened to the interesting tidbits they all shared about the woodlands and wildlife along the river. Belted kingfishers and a great blue heron dove for food in the rippling water. Ashe pointed out an Osprey's nest of sticks high atop a dead tree at the edge of the timberline where three white tail deer grazed.

"Yikes, is that a rat?" I asked, pointing toward a muddy bank where a rodent crouched and nibbled on something.

"It's a muskrat," Mason said, passing the piloting duty to Kate, then sitting beside me. "Are you enjoying our river cruise?"

"Very much. The scenery is breathtaking and it's just so peaceful. I really needed this."

"A day on the river is good medicine. Flying has that same effect on me. You should let me take you up sometime. I really think you'd enjoy it."

"In that little kite plane of yours?" I shook my head. "Not a chance."

He laughed. "I'll take you up in my two-seater."

"I doubt I'd be a fan of either one."

"You might be surprised," Chloe said, joining our conversation. "Mason took me up once and it was a thrilling experience."

"Me, too," Maggie said. "If you ever wondered what it would feel like to have wings, let Mason take you up in his plane. It's a fabulous experience."

Just thinking about it gave me a bit of vertigo.

"Hey, you guys, there's an eagle," Sophie said, directing our attention ahead to a tree jutting out of the water.

The instant I spotted it, I slipped my phone from my bag and zoomed in on the eagle. It looked so regal with its head tilted slightly up as if posing for my video or perhaps just listening for our approach. It seemed to look right at me before leaping off the tree. Its expansive wings swept out away from its body, flapping with such grace I felt transported by the creature's magnificence. The eagle soared higher, then turned and headed away from us, showing its beautiful white tail as it disappeared into the tree line.

As we passed a small group in kayaks, we called greetings to each other. Sunshine sparkled on the water as I scanned the riverbanks. Hiking trails meandered in and out of the woodlands girding the river. Kate pointed out a stretch of silver maple populating a floodplain forest. She said she'd spent her early teen years hiking and canoeing with her family. When I asked if she'd ever met a black bear during her hikes, she said she hadn't but confessed she'd be more concerned crossing paths with a fisher or a skunk.

"Or a coyote," Sophie added. "That was my biggest worry as a kid. I was the youngest and smallest one in our group."

"Yeah, but you were the fastest runner," Kate said. "I suspect a coyote would have feasted on those of us you left behind."

I studied the marshy inlet and woodland beyond. "I can imagine the types of creatures living in there. Have you ever seen a moose?"

"Once," Kate said. "Mostly we see white tail deer, racoons, otters, rabbits, and small critters like squirrels and chipmunks."

Ashe negotiated the craft close to a small beach-like area, then used the power-pole to anchor the boat before cutting the engine.

"Time to cool off," Mason said, standing to pull off his shirt.

His bare athletic torso created a deep longing in me, and I looked away, a little shocked at my own intense reaction. The rippling surface of the river beckoned, and I could see the loamy bottom dotted with small stones. When I turned back, Ashe had shut off the engine and was shrugging off his shirt. The girls were standing, too, and stripping down to their bathing suits.

"Last one in buys dinner!" Maggie said, unlatching the access gate and dropping the stairs into the water. She bopped down the steps and slipped into the water, followed by Ashe and the girls.

"Coming in?" Mason asked, dropping his sunglasses in his hat and setting it on the console.

"Yeah, sure. I'll be right behind you," I said, because the thought of disrobing in front of Mason made the day seem twenty degrees hotter. With a nod, he descended the ladder and joined the others in the water, and I followed a moment later.

I wasn't a strong swimmer like the rest of them, so I stayed a little closer to the boat. Plus, I kept wondering what sort of creatures were in the water with us. When I doggie-paddled past Mason, he winked.

"Heads up!" Ashe tossing ball to Kate. She batted it to Chloe, who popped it high in the air.

"Got it!" Sophie called as she executed a powerful downward spike toward Maggie.

With a yelp of surprise, Maggie dove sideways. She surfaced wide-eyed and sputtering. "Jesus, girl!"

Sophie raised her hands in apology. "Sorry, I had a momentary flashback from my competitive volleyball days. I'll play nice."

"That's no fun," Ashe said, just before dunking Maggie.

For the second time, she surfaced, but this time with a snarl on her face. "Okay, big brother." She dove toward him, but he dragged Kate in front of him.

"Don't use me as your shield," Kate said, pushing away from them.

Maggie's eyes flashed as she stalked Ashe. "Ohhh...you're

going down!" she said, then leapt forward, wrapping her arms and legs around Ashe, dragging him under water.

After a moment of sloshing, he came up laughing and pushed her away. "Jesus, Maggie, you're like wrestling a freaking octopus."

Our laughter spread like sunshine across the churned-up water. I couldn't remember the last time I'd played like this. It would have been sometime in my teenage years, but it wouldn't have been with my sister. We'd never shared the close bond that Maggie and Ashe shared.

A beachball approaching my face snapped me out of my introspection, and I knocked it away just inches from my sunburned nose.

"Nice cat-like reflexes," Mason said, tapping the ball high in the air and sending it toward Chloe.

Snared in his gaze, I felt like a cat, purring each time he looked at me, arching my back toward his hand whenever he was near. The man was catnip, and I felt feral and in heat when he was around.

"Heads up!" Kate shouted, and I reacted in time to bat the ball to Maggie who whacked it right back to me.

"Just keeping your head in the game," she said, snapping me out of my preoccupation with catnip, an enticing treat but one I needed to steer clear of.

The seven of us played ball and swam in the river for a long time. Finally, Ashe said his stomach was growling and it was time to eat.

After our refreshing swim, we dried off and ate lunch. I'd just popped a juicy strawberry in my mouth when Ashe told everyone about my boss showing up and how I'd dropped him to his knees with a finger lock.

"She did not," Maggie said with a laugh, and I could tell they thought Ashe was joking with them.

"She sure as heck did," he insisted, then released a belt of laughter. "Walter looked like a mob boss in a gangster movie when he thumbed toward the door and told the guy to *scram*." By the time Ashe finished the story, their laughter flooded the boat and flowed over the railing.

All eyes were on me as I chewed and swallowed, but I didn't feel embarrassed at all. I felt proud of standing up to the dumbass.

"Dang it, I wish I could have seen that," Maggie said, "especially after hearing you tell him off and quit your job at the gas station."

"Yeah, now I wish I'd had video surveillance in the shop so I could send a copy to my former co-workers," I said.

After lunch, we continued our journey downriver. Mason told me the Dunwith River stretched for miles through wetlands and forests populated with pines, spruces, and larches. As we navigated past shaggy river grasses, reeds, and thick rushes, he navigated the boat into a marshy nook and cut the engine.

Ashe turned off the music, and everyone grew quiet.

In the sudden stillness, we listened to the sound of buzzing insects, the twittering and chirping of lively birds, and small blips and splashes here and there as small creatures slipped into the water. A red-winged blackbird called repeatedly for a mate, and a pair of mallards paddled through the cattail reeds nibbling scraps with their flattened bills.

Deep within a cluster of rushes came the call of a loon. I felt so connected with that long mournful wail, tears surged to my eyes. An answering call came from farther away. The birds were calling to each other, asking *where are you*, and I wanted to say *I'm here. Finally. I'm right here where I'm supposed to be.*

Chapter Twenty-Four

I sequestered myself in my shop, working around the clock on the sculpture for the town. Maggie, Kate, and Chloe all texted invites to lunches and girl gabs, and I replied promising to catch up with them as soon as I got far enough along on the sculpture to feel comfortable taking a break. Mason stopped by to ask me out to dinner, but I told him I was too busy to eat, so he started bringing take-out two nights a week and convincing me to take a twenty-minute break. The tasty food and his charming sense of humor was a welcome distraction from the chronic anxiety twisting my gut in knots.

Walter understood I was pressed for time but insisted on popping by for a few minutes each morning with coffee to make sure I was still standing and to cheer me on. I missed our time together and promised him we'd get back to our more leisurely coffee dates as soon as I finished the main structure of the sculpture.

Tyler had called to let me know he was settled in his dorm and might pick up a part-time job at the local café. And Eli had called yesterday to let me know the paperwork and transfers for my business had been completed and payment was made to Walter's account. It was finally done.

After the initial thrill I felt over owning a business, I experienced another twist of anxiety. My savings account was depleted to almost nothing, and I'd turned away a paying job because it would have required me to do repair work at another facility. But I was so short on time to make the sculpture, I simply couldn't afford to spend two weeks on the repair job. Probably not my best business decision, but I needed to complete the sculpture first. For my new community. And for me.

By the end of the third week, I'd lightly tacked up the main structure of an eagle on a tree branch preparing to launch into flight. The main body of the tree was taller than I'd anticipated, and with the eagle perched on top it created a tipping hazard. It was too dangerous for me to continue working on it without ensuring I wouldn't end up crushed by a toppling tower of metal. I needed to move the piece to the center of my shop where I could use the overhead hoist to keep the sculpture upright so I could create a wider, heavier base and complete the project.

Mason had texted that he was bringing subs over for our bi-weekly meal, and I needed to get upstairs and shower before he arrived. But I wanted to get the sculpture moved first, so I climbed onto my forklift and sat unmoving as my weary brain tried to figure out the safest way to move the top-heavy sculpture. Finally, I decided to lift the sculpture from its base which was a metal pallet-like frame I'd tacked together from angle iron. I slipped the forks in and lifted slowly. The sculpture shifted slightly but seemed secure, so I elevated the forks a few inches and slowly backed in a half circle. As I started forward, the forklift stuttered as if about to stall, then it suddenly shot ahead as if I'd hit the accelerator pedal. The sculpture teetered and shifted sideways with a screech of metal against metal.

I hit the hand lever to lower the forks, hoping I could trap the base between the forks and concrete floor to steady the sculpture, but in my panic, I'd pushed the lever in the wrong direction. The forks rose, and the sculpture tipped sideways and crashed to the floor, twisting the metal base around the forks and rocking the machine so violently I feared it would tip over.

For an instant, I thought I was hallucinating or having a waking nightmare brought on by fatigue. But the ringing in my ears and thudding in my chest assured me the worst had really happened. My sculpture was a twisted, mangled mess of metal.

"Jesus, Andie! Are you okay?" Mason called as he bolted inside with a takeout bag clutched in his hand. "My god, what happened?"

Tears welled up in my eyes, but I angrily blinked them back. I shut off the forklift and stared at the destruction. My chance to create something of my own and contribute to an important endeavor in a community I loved had just become a pile of scrap metal.

Mason clasped my arm. "Andie, are you hurt?"

I shook my head, fighting tears.

Without a word, he just reached up and pulled me off the forklift and into his arms. "Please tell me you're okay," he said, holding me gently.

I nodded because my throat was too filled with anguish to speak. He just stroked his hand down my back as I struggled to pull myself together. I expected him to say I shouldn't be working alone, that the work was too dangerous, and maybe express a dozen more concerns, but he just held me.

When I finally straightened my shoulders and drew away, he said, "How can I help?"

I glanced at the tangled mess of metal and couldn't bear the pain. All I wanted in that moment was to escape. "Take me up in your plane."

He arched an eyebrow, a mixture of surprise and doubt in his eyes.

"Please. I need to get out of here. I need to do something that will take my mind off this mess."

"Would you rather just go for coffee or a drink?" he asked.

"I would only sit there thinking about this. Please, if it's okay to fly, will you take me up?"

"It's okay, and I'd love to."

"All right. Can you give me a few minutes to clean up?"

"Of course. Take your time," he said. "I can wait."

Shaking from the accident and fatigue, I asked him to close the overhead door then follow me upstairs to my apartment. He completed the task, then sat on the sofa while I headed to the bathroom to shower.

I refused to let myself think about anything but getting washed and dressed. I would face the problem tomorrow, after a night of rest, after giving myself permission to step away for a few hours.

When I slipped into my bedroom to get dressed, the sight of my bed was almost too much to resist, and for a moment I regretted asking Mason to take me flying. But I knew if I crawled into bed, I'd have nightmares or I'd wake after a few hours in a panic because of the stress I was under. So, as Mason had suggested, I dressed in layers and put a zip up sweatshirt in my shoulder bag.

"Do you want to eat before we go?" he asked when I returned to the living room.

My stomach was still twisted in knots. "I'd rather wait until we get back, if that's all right with you."

"Absolutely," he said, then gave me a sweet smile. "Ready?"

"As I'll ever be," I said, trying hard to return his smile.

We left my apartment and arrived at his airport hangar within ten minutes. Rita had installed the man door in Mason's hangar which is why I hadn't been in it until now, but I was immediately impressed when he turned on the lights.

"I didn't know a tricked-out hangar was a thing," I said, taking in the efficiency apartment-like set up at one side of the large hangar. A tiny kitchenette with a microwave, a coffeemaker, and a refrigerator where Mason put our subs, bordered a lounge area complete with sofa, end tables, and a flat screen television sitting atop a large area rug.

"There's a bathroom in there if you need it," he said, pointing to a boxed in area with a closed door at the corner of the hangar. "Make yourself comfortable while I do my preflight inspection. There are beverages in the fridge and snacks in the cupboard."

Grateful for a chance to sit down, I sank onto the thick cushions of his sofa. My first thought was I could fall asleep right there. As he pulled the beautiful plane out of the hangar, I felt my body unlocking. By the time he finished his inspection and returned a few minutes later, I'd become part of the cushions.

"Last chance to bail," he said, smiling down at me.

"Just promise we'll survive so I can sit on this sofa again. These cushions are divine."

"We'll survive," he said, pulling me to my feet. "And we can sit here to eat when we get back."

Pulling on my sweatshirt, I followed him outside and waited while he closed and began to lock the hangar door, but he paused suddenly as if he'd forgotten something. "I'll be right back," he said, then he disappeared back inside the hangar.

I stood next to his red and white airplane on the large concrete slab in front of the hanger. The concrete gave way to a narrow, paved taxiway that ran the length of a long, wide grass runway. I heard the distant sound of a propellor clapping the air and fast approaching. I glanced up and spotted a plane heading toward the airport. As the sound of the propellor and engine got louder, a blue airplane descended and cleared the large yellow cones at the end of the runway. The wheels of the landing gear began to spin as they kissed the blades of grass, so close I could see the pilot in the cockpit. Mesmerized, I watched as the plane rushed past me and came to a slow rolling stop.

"You aren't losing your nerve, are you?" Mason asked, his sudden appearance giving me a little start.

"Not yet."

"I'm glad to hear that." He escorted me to the right-side of his plane, where I saw the word "EXPERIMENTAL" below the door. "Is this thing safe to fly? I don't want to be part of any experimental flight."

"That's just a classification for aircraft not built by a factory. But my plane is inspected, and an airworthiness certificate was issued by the FAA."

"If it's not built by a factory, who built it?"

"My father and I assembled it fifteen years ago. I've been flying it since we built it, and it's safe. But no pressure if you've changed your mind."

I considered it for a moment while surveying the length of the airplane, assessing the craftsmanship I knew nothing about. "I'm putting my life in your hands," I said, knowing that I needed to do this more than I needed to be cautious or scared right now. Following his instruction, I grabbed the overhead bar inside the cockpit with my left hand while placing my left foot on the tire. Then I pulled myself up to place my butt on the seat. Pivoting on my backside, I lifted my left leg over the control stick and pulled my right leg inside. "Whew, it's a challenge to wiggle into this thing."

"You'll think it's worth it when you fly the plane," Mason

said, reaching across my waist and shoulder to fasten the four-point harness seatbelt.

"No way. Flying this kite is *your* job."

"Put this on," he said, handing me one of the beige helmet headsets that had been hanging from a hook behind the seats. He walked around the rear of the airplane and climbed in through the left door. Sitting shoulder to shoulder in the compact cockpit, he secured his seatbelt harness and put his helmet on, "Test, test. Can you hear me?"

"Aye, Captain."

He smiled. "All right let's get this girl warmed up. Clear prop!" he said before pushing the start button. The engine roared to life, and I was glad to have the headset on to protect my ears.

"While the engine is warming up, let me show you a couple of things so you have a better understanding of what's going on while we are flying."

I wondered if this was his usual schtick when in flight instructor mode, or if he was trying to make me feel more comfortable.

"There are two control sticks and two sets of rudder pedals so that the plane can be flown from either the right or left seat," he said nodding to the stick between my knees and the pedals near my feet. "Whatever I do on my side will cause your stick and pedals to do the same thing, and vice versa," he said, moving them back and forth to demonstrate. "So please don't touch or move yours unless I say you have the controls."

"I won't want the controls."

He laughed. "You might change your mind once we're in the air.

I pointed to a gauge with a needle indicator positioned above a horizontal tube with a ball in it. "What's that ball in a tube thingy."

"It's a turn-slip indicator. The needle gauge reflects our turn, and the 'ball in a tube thingy' tracks our slip. In a nutshell, they show if our turns are uncoordinated and help us prevent skidding turns."

"I assume we don't want to skid?"

"Correct." He pointed out a bunch of gauges and demonstrated how the pedals move the rudder on the tail, causing the nose of the plane to move right or left. Then he said moving the control stick side to side controls the flaperons on the back of the wings, which rolls the plane and aids in turning. "If you push the control stick forward, or pull it back, the elevator on the tail moves up and down, in turn moving the nose up and down which controls the pitch of the plane. And this is the throttle. Which of these makes us go faster?" he asked.

I rolled my eyes. "I can't even remember half of what you just said or what the gauges are much less what all these pedals and levers do. But for the sake of playing along, I'll say the throttle makes you go faster."

"Common mistake. During flight, the throttle provides altitude by causing more airflow over the wings which creates lift," he said, demonstrating the upward angle with his hands. "Everybody gets that wrong initially, but it's an important point to remember."

"Okay, but why do I need to know that?"

"Well, what if I have a heart attack while we're in the air?"

A flush of panic rushed through me. "Oh my god! I never even considered that."

He laughed. "I was toying with you."

"Jeez, now that's all I'm going to be able to think about."

He gave my knee a gentle squeeze. "I'm sorry. I'm perfectly healthy, Andie. I promise to keep you safe and treat you to an amazing adventure."

"You'd better. I'd at least like to see my son graduate

college." We sat for a moment, as if he was giving me time to back out if I wanted. "All right, Captain, continue my crash course just in case you decide to croak in the air."

"I won't croak, but since you're interested, just remember if you push the nose of the plane down with the control stick, you go faster. If you pull the stick back and lift the nose, you create more drag, in turn becoming less aerodynamic which causes you to slow down."

"That sounds easy enough."

"It is, in theory. But if you pull the stick back too far, raising the nose high, the wings can't create enough lift, so the plane stalls, spins, and crashes."

"Dang it, now I'm scared again. And confused."

Mason slipped his warm hand over my clenched fist. "We'll be fine, Andie. I've spent my life flying planes. I've got this. Just enjoy the ride, okay?"

"All right, but let's go before I chicken out."

After checking the temperature gauges, he taxied the plane to the end of the grass runway. "We're configured and ready to go. Are you?"

"As ready as I'll ever be," I replied hesitantly, folding my hands in my lap, reminding myself to avoid touching the control stick or rudder pedals.

He pushed the button on the control stick and made a radio call. "Dunwith Valley area traffic. This is red experimental Kitfox, Four-Two-Two-Romeo, departing runway two-seven. Dunwith."

He gave me a wink, then pushed the throttle forward. "And we are rolling. Full Power. One Mississippi. Two Mississippi." The unexpected acceleration pushed me back in my seat. "Airspeed alive. Stick forward. Tail up. Three Mississippi. Wings are alive." I could feel the small plane begin to heave as if trying to break free of gravity, where I'd been dwelling for too long. "Pull flaps. Rotate. And we are off," he said.

As the plane climbed, my helmeted head felt heavy and pushed against the seat back.

"We'll level off once we've cleared the trees at the end of the runway," he said, his confident voice reassuring me that he was in full control.

The power of the plane and our upward climb pressed me back in my seat, and all I could see was the red and white engine cowl in front of us and the gorgeous blue sky. As the plane began to level out, my body grew lighter, and soon a feeling of soaring on my own wings sent a wild thrill through me. "Oh my gosh! This is crazy!"

"Crazy good, or crazy bad?" Mason asked, glancing at me with concern in his eyes.

"It's amazing!"

My reply seemed to please him. "Today's unseasonably warm weather makes it more difficult to gain altitude when taking off from this elevation, so our climb out is slower. Think of it as having less dense air for the propeller to bite into and keep us moving. Crashes happen when pilots neglect to take density altitude into consideration when taking off from higher elevation airports."

"I'm duly impressed," I said. "I had no idea how involved and complicated it was to pilot an aircraft."

Mason's knowledge and skill reassured me, and I felt myself relax. The tension of the past several weeks began to peel away like old skin cells, and I imagined them being blown away in the prop wash as we soared through the sky. To finally distance myself from everything I'd been carrying on my back, my heart, and my mind for the past year was an unexpected gift.

The right rudder pedal in front of me moved forward as the stick followed in unison, causing us to bank right. Out the side window I saw Fern Park in the center of town, and the sparkling Dunwith River cutting a winding path through the dense Adirondack Forest. As we leveled out, Mason pointed below. "If you want to know the condition of your roof, now's your chance to see it."

I looked out the window and saw my shop. Suddenly, it hit me that it was really mine. "Eli called yesterday to tell me the paperwork and transfers for my business were done. I own it now."

Mason glanced over with a warm smile. "That calls for a celebration."

"Only if my roof is in good shape," I said, straining to examine it from above.

"It's a metal roof, and from what I can see, it looks perfect."

We followed the serpentine river lined with several specialty shops and eateries I'd yet to explore. As we meandered north past the Winery, we banked right giving me a full view of the downtown area out of my side window.

"A couple of miles ahead, you'll see Chloe's place," he said. "Have you been out to Kate's house yet?"

"Yes. It's gorgeous."

"We'll be flying over it soon."

The farm fields, rooftops, trees, and country roads passed below us as the stick and left rudder pedal began to move. A couple of minutes later, he said, "There's Kate's place, and I think that's her on the dock."

As we circled in a lazy figure-eight, I peered out Mason's side window and saw Kate's cottage and the small mountain lake glistening below us. She was standing on the dock as we made our second pass.

"Her place is even more beautiful from this vantage point."

"Yeah, flying gives you a different perspective on everything," he said. "When I'm in the middle of a mess, I like to fly and gain some distance from the problem. Suddenly, it seems less significant."

I understood what he meant, but even soaring on the wind didn't lessen the significance of losing my sculpture and weeks of work.

As we turned back, we passed over farm fields and thick forest. The sudden drop of the airplane flipped my stomach, and I released a yelp of surprise. It felt as if we'd just hit a ditch.

"It's just afternoon thermals," Mason said. "When hot air over an open field rises and meets cooler air over the trees, it creates turbulence. Place your hand on the control stick and your feet on the pedals, and you'll be able to feel what I'm doing here."

"Won't that mess with your control?"

"Not if you don't resist against my movements."

"Okay," I said, slipping my fingers around the leather-wrapped control stick and gingerly placing my feet on the pedals. The airplane slowly banked left, then right, and then left again. I could feel him pushing the stick, my hand following, and the plane responding in turn. All I could focus on was how he gently worked the controls and the warmth of his shoulder against mine.

"Let's see how you do on your own," he said. "You've got the controls."

"Wait! What?"

He lifted his hands to show me he wasn't navigating. "You've got the controls. I'll manage the throttle. Just follow the curves of the river."

"Oh my god, please keep your hands and feet on the controls."

"I will, but you're managing them. I'll take over if needed."

"I can't remember what the pedals do."

"Just apply gentle pressure to the right pedal if you want to go right or to the left if you want to go left."

"Oh boy." I released a slow breath. Gently pushing the rudder pedals in the direction that I wanted to go, I attempted to follow the blue-green waterway as it meandered its way through the tree-lined terrain below.

"Add a touch more flaperon as you turn. I'll demonstrate. I've got the controls," he said.

I relaxed my death-grip on the stick and let Mason resume control of the plane. "Watch the ball on the turn-slip indicator," he said, pointing to the ball-in-a-tube thingy I'd asked about earlier. He applied left rudder pressure, and the ball rolled to the right side of the indicator. "Now watch what happens when I apply left rudder and follow along with the control stick to the left." The ball centered and remained between the two lines in the indicator. "If the ball moves to the outside on a turn, it shows that we are in a skid, which can be dangerous. Now you try. You've got the controls."

"I don't want them, but I guess I've got them," I replied, trying to sound confident while my heart was pounding.

He laughed. "Relax, Andie. I'm right here. Just have fun with this. Follow that sharp S-curve in the river there," he said, pointing ahead. "Remember, use both rudder and stick."

I envisioned that we were driving down a highway and focused on keeping my movements small and my touch light. The curves of the river flowed below us as we banked gently right, left, right, then straightened out again.

"Nicely done," he said. "Head toward that field while I add a little more power to give us some altitude."

"Okay, but don't you dare let go of the controls."

"I'm right here." With that, the engine roared as we climbed higher above the trees and a large dairy farm several miles south of Dunwith. I'd driven past that farm multiple times during my years as a road warrior selling welding supplies. From this altitude, the sprawling farmlands I'd driven past looked like tiny brown and green patches on the vast canvas of the surrounding Adirondack Mountains.

As I navigated across the field toward a forested area crisscrossed by rivers and tributaries, it felt as if I'd sprouted wings. I was so lost in my moment of bliss that the sudden drop of the airplane startled me. I pulled back on the control stick, but Mason's firm hand blocked me from doing the very thing he'd cautioned me not to do. "Ohmigosh, I'm sorry."

"No harm," he said. "I expected your reaction because it's natural, but it's the wrong one in a plane. The turbulence is going to continue for a bit, so I'll take it from here."

We were thrust upwards, then dropped down, then thrust back up repeatedly for several minutes before things smoothed out. Then Mason pulled the throttle back and pushed the stick forward, pointing the airplane down toward the Dunwith River below. Millions of years of flowing water carved the deep canyon between two of the Adirondack Mountainsides where we were headed. Pushing the control stick over his right knee, we descended with a sharp turn between the two mountains. The river now meandered directly below us as we banked left and right along the waterway.

"Is that where we anchored the pontoon boat?" I asked, spotting the pretty inlet where we'd gone swimming.

"Yes," he said, manipulating the pedals and control stick as we followed the winding riverbed. "When the river is low this time of year, there's a gravel bar I land on. We could set down there and eat our dinner if you like."

Hints of red and gold in the woodland trees heralded fall was rolling in. I hadn't expected this sort of adventure, but I loved the idea—until I saw the small loamy patch of stone below. "That gravel bar doesn't look big enough to land a plane on."

"It is, but if you'd rather eat at a picnic table in the park or back at the hangar, just say the word."

"Go for it, hotshot, but I'm trusting you to keep us out of the river."

He grinned. "We'll circle around and land on the next pass," he said, pushing the throttle forward. The engine growled, and he pulled back on the control stick causing us to climb out of the ravine. Watching his tan hands manipulate the controls made me think of how they'd felt on my waist when we danced, and on my back when he'd pulled me into his arms and kissed me.

"Look at that," he said, motioning out the window on his side.

The dark-tipped feathers of a bald eagle splayed like fingers grasping the thermals. Its white tail feathers buffeted in the breeze as it soared on spread wings and scanned the river below. Seeming oblivious to our presence, or unconcerned that we were sharing airspace, it circled slowly.

I knew then that I couldn't have captured the creature's beauty in the short time I had to work on my sculpture. Perhaps the accident that destroyed my hard work, however devastating, might have spared me ultimate disappointment.

"Here we go," Mason said, nodding toward the gravel bar below as we descended. The roar of the engine became quieter as the plane touched down, gravel crunching beneath the tires as we rolled to a stop. He cut the engine with a satisfied smile. "Told you we could land here."

"That you did," I said with a laugh.

After we removed our headsets and unbuckled the harness seatbelts, Mason leaned across me and released the doorlatch lever. As it swung upward, a rush of fresh mountain air filled the cockpit, and I inhaled deeply as we each stepped out of the plane.

The sound of flowing water making its way around rocks and fallen tree branches mingled with birdsong coming from the forests girding the river. The serenity of the place was a balm for my tattered spirit. While Mason was busy with the plane, I stood scanning the ravine, the sparkling river, and the rugged beauty of surrounding forest. Closing my eyes, I tilted my face toward the rays of the late afternoon sunshine and absorbed its rejuvenating warmth.

"Dinner is served," Mason said, garnering my attention and reminding me I was not alone. He had spread an orange and silver emergency blanket under the wing of the airplane and topped it with what appeared to be an open sleeping bag. Our wrapped subs lay in the center of the spread. "Table for two," he said, wearing a boyish smile.

His desire to make the evening special was as sweet as Walter's warm-hug coffee. "Well, this certainly beats a picnic table in a park."

We sat on the spread and ate our dinner. It felt wonderful to be away from everything, to experience nature on the wings of Mason's little plane and dine on a blanket with the river flowing around us. "I must be hungry because this sub tastes better than any meal I've had in a long time."

Our eyes met, and he smiled. "Everything tastes better when you are sitting next to an airplane on a gravel bar."

"Ah, so that's why I'm enjoying this so much," I said, but I knew it was as much from the charming man sharing a picnic blanket with me as it was from the peaceful setting. "Now, if we just had popcorn, I'd be quite content."

"Hmm, popcorn or tortilla chips," he said, moving his hands as if weighing the options.

"No contest. Popcorn wins every time. I could eat it every

day, and I might as well confess right now that I never share my popcorn. Not even with my kid."

"Duly noted," he said with a laugh.

As we ate our dinner, Mason shared stories from his years of flying commercial jets, telling me about irrational passengers and horny flight attendants that had me laughing, and about aircraft and navigational issues that nearly put me off flying commercial altogether.

After we finished eating and storing the trash in the plane, we settled back on the sleeping bag. For a long time, we simply listened to the babbling river and enjoyed the peaceful surroundings. As hues of pink and orange colored the sky, the setting sun cast long, dark shadows across the riverbank, and our conversation flowed as effortless and unrestrained as the river.

Leaning against the wheel of the Kitfox, Mason asked why I'd moved to Dunwith. I shared a little about my past, steering clear of my family and divorce issues, and confessed my desire to do my scrap metal art full time. I swiped on my phone and showed him images of several sculptures by John Lopez and Karen Cusolito that inspired me.

When he remembered my mentioning Cusolito during our lunch break at the airport and that I'd been utterly enthralled with her "Ecstasy" sculpture, I was surprised and deeply touched. I hadn't shared this much of myself or my artistic passion with anyone since my father and I worked on our last sculpture. For Mason to not only recall our conversation but understand how such spectacular works of art moved me so deeply felt surreal.

I shared my excitement over creating a sculpture for the town and how devastated I was by the accident and seeing the destruction of weeks of hard work. He listened as if hanging on every word, as if deeply interested in my work and my life, as if he truly cared about me. I'd never experienced that connection before and maybe that's why everything came pouring out of me. "Oh my god, I just realized I've been blathering on like a self-centered idiot. I'm so sorry."

To my surprise, he cupped my jaw, his fingers warm against my face and neck. "Andie, you are the most fascinating person I know, and I love every word coming out of your beautiful mouth," he said, his earnest blue eyes surveying my face as he leaned in and kissed me.

I sank into the kiss willingly, wantonly, welcoming his thrilling touch. As he deepened the kiss, I slipped my fingers into his hair and guided him down on top of me as I lay back. I trailed my hands over his shoulders, reveling in the feel of his muscles flexing as he moved against me. I ached for more. I needed more. I wanted this piece of myself back.

But he broke away with a gasp, his eyes dark with need as he gazed down at me. "If this isn't what you want, I need to stop now."

"If this wasn't what I wanted, you'd already be in the river."

With a moaning sort of laugh, he rolled me into his arms and buried his face in my neck. "You smell amazing."

He *felt* amazing. The warmth of his lips moving over my neck and jaw sent streams of hot desire through me. I pressed against him, aching and throbbing and yearning as his hands traveled my body. Needing to get closer, we peeled away our clothing. I arched lustfully into his masterful hands, exposed my neck to his searching mouth, and opened my body to his probing exploration.

With a low moan, he slipped between my thighs, and we were lost in each other, in the feel of our bodies rocking together, in the mounting pressure and pleasure that built like a storm surge, and finally, in the sound of our blissful release and ragged breathing being carried away on the flowing river.

Chapter Twenty-Five

We'd made it back to Mason's hangar before dark, but it was nearly midnight when I showered and climbed into my bed. But my head was filled with memories of flying in Mason's plane and soaring in his arms during the most thrilling sex I'd ever experienced.

I wondered if our sexual encounter had rocked his world as it had mine. I finally understood why Kate was such an avid proponent of the friends-with-benefits relationship. To be able to enjoy Mason's friendship and interludes of thrilling sex without the obligatory bonds of a committed relationship was exactly what I wanted right now.

But it made me think about Clark. Our sex life had been good, or at least good enough. But he'd never seemed content with life. I repeatedly asked if everything was all right, and he'd answer *Yeah*, and I'd drop the subject. It was after a big car show, when he seemed depressed and lounged around the house for a week, that I finally asked if he was okay. He looked at me and said, "I just keep thinking, is this all there is?"

Everything inside me dropped to my feet like rubble. I wondered, how he could feel dissatisfied when everything we did was for him. We ate the food he liked, watched the sports programs he enjoyed, went to the events he chose. He had expensive toys and could spend his time in any manner that made him happy. What more could he have wanted? Did I mean nothing to him? Did I bring no joy or light to his life? To have his dissatisfaction so blatantly stated and know how little value he placed on our relationship broke me. It didn't matter now because my life was here, and I was focused on moving forward, but the wound was still raw.

It was futile to stay in bed, so I dressed, then headed downstairs and turned the lights on in my shop. The instant I saw the twisted pile of metal dangling off the forklift, I moaned in despair.

I had used a light touch when tacking the sections together so the welds would be easier to break or cut should any adjustments be necessary. I thought it would make the job go more quickly but those light welds had left the sculpture vulnerable to bending and breaking apart. No matter how I envisioned salvaging the sculpture it simply wouldn't work because the process to fix it would take longer than just starting over with a new sculpture.

The commemoration ceremony was one month away and there was no way I could buy more material, cut and clean the sections, then start the sculpting process all over again and finish it in thirty days. Defaulting on the agreement I'd made with the town meant I'd have to refund the money they'd given me to purchase the materials. Money I no longer had. But worse than that, I felt utterly defeated because I was going to let everyone down; my new community, and myself.

My eyes flooded, and I felt as broken as the sculpture, but I swallowed an angry sob. My father wouldn't have allowed me to blubber over a mistake or wallow in self-pity. He'd have told me to take a break, get some rest, then get off my ass and solve the problem.

But I was too disheartened, disillusioned, and desperate to think clearly, so I distracted myself by going through the boxes Chloe and I had picked up at my house. They were still sitting in the corner of the shop beside the tarped sculpture my father and I began so long ago. I couldn't recall what I'd packed in the boxes, but the first one held college textbooks and course notes. I didn't know why I'd bothered to keep any of that stuff. It seemed a lifetime ago when I'd ventured off to college thinking I knew so much about welding and art only to discover I'd barely scratched the surface. My father had prepared me well, though, introducing me to welding and design basics, helping me understand form, nourishing my creative thinking, and teaching me how to be a problem solver.

The second box was full of Tyler's baby clothes that made me smile and cry and wonder why Clark hadn't dropped the box at the donation center as I'd asked him to do years ago. Had he hoped we would need them for another baby? Or had he just tossed the box aside as he'd done with so many of my requests? I promised myself I'd look through the clothing later to see if the items could still be donated.

In the third box I opened, I found the first scrap metal sculpture I'd made with my father. It was a little horse made from nuts, bolts, and springs. He'd taken me to a local scrapyard where we'd selected the items. My sister's favorite thing was shopping with my mother at the local mall, but mine was visiting scrapyards with my dad. Those trips with him were some of my fondest memories. My old journal was in the box, too. Sitting on the floor with my back against my worktable, I opened it to the first page where my father had written a list before he'd given me the journal.

1. *Be a problem solver*
2. *Throw some of it away*
3. *Try something new*
4. *Add another piece*
5. *Get out of your own way*
6. *Get a new perspective/view/angle*
7. *"...the whole is something besides the parts..."*
   Aristotle
8. *Work from your head, sculpt from your heart*
9. *Find the lost or missing pieces*

Drawing my fingers over his slanted writing, I could almost hear him telling me to get up and figure out how to fix the problem. With a hard sigh, I pushed myself to my feet and put the journal on my workbench. Time to face the music, or more aptly the mangled mess still dangling off the forklift.

Using my handheld angle grinder, I began the long process of cutting through the twisted sheet metal. I wasn't sure what had caused the mishap. I'd been careful lifting and moving the piece, but something had gone wrong with the forklift causing the sculpture to topple.

By the time I'd cut and pulled the wrenched base of the sculpture off the steel forks, sunlight was streaming in through the windows. I arched my aching back, then opened the man door, hoping the cool morning air would revive my weary brain.

When I returned to the forklift a few minutes later, I immediately spotted part of the issue that had caused the sculpture to topple. It was one I'd known about but had been too fatigued at the time to remember. Back when I was cleaning up the mess that Walter had made in the shop, I'd noticed that one of the forks on the lift was bent. That slight downward bend must have tilted my top-heavy sculpture just enough to unbalance it, and the sudden surge of the engine, another part of the problem, had sent the whole thing crashing to the concrete floor. My panicked reaction and mishandling of the controls had finished it off.

This was my fault because I hadn't remembered the fork was bent, and because I'd worked myself into a state of exhaustion. My own impatience had made me push on when I should have taken a break, and it caused me to make a fatal mistake. The sculpture was truly trashed. It seemed I'd failed at my art career right out of the gate. I might as well order my business cards right now because it appeared I'd be running a metal fab business rather than creating metal sculptures.

A sharp bark and clicking of claws across the concrete floor drew my attention to Louie who was almost at my side. He plopped his butt down and gazed up at me with adoring eyes.

"Hello, sweet boy," I said, kneeling to give him a body rub. "How's my favorite guy this morning?" His reply was an excited wheeze. "All right, come on," I said, heading for my workbench where I kept a container of doggie biscuits.

As I gave Louie a biscuit, Walter stepped inside with a squinty smile and a coffee mug in each hand. "Good morning!"

"It is now, thanks to my two favorite guys," I said, striving to shrug off the heavy weight of failure.

"How's the sculpture coming along?" he asked, just before his gaze fell on the bent and twisted debris lying on the floor. The smile slid off his face and his eyebrows pinched as he looked me over with concern. "What the devil happened here?"

"I had a little mishap with the forklift," I said, trying to assuage the concern etching his face. Walter was the only person I'd allowed to view the sculpture, mainly because Louie would bolt into the shop and Walter would follow him inside each morning for our coffee date. Walter had been tracking my progress and seemed so invested in my work, I suspected he'd be as disappointed as I was over the loss.

"That is more than a mishap, Andie. Are you okay?"

"I'm fine. Really, the only damage was to my sculpture."

Shaking his head, he surveyed the heap of scrap on the floor. "What a terrible shame," he said. "I'm so sorry."

I expected him to ask what I was going to do now, or if I knew how I was going to fix the sculpture, but he just suggested we go out to the patio and have our coffee. It was as if he knew it was too painful for me to discuss the situation and that I didn't have any answers. After we sat, Walter told me that the plants we'd moved from my apartment to The Grove were thriving in the open dome-covered gardens. He talked about the comedy night, theater production, and other upcoming events happening there this fall. I'd seen them listed on the Board but didn't have a chance to comment because he switched the thread of conversation so abruptly it gave me whiplash.

"You know, Rita hit a whale of a problem on one of her big projects, and she called herself a fool for taking the job. I suggested she refund the client's money and tell them she couldn't do the work, but she said she'd made a promise, and she would dang well keep it." A lopsided grin lifted his cheek. "Anytime she encountered an issue on a project, she'd pace through her shop, tapping a tape rule against her palm or gnawing on her pencil, talking and debating with herself sometimes for days until she'd finally spit out an answer. So maybe if you think on this for a spell you'll find a solution," he suggested.

I wished it were that simple, but time to pace and think was the one thing I didn't have. But like Rita, I'd made a promise to the town, and somehow, someway, I needed to find a way to honor it.

Chapter Twenty-Six

After Walter and Louie left, I was kneeling beside my scrap heap on the floor, trying to determine if I could salvage any of the pieces when Maggie came through the door.

"Oh, girl." She opened her arms and pulled me up into a hug. "Mason came by this morning and told me what happened to your sculpture." She stepped back and glanced at the mess of metal on the floor. "How can I help?"

I shook my head. "You can't, but thanks for asking."

"Can you fix it?"

My throat tightened, and I shook my head.

"Well, crap," she said. "Can you start over?"

I shrugged. "I could, but I don't have enough material."

"Maybe I can help. What do you need?"

"Got any spare nuts and bolts or bicycle sprockets and chains?" The confused look on her face told me I was being petulant when she was simply trying to help. "I need scrap metal. You know, common junk I can repurpose?"

"Don't you have tons of that stuff in here?" she asked, glancing at the shelving unit where I stored the cut scraps of sheet and bar stock.

"That's not the kind of scrap I need."

"Okay, what do you want, and how much of it will get you back to work?"

"I'm touched by your desire to help, but I'm basically out of time to do the project."

"The commemoration is a whole month away, Andie."

"Yes, that's just four *short* weeks."

"Or thirty *long* days," she countered. "Andie, people don't fail because of setbacks. They fail because of what they're *unwilling* to do. So, if you're *willing* to keep going, I'll help you. Give me a list of what you need, and you'll have plenty of it by the end of the weekend."

"That's highly improbable."

She cocked her head and gave me a haughty look. "Not for me." She linked her elbow with mine and turned me toward the office. "Make a list right now so I can get the word out that we're having a community scrap drive for a great cause. And tell me where you want everything delivered."

I stood indecisively, wondering if she could really do it, and if I could possibly honor my commitment.

"Come *on*," she said, tugging me forward. "We can't waste a minute."

An understatement, I thought, the sound of a ticking clock filling my head as we went to my office. I scribbled fast, filling a notebook page with examples of the kind of scrap materials I needed, basically anything except major appliances in this case, then handed it to her.

"All right. You can expect things to start showing up as early as this afternoon."

I couldn't believe she would accomplish her goal, but I just gave her a nod. "That would be fabulous, Maggie, but if I'm interrupted each time someone drops off materials, I won't get any work done.

I'll need to work every second of every day to have any chance of making this happen. So would it be okay if I put some barrels and bins out front and just have people leave their items there?"

"Absolutely, and good thinking. I'll put a sign on your door instructing everyone to leave materials in the bins, and I'll also add the same instructions to the notice when I post it on the Board."

"Do you really think you can make this happen?" I asked, because if she was committed to a scrap drive, and the community supported the project at the level she believed they would, then there might be a sliver of hope for me to honor my work-for-hire contract. I'd need to create a new design *fast*, but I couldn't do that without knowing what kind of materials I'd have to work with, so I felt hamstrung.

"It's *going* to happen," she said interrupting my circular obsessing. "You'll be buried in junk by Sunday. Just put your bins out front and let me handle this." After giving me a quick hug, she got in her van and left me standing in the wake of her swirling energy.

I did as she asked and used the forklift to move a metal barrel and two steel bins out front, hoping at least one of them would fill with a wide assortment of scrap metal that I could repurpose. I'd just parked and shut off the forklift when my phone dinged that I had a message.

It was an alert from the Board. Maggie had already posted the notice for an *Urgent Community Scrap Run - Items needed IMMEDIATELY* it said, noting my long list of items. *Scour your attics, barns, and garages right NOW, and contribute to the sculpture that will stand in Fern Park to commemorate our amazing community. Be part of our Done With evolution!* She'd added.

Reading her notice lifted my spirits. If anyone could make

this happen, Maggie and this amazing community could. I just had to believe I could do it, too.

Desperate for inspiration, I flipped through the old journal my father had given me. My early sketches and handwriting were barely legible but made me smile. As I turned the pages, I noticed how I was evolving as an artist under the gentle tutelage of my father. He'd seen that side of me early on and had nourished it. He'd never suggested I become a lawyer or doctor as my mother had done on numerous occasions. He simply told me to go where my passion might lead me.

Why had I allowed that piece of myself to get buried?

"Andie? Are you in here?" I heard Walter call from the open doorway.

I looked up to find him heading inside with Louie. The little scamp had something clamped in his mouth as he trotted toward me. He dropped the item at my feet, and it hit the concrete floor with a metallic clink. "What's this?" I asked, then realized it was a pair of needle nose pliers. I glanced at Walter. "Those are Rita's pocket pliers."

"They're for your scrap drive," he said. "I saw the notice a few minutes ago and wanted to be the first one to contribute."

"But those are *Rita's* pliers," I said again as if he hadn't heard me the first time.

"Yes, they are," he replied. "Rita would love the idea of her favorite pliers being incorporated into a piece of art. And I think it's the perfect way to memorialize my wife and her passion. It would give me great comfort to know that someday when I'm gone, Rita's pocket-pliers won't be tossed in a donation box or scrapyard, so please say you'll use them in your sculpture."

I was dumbstruck that he was giving them up, especially after he'd trashed the entire shop looking for them. "Are you sure about this, Walter?"

He gave a firm nod. "Please, Andie. Will you use them?"

"I'd be honored, thank you," I said, picking them up, then wiping them on a rag to remove Louie's slobber.

Warmth filled Walter's eyes. "I brought coffee if you're interested," he said, holding up our usual travel mugs. "Got time for a visit?"

I didn't, but I missed them. Our morning visits had been short because I'd been working on the sculpture I'd just destroyed. Now, if Maggie rounded up enough scrap for me to start another project, my coffee dates with Walter might have to be put on hold. "I'm always interested in coffee. Especially yours," I told him. "And we'd better take advantage of our visit now because I probably won't have time for coffee breaks when I start the new sculpture."

When we stepped outside, we found Maggie duct taping two posterboard signs on my overhead door. One said *Artist at work. Do not disturb.* And the other said *Leave all items in the bins.*

"I hope I don't have to open my door," I said.

"You shouldn't anyway because an open door is an invitation for people to visit or to snoop, neither of which you need right now. Your job is to stay inside and do your work."

"Yes, ma'am," I said, giving her a mock salute, then I thanked her for making the signs.

She greeted Walter and scratched Louie's head. "I've already had some calls from people who will be dropping stuff off today, so this is happening, Andie. What else do you need help with?"

As hopeful as I was, I still doubted she'd gather enough scrap material for a full sculpture, but I said, "It would help if the items could be sorted, disassembled, and cleaned up a bit, so if you know anyone looking for work, I'll pay them." At this point, I'd be willing to sacrifice my last bit of savings if it would enable me to create a sculpture and honor my contract with the town.

"I have people," she said, "and you won't need to pay them."

"That's right," Walter chimed in. "I helped Rita in the shop, so I can give you a hand with any of that work."

"All right, depending on how much scrap comes in, cleaning and sorting can start on Monday, but don't complain if I take advantage of you two."

"I won't complain, Andie, if you quit bemoaning your situation and get your whiney self moving," Maggie said, making me cringe and Walter laugh.

She was right, though. I needed to stop looking at the destruction and start looking for the solution.

* * *

All I'd accomplished after a night of sketching ideas was a lot of wasted paper. I'd slept for four hours and gone back to my worktable early this morning hoping my brain would cooperate and produce an answer. But the constant banging and clanking of junk being dropped into the bins outside, a wonderful yet distracting noise, made thinking impossible. I needed to go someplace where I could think and get inspiration.

So, I called Mason and asked how long it would take to fly to Albany.

"Depending on the plane, I can get us there in under an hour," he said.

"That fast?" I felt a bump of excitement. "How much would it cost to hire you and your plane?"

"Usually a few hundred dollars, but I need to deliver a part to my buddy out that way in a couple of days, and you could hitch a ride for nothing."

"That would be wonderful, truly, but the event is today. Thanks anyway."

"Are you going to the Scrap Metal Madness event you mentioned?"

I was truly shocked and deeply flattered that he remembered. "I was considering it, but I can't afford the time to drive there and back or the cost of hiring your services."

"I could make the delivery today and you could ride along."

"Really?" I asked, hoping he wasn't joking with me. "You can just take off whenever you like?"

"Not always, but my schedule is open today and I'm available. I've got the part my buddy needs, so I can make the delivery early. What time do you want to go?"

I suspected I was taking advantage of his generosity, but I was desperate for inspiration, and the thought of spending a little time with a man who could keep me from obsessing about my troubles was impossible to pass up. "As soon as you can be ready."

"All right. Be here in one hour."

"Thank you," I blurted, then ended the call and sprinted upstairs to shower.

* * *

I worried things might be awkward between Mason and me, but he seemed his casual, friendly self. We'd been in the air about fifteen minutes when he said, "We don't have to talk about this, but I need to know if you have any regrets over our intimate moment on the gravel bar."

Although his question surprised me, he was so forthright and open, I replied in kind. "None. It was nice."

He smiled. "Nice wasn't what I was going for. I'll have to do better if there's a next time."

I laughed but wondered how he could sit there all sandy-haired and gorgeous with his blue eyes holding my gaze and think there wouldn't be a next time. If the man wasn't piloting the plane, I'd climb on his lap right now. But I kept my lustful thoughts to myself and gave him a noncommittal shrug. "I suppose there could be a next time. Depends on how many sandboxes you play in."

He burst out laughing. "If a sandbox means what I think it does, I can assure you I'm quite content building sandcastles in one box."

I snorted. "This conversation is getting a little weird."

"Definitely," he said. "Mind if we talk about something else?"

"Please. Tell me about this plane," I said.

He gave me a brief overview of its speed and how it differed from his light sport aircraft, then asked me about the event we were heading to. The rest of our short flight was fun and our conversation casual. After we touched down and navigated to a hangar, we picked up my reserved car rental and drove to the event.

The town had closed off a street near Bayhill Park where the event was taking place. Crowds of people in T-shirts and sunglasses were milling about, some nibbling on vendor food while viewing the mile-long display of artistic creations. The smell of fried dough, popcorn, and burgers filled the air as we paid the entrance fee. A four-piece band playing country music drew Mason's attention, but my gaze barreled ahead, leaping and looking at the variety of metal sculptures positioned along the street as far as I could see.

Mason's chuckle drew me around in search of what he found humorous. But his gaze was fixed on me. "Andie, your eyes are flashing like lightning bugs, flaring up with each new sculpture you see."

I wrinkled my nose, a little embarrassed over my obvious excitement. "I should have warned you that I can't control my enthusiasm at these shows."

"Watching you is the best part of the event as far as I'm concerned," he said, his gaze roving my face. "Pretend I'm not here and enjoy yourself."

Ignoring Mason's presence and how my body gravitated toward his was impossible, but I was here to feed my artistic passion, not my sexual craving. So, I turned my attention to a five-foot tall sculpture of an otter with whiskers.

"That is incredible," Mason said, giving the piece an encompassing look.

I agreed but took my time noting the details of the sculpture and admiring how the artist used eighth-inch stainless steel wire to fashion the figure. It was a simple structure in terms of concept and design, but the work was executed with a skilled hand.

As we moved on, Mason would comment on the aesthetics of the sculptures, noting how creative they were and marveling at the amount of work involved to make them. I took a deeper look, observing the variety of scrap metal used, how the pieces were placed or reshaped, how they formed the whole of the sculpture and made it more interesting, and whether the welds were clean or if the artist hadn't yet perfected that skill. The artistic displays drew me from one sculpture to the next and the next in a trans-like state, completely absorbed in every detail.

Mason bought drinks for us while I talked to the artists, asking questions about their process, about the number of hours invested in each piece, if they had their own shops and if creating sculptures was their full time job. Only one artist was working on commissions and creating metal art pieces full time. I could see she was highly skilled, and her sculpture was an exemplary piece of work. But several of the part-time artists were just as skilled and their work was outstanding, which made my desire to do this full time seem like a foolish dream. I wasn't even sure my skill could measure up. And that drove a wedge of anxiety into my stomach that made eating lunch impossible.

I continued to wander from sculpture to sculpture while Mason grabbed a slice of pizza for himself and caught up with me a few minutes later. "I thought you might like this," he said, handing me a jumbo-size paper cup.

When I saw it was filled with buttered popcorn, I smiled. "Thank you, but I hope you don't expect me to share this with you."

"Didn't even cross my mind." His playful wink whisked my thoughts back to our night on the gravel bar and our fun conversation and passionate sexual encounter. "I just thought popcorn might add to your enjoyment of the exhibits."

"That goes without saying. Popcorn brings pleasure to everything," I said, dropping a piece in my mouth.

"Duly noted," he said. "I'll bring popcorn the next time I visit your sandbox."

My burst of laughter ejected the piece of popcorn from my mouth. It hit Mason in the chest and stuck to his shirt.

A slow smile lifted his lips as he flicked it off.

Heat suffused my face, but I refused to give in to my embarrassment. "Sorry. I hadn't meant to share that with you."

He cupped my face in his warm palms. "Please don't change a single thing about you," he said, then lowered his mouth and kissed me. When he lifted his head, he licked his lips. "Butter and salt, the perfect combination."

"Nothing better," I said, casually sticking another piece in my mouth, but my body vibrated and my mouth longed for more than popcorn.

With Mason's hand on my lower back, we navigated our way through the crowd. I reminded myself I was here to get inspired by creative art, not talk about sandboxes and salt-and-butter kisses.

I needed to observe and explore the sculptures, the ideas and execution of the artists' vision, and hopefully fill my creative well.

I took my time with each piece of art on display. I tried to see the art through Mason's eyes, to become a spectator and simply enjoy the exhibits, but it was impossible. I knew too much about metal, welding, and sculpting to not see every detail. Where Mason saw a life-size horse, I saw hundreds of horseshoes welded together to create the sculpture. Where he saw a turkey, I saw springs, sprockets, and diamond grating. I simply couldn't take in the whole piece without seeing all the parts, without mentally calculating how they were assembled, and without wondering which came first for the artist, a bin full of scrap metal or the idea for the sculpture.

I loved the big, intricate sculptures and wanted to create something on that scale for Dunwith, but time was so short. I thought about my own sculpture, the one I'd started with my father. I wondered how it would compare to the art being exhibited here. It had been so long since I'd worked on it or even laid eyes on it, I couldn't even pose a guess as to its merit. But I remembered the joy of working on it, the thrill of seeing it evolve, and ultimately the heartbreak of hiding it under a tarp because it was too painful to look at.

But now, after viewing so many imaginative pieces of art, my burning curiosity to see how mine compared overshadowed my lingering grief.

By the time we'd made our way through the exhibits and back to our entry point hours later, my mind was chaotic, and my popcorn was long gone.

"So which sculpture did you like best?" Mason asked on our

flight back. "My favorite was the otter," he said, "but maybe because it's my spirit animal."

I glanced at him. "Do you really have a spirit animal?"

"No, but if I did, I'd choose an otter. Did you know they can hold their breath under water for up to five minutes?"

"I did not. All I know is they're cute as hell."

"They are, and they're smart, too. They can juggle rocks, and some otters will keep a favorite stone in their fur-lined pouch for their entire life."

"Is that true?"

"Yep, and they sleep holding hands so that they don't drift apart."

"You're making this up."

"No, it's true. They call it a raft of otters. Sounds like a good way to live life. But what about you? Do you have a spirit animal?"

My brain was cramping from our odd conversation. "I don't think so. I mean, how does one know?"

"Not a clue," he said, shrugging one muscular shoulder. "I was just trying to turn your thoughts from whatever put that deep scowl between your eyes. Is something on your mind?"

"Yes. I'm scowling because my popcorn is gone."

His laughter was so warm and intimate, I yearned to feel his body melt into mine. "Next time, I'll see what I can do about in-flight popcorn service."

Chapter Twenty-Seven

As I pulled the tarp off the sculpture I'd started with my father, memories flooded in. I'd just entered tenth grade when we began the project because I'd fallen in love with a Siberian Huskey my friend had. I wanted a dog of my own, but my mother was severely allergic to pet dander and couldn't have pets in the house. I was crushed, but my father put his arm around my shoulders and walked me out to the shop. He said we would make a dog out of scrap metal. That wasn't at all comforting, but as he sketched out the idea, the project and its lifelike size drew me in.

I named the sculpture Titan, which my father deemed quite fitting for a dog made of metal. We worked on Titan in fits and starts, having to steal minutes between my father's busy job, endless family obligations, and my schoolwork and events. Sometimes, when life or my mother demanded our time, Titan sat untouched for months. I was nearing the end of my senior year, almost three years later, when my father and I added another form to the sculpture. Using quarter-inch wire and slightly heavier metal rods, we fashioned the skeletal cage of a young girl walking beside the dog.

We'd been close to finishing the dog part of the sculpture and were preparing to start fleshing out the girl, but we stepped away again for me to take my Australian adventure after college graduation, and as it turned out, for my father to take his one-way trip to a painful death.

Looking at the piece now, I could see that the work was surprisingly good. Spectacular even. I drew my fingers over Titan, reacquainting myself with his powerful haunches and sloped back, his thick neck and raised head. My father and I talked about Titan as if he were a living creature because to us, he was. Every piece of him was selected with thoughtful consideration. Every conversation about him was filled with excitement and joy. Every weld holding his body together was placed with care by my own hands. And I suddenly realized that my father hadn't done any of the welding on the sculpture. He'd coached me and assisted me when I needed him to hold a piece or help me shape it, but otherwise the work was my own. The two of us spent innumerable hours scouring scrapyards, garage and yard sales, and barn and estate auctions looking for scrap metal, for pieces of Titan. My father would come across something fun, like a bicycle sprocket, and show it to me. *What do you think we can do with this?* he'd ask. I'd give it deep consideration, imagining how that one unique piece would bring Titan to life. The more we looked, the more we found, and the easier it was to imagine how each unique piece would fit and become part of the whole. Those days with my father were some of the best moments of my life.

We loved scrapping, as we called it, and working on Titan. I wondered why we'd let him linger unfinished for months at a time. I recalled our last discussion, how my father felt the sculpture wasn't quite right, that it looked good but felt off somehow. I couldn't see it. My father would never point out issues. He'd simply let me study the piece and figure it out for myself. In this way, he trained me to see with an artistic eye, to evaluate a piece in minute detail and as a whole entity.

As I studied our sculpture, I still couldn't ascertain what had felt off to him because all I could see now was a project with the potential to replace the one I'd destroyed. *Use what you have,* my father would say repeatedly. The concept I'd pitched to the council was for a sleeker more polished sculpture, but that option was gone. I hoped the board wouldn't run me out of town for changing things up on them without their approval, but there were no other options I could offer them. And as I closely inspected my scrap metal sculpture, I believed it would be far more appropriate for this progressive community.

But only if I could finish it in time.

Titan would require modifications and some finishing work. The girl walking beside him was supposed to represent me, but when my father died, she'd been left unfinished, too. The girl was just a skeletal form that would require hours of work and scrap materials I didn't yet have. Transitioning the girl into an adult female form would require even more time, but it felt necessary for her to represent the nurturing yet powerful aspect of the female spirit that was so alive in this town. I would work on her first, then finish the dog.

Taking up my sketch pad, I began making adjustments on paper that would hopefully save me valuable time during the physical process. My father's words of advice were ever present. *Plan first. Prep well. Work smart.* The clanging, banging sounds of metal being dropped into the bins out front grew less frequent as the evening gave way to nightfall. Tucked in the back corner of my shop, I measured and sketched and tweaked my plan until my eyes burned with fatigue. Then I set up welding screens to shield my sculpture from any visitors to my shop. I needed to do the work in private, alone, just me and the voice of my father. From this point on, the only person who would view my work before the unveiling would be me. And probably Louie.

* * *

I had allowed myself four hours of sleep, a hot shower, and a steaming mug of strong coffee before heading outside to see what scrap items had been deposited in the bins. The bluish dawn light made it difficult to inspect the variety of scrap collected, but I saw enough to be utterly impressed with Maggie and the Dunwith community. Within one day Maggie had acquired the amount of scrap it would have taken my father and I a year to collect. I could hardly wait for full daylight when I could root through the bins and select pieces for my sculpture. But I had plenty of prep work to do before then, so I headed inside, geared up, and started severing the skeletal body of the female sculpture from her legs that would need to be lengthened. I placed the cut section on the floor, then removed the arms from the torso, both of which would need to be extended and reshaped from a lanky teen body to that of an adult female.

It was almost physically painful deconstructing the work my father and I had done together. But this sculpture was no longer about a girl and her dog. As I viewed her lying on the concrete floor in pieces, I promised to weld her back together so she could never again be broken. I wanted this piece to tell a new story about powerful women standing up and standing out, and most important, standing for others.

Closeted in my welding nook with protective gear shielding my eyes and ears, Louie's sudden appearance startled me. Knowing Walter wouldn't be far behind, I set aside my hand grinder and slipped off my head gear. "Come on, sweet boy, your treats are on my workbench," I said, stepping from behind my screens before Walter could approach. I greeted him with a wave and pointed toward the door. "I'll be right out," I called, scooping up two treats for Louie who was already nudging my legs.

Walter gave me a nod and stepped back outside. I followed him out and was greeted with his lopsided smile. "I know you don't have time to visit but I figured you could use a cup of coffee."

"Always," I said, enjoying a brief respite in the morning sunshine with my favorite guys.

He glanced at the steel bins. "Looks like they're filling up. What can I do to help?"

I shrugged and slipped Louie a treat. "I'm not sure. I haven't had a chance yet to see what's in the bins." I didn't want Walter digging through scrap bins or moving heavy pieces of metal. I wanted him to stay safe and healthy. "Bringing me coffee is more than enough."

He wrinkled his nose. "I'm strong as an ox and just as stubborn, so I plan to help out here," he said. "And Mason should be along soon to lend a hand, so the two of us can help in some way. Please just tell me what we can do."

It surprised me that Mason would be coming by, but I was glad. I needed every available helping hand. "Okay, if you two can sort the scrap it would allow me to quickly see what I have to work with."

"We can do that. What'll work best for you?"

"Put pipe and tubing in one pile, gears and round shapes in another, springs and spiral or curved shapes can go together, and small pieces in another. Just do whatever makes sense to you."

"Do you care if stainless, aluminum, copper and such are in the same pile?"

"Nope. Just sort by shape, and I'll select what I need. Do you have gloves and eye protection?"

"I have everything in my cart," he said, thumbing toward his scooter.

"All right but promise me you won't overdo it."

"I'll be fine, Andie. Now quit pestering me and get back to work," he said, feigning a bossy scowl.

"Yes, sir." I popped a kiss on his wrinkled cheek that made his eyebrows lift in surprise before he pulled me into a hug. When he released me, I knelt and scratched Louie's neck. "You make sure this ornery cuss doesn't misbehave and hurt himself," I said, then headed inside.

As I pulled on my protective gear, I wondered why Mason hadn't mentioned he was coming over to help this morning. Had he and Walter set this up on their own? Or was Maggie already scheduling helpers for me? Whatever the case, I couldn't think or worry about anything other than fabricating the sculpture.

Face shield down, ear protection secured, gloves on, I got to work.

* * *

People came and went all week, dropping off scrap, or helping to sort and clean the pieces I'd selected. Bobbie Jo, Sophie, Beth, and my gal pals all popped in and out to lend a hand, as did Mason and Ashe. Several of Maggie's helpers were strangers to me. A crew wearing T-shirts saying *Because it's the Right Thing To Do* showed up in small groups over the course of several days. I also recognized a few faces from The Grove that Walter had likely rounded up to help. They would line up their scooters out front like a motorcycle gang and make nearly as much noise hollering to each other or cackling with laughter.

The only time I spent outside was to view and select scrap, but other than a hello and thank you to whoever was there, I didn't stop to talk with any of them. I couldn't spare a single moment. My breaks consisted of two-hour naps, ten-minute meals delivered by friends, and five-minute showers, which I skipped far too often.

Two or three times a day, I looked through the sorted scrap piles, visualizing how the angles, curves, and jagged pieces would nest together, and how the unique textures would bring my sculpture to life. I filled crates with nuts, bolts, rings, chains, gears, disks, springs, metal grating, and other items that needed disassembling and cleaning. In another box, I placed pieces that were ready to be cut or shaped and would be welded into the morphing body of my female sculpture.

It was late evening when I finished re-creating her skeletal form with metal tubes, rods, and quarter-inch wire. My fingers were cramping, and I had a crick in my neck, so I pulled off my welding mask and set it on the floor at my feet. I was beat. And sore. I wanted to soak in a hot bath, then sleep for a few hours, but I simply had too much work left to do. My lady of steel was finally ready to be fleshed out, and I would give her a metal exterior that could withstand even the strongest of storms. She would not bend in the face of adversity or break under the oppression of societal pressure. Not my iron woman.

My heroic vision of her made me laugh, then shake my head. Exhaustion was apparently taking its toll, so I gave in and slogged upstairs for a short nap. But I couldn't sleep. It was past midnight, and yet my brain wouldn't stop darting around, knowing there was something important I needed to find. I knew staying in bed was just wasting my time, so I returned to my workstation and continued sculpting.

For days, I shut myself away, bending, cutting, twisting, crimping, angling, grinding, nesting and layering each piece as I shaped and tacked up iron woman's legs. I hammered and welded until my vision blurred and my clothing was drenched with sweat. In the early morning hours, I would slog upstairs, drop my sodden clothes on the bathroom floor, and cry as I showered. I was happy and miserable at the same time. After years of denying myself a place where I could create art, I had my own shop. I had a project I was excited about, but the impossible deadline was an unbearable weight.

I worked in that manner day after day, night after night until I lost all concept of time. People appeared and disappeared. My friends forced food on me when I forgot to eat and pushed me into bed when I was too delirious to argue.

Walter worried and fretted and warned that Rita had pushed herself so hard once that she'd ended up with mono. He assured me I did not want mono, and I agreed, although I knew it was exposure to the virus, not the work, that had made Rita sick. But the scale weighing my workload against the time remaining to accomplish the task was heavily tilted, and not in my favor. It was either risk my health or utter failure.

Tyler texted a few times to say all was well and he was enjoying his animation class. I was glad and relieved and wanted to hear all about his experience, or to ask him to visit, but thinking about anything other than where I would place the next piece of scrap metal was beyond me at the moment. So, I replied with emojis, shorthand for the text-challenged or mentally and physically exhausted.

My brief replies must have worried him because he called me. My son actually picked up the phone and *called* me. Deeply concerned, I answered.

"Mom, are you okay?" were the first words to come through the phone.

"What? Yeah, why?" I asked, wondering if my words sounded as slurred as they felt coming out of my mouth.

"Well, your texts were weird. And you didn't even acknowledge my birthday. Have I done something to make you mad?"

I felt mad in the out-of-my-mind-insane way due to exhaustion. "Oh, honey, I'm so sorry. I completely lost track of time. I'll send your gift just as soon as I finish my project."

"What project?" he asked as if he didn't believe me.

That he didn't remember me telling him about my sculpture or that the town had commissioned a piece of art from me didn't surprise me, but it hurt. "I'm working on the sculpture I'll be unveiling in, wait, what day is it?"

"What?"

"What day is today?"

"God, Mom, what's going on with you. Are you drunk?"

I laughed a little, but my eyes welled up because he sounded more disgusted than concerned. "I'm not drunk. I'm wrung out and sleep deprived. I've been working round the clock. That's why I've lost track of the date."

"It's Tuesday morning, October 1st."

"Oh my god." My heart gave such a hard jolt I felt my chest shudder. The unveiling would take place in five days. I had four days to finish the sculpture, move it to Fern Park, and mount it on the concrete pad awaiting its arrival.

"Mom, you're kind of freaking me out. Could you please say something normal?"

"Love you, Ty, but I've got to go," I said, then hit the end call button and gave in to a full-fledged panic attack. I raced for the door and burst outside, gasping and gripping my chest. My knees gave out, and I plopped down on a step stool someone had brought to sit on while cleaning scrap metal. I planted my elbows on my knees, pressed my hands to my eyes, and rocked my legs side to side. *Just breathe. In for four...hold for four...out for four...in for four...*

"Andie, are you okay?"

I heard Maggie's voice but couldn't tell where it was coming from.

"Hey," she said, her voice suddenly in my ear as she gave my shoulder a shake. "What's happening here?"

"Can't breathe," I gasped between the waves of panic rolling over me.

"Did something happen? Did you breathe in something toxic?"

I shook my head. "Just need a minute." *In for four...hold for four...*

"Jesus, girl, you're a hot freaking mess."

I nodded and would have told her I was an utter disaster had I been able to catch my breath.

"Like it or not, you are taking a break. I mean it, Andie. You can't continue like this."

"Have to," I said, panting like an overheated canine.

"Nope, not happening."

"Only four days left to finish the sculpture."

"Then we'll double down on helping you. I'll get Kate and Chloe to come over at six and we'll do whatever work you need done. But right now, you're going to go upstairs, take a long-overdue shower, and get some sleep before you have a heart attack."

I lifted my head and looked at her through bleary eyes. "Walter said I might get mono."

"What?" Her mouth teetered in a half-smile as if she didn't know what to make of my nonsensical gibberish. "You've been alone in your shop, so I doubt you've been exposed to the virus."

"Good." I gulped in a breath, then released it in a single blast. "That would suck, though."

"Okay," Maggie said with a laugh. "Whatever disaster decides to strike you down, I'm pretty sure it's imminent if you don't get some rest. So just go to bed, will you?"

I nodded. My body trembled with a fatigue so deep it hurt.

"But, Andie, you really need to shower first."

I snorted because I felt as disgusting as I must look.

She slipped her hand beneath my elbow and hauled me to my aching feet. "Come on. I'll get you upstairs to the bathroom."

"You're a good friend, Maggie."

"Ah, jeez, don't get sentimental on me."

When she guided me inside and headed for the stairs, I shook my head. "Use the lift."

She looked at me. "That's the first intelligent thing you've said in days."

"I'm too tired to take offense."

"Good, then I might as well tell you that your hair is a rat's nest. We might have to shave your head."

I laughed and cried and hugged her arm. "Thank you for making me laugh when I feel like weeping."

"You *are* weeping," she said, hugging me back. "In fact, you're a blubbering mess right now, but don't worry, Andie. I've got you. Get some rest and we'll have our girl gab in your shop tonight."

"Really? With beer, too?"

"Yes, and food," she said, opening my apartment door.

"Oh, I miss our girl gabs."

"Me, too," she said, walking me to the bathroom. "And we'll get plenty of work done tonight while we're hanging out, so you don't have to worry about falling behind."

"You're the best, Maggie. I almost wish I had lesbian tendencies because you would be my perfect mate."

Her laugh echoed in the bathroom. "Well, I'd have to be of the same persuasion to make it work, so looks like we're stuck being friends."

"That's all right, I'll take a great friendship over a romantic relationship any day."

"Me, too. Now please get your stinky self in the shower, then go to bed." With that, she closed the door.

Chapter Twenty-Eight

I'd finished sculpting iron woman's torso and head, but I had saved her arms and shoulders for last because those body parts would be my biggest challenge. I wished I could just toss a cape around her shoulders and make her a superhero, but iron woman deserved my best effort. With only days remaining until the unveiling, I clamped my fingers around my throbbing forehead, scouring my mind for a shorthand way to create the intricate curves and valleys that would define her upper body.

As I picked through two crates of cleaned scrap, searching for the right combination of items, an idea struck me so abruptly I shrieked. "Oh my god!" I was so lit up by the discovery that I bolted around the screen and was met with seriously concerned expressions on my friends' faces. "I need quotes from you guys."

For a moment, all I received were blank looks from Chloe, Kate, and Maggie who were cleaning the pieces of scrap metal I'd selected earlier.

"What the hell, Andie? You just scared the bejesus out of us. We thought you cut your freaking hand off or something."

"Sorry. I had a brainstorm that's going to save me hours of work, but it's also a great addition to my sculpture. Before you ask, I can't share it until the sculpture is unveiled. But I'm going to need quotes that represent Dunwith, our community, our mindset, female empowerment, equality, inclusivity, and that sort of thing."

"Okay," Maggie said. "How about *women should rule the world?*"

"That goes without saying," Chloe said, and we all nodded in agreement. "Andie, are you ready to take a break and join us?"

"Give me an hour," I said, backing away. "Will you please come up with some quotes? Shorter is better, but I'll take meaningful or powerful over short." Without waiting for their acknowledgment, I pivoted on my boot heel and ducked behind my screen.

"It's like working for the Wizard of Oz the way she hides behind that curtain and issues commands," Maggie said.

I smiled. "I heard that."

"Good, now I know you'll hear me when I tell you it's time for a break."

But an hour later, I didn't hear her because I was hammering and reshaping the eagle's wing I'd scavenged from my destroyed sculpture. It was the sight of a towel landing at my feet that got my attention. Setting aside my hammer, I pulled off my head gear and gloves, then joined my friends for our girl gab.

Maggie sat on an overturned bucket, taking a long draw on a bottle of beer. Chloe was parked on a spool of welding wire, and Kate sat on an old wooden tool chest that, according to Walter, had belonged to Rita's father. Cleaning rags dangled from their oil-stained hands, and their faces were smudged with grease. Dressed in jeans, work boots, and ball caps, they looked like a crew on an oil rig. A tarp was spread across the floor between them where they'd placed the scrap metal they were cleaning while I'd been working on the sculpture.

"Pull up a bucket," Maggie said, gesturing to an overturned five-gallon pail like the one she was sitting on.

"You ladies have been busy," I said, gratefully sinking onto the pail.

Maggie handed me an ice-cold beer. "Told you we'd double down and get you caught up."

"That you did. I owe you all big time," I said, toasting them with my beer bottle before tipping it to my parched mouth. After another draw on my beer and letting the cold, effervescent brew cool my throat, I asked, "So what part of the girl gab scoop did I miss?"

"Nothing yet because Kate refused to share her news until we were all present," Chloe said, shooting an accusing look at Kate.

"Fine, I'll tell you now." Kate pushed to her feet and stepped onto the wooden tool chest as if taking the stage. "I would like to announce that at ten o'clock this morning I finished the first draft of my fantasy novel."

"That's spectacular, Kate!" Chloe stood and hugged Kate around the waist.

Maggie launched herself up to wrap them both in an awkward hug. "Absolutely amazing, Kate."

I pushed to my feet and threw my arms around the lot of them because they were so wonderfully silly and because I understood that Kate had accomplished something far greater than writing a book. She'd conquered self-doubt, distractions, opposition, and exhaustion to create something meaningful from a simple thought or idea. "You must be flying right now."

"I feel invincible!" Kate said, thrusting her fist in the air, forcing us to take a step back.

Maggie raised her bottle. "To Kate, one serious badass."

"I think we're all badass women," Kate said, stepping off her mock stage. "Making it this far in life without losing our minds is a feat in and of itself."

"For sure," Chloe said, plopping down on the spool of welding wire. "Just thinking about all the shit we've been through makes me wonder how we're all still standing."

Maggie gave Chloe's shoulder a squeeze, then fished a beer from the cooler. "Anyone else ready?"

"I am." I'd slugged down the first one because I'd been parched, but I'd sip this one because I still had work to do. "So, what now, Kate? What happens after you finish the draft of your book?"

"A much-needed break. My book needs work, but I need a rest and some distance before I can see it with fresh eyes."

"I like that," I said, realizing that the breaks I'd taken with my friends, particularly with Mason, soaring through the sky in his plane and viewing an eagle from above, had given me a new perspective. The experience had enabled me to view the mangled eagle's wing of my sculpture with fresh eyes, to envision it as a shoulder wrap for iron woman. I was so excited by the idea I yearned to share it with my friends, but instead, I asked if they'd come up with quotes for me.

Kate exchanged a grin with Chloe and Maggie before she picked up a tablet they had taken from my desk. "This is my quote," Kate said. "Stop supporting or tolerating bigotry and misogyny."

"Not exactly what I was looking for, but I like it."

"Okay, this one is Maggie's. *My Body, My Gun, Your Choice.*"

I laughed, loving the twist on the *My Body, My Choice* quote that was co-opted by arseholes claiming *Your Body* was *Their Choice.*

"You know we really don't hate men, right?" Chloe asked.

"We're just having a bit of private fun at the expense of the misogynistic arseholes who deserve it."

"That goes without saying," I said. "But did you manage to come up with any quotes I can actually use on my sculpture?"

"I have a list of several appropriate for public consumption," Kate said. "Here are a few: *We will stand for others. We will use our collective voice. We will not be silenced. We will celebrate and protect all living things.*"

As she continued to share them with me, I knew they were perfect for my sculpture, and if the world would embrace even half of the ideals and values this community exemplified, perhaps we could regain our humanity and save our beleaguered planet.

* * *

Although I'd planned to partake of our girl gab for only thirty minutes, it was nearly an hour later when I left my friends to their work and returned to my own. I opened my laptop on the workbench and placed an order for three-quarter-inch stainless steel letters that I would need for the quotes I planned to add to my sculpture. Then I sent Kendra, my contact at the company, an urgent email stating I needed the order expedited and sent next-day air.

I'd just picked up my hammer when Maggie yelled over the screen that they'd finished cleaning the parts and were putting the boxes on the other side of the screen for me. I thanked them for their work and the beer and said I owed them all big time. They promised to collect on that debt and warned me not to work all night. Maggie said she left a little gift for me in my apartment, then they headed back to their own lives.

Feeling incredibly fortunate to have them in my life, I went back to work with a smile on my face. For two hours, I reshaped and wrapped the partially folded eagle's wing around iron woman's shoulders and most of her right arm, so it draped like a feathered shawl. With her bold stride and raised chin, she was coming to life beneath my mallets, pliers, and welding torch.

Hours later, when I finally slogged upstairs to my apartment and turned on the lights, I immediately saw Maggie's gift. While I'd been working, she'd hung curtains and placed pretty area rugs in my kitchen and living room and had done the same in my bedroom and bathroom. My space was so cozy and inviting, I wished I could spend time relaxing here rather than rushing through showers and short naps. Soon, I promised myself. After the unveiling, and a couple days of sleep, I would host a party in my apartment for my friends.

* * *

Thursday afternoon, I was gluing the stainless letters onto the eagle wing feathers when I heard a yelping screech outside that raised the hair on the back of my neck. Alarmed shouts filled my ears as I bolted for the door.

Outside was a melee of activity. Louie was yelping in obvious pain as Walter scooped him into his arms. A lady from The Grove was sobbing and apologizing, shaking so badly she could barely get off her scooter. Another elderly resident hobbled toward his scooter calling over his shoulder that he'd take Walter and Louie to the vet.

That's when I saw blood covering Louie's leg and the fear on Walter's face as his sweet boy panted in his arms.

"Oh no," I whispered. Dread wrapped my body like winter slush around bare feet. "I'll get my keys," I said to Walter, then raced inside with my heart hammering. I returned in seconds, shaking and out of breath as I guided Walter to my beater car at the edge of my lot. "What happened?"

"Hattie backed her scooter into Louie," Walter said, his jaw quivering as he sank onto the seat. "This poor boy tried to scramble out of the way, but he's an old guy like me. We can't move that fast, can we, buddy?" he asked, directing his question to Louie who whimpered and panted in obvious agitation.

I hurried around to the driver's side and cranked the engine to life, then did my best not to hit anybody as I backed out.

Thankfully, the vet's office was only a few blocks away, and they took us in immediately upon seeing Louie's injury. Assisted by a young vet tech, the doctor performed a gentle physical exam while Walter stood beside the table, his face a mask of fear. If Walter lost Louie, his best friend in the world, after suffering the loss of his lifelong love, I feared it would kill any light left in the man. The thought of losing either of them gutted me.

"I'm not noticing any tenderness in Louie's abdomen or ribs, which is a good sign," the doctor said. "I suspect he has a femur fracture, but we'll need an X-ray to confirm it."

"Can you fix a femur fracture?" Walter asked meekly, as if terrified the answer might be no.

"Usually, but treatment depends on the fracture. Let us take a look and we'll have better information for you in a few minutes," she said, then gently lifted Louie in her arms, taking care to support his injured leg. "We'll get you feeling better soon, little man."

Walter and I waited in the small, private room, both of us too shaken and worried to speak more than a few words. When the vet returned several minutes later without Louie, she assured Walter that Louie was okay and was being prepped for surgery. "Normally, we schedule all surgeries, but Louie has a femur fracture that requires surgery now. He also has a gash on his leg that will need a few stitches. We've given him a light sedative to make him more comfortable while we wait for bloodwork results, which we'll have in a few minutes. At that point, we'll take him into surgery, which will likely take about two hours. He'll need to stay the night and have his activity restricted for approximately six weeks."

Walter's face was so pale and drawn, he looked ancient. "Can we see him before surgery?"

"Of course. I'll have a vet tech take you back to his kennel," she said, then left the room.

"I'm so relieved they can fix his leg," I said, hoping it gave Walter some measure of comfort.

"I am, too." He gave a slight shake of his head. "But Louie's not going to like being cooped up. I suspect his recovery will be hell for both of us."

I smiled. "Maybe I can fabricate a wheeled cart for him like they have for disabled pets."

Walter's eyebrows peaked, the first sign of life in his face since Louie got hurt. "That would be something, wouldn't it?"

A vet tech popped his head in and said we could see Louie now. We followed him to a quiet area at the back of the building where three other dogs were resting on padded beds in various size cages. Two exam tables sat in the middle of the area with a double sink and glass cases containing medications lining one wall, and a counter with three computer monitors along the other.

"Here's Louie's penthouse," the vet tech said, then told us we'd have about ten minutes to visit before they would need to take Louie into surgery. "You can crack the door open a bit, but it's best if you don't get him excited."

Walter opened the door a little to slip his trembling hand inside. He stroked Louie's snout. "Hey, buddy. I'm sorry I didn't keep you safe," he said, his lips bunching as a tear wet his cheek.

Tamping down my own emotions, I gave his boney shoulder

a gentle pat. "Louie will get through this. And I'll be right here with both of you," I said, letting Walter know he wasn't alone. I slipped my fingers through the metal cage to stroke Louie's front paw. His toes curled around my finger as if to give me a reassuring squeeze, and my heart melted. Louie's eyelids drooped and his head sank back down on the pad. Seeing that the sedative was helping Louie relax was a huge relief.

"You don't need to stay," Walter said, glancing at me. "I know you need to be at your shop."

"No, I need to be here with you. I'm not going anywhere, Walter. I couldn't concentrate on anything but you and Louie anyway, so I'm staying right here."

Walter didn't say anything, just reached over and gave my hand a squeeze.

We stayed with Louie, talking softly to him, until the same vet tech came back to let us know they were ready to take Louie into surgery. We were directed to the waiting room where a middle-aged man sat with a small carrier containing a gray tiger cat. A young woman across the room was coaxing what looked like a wolfdog onto a floor scale to get its weight. She laughed when the vet tech said the dog outweighed her by ten pounds.

People came and went, bringing their cats and dogs for vaccines and exams, or to pick up prescription foods and medications. Walter and I tried to converse, but neither of us succeeded at small talk. My head was filled with worry over what might be happening to Louie in surgery, and my gut was knotted with anxiety over my encroaching, impossible deadline. It felt like days passed before a vet tech finally took us back to a private room, but he assured us it had only taken two hours and fifteen minutes for the surgery, and that Louie did very well. He went over the lab results and the X-rays and told us the doctor put a percutaneous pin in Louie's femur that would be removed once the bone mended. They'd be keeping him at least one night and would go over care and other instructions when they discharged Louie.

Walter seemed a little stunned as we followed the vet tech back to Louie's penthouse kennel. Louie's eyes peeped open, but he was still heavily sedated and immediately drifted off. We were able to spend a few minutes with him before they asked us to leave him in their capable hands.

By the time we reached the parking lot, Walter was wiping his eyes with a bunched up handkerchief. "Don't seem right leaving my boy all alone in there."

"I know," I said, hugging him. "But with the meds they're giving Louie, he'll surely get more rest than either of us will."

A half-laugh tipped Walter's mouth, then he sniffed. "That's for sure. Should have asked the vet for a sedative for myself."

"He'll be okay, Walter. They all know and love Louie, and they'll take good care of him."

"I know. Just feels like half my body is missing."

"Why don't I drop you at your apartment and you can get your scooter tomorrow?" I suggested as I pulled out of the parking lot.

"I don't think I can stand being there without Louie. I just can't," he said, a tortured expression on his face. "Maybe I could stay at your shop for a while?"

"Of course. Whatever you need."

Apparently, what Walter needed was the comfort of his old home because he asked if he might rest on my couch for a spell. I had lost nearly six hours of the day, but Walter and Louie were my guys, my family, and my heart ached knowing our sweet boy was injured.

It was heading toward late evening when I suggested Walter

spend the night. When he readily agreed, I knew he didn't want to be alone. I put out fresh towels for him on the bathroom vanity, and after he cleaned up, I sat with him until he fell asleep on my new sofa in his old home.

Chapter Twenty-Nine

L ate Friday afternoon, Walter refused to let me take him to the vet's office to pick up Louie. He said his friend from The Grove was taking him over and that I needed to stay put and finish my work. I didn't really have a choice, but I made him promise to let me know when they got home and how Louie was doing. An hour later, he texted two photos of Louie at home, looking humiliated in his kennel.

I was down to my final night to finish my sculpture. Every muscle in my body felt contracted with anxiety, and the urge to hurry, hurry, hurry thrummed hard through my veins.

Steering my mind back to work took effort and constant vigilance. Carefully, I glued stainless lettering to the metal feathers of the eagle's wing to create words like *inclusivity, individuality,* and *impartiality,* and phrases like *An evolved & enlightened community, Un-learn bias,* and *Be kind.* Finally, I glued on my favorite phrase *Forever Wild,* the motto for the beautiful Adirondacks region, across the scapular part of the wing which wrapped wild woman's shoulders. The letters were twice as large as the others and would stand out as a statement for our community. The feathers, cut from weathering steel, would eventually turn rusty shades of orange and brown, making the silver stainless steel letters pop in contrast, and highlighting the quotes my friends and I had come up with during our girl gab.

I wish I had been introduced to empowering quotes, like the ones I'd just glued onto my sculpture, when I was a teenager. If I'd have known that the only thing I would ever need was my own authentic voice it would have saved me decades of feeling lost and alone. I wouldn't have given myself away. I wouldn't have let anyone bury, steal, or erase pieces of me.

As the hours dwindled down and hints of dawn light seeped in the window, I pushed on without sleep. In four hours, Hank from the town barns would arrive to help me move my sculpture to Fern Park. But it wasn't ready.

I needed more time, so I texted Leila, apologizing for the early hour and for messaging her on a weekend, but told her the sculpture wouldn't be ready to move until the end of the day. Her reply was brief but said she'd have Hank call me to schedule a time.

Lazer focused on my work, I shaped, nested, and layered disk-shaped washers, sprockets, three old keys, one metal lock, two horseshoes, a monkey wrench, a triangular-shaped piece of perforated stainless sheet, and a multitude of other scrap pieces onto iron woman's arm and torso until I'd fully fleshed her out.

Just after nine, Hank called to ask what time I wanted to move the sculpture. His question caused such a torrent of stress in me, my eyes burned with tears of frustration. "I have a few things to finish up yet. Is there any way we could do this in the evening?"

"Well, I'm not actually working today. It is Saturday, you know."

I nodded but couldn't reply. After everything my friends and community had donated to the creation of this sculpture, I could not fail them.

I couldn't.

"How late are you thinking?" he asked.

Stretching my neck to ease the tension in my throat, I said, "Seven-thirty, maybe?"

"It's kind of late. We might run out of daylight, but I guess I can't move something that isn't ready to go. All right. I'll let Leila know our plan. See you this evening," he said, and ended the call.

I hoped he wasn't upset, but Walter's call redirected my attention to more pressing concerns. "Is Louie all right?" I asked, hoping his first night home hadn't been too rough.

"Thanks to the meds, our boy made it through the night without too much fussing," Walter said. "I watched and worried all night, but it was worth the lack of sleep to have him home."

"I'm sure. Is there anything you need?"

"We're just fine, Andie. Louie is taking this surprisingly well, and the pain meds make him drowsy, so he seems content enough to stay tucked in his bed. I called to let you know we're well so you can focus on your work. How are you coming along?"

"Racing the clock as you know."

"Then I won't keep you another second. Just keep working, Andie. You can do this."

He ended the call then, and I began the laborious task of finish welding and grinding iron woman's peaks and valleys, slowly revealing the power and grace of her form. I didn't finish until late afternoon. Then I turned my attention to Titan.

"All right, this is it, Dad. Last chance to tell me what's off with my work," I said, my voice hoarse with fatigue.

As I studied the sculpture, I mentally reviewed the list my father had written in the front of my journal. *Try something new.* I had. I'd tried a new sculpture, and I'd destroyed it. *Throw some of it away.* I had scrapped everything except one wing. *Be a problem solver.* I had solved my problem by resurrecting the sculpture my father and I had started, and I would now use to replace the one I'd destroyed. *Add another piece.* I'd added the eagle's wing as a shawl around iron woman's shoulders. *Get out of your own way.* I was too tired to move, to get out of anyone's way, but I knew that's not what my father's words meant. I was my own biggest obstacle every time I doubted the work or my ability. I needed to *Get a new perspective* as he would often tell me, and I was trying to do that now as I studied Titan.

My dog of steel made me think about sweet Louie and how small he looked tucked in a kennel at the vet's office before his surgery. Remembering the feel of Louie's little, round paw cupped in my palm and the way he curled his toes as if to give my hand a squeeze, tugged at my heart—and at my brain, and an inkling of understanding slowly seeped into my mind.

Titan's feet were too long.

I scrubbed my burning eyes with my fists, then leaned in and looked more closely. Was that what my father thought was off about the sculpture, that Titan's feet were too long? Or was it Titan's nose that I now realized was too stout for a Siberian Huskey. When my dad and I were actively working on the sculpture, I suspected he was just being overly critical, but I could see the issues now. Titan's head was too thick, and his nose was too short and blockish for that of a Huskey. It was so glaringly obvious to me now, I wondered why I hadn't been able to see it at the time.

Had my father been waiting for me to fully recognize that I'd been creating a primal beast more suited to my wildish nature than a domesticated dog? Had he intuitively understood that his daughter would be more at home trotting forest paths with the wolves?

How had I lost that part of myself?

Grief, I suppose. My loss had been so great when my father died it cloaked every aspect of my life. I'd felt numb and lost in a barren landscape so foreign to me I didn't know how to survive. Like an injured animal, I sought comfort where it was offered. I was at the mercy of the one providing sustenance and care, and I'd been severed from my natural environment for so long I'd lost my innate nature. Is that why I hadn't understood my inner yearning was for a space where I could roam and explore and create?

I understood it now. I was a creative creature. And Titan was a wolf.

My wolf.

Work from your head, sculpt from your heart. With my father's words in mind, I cupped Titan's beautiful head in my hands and promised I'd liberate him. I made small, precise cuts beneath Titan's jaw and tilted his head up as I knew any self-respecting wolf would want. A few more cuts opened his mouth so he could howl and communicate with his pack. And finally, I knew exactly where Rita's pocket pliers were meant to go. Placing the handles forward toward the front of Titan's open mouth made him look as if he was howling. The pointed tip of the plier created the hinge of Titan's jaw.

Rita's pocket pliers were now prominent and visible in the sculpture and gave Titan a commanding attitude that matched Rita's own. Pleased with the effect, I welded them in place, then smoothed out the welds with my grinder and added a finishing pass with a polishing pad.

At ten minutes after seven o'clock, as I laid down my grinder for the last time and pulled off my gloves, a guttural sob burst from my mouth. After all the hours of excitement, fear, anticipation, self-doubt, panic, hope, and exhaustion, I'd finally done it. I'd finished the sculpture that had haunted me for more than twenty years.

And I'd kept my promise to my father.

Chapter Thirty

Hank, a middle-aged heavy equipment operator for the town, drove an industrial forklift into my parking lot at seven-thirty sharp where I was waiting for him. He cut the motor and stepped off the machine, squinting as his eyes scanned the inside of my shop. "Ah, you did say you'd be ready now, didn't you?" he asked, apprehension thick in his voice.

"Yes, and thanks for coming on your day off."

"Well, the town would be mighty disappointed if they don't see a sculpture sitting in the park tomorrow morning."

"Then we'd better get to work." I directed him to the back corner of my shop where Titan sat concealed beneath an opaque blue cloth drape provided by the town. "I don't know how much it weighs, so I could only pose a guess."

"No matter. That beast out there can lift thirty thousand pounds," he said, gesturing to the crane-forklift combo sitting in my parking lot. He gave my sculpture base another close inspection, followed by a quick nod, then headed outside.

It took forty-five minutes to move my sculpture to the park and another hour to mount it on the platform. Although I'd made sure to use the same bolting pattern for Titan's base as the sculpture I'd originally planned, one of the mounting brackets was slightly off from the bolt hole. I heated the metal tab with a torch and hammered it until it aligned with the hole. At that point, I sent Hank home since his part of the install was finished, then I filled the holes with epoxy and set the stainless steel bolts to secure the sculpture to the concrete base.

The park was illuminated by glowing lanterns on steel posts, and I was delirious with fatigue when I finished. I sat on the concrete pad and leaned my aching back against the drape covering Titan. I'd imagined sharing this moment with my friends, but my wobbly emotions made me glad to be alone.

I sniffed and backhanded my moist eyes, then smiled and released a watery laugh, then cried again because my father wasn't here to see our finished sculpture.

* * *

Sunday morning, I rose early and went for a run along the river. Starting slowly, I let my tight muscles warm up, then stopped at a picnic area to stretch and unlock my abused body. I moaned aloud because it felt so good to be outside in the crisp morning air instead of tucked behind a welding screen. I savored every minute of my thirty-minute jaunt, promising myself another run tomorrow and that I'd start visiting some of the shops and restaurants along the river.

After a quick shower at home, I drove to the café where I bought two large coffees to go, then went to The Grove and knocked on Walter's door. The sound of Louie's bark made me smile. Seeing Walter's surprised face when he opened the door had my heart swelling with love.

"Got time for a coffee date?" I asked, lifting my hands to show him I'd brought two cups.

"Good gracious!" he said, his eyes lighting with delight. "What a wonderful surprise." He stepped back to let me inside.

I handed him a cup of coffee. "Delivery from the Maple Leaf Café."

"Best coffee in town," he said, and I immediately thought of the day I met Maggie at the Tamarack gas station, and she took me to the café for coffee.

I couldn't bear to think what direction my life might have taken had I not met her that morning. If not for Maggie, I wouldn't have met Kate and Chloe or experienced their girl gabs. I wouldn't have stayed in town long enough to weld Beth's railing and remember how much I loved that kind of work, or for Walter to convince me to buy his business. I wouldn't have met all the wonderful people who'd become my friends. I wouldn't have flown in Mason's amazing planes or made love on a gravel bar. I wouldn't have had coffee dates with Walter and Louie or experienced the ocean of love they gave me.

"Can you stay for a bit?" Walter asked.

"I sure can." I sat my cup on the table. "I have a special delivery to make first," I said, then crossed to Louie's kennel on the living room floor. His tail thumped the side of the cage. "Don't get up, sweetie." I glanced at Walter first to see if it was okay to give a treat to Louie. At Walter's nod, I opened the door and gently rubbed Louie's head and ears. "Here you go, love."

He lipped the treat and licked it into his mouth, leaving a swath of slobber across my fingers. I laughed and felt my heart bursting with love. I spent a few minutes administering adoring affection in the form of gentle petting. When his eyes were drooping, I quietly closed the door and headed to the kitchen sink to wash my hands.

"We got one of those little doggie wheelchairs from the vet," Walter said, "so Louie can be mobile without hurting himself. I strapped the contraption on him for a couple minutes last night, and Louie didn't know what to make of it." Walter's shoulders shook with laughter. "He kept looking behind him, but he got the hang of it after a few minutes and didn't seem to mind too much. He moseyed around the living room for about five minutes before heading back to his bed."

"I wish I could have been here," I said, a twinge of pity in my heart for the little guy. "I feel so bad for him."

"Oh, Louie's a tough boy, and he'll be back on his own four paws before you know it."

"I'll probably celebrate that day as joyfully as Louie will."

Walter smiled. "Me, too." After a pause, he said, "I saw a photo on the Board this morning of a large, tarped sculpture in the park awaiting an unveiling today. Looks like you beat the clock."

"By twenty whole minutes," I said, feigning arrogance, as if there was never any question.

Walter released a belt of laughter. "I can't tell you how much I'm looking forward to seeing your work. I know it will be amazing."

I wish I'd been able to keep my work to myself for a while like Kate was doing with her book. She would be able to revise her work, an opportunity I wouldn't have. But I had given it my best effort, and Titan would have to stand on its own now.

Chapter Thirty-One

F ern Park was milling with people when I arrived. They spilled out into the streets girding the grounds, their conversations and boisterous laughter a backdrop for the live band playing on stage. The smell of roasting veggies and fresh baked bread, my favorite foods that always made me hungry, twisted my stomach into a queasy knot.

I wanted to rush back to the quiet privacy of my shop where I could practice square breathing until I calmed down. But Leila and Mayor Savanna had seen me, and they were beckoning me to the small stage erected near my sculpture.

Suddenly, I questioned my decision to wait until the last minute to arrive. Perhaps I should have come early. Maybe it would have given me time to settle my nerves. But that would have meant talking with people, and I hadn't felt capable of conversation. My mind had been spinning all morning wondering what I would say in my speech, one I didn't want to give but, as the artist, was expected to do.

As I approached the stage, the mayor signaled the band, and they stopped the music. The abrupt ending of the song followed by Mayor Savanna's voice over the PA drew everyone's attention.

"Today is *Done With Day*," she said, and was rewarded with applause and cheers that rippled across the park. "As a community, we are actively choosing to be open-minded, forward-thinking, compassionate individuals," she said, then paused to let another round of applause and cheers die down before she spoke again. "We are choosing to be environmentally conscious, making it a priority to protect our planet and wildlife. Dunwith is an inclusive community where we celebrate our differences and support each other. To commemorate this special day, we've commissioned a sculpture by our own resident artist Andrea Arness."

She waved me onto the stage, and my legs felt like sandbags as I climbed the steps.

"By marking our *Done With Day* with a physical sculpture," she continued, "we are cementing our commitment to inclusivity and equality and showing the world that we're proud to be an enlightened community!" The crowd roared so loudly I felt the wooden platform vibrate beneath us. After a long moment, she held up her hand for silence. Once everyone had settled, she said, "You might have noticed that this important event and the unveiling of the sculpture is being covered by our local news station. It will also be broadcast to its affiliates. This means we are about to make a statement to the world, or at least to anyone who watches the broadcast," she said, eliciting cheers and laughter.

I'd had no idea that a television news crew would cover the event, and it amplified my anxiety. My heart pounded harder and my vision blurred.

"Now, without further ado, the artist will share a few words with us before the sculpture is unveiled," she said, then pressed the microphone into my trembling hand.

The park grew quiet, and my mouth went dry. I'd considered a few thoughts I might share at this moment, but I couldn't pluck a single intelligible word from the slurry swirling through my head. Suddenly, a loud *Hee-haw* from somewhere in the crowd sliced through my panic and created a ripple of laughter from the audience.

For a moment, I thought I was being heckled, but then I saw my son standing near the front of the crowd, grinning and flapping his hand by his head like a donkey ear. He was letting me know he was here for me, that I hadn't lost him, that I could do this thing that scared me. And so, I dragged in a deep breath and returned his smile with a wobbly one of my own to let him know I'd received his message.

"It's an honor to have my first life-size sculpture stand right here in Fern Park," I said, addressing Leila and Mayor Savanna who were holding the cords that would release the drapes covering my sculpture. "Thank you and the other council members for trusting me with such an important task."

I couldn't hear their replies over the smattering of applause, but I read their lips as they thanked me in return.

Facing our audience, I said, "Creating this sculpture was a complicated journey, and one I couldn't have completed without the support of this amazing community." A murmur rolled through the park. "Your generous donations of scrap metal and the hours many of you spent sorting and cleaning materials enabled me to finish the work in time for this celebration. I need to give a special thanks to Hank in our streets department for working late last night to help me mount the sculpture. Without him, it would still be sitting in my shop."

Laughter and shoutouts to Hank sounded across the park.

"Before I share my vision for the sculpture, I must also thank my steadfast friends," I said, giving a nod toward Maggie, Chloe, Kate, Ashe, Mason, and Walter who were standing a few feet from the stage, and to Sophie, Bobbie-Jo, and Beth who were standing left of the stage, "for pushing me when I might have given up, for feeding me when I was hungry, for making me go to bed when I was too weary to work, and for giving me a team and family to lean on. And finally, I'd like to thank my son, Tyler, for that loud *Hee-haw* that reminded me why I'm here."

The collective burst of laughter gave me a moment to catch my breath and gather my thoughts along with a bit of confidence.

"*It's a wonderful life* was my son's favorite Christmas movie when he was young, and I loved its message that every person matters. We each create ripples that affect others. If Dunwith is your home, you are extremely fortunate to live in a place that values community and celebrates life in all its forms and iterations. That is remarkably rare and so are those of you who champion and support this ideal. Your kindness and compassion make a difference. Your actions make ripples that change lives. *You* matter."

I had to wait for the applause to settle before I could continue. "Sometimes an artist knows from the beginning what they're after, or what they want a piece to look like. Other times, they have to pull it apart and rework it many times before the piece will reveal itself. As you view this sculpture, you'll see materials you donated, pieces of your life you willingly gave to someone in need. Some of you will see the parts you cleaned and prepared, the work you did with your own hands. For me, this sculpture was a community effort that will stand as a symbol of our ideals and represent the wild beauty of this amazing community. So now, with great joy, I'd like to present... *Titan*."

A loud drumroll erupted from the bandstand and rolled across the park as Leila and Mayor Savanna pulled the cords to release the drapes. They fell away like silk scarves, and the bright, ringing crash of cymbals filled the air as *Titan* was finally revealed.

A collective gasp burst from the crowd followed by a roar of applause that grew to a thunderous level as the mayor and Leila pulled the drapes away from the base of the sculpture.

My heart pounded and I grew lightheaded, and all I could hear was blood whooshing through my ears. Slowly, words like *wow* and *amazing* and *ingenious* started seeping through the pulsing noise in my head.

Mayor Savanna and Leila both hugged and thanked me, their effusive praise bleeding in and out of the surrounding noise. I experienced such a surge of relief, I could barely form an intelligible sentence. I'd anticipated and lived for this moment for weeks, and now that it was here, I just wanted to go hug my son and hang out with my friends. But the news anchor nabbed me for an interview, and I knew this was an important opportunity to talk about Dunwith leading the way for other communities to evolve. And in a deeply personal way, it was my moment to let people know that Evergreen Metal Sculptures was open for business. I could finally order my business cards.

The reporter tucked us in a nook behind the stage for the interview, but we could hear people milling around the sculpture, drawn into a game of identifying the items I'd used to create it. I could list and locate every piece I'd used and explain why I'd chosen those particular items, but I didn't share any of that in my interview. After talking about Dunwith and the reason for our *Done With Day* celebration, I answered questions about my sculpture. I talked about my vision for the piece, the tools I used, and how long it had taken to create it. For me, it had been a journey of more than twenty years, but I simply said it took a few weeks of very long days.

Half an hour later, after my short interview and twenty minutes of fighting my way through the crowd of people eager to congratulate me or compliment my sculpture, I finally found my son.

"Hey, Mom! You looked shocked to see me," he said, smiling and seeming pleased with himself as he gave me a hug.

"I certainly was! Please tell me everything is okay."

"Yeah. The guys and I just wanted to come to see your sculpture and check out Dunwith. *Titan* is, well it's, wow!" He shook his head as if he couldn't believe I'd really made it. "It's amazing, Mom. Really. I'm kind of blown away."

I laughed. "Now *you* look shocked."

"I am!" he said. "I had no idea you could do that sort of thing. The guys and I were checking it out while you were being interviewed. How did you know where to place all that stuff to create a person and a wolf?"

"I just guessed," I said, half-kidding, and pulled him back into a hard hug. "Thank you for being here and for saving me from the meltdown I was about to have on stage."

"I was just returning the favor, Mom."

My heart flooded with warmth knowing he hadn't forgotten our Hee-haw game and the special moments we spent together. "I'm so glad you're here, hon, but don't you guys have classes tomorrow?"

"Well, yeah, but not until afternoon. Can we crash at your place tonight?"

"Tyler, it's your home, too, and your friends are always welcome." I released him and greeted the boys I'd watch grow up with my son, with a hug.

"Thanks, Mom. We're going to grab something to eat now."

"Okay but come back when you're finished because I want to introduce you to a few people. I'll be right over there," I said, pointing to a beer tent where Chloe and Kate were standing. I noticed Maggie behind them but couldn't see who she was talking with.

"We'll be back in a bit," Tyler said, then strolled off with his buddies, but their rubbernecking told me they were looking for more than food.

"To be that young again," Walter said, coming up beside me.

"Oh, shoot, I wanted to introduce you to my son," I said, watching Tyler and his friends disappear in the crowd. "Ah, well, he'll be back. Walter, are you able to stay?"

"Hattie is sitting with Louie, so I'm a free man for an hour or so."

"Then would you like to get a beer with me? I'm parched!"

A mischievous smile tilted Walter's mouth. "You bet," he said, adjusting his ball cap to shield his eyes from the sunshine as we made our way to the tent.

While my friends complimented my work and the sculpture, Walter stood beside me with one trembling arm around my shoulders but rock solid in his support. This beautiful man and his sweet, slobbery dog had salved the wound in my heart and given me another chance to have a family and a place of my own where I could finish my sculpture.

"*Titan* is an extraordinary piece of work," Walter said, his voice graveled with emotion as he gave my shoulders a squeeze. "Rita would love how you used her pocket pliers."

"You saw where I placed them then?"

"I did. I was standing right there when they unveiled your work, and I didn't leave until a few moments ago when I came looking for you. Your passion and talent are evident in every bend and weld you made to create that exemplary piece of work. You found your calling, Andie."

A joyful current surged through me as our friends echoed Walter's praise. Someone slipped a beer in my hand, and someone else gave me a hug. Maybe Kate? My attention was splintered in so many directions I floated through several minutes of conversation.

Tyler returned, saying he already liked Dunwith and that he and his friends would be coming back during one of their college breaks to check out more of the town. I introduced him to Walter and my friends, then my son strolled off again with his buddies and a couple of teenage girls they'd met at a vendor stand.

"The band is back from their break," Maggie said, slipping her arm through mine. "Time to dance and celebrate your big moment, girlfriend."

Kate and Chloe joined us in the milling throng, then Ashe and Mason. Walter gave me a twirl and a hug, garnering a promise to meet him for our morning coffee date, then he headed home to Louie.

The band played and the crowd sang along, and I danced with a beer in one hand and a smile on my face.

"I'm glad to see you smiling again," Maggie said, raising her voice to be heard over the music.

"I was just thinking how my worst day led to a great new life. Thank you for hitting on me at the gas station."

Maggie laughed. "Well, thank you for letting me pick you up, and for that gorgeous sign you made for me. No one can walk by it without coming inside to see what's so foxy about my boutique."

"I suspect that's immediately evident when they see you and Jill," I said with a laugh. "But I should be thanking you because that sign got me this gig. And I've already been given two business cards today from people interested in signs."

The crowd squashed us close to Chloe and Kate who told me not to forget about them when my business started booming.

"I'd never forget you ladies. You're my wolf pack, my forever wild friends."

"Ooh, I'd love to be a wolf with a poofy tail," Maggie said, swishing her hips and butt.

I laughed. "Okay, Maggie, someone has to show you how to bounce your booty," I said, dropping into a squat with a shoulder-grooving-butt-popping-bounce that had them laughing and shouting *Git it, girl*.

For those brief seconds, I felt outside my body, so untethered and free of the cage I'd unwittingly crawled into a lifetime ago I barely recognized that uninhibited side of myself. I felt playful, empowered, and alive! I shook off all the ragged, jagged pieces of my grief and tossed off the oppressive seriousness that had cloaked my life for so long. I moved into a less provocative dance and faced them. "And that, my friends, is how it's done," I said, laughing out loud because I'd shocked myself and delighted these crazy, wonderful women.

"You just witnessed that, right?" Maggie asked Mason, who was watching with surprise in his eyes and a smile on his face.

"Yes, I did, and it's something I'll never un-see," he said, toasting me with his drink as the band dropped into a slow dance.

"Next girl-gab is at your place," Maggie said, "and you're going to teach us how to do that."

"Okay, but you don't have enough booty to bounce." I started to follow them to the beverage tent but found myself guided back around by Mason's gentle hand on my elbow.

"One dance?" he asked.

I smiled and slipped into his arms. "Thought you'd never ask."

God, he smelled good, his muscled body hard and warm against my own as he drew me close. Tonight wasn't the night to partake of his pleasures, but I fully planned to do so when my apartment was free of teenaged boys. Because I deserved passion and fun in my life.

"Your sculpture is spectacular," he said, "and your speech was really powerful."

All I remembered was the thudding of my heart as I gazed down at the smiling faces of my friends and Walter and Tyler, my *people*, supporting me and cheering me on.

As Mason drew me closer, I looked over his shoulder and saw my iron woman standing tall and proud. She was fierce and beautiful with her eagle's wing shoulder wrap and her wind-tossed hair flowing behind her, a *wild* creature with an iron constitution. Her determined stride and steely resolve would be a symbol of strength for all women to stand strong in every storm.

And I looked at Titan, so regal with his powerful haunches flexing as he walked beside her, his mouth open and snout lifted to the wind, and I knew my magnificent wolf was finally free to howl in all his wildish glory—and so was I.

I'd found a forward-thinking community, real friends, my passion, my independence, my self-respect, and my own voice. In resurrecting my passion, I'd found the broken, lost, and stolen pieces of myself and welded them back together to create a strong, empowered woman.

My father would ask. *Did you find the lost or missing pieces?*

And I could finally answer *Yes*.

I found the pieces I wanted to keep.

Also by Wendy Lindstrom

Done With

Done With

Found Pieces

The Second Chance Brides

Always and Forever

Twice Loved

Then Came You

Only You

My Heart's Desire

The Greatest Gift

My Forever Love

Chances Are

A Moment Like This

Lost in Your Love

Second Chance Brides Special Collections

It Had to be You Collection (Books 1-3)

Anything for Love Collection (Books 4-6)

From the Moment We Met Collection (Books 7-9)

The Grayson Family

When I Fall In Love In Love

Shades of Honor

The Longing

Lips That Touch Mine

Kissing in the Dark

Sleigh of Hope

Leave it for the Rain

The Promise in Your Eyes

Captured by Your Love

Until I Found You

The Graysons Collections

Grayson Series Collection One (Books 1-3)

Grayson Series Collection Two (Books 4-6)

Grayson Series Collection Three (Books 7-9)

About Wendy Lindstrom

Wendy Lindstrom is the RITA award-winning and *New York Times* bestselling author of the Grayson family saga, a captivating series of feel-good, emotionally powerful novels. Her books are unforgettable, heartwarming stories about enduring friendships, family bonds, and romantic relationships between strong, complex characters living in a charming small town in America.

Fans of uplifting, binge-worthy historical romance will love Miss Lindstrom's popular Grayson family series, a #1 storewide bestseller on Barnes and Noble, and a *New York Times* and *USA Today* bestselling series. Romantic Times has dubbed her "one of romance's finest writers," and readers rave about her enthralling characters and the "awesome underlying emotional power" of her work. The Grayson Brothers series is a must-read for those who love stories that uplift and warm the heart.

For more information about the author, her books, and to get the behind-the-scenes scoop at her Rustic Studio—a world much like the Grayson world—visit her website and also subscribe to her engaging newsletter where she shares personal stories about the magnificent wildlife at her Rustic Studio, her insights on writing, her tiny house obsession, landscaping her beautiful water-garden, her passion for great books, her love of martial arts, and other fun subjects.

You can also follow her on BookBub.

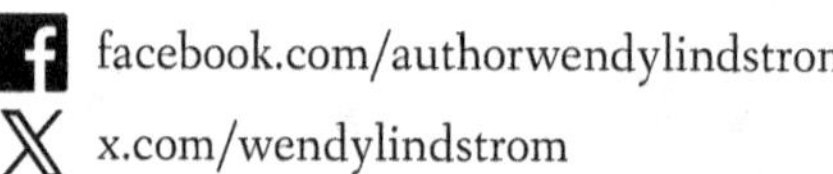

A small press bound by the belief that every voice matters.

Sign up for our newsletter to learn about new releases and more.
https://oliver-heberbooks.com/subscribe/

Follow us on social media:

facebook.com/oliverheberbooks

instagram.com/oliverheberbooks

amazon.com/oliverheberbooks

youtube.com/@OliverHeberBooksPublisher